THE TRUTHFUL WITNESS

JAMES CHANDLER

SEVERN RIVER PUBLISHING

Severn River Publishing
www.SevernRiverBooks.com

This is a work of fiction. Names, characters, businesses, places, events and incidents are either the products of the author's imagination or used in a fictitious manner. Any resemblance to actual persons, living or dead, or actual events is purely coincidental.

ISBN: 978-164875-452-4 (Paperback)

ALSO BY JAMES CHANDLER

Sam Johnstone Legal Thrillers

Misjudged

One and Done

False Evidence

Capital Justice

The Truthful Witness

Conflict of Duty

Never miss a new release!

Sign up to receive exclusive updates from author James Chandler.

severnriverbooks.com/authors/james-chandler

For David and Aaron, my sons-in-law.
I couldn't be prouder of you.

PROLOGUE

Last Wednesday, April 9

Grant Lee didn't need this. Yesterday he had finished the grueling murder trial of Mike Brown, heir to the Ukrainian Cryptocurrency Exchange, whom Lee had charged for the murder of his father-in-law and benefactor, Maxim Kovalenko. Brown, defended by Sam Johnstone, had somehow been acquitted; Lee was still raw and didn't want to talk with anyone, but the extended family of retired judge Preston Daniels had been calling non-stop and the staff could no longer hold them off.

Daniels' ailing wife Marci had passed away yesterday, as well. It wasn't unexpected—she'd been ill for some time, and Lee suspected the calls stemmed from a grieving family looking for answers he didn't have. As chief deputy county attorney for Custer, Wyoming, returning calls like these was part of the job. Besides, if Daniels' family had some influence, as he suspected, being as responsive as possible was best—especially if he decided to challenge County Attorney Rebecca Nice in the upcoming election.

He'd asked his assistant to schedule a videoconference, and when the bleeps and boops finally ceased, he was face to face with a heavyset, teary-eyed woman. Beside her and holding her hand was a man Lee assumed was her husband. They were seated at what appeared to be a table in a well-appointed kitchen. Good. Perhaps he could hit them up for a contribution when the time was right. He clicked the icons to start his camera and activate his microphone.

"Good morning," Lee began. "I'm Grant Lee, chief deputy county attorney in the Custer County Attorney's Office."

"Good morning," the woman said. "I'm Miriam Baker. I am—was—Marci Daniels' sister. This is my husband, David," she added.

"How can I help you?" Lee asked.

"We wanted to talk with you about Marci's death."

"I understand," Lee said. "What would you like to know?"

"Well, we understand my sister died from a drug overdose," Miriam said, dabbing at her eyes with a tissue.

The drugs used in treating cancer and its associated symptoms were powerful. "I haven't seen anything official, but I heard the same thing. What would—"

"What are you going to do about it?" Miriam blurted. "He killed my sister!"

"Excuse me?"

"Press. Press Daniels killed my sister! I've been worried about this for months. She was doing fine, then he decided to take her to Mexico for all kinds of ridiculous treatments. Those people don't know anything," she said dismissively. "Then, as she got worse—just like we all knew she would—" She broke down and her husband put his arm around her shoulders. When she had composed herself, she continued, "He started saying things like, 'She wants to die with dignity.' Well, we were smart enough to know what that meant. We tried to get her to leave, to come out here to California to stay with us, but she wouldn't."

Lee watched as Miriam loudly blew her nose and wiped her eyes. When she had taken a deep breath and appeared momentarily composed, he asked, "What would you like me to do?"

"Arrest him!"

Lee shook his head in what he hoped was an understanding manner. "I'm afraid that's the job of the police," he said. "I know that they routinely do—"

"I don't care about routines," Miriam said. "This is murder! There are no routines. Get the law to do a proper investigation, and you'll find out he killed her to be rid of her."

"That is a very serious allegation," Lee observed. "And one that would be decidedly difficult to prove."

"Mr. Lee, my wife is not a hysterical woman," David said. "I can vouch for everything she is saying. Press . . . well, toward the end there, I think he was exhausted and hopeless and I think he just decided they'd both be better off with her dead."

Miriam wailed and Lee felt his stomach tighten. "Okay, let me do this. I'm going to talk with the medical examiner and the chief of detectives—"

"You already know what he's going to say," Miriam scolded. "Talk to Press! He'll tell you he killed her!"

Doubtful. "Okay," Lee said, looking at his watch. This hadn't gone according to plan. "Look, I've got a meeting here in a few—"

"One more thing," Miriam insisted, holding up her hand.

"Yes?" Lee tapped a pencil on his desk.

She wiped her eyes with the back of her hand. "Marci had a million-dollar life insurance policy. Never worked a day in her life. Who has a million-dollar insurance policy when they never worked? You need to investigate this!"

Interesting. "I will," Lee promised. "But right now, I've got to get to court. I'll be in touch." Hanging up quickly, he called for a young attorney in the office, Aiden Cates. "Please call the medical examiner and tell him I need to talk with him about Marci Daniels as soon as possible—here or there, I don't care. And get ahold of Chief Lucas; I need to speak with him, too."

Sergeant Ashley Miller of the Custer Police Department took a long pull from the cigarette she had mooched off a patrol officer and held the smoke in as long as she could before exhaling. She looked in the car's rearview mirror and smoothed her hair.

"I didn't know you smoked," said Mike Jensen, a corporal with the patrol division. He had been a finalist for the sergeant of detectives job she now held but had shown no subsequent bitterness.

"I don't. I quit when I left the Air Force."

"Yeah, well . . . It's not every day you question a retired judge."

"No, it isn't," she agreed.

"Judge Daniels can be a real hard-ass, too," he said. "And with his wife's passing he might be a real prick."

"Thanks, Jensen—got any more good news?" The thought of interviewing retired judge Preston Daniels about the circumstances regarding his wife's passing had her on edge. She didn't know him well; she hadn't been in town long. Until recently, she had been a patrol officer in Casper. She had applied for the job in Custer on a lark and—to her unending surprise—had gotten the nod. She was becoming more comfortable with her responsibilities and was justifiably pleased with her ability to deal with high-stress situations most days, but this was different. Judge Daniels was a legendary figure in Custer. She'd met him on a couple of occasions and found him pleasant enough, but intimidating.

As she understood it, within an hour of his wife's death, Daniels' sister-in-law had been on the phone with anyone she could get ahold of, alleging the judge had killed his wife of forty-five years. Apparently, she'd called the county attorney's office and eventually spoke with Grant Lee, who had called Chief of Police William "Buck" Lucas. As the stuff rolled inexorably downhill, he had been on the phone with Miller almost immediately. She'd explained that she'd been onsite shortly after Marci Daniels' death and saw nothing untoward, but the sister-in-law had raised enough hell that Miller had been ordered to follow up.

The nicotine hadn't helped, of course, and her hand shook visibly as she looked at her watch. It was time.

She exited the unmarked car, dropped the lung dart, and crushed it with a boot. "Let's do this," she said to Jensen, and the two walked briskly up the sidewalk to Daniels' home, Miller lamenting the moment of weakness that resulted in her imbibing in her first smoke in seven years. Everyone in town knew where Press and Marci lived, and she noted weeds in what she could tell was once an immaculate lawn. She rang the doorbell and waited until the door was opened by a thin, blondish woman of about thirty-five. Miller showed her badge.

"Detective Sergeant Miller, Custer Police. This is Corporal Jensen. We'd like to talk with Ju—er, Preston Daniels, please."

"I know you," the woman said to Jensen, ignoring Miller.

"Julie Spence," Jensen replied. "It's been a while. How are you doing?" he asked without thinking.

She teared up quickly. "I mean . . . but I've been doin' good."

He nodded his understanding. "Excellent."

Miller watched the exchange with little interest. "Mr. Daniels?" she asked Julie.

"I'll have to see if he is available," Julie said. "He's been sleeping. I think the doctor gave him something after . . . you know."

"It's important that we talk with him," Miller said. "You want us to come with you?"

"Oh . . . No, I'm sure I can wake him." Julie stepped to the side. "I'll be right back if you'll wait in here."

Miller and Jensen entered and looked around the entryway. While she waited, Miller studied walls adorned with framed photographs reflecting the couple's life together, depicting them in faraway places Miller recognized but had never seen in person: the Eiffel Tower, Niagara Falls, and the Bay Bridge. In others, the smiling couple were pictured in front of notable Wyoming landmarks: the Tetons, Devils Tower, the Cheyenne Frontier Days arena. In each, the much-taller Daniels had an arm around his lovely, petite wife.

Miller, engrossed, was startled when Jensen spoke. "Our condolences, sir." She turned to see Daniels standing behind her.

"I loved her so," Daniels explained to Miller. He shook his head sadly. "But I think that sometimes we get so busy living that we forget to love. I should have spent more time on her." He stepped forward and pointed to a faded photograph portraying the obviously young couple on a beach. "Hawaii, 1976." He wiped an eye with his index and middle fingers, then turned to her. "She was so pretty. I was enthralled," he added wistfully, then—perhaps recognizing her discomfort—he apologized. "I'm sorry. Still struggling."

"It's okay, sir," Miller said. Recognizing her mistake in deferring to a man she was about to question, she tried to sound authoritative. "We need to ask you some questions. Is there a place we could talk?" she asked, indicating the lurking Julie with her head.

"Certainly." Daniels gestured toward the door to a carpeted room. "We can meet in my home office. Coffee?"

"Thank you," Miller said. "Black is fine."

"Corporal Jensen?" Daniels asked.

"Black, sir."

"Julie, would you mind?" Daniels asked. When she had departed to retrieve their coffee, Daniels looked to Miller. "She has agreed to stay on for a while. Help me tie up loose ends, you know."

Miller smiled and retrieved a notebook and pen from a pocket as they waited for Julie to return. Jensen sat quietly, looking at his hands. When the coffee mugs had been placed in front of them, Julie left quietly, closing the door behind her. Daniels retrieved a flask from a credenza behind his desk, poured a healthy shot into his coffee, and replaced the flask, then sipped appreciatively before looking at Miller abruptly. "How can I help you, Detective?"

"I want to begin by passing on to you the condolences of the entire department. We're very sorry for your loss."

"Thank you," Daniels said. "But?"

"But we're here to ask you some questions—clear some things up, you understand." Miller hoped he didn't hear the quaver in her voice. The nicotine had her anxious.

"What would you like to know?"

"Well, as I understand it, you administered a dose of morphine to your wife at approximately three p.m. You then took a nap and came in to check on her—is that right?"

"No, not quite," he corrected her. "I wasn't feeling well myself—some kind of bug or something. The morphine is kept in a safe. I'm the only one with the combination. I got her medication out and set it in the pantry for Julie to administer—we took a class together. Julie writes down the time she gives—gave—medication to Marci on a little pad I have. Marci would normally nap for about two hours after the morphine, so when I got up I looked at the time Julie had recorded . . . I thought she was sleeping . . ." He drew a long breath and then released it. "At the three-hour mark I went in to check on her and—"

"What made you think she was sleeping?"

Daniels swiveled in his chair and again reached into the credenza. Miller was afraid he was going for the flask again until he withdrew a small video monitor and showed it to her. "It's a baby monitor," he explained. "I kept an eye on her with this. That way I didn't wake her up by walking in her room—our room." He smiled wryly. "She said I walk like an elephant."

"So, she slept too long?"

"Yes."

"What did you do then?"

"I went in and checked on her. I didn't see her breathing. I went to her bedside and put my hand in front of her mouth and nose. She wasn't breathing. Her skin was cool."

"What—"

"Her eyes were open," he continued. "She looked . . . at peace for the first time in a long time. She was out of pain."

"What did you do then?"

"I closed her eyes and then I called 9-1-1."

"What did you tell them?" Miller asked, knowing full well what he had told them. She had listened to the phone call half a dozen times.

"I told them I needed help. I told them I had killed my wife."

Miller made a note. "You have to know that was odd phrasing," she said. "Why did you say it that way?"

"Because when I saw she was . . . dead, that's when I realized I had forgotten to switch out the morphine."

"I don't follow."

"The day before she . . . died, the doctor had increased the prescription for diazepam. She gave me a new prescription for morphine—syringes pre-loaded with a lesser amount. I was supposed to swap them out. I—I forgot. Julie gave her what I left out."

"Then what?"

He was fiddling with his wedding ring. "Then, I—I know this will sound strange . . . I lay down in bed next to her and waited. I—I just needed

to be next to her one more time. Forty-five years, you know?" He took a
ragged breath and looked up at her.

"You told the first responders you killed her?"

"Oh, yes. I'm sure I did."

"Did what?"

"Told them I killed her."

"Did you?"

"Oh, I see what you mean," he said. "Well, I'm the one who left the
wrong medicine for Julie to administer. I'm the one who left Marci alone in
her bed and didn't check on her until it was too late. I'm the one who didn't
make her go to the doctor two years ago when she first started feeling
poorly. I'm the one who wore her out with the trips to Mexico. Don't you
see?"

Miller nodded. "I do. You're saying you're responsible for her
death—"

"Indisputably."

She was pushing hard on the pad with her pen to conceal her shaking
hands. She looked at Jensen before she asked the next question. "But you're
not saying that you actually *killed* her, are you?"

"Detective. Words mean things," he lectured. "Of course I killed her. Of
that, there can be no doubt. Are you asking me if I murdered her? Because
there is a difference."

"Yes. That's exactly what I'm asking."

He snorted. "Of course not. I would not do such a thing. I need—
needed—her."

She met his gaze. "I'm told that you said on more than one occasion that
she'd be better off dead."

"I'm sure I did—but that was just frustration," he explained. "Have you
ever watched a loved one die?"

"I have not, but—"

"You think you've had bad days? Well, caring for someone who is
terminal creates bad days on an unimaginable scale. Watching someone
you care about waste away sucks the life out of you. The constant visits to
doctors, and blood draws, and tests, and consultations—all the while
knowing that she didn't or wouldn't have wanted to go on this way. She told

me a hundred times she wished it could all be over, but we kept on. I know now it was all for me—because I selfishly wanted her to live!"

"It must have been horrific," she sympathized. "Are you sure you didn't just speed up the process a little to make it easier on her?"

"No," he said, then turned his attention to Jensen. "Jensen, are we done here?"

"I'm running this interview, *Mister* Daniels," Miller said. "We'll be done when I say so. You told the 9-1-1 operator and the EMTs and everyone else you 'killed her.'"

"I have already addressed that, Detective. I'm a judge—was a judge. Words mean things." He drank deeply and turned again to the credenza.

"Indeed. But you must understand that those very words, when combined with the M.E's findings and . . . things . . . said by others . . ."

Daniels turned back to her. "My sister-in-law."

"Among others," she hedged.

"Detective, you have to understand that Miriam is . . . well, histrionic, to use a psychiatrist's term of art. The layman would probably say she is a meddling, bothersome, interfering pain in the ass."

"She may well be, but she says that you told her on multiple occasions that Marci would be better off dead."

"No, I said *Marci said* she would be better off dead—you understand the distinction, don't you?"

"She also said that you had a large life insurance policy on Marci, and that taking care of her drained the family savings."

"Both of those are true," he replied, shifting forward in his chair. "But let me ask you: did she tell you the insurance policy was purchased with money from her mother's estate, and that Marci purchased it long before she got sick?" Seeing Miller's non-reaction, he continued. "Did she tell you that I would have spent every damned penny I've got and would live in a freaking box down by the tracks if it meant Marci was alive? No?" He poured himself another shot and took it. "Detective, Miriam has been married four times—did she tell you that? Miriam doesn't know any more about love or marriage or caring for someone than she does space exploration!" He pounded his fist on the desk for emphasis.

When Miller took her eyes off Daniels' clenched fist, she could discern a small vein throbbing in his forehead. "I'm only trying to get some things cleared up," she said.

"I understand that," he said. "But it's important that you understand the source of these allegations—it's personal."

"Meaning?" Miller asked.

"Meaning I married her baby sister and moved her out of that woman's orbit forty-five years ago. She's never forgiven me because . . . well . . . Miriam and I dated before I met Marci. Now, what else do you want to know?"

"A couple more questions. Could Marci have given herself—"

He was shaking his head vigorously before she could finish the question. "Marci couldn't get out of bed by herself, and I doubt she even knew where the meds were kept."

Miller made another note and then looked at him directly. "How is it that you could have *forgotten* to change the syringes?" That one hit home; he sank in his chair.

"I—I don't know," he said. "I've asked myself that a thousand times. I mean . . . I'm tired and everything but . . . I can only tell you I didn't." He removed his glasses and wiped his eyes with a thumb and index finger. "No excuses."

"This Julie Spence—how did she come to be in your employ?"

"I was getting tired, so I contacted a home health agency here in town. They recommended Julie," he added, smiling wryly. "Honestly, my first reaction was to reject her because I knew her in my prior life. She's an addict and I was worried about having her in my house—especially around drugs."

"What changed your mind?"

"The agency was extremely high on her and . . . well, Julie and I talked; she said I had saved her life," he explained. "She'd had some trouble and some challenges that she appeared to have overcome and . . . and, well, what kind of person would I be if I didn't give her an opportunity? Most important, Marci really liked her."

"And how did it work out?"

"Wonderfully! Like I said, Marci liked her. They would talk for hours." He looked out the window and then back to Miller. "Julie was pleasant, always on time, and she looked after Marci like she was her own mother. You know, we never had any children, and Julie was about the age our children might have been. They just seemed to hit it off."

"And you and Julie—" Miller began.

"Nothing," Daniels said. "Not a damned thing. And you can tell Miriam I said that. Call it flat denial, call it an angry rejection, call it whatever you want. But tell that meddling bitch I deny an affair with Julie, and while I accept responsibility for Marci's death, I didn't murder her."

Miller and Jensen exchanged a look. "I think that will do it for today," Miller said, standing. "We'll see ourselves out."

Daniels didn't respond; instead, he turned and opened the credenza door. Outside, as they walked to the car, Jensen shrugged. "I believe him. He's so irascible I have to believe that if he would have killed her intentionally, he would admit it."

Miller side-eyed Jensen. "On the other hand, how in the hell do you forget to change out medication? He's obviously an incredibly bright guy."

"He's been fighting this with her for two years. Maybe he just—"

"Put her out of her misery?" Miller finished.

"I was going to say wore out and forgot," Jensen countered. "I just . . . well, he's not young."

"You're not arguing he has dementia?"

"No, I'm just saying he might have gotten physically, mentally, and emotionally worn down. I just can't see him—"

"—putting her down like an old housecat?"

"Right," he said. They were looking at each other over the roof of the car. "What are you thinking?" he asked.

"I'm thinking that unless Julie rats him out, the best we could do is involuntary manslaughter," she said. "But you know as well as I do that Grant Lee will want more than that."

"Yeah," Jensen agreed. "I'm kind of glad you got the job—you get the great joy of explaining what we've got to him."

Miller smiled. "You drive," she said, tossing him the keys. "I need to think about this."

Aiden Cates was a twenty-six-year-old who before being asked habitually reached for his identification to prove his age on the rare occasions he purchased alcohol. On this Thursday morning, the young attorney was in conference with Grant Lee, for whom he had enormous respect.

"This could be big—huge, even," Lee said. "If we can bring a case against a retired judge, it will be statewide news. We get a conviction, and our careers will be made."

"It's going to be difficult," Cates surmised. Why, he wasn't sure, but it seemed like the right thing to say.

Since his call with Miriam Baker, Lee had spent time with the medical examiner and Miller, who seemed skittish as hell. "What are you afraid of?" he had asked.

"I'm not afraid of anything, but I'm not sure that we have enough to charge him with anything beyond involuntary manslaughter—if that," she had said.

"He admitted that he didn't change out the meds."

"True."

"He admitted that he didn't check on her for almost three hours."

"Yes, he did, but—"

"He admitted that he had talked about ending her pain or whatever."

"Well, yeah, but I think—"

"He admitted she had a large insurance policy."

"She did, but she bought—"

"Then you've got a motive, an opportunity—"

"Why are you interrupting me?" Miller demanded.

"I'm not interrupting—"

"You are. You are asking questions and not allowing me to respond fully," she countered. "I'm not some defendant on the stand and I don't work for you, Counsel. I'm not going to put up with it."

Lee had been taken aback. "Look, I'm sorry if you think—"

"No," she said. "Don't drop the mansplaining crap on me. I'm looking into charges, and I'll bring charges to your office when I'm damned good and ready—meaning when I am convinced that he committed a crime and when I've got enough to prove it, and not before." She had stomped out, leaving Lee speechless.

He sipped coffee, recalling her anger. Perhaps he should talk with Lucas. He looked to Cates and finally commented on the young lawyer's observation. "Perhaps. But they all are. How difficult it's going to be will depend on the level of cooperation we get from some of these agencies—the police department and the medical examiner's office, specifically. Christ! He made the 9-1-1 call and admitted killing her!"

"I heard, but couldn't that be taken a number of ways?" Cates asked.

"It could, but assuming he meant what he said—and we'll find that out soon enough—we've got an admission, or at the very least a statement against interest. The M.E. hasn't released his report yet, but he did say that she almost certainly died from an overdose, and Daniels admitted to Miller she couldn't have administered the drugs herself. That means someone—Daniels or that Spence woman at his direction—administered a fatal mixture of diazepam and morphine to Marci. The uncontroverted facts are damning."

Cates looked around the spartan office. He hadn't been in many lawyers' offices, but Lee's was the only one totally bereft of personal items. "So it will come down to motive, and he's a judge!"

"*Was*," Lee countered. "I know that, and for that reason I specifically told the chief that Daniels needs to be treated like any other suspect and that he needs to light a fire under his people—especially Miller." He stood and walked around his office, looking at his bare walls. "What the criminal justice system in this county needs is leadership—real leadership," he added, pointing toward the office of Rebecca Nice, the county's elected prosecutor. When Cates nodded as if he understood, Lee continued. "I already told you: a case like this could make us. On the other hand, there is a lot of risk associated with taking it on—if we fail, our shit is weak. Are you up for this?"

"Of course," Cates said, having no idea what *this* might entail.

"Good. Now here is what I need you to do." Lee then explained a series of actions and interviews he wanted Cates to undertake. "One more thing: I need a bench memo about a possible change of venue, and one covering the procedure to swear off a judge. If Daniels is arrested, he'll hire Sam Johnstone, and I want to be ready when Sam files a motion for a change of venue; plus, I'm thinking I'm going to swear off Judge Bridger if he doesn't recuse himself."

Cates nodded. "Is it true that when the cops got there, the judge was lying in the bed with her?"

"Aiden, I'm only going to say this one more time: he's not a judge. He *was* a judge. Now, he's just another suspect. Get that straight," Lee corrected. "But yeah, it is true. Why?"

"That's so creepy!" Cates shivered involuntarily. Then he looked to Lee. "So, you want me to do this stuff, like, today?"

"Like, yeah," Lee replied sarcastically. "Why wouldn't I?"

"Well, I've got that other stuff you gave me," Cates began. "I mean, I've—"

Lee stared hard at the young attorney. "I hear you. But there are twenty-four hours in a day, Aiden." Cates was a pleaser—that was one of the reasons Lee had insisted Rebecca hire him. "This is an important mission and I need you on it. Can I count on you?"

Cates withered under Lee's stare. "I'm on it," he said simply.

"Good," Lee replied. "Tomorrow will be fine." Indicating a stack of paperwork on his desk, he eyed Cates. "I've got stuff to do myself. I think you'd probably better get started, eh?"

Cates took that as his cue and stood to leave. As he turned to the door, he heard Lee say, "Close it. See you in the morning."

After Cates departed, Lee walked down the hall for an unscheduled office call with Rebecca. He explained his initial discussion with Marci's sister, his conversation with the M.E., the results of Miller's interview with Daniels, and the status of her burgeoning investigation. It all pointed to one thing: Daniels had unlawfully killed his wife. The only question, really, was the degree of culpability. "We've got to charge him!" he implored. "There is more than enough evidence to support a charge of manslaughter—at a minimum."

"There is simply no way that Preston Daniels murdered his wife,"

Rebecca replied. "I've known him for twenty years. No way. He's a crusty old judge, but inside he's a very kind and caring man."

She couldn't be this naïve. "Kind and caring people kill other people every day."

"He was a doting and dedicated husband—I saw it with my own eyes," Rebecca explained. "When Marci first got sick, we all took meals to the house. I sat with them one evening. I saw the love in his eyes as he cared for her. We should all be so lucky."

"Things change, boss. She's been sick for a while. Maybe he ran out of gas. He says he hated seeing her suffer. Maybe he wanted the money. Then there's that Spence gal. Who knows? What we do know is that she died of an overdose—a mixture of drugs she was incapable of giving herself."

"Do we really know that?"

"Absolutely. We know the drugs were kept in a safe and that she was not ambulatory, so we know she could not have gotten up, gone to the safe, obtained the drug, and self-administered. Both Daniels and the Spence woman said she administered what Daniels provided for her."

"But how are we going to prove intent?"

"We don't have to—even if he had no intent, we've got enough now for involuntary manslaughter. But I think we can: Daniels says he provided the dosage, then took a nap. Admits that when he awoke, he didn't check on his wife. He says he figured she was sleeping." He watched her closely, seeking a reaction. "That's involuntary manslaughter. Add the motive—a million-dollar life insurance policy and maybe an affair—and we're looking at voluntary manslaughter, maybe murder." He knew she would need a push. "Look: with the evidence we have—if anyone found out, I mean . . . it would look like we didn't file because of who he is."

"We're not filing until I say so," she said. "I don't need to remind you I run this office. And I don't want to hear or read about the evidence we have —do you hear me? And the idea of an affair is absurd."

"It happens all the time."

"Not to Marci Daniels, it didn't. Don't file without my prior permission."

"Got it," he said. "But what do you want me to tell the media?"

"Nothing! Not a word. That's my job. I'll think of something."

"Well, think quick, because the pressure's on," Lee advised. "People want answers."

"Who?"

"Well, her family, for one. They are raising hell," he said. "And I don't have to remind you this is an election year—"

"Then don't." She was watching him closely. "Why are you talking with her family?"

"Because they were calling non-stop," he explained. "I deemed it my responsibility—don't you agree?"

"No!" Rebecca slapped the desk in front of her for emphasis. "If I thought someone should have returned the calls, I would have done it myself. The public doesn't run this office—I do!"

"I just thought that—"

"How about outside the courtroom you let me do the thinking?" she snapped. "Grant, you've got some trial skills—I'll admit that. But I didn't hire you to run this office, thank you very much."

"I understand."

"And I'm going to tell you something else. If we arrest Judge Daniels, we are going to have a tiger by the tail in Sam Johnstone. If you think he was hard to deal with while defending some billionaire's kid he didn't even like, well, if he gets fired up, he'll be a formidable foe."

"I can handle Johnstone," Lee said. Seeing Rebecca's doubtful look, he insisted, "I can."

She sighed audibly. "Right. And I'll admit it is beginning to look like you might get another shot to prove it. But don't push it. Do not—I say again, do not—file charges against Preston Daniels without me personally seeing and approving the warrant. We cannot afford to dick this one up. Now, I've got some calls to make." She picked up the phone, pressed a pre-programmed number, then swiveled in the chair so her back was to him.

The next morning Lee was in his office talking with Cates when Rebecca stomped in unannounced and slammed the door shut behind her. "I told you not to file on Daniels without my permission!"

"Aiden, can you give us a minute?" When the young attorney had sprinted from the room, Lee looked to Rebecca. "Rebecca, I haven't *filed* anything," he assured her. "Now, I'll be the first to admit that—"

"Do not quibble with me!" she interrupted. "I've been told affidavits of probable cause and an Information have been prepared. You have undermined me and disobeyed a direct order!"

Lee sat back in his chair, appraising his boss. "I'm the chief deputy. I asked the police department to prepare affidavits of probable cause based on what they have now. Cates is working on an Information—that's only prudent. That's all I've done to this point," he said carefully. "We would do that for any other case. If I—"

"This is *not* any other case! You ordered Cates to draft an arrest warrant, as well!"

That was true, but because it hadn't been served, he hadn't technically violated her order. "I've only done what I thought was the right thing to ensure we are prepared just in case you—"

"You are attempting to skirt my orders," she argued. "You are in the process of undermining me."

"Rebecca, the evidence is in. He killed her. He has admitted it to those closest to him. She died of an overdose she could not have administered herself. Her sister says he had spoken of putting her out of her misery, and she was insured for big bucks. They were having financial problems as a result of her illness."

"But there are considerations you haven't taken into account," she said. "You will wait until I give you an explicit go-ahead before going any further." She looked at him expectantly.

Lee leaned forward in his chair to face her, interlocked his fingers, and placed his hands on his desk. Now was as good a time as any. "I'm not going to do that," he said levelly. "We need to move forward. It's the right thing to do. It's time that we begin to enforce the law equally."

The color had drained from her face. "Grant, you have no idea what you are doing here. I've known Press Daniels for years. No way did he kill his wife. No way. There had to have been an accident. We need to investigate this further. We can take another look when we've completed a full investigation."

"I'm satisfied with the evidence," he said. "Otherwise, I wouldn't be moving forward."

"And I'm telling you that you don't have the full picture!" She took a deep breath. "Now, I am ordering you to cease and desist until I give you the go-ahead."

This was it, then. "I'm not going to do that, Rebecca."

She sat back in her chair. "I can fire you."

"You can, but it would be a big mistake."

"Why do you say that?"

"Because if you fire me, it will come out that I was let go for planning to file charges against a well-known, powerful figure in town," Lee explained. "The public will find that I had good cause and was stopped by you. It will look like you are covering up for him."

"No, your dismissal will be for insubordination," Rebecca stated.

"You can try and explain that to the voters, sure." Lee shrugged and watched as Rebecca considered her options.

"You are being both insubordinate and disrespectful. I have no choice but to fire you."

Time to be frank. "I don't think so. I fully intend to file to run against you this fall. I told Aiden that this morning, and I told him moments ago that I intended to tell you the next time I saw you. Now if you fire me, it will be clear you did so as retribution for my having the gall to tell you of my intent to challenge you—and that's against the law, as you well know."

Her eyes narrowed. "But that wouldn't be true. I already told you—"

He smiled. "I guess we'll just have to sort that out during the lawsuit," he said. Her face fell, and he knew she was finished. "For the record, I think my number one issue might well be my opponent covering for a well-known figure by forbidding me from filing charges despite overwhelming evidence of some degree of guilt. How do you think a law-and-order-starved voting public will see that?"

"I can explain," she said lamely. "The people . . . the public knows I am a careful and considered prosecutor."

Time to finish her off. "What the voters have seen is a series of acquittals by juries who have been let down by your office. I'm not supposed to tell you this, but I think it's fair. I have already been informed that when I throw my hat in the ring, I will have the support of the sheriff's office and the police department." It wasn't true, but she couldn't know that. "They are just waiting to see if you file before making their endorsement."

He watched as she gulped air and held it for a moment. "You rat bastard! Behind my back—"

"Well, to some degree," he acknowledged. "But this is really about the public good."

"Don't lecture me! You know nothing about this community or its needs. What you know is that you think you are good at trying cases and that you're on some sort of mission to save the planet! Well, I'm here to tell you that bullshit isn't going to fly."

He nodded. "I'm sure it's a shock to you and I understand how you might feel. But I think that if you give it some thought, you'll know what to do."

"You are a condescending sonuvabitch!"

He reclined in his chair, steepling his hands against his lips. "I don't think there is any need for ad hominem attacks, Rebecca. You are better than that. Why don't you think it over? I want to remind you that if you fire me now, it will be a violation of statute. Besides, I'll run against you, and with the backing of the police and sheriffs, well—"

His door slammed shut behind her. He smiled and drank tepid coffee from a cup he'd purchased online some time back. It was labeled "World's #1 Lawyer."

As Judge Melissa Downs read, Lee sat opposite her with his long legs crossed. Although she hadn't been dealing with him long, she had already developed an extreme dislike for him—it was all she could do to try and hide her feelings. He was an arrogant, pseudo-intellectual twit, and not half the trial lawyer he imagined himself to be.

She took off her readers and placed them carefully on the desk, then rubbed her temples with her index and middle fingers. "You have got to be kidding me!" She had been a circuit court judge in Custer for a couple of years now. Before that, she'd been living in Cheyenne, happily married and practicing civil litigation until one day her husband of almost ten years decided he needed to find himself. He left her, their then-nine-year-old daughter Emma, and his job as a banker to become a kayaking guide in Colorado. In response, she'd thrown her hat in the ring for a judgeship occasioned by her predecessor's suicide. Having now occupied the bench for almost two years, she was beginning to feel comfortable with most of her duties. But this was different.

She looked up from the arrest warrant. "When this goes public, the shit is going to hit the fan!"

"Probably," Lee agreed. "But you've read the affidavit." He pointed at the document on the desk in front of her. "There's more than enough there."

"Looks entirely circumstantial to me, Counsel," she countered. "To the point that I cannot believe Rebecca Nice is going along with this."

"I don't know that she has a lot of choice."

Downs was taken aback. "What are you talking about? She's the county attorney."

"Judge, I think there is more than enough evidence to justify his arrest," Lee replied, ignoring the question. "Of course, if you disagree, I can find another judge."

In Wyoming, the circuit court was the lower trial court. Accordingly, Downs had jurisdiction over misdemeanors, civil matters where less than fifty thousand dollars were in dispute, and civil orders of protection. In addition, she signed most search and arrest warrants and was responsible for conducting the initial appearances for and setting bond on defendants charged with felonies up to and including murder. If she signed this, it would soon be her responsibility to see and set bond for Daniels following his arrest. The thought of doing so gave her butterflies; when she had arrived, Daniels and his wife Marci had taken it upon themselves to welcome her and Emma to town. With his help, she had gotten her feet under her and—up until right now—felt competent to handle most anything that would come before her.

Some time back, at dinner and with a couple of drinks in him, Daniels had opined that she would know she was a good judge when she ruled against someone she cared about, or for someone she despised. With that occasion now presenting itself, she was concerned about her ability to follow through. "Let me take a look at it," she said. "I will have my assistant call you here in a few."

"Judge, it is Friday afternoon. If you don't sign it—"

"Counsel, if I didn't know better, I might take your insistence as a threat. You wouldn't come into my chambers and do that, would you?" Without awaiting a response, she continued, "Now, I explained to you I am going to take a look at it. Is there anything else?" Lee appeared ready to say something, but perhaps thought better of it and closed his mouth tightly. "Thank you," she said. When he had departed, she called a mentor judge in another district. This was going to be a shitshow no matter how she played it, but another opinion couldn't hurt.

Despite the April sleet and snow, Lee's face was hot and his hands were sweaty. Momentarily, his career path would fork. Just an hour ago he had presented Chief Lucas with an arrest warrant signed by Downs ordering the arrest of Daniels. The chief was livid, but after throwing a minor temper tantrum he'd seen the writing on the wall and agreed to arrest Daniels. "But not until after the funeral," he had said.

"Fair enough," Lee had replied. "But if it's not done by close of business today, I'll go to the sheriff to get it done, and then on Monday I'll request a meeting with the city council."

Lucas' face had turned beet red, and Lee had seen a vein in his neck throbbing. "Don't you threaten me, Counselor! You have no idea what the arrest of Judge Daniels will mean to the people of—"

"The people want all criminals treated alike," Lee had said. "And if you feel differently, let me know."

Hours later, at Marci's funeral, Lucas had situated himself next to Rebecca, who was reluctantly sharing a back-row pew with Lee. As Lucas whispered in her ear, no doubt to inform her what was about to go down, Lee side-eyed the pair. When Lucas had finished his whispering, Rebecca looked at Lee and slid down the otherwise unoccupied pew until she was in his bubble. He could smell the garlic from whatever she'd had for lunch.

"You sonuvabitch!" she hissed. "Today—of all days?"

"Yeah, it's kind of tough," Lee admitted. "But I think you knew this was going to happen, and I think you'll agree that public safety is paramount in these situations—won't you?" She blinked back tears of frustration, and when the family entered the sanctuary, she slid back down the pew. Lee noted that Sam Johnstone and Cathy Schmidt were sitting up front with Daniels. This would be delicious.

When the long service was over, Rebecca stood and departed without a word to anyone. Lee forced what he felt was a sorrowful smile and offered it to other mourners as he followed her outside. Unable to overtake her, he watched as she marched to, entered, and started the small sedan, backed out of her parking spot, and sped away. He walked slowly to his own car and waited. When at last the procession headed for the cemetery, he positioned his car at the tail end of the line of vehicles.

At the cemetery and from afar, he watched the somber graveside service. When the last of the cars filled with tearful mourners finally departed, he felt his pulse quicken. Trailing Daniels' car out of the cemetery, Lee smiled when he observed two police cars slip in behind it, and he wondered whether Sam—who was driving—had any idea he was being followed. As the miles passed, Lee began to wonder when the cops would make their move—or if they would make it at all. They had better; he had made clear to Lucas the cost of failing to act. Had Rebecca countermanded him? Doubtful—she didn't have the intestinal fortitude.

He was about to call Lucas when Sam turned into a liquor store parking lot. Lee thrilled as the sirens wailed and the squad cars lit up. He pulled over and jumped out of his car, exulting in the spectacle despite the sleet stinging his face. Standing beside his car, he watched as the arresting officers yelled instructions he could not hear due to the high wind.

Lee saw Sam warned off, then watched as a protesting Daniels was taken into custody. He walked around his car and sat on the hood for a moment. Changing his mind, he walked to the center of a parking lot adjacent to the liquor store and stood quietly, certain he'd eventually be seen. He watched Cathy and Sam embrace, and when he was certain Sam had noticed him, he executed what he felt was a smart faux salute, then turned, put his hands in his pockets, and walked back to his car, triumphant.

1

The arrest of Sam Johnstone's mentor Press Daniels had Sam feeling restless, irritable, and discontented. He pouted and slouched around the house until he sullenly looked in the refrigerator and found only a jar of jalapeños, a stick of butter, a pitcher of sweet tea, and a rotting onion. Despite knowing he was only one drink away from disaster, he drove to the Longbranch Saloon—ostensibly to order food to go. Jamey Johnson was playing on the jukebox, and he hummed along, enjoying the bar's smoky haze. When he ordered a longneck and whiskey back, owner/bartender Gino Smith asked him three times if he was sure. Three times he assured Gino he was fine. "I'm okay—really."

Two hours later he had downed four or five tall beers and an equal number of shots. He was halfway to feeling all right . . . and he only felt right when he was wrong. Before he left the bar, he walked to the men's room and practiced walking heel-to-toe, turning around, and reciting the alphabet backward in an effort to gauge his probable success on the standardized field sobriety tests used by law enforcement—just in case. He was pleasantly surprised that he had remembered the drills so well and headed for the bar to pay his tab. He had no business driving, of course, but risk was part of the kink for an addict/alcoholic. He paid his tab, tipped big, and purchased two small bottles of vodka "for the road," assuring a grim-faced Gino he was good to go and that he could make it home safely.

"Damn it, Sam," Gino groused. "You get busted, and the police report and the newspaper will note you'd been drinking here." Sam had assured Gino he was fine, then grabbed the Styrofoam container with his cold food and walked unsteadily out the door.

Now, as he neared the turn on a darkened road approximately one mile from his apartment, he uncapped one of the miniature bottles of vodka he'd purchased, drained the contents, and tossed the empty out the open window, enjoying the feel of both the icy April evening air and his burning esophagus. Keith Whitley was on in his old truck's CD player, and Sam sang along until flashing blue lit up his cab, bringing him out of his reverie. He looked in the mirror, and upon seeing his reflection cursed himself and slapped at the offending glass, then took deep breaths in an effort to control the onrush of adrenaline that always accompanied drinking trouble.

The stakes were high—a conviction for drunken driving would imperil his career as an attorney. More importantly, it would disappoint everyone who had cared enough to help him when he was struggling. Relapse was neither inevitable nor uncommon, of course, but in Sam's case it was predictable—he'd been "too busy" to meet with either his VA counselor, Bob Martinez, or his AA sponsor of late. His secretary, Cassie, would scold him mercilessly.

Forgetting to signal, he steered his truck uncertainly to the side of the road, put it in park, and pounded the steering wheel in frustration. All the work, all the effort, all the people who had faith in him. He should have called Bob. He should have called his sponsor. Hell, he could have talked with Cathy, Cassie, or someone—anything but go to the bar. How many times had he listened to a man or woman in a twelve-step meeting lament their actions while smugly thinking it would never happen to him? He struggled to retrieve his driver's license from his wallet and was searching through his glovebox for his truck's registration and insurance card when he felt a presence at his window. He prayed it wasn't an officer he knew.

"Evening, Sam."

Christ. It was Ron Baker of the Custer Police. "Hi, er, Ron," Sam replied. "How you doin'?"

"I'm well, Sam. Do you know why I pulled you over?"

The proper response was, "I have no idea, Officer," but this was Baker. Sam shrugged. "I was probably speeding."

"Well, that and weaving all over the road," Baker replied. He made a show of sniffing the air in Sam's truck. "You been drinkin'?"

Again, the proper response was, "Of course not." "A little," Sam admitted, somehow incapable of following the legal advice he had provided innumerable clients over the years.

Baker nodded. With a traffic violation, the smell of booze, and an admission to drinking, he had reasonable suspicion, enabling him to extend the traffic stop to investigate possible drunk driving. "Well, how about you step out and we'll do some tests to make sure you're okay to drive —sound good?"

"You bet."

When Sam unsteadily exited the car, the remaining bottle dropped on the ground at his feet. He struggled to retrieve it while Baker watched. "I'll take that," he said, extending his hand when Sam had finally picked the small vodka bottle off the ground. "Did you toss one of those out the window a ways back?"

"Maybe," Sam admitted, feeling extremely fatigued. He turned to face Baker and noticed a line of cars driving slowly past. It seemed he knew the face of every driver and occupant.

He looked to Baker, who was shaking his head. "Sam, are you okay?"

Another day, another bad decision. He'd been sober for months, but remained halfway between who he was and who he wanted to be. "I—I'm fine," Sam replied. "A little tired, is all. Leg's hurting," he lied, knocking on the prosthesis. "Let's just get this over with." He heard himself say, "Letth" and "thith."

"Okay," Baker said. "Before we get started, could you turn off the music?"

"Do what?"

"The music. Turn off the music on your phone."

Sam turned off his phone. "There," he said, but when he looked up, he didn't see Baker. Instead, he saw the stark white walls of the small bedroom in his apartment.

He was home. And sober. It had been a relapse dream—and not the first he had experienced, of late. He swung his remaining leg over the side of the bed, then reached for and shakily donned his artificial left leg. In so doing he felt slightly repulsed by the soaking wet T-shirt sticking to his body.

Later, in his kitchen, he texted his sponsor. *Got time for a call?*

Hours later, Sam was in his office trying to focus. The events of the past week had brought a whirlwind of emotions—never a good thing for a recovering addict/alcoholic. Last Tuesday his client Mike Brown had been rightfully acquitted of the murder of his father-in-law, billionaire cryptocurrency mogul Maxim Kovalenko. Hours later, Marci Daniels had died following an extended illness. On Saturday afternoon, he and Cathy Schmidt had attended Marci's funeral and graveside services with Daniels, only to stand by helplessly as Daniels was arrested for her murder. Daniels' arrest was unnecessary, gratuitous, and provocative.

Now, two days later and despite prayer and meditation, Sam's fury at Lee hadn't abated and had probably contributed to last night's relapse dream. Still shaken hours later, he had to remind himself to breathe. Later this morning, he would enter an appearance on Daniels' behalf and this afternoon he would join Daniels in court for his initial appearance in front of Judge Downs. Try as he might to focus on the task at hand—crafting an argument to convince what he anticipated would be a highly skeptical judge to release an accused murderer on pretrial release conditions—his thoughts were clouded with memories of Marci and Press. They'd been like the parents he hadn't had since his mother's death decades past. After Daniels' retirement and even during the early onset of Marci's illness they had him over from time to time. He'd sit on the couch and listen to Marci give Press hell and marvel that the old judge had someone to tell him what to do—just like everyone else. Following each visit, Marci would send Sam home with plates and plastic containers full of food. "You've got to eat, young man," she would say. "You're too thin."

The change in her had been gradual but drastic. Loss of weight, loss of hair; ultimately, she had turned a sickly gray color. Daniels' degradation had been just as marked; he'd gone from curmudgeonly to flat-out angry, and the change in his appearance had been a topic of discussion in town. For a time, Daniels had attempted to continue some part-time legal work for Sam's firm as an "of counsel" attorney, but frequent trips abroad to attempt risky, unapproved-in-the-US treatments for her advancing cancer had taken their toll. At last, when he'd been too worn down to work or care for Marci alone, Daniels had brought on Julie Spence, a recovering meth-amphetamine addict and home health care assistant upon whom he came to depend. But by then it was too late, and last week Marci had passed.

Until Daniels' arrest, Sam assumed her death had been a natural one. The arrest of the respected judge sent a shockwave through Custer and resulted in national headlines and an influx of out-of-state visitors, as "Judge Accused of Murdering Wife" was the kind of story that had editors sending members of their ever-decreasing staffs to small-town Wyoming in search of a story sure to titillate readers.

Sam stood and walked to his window, moving the blinds so he could see the street in front of the courthouse some distance away. Constructed in 1932, the courthouse was finished in what Sam had been informed was a "classically modern" architectural style. The front view was of a symmetrical, commanding structure of cut limestone dominated by six evenly spaced ionic columns, two of which framed enormous double doors that concealed metals detectors staffed by court security officers assigned by the county. To Sam, the effect was one reminiscent of the depository at Fort Knox. On the north side of the building was a circular drive where an area of well-manicured lawn was dedicated to local veterans from the nation's ever-growing list of wars, conflicts, and foreign military interventions. There, local artists had been commissioned to create representative sculptures. The result was an architectural mix that was the stuff of nightmares, interest, or amusement, depending on one's viewpoint.

In the foreground, plastic cones cordoned off the parking spots that would soon be occupied by national media eager to satiate an increasingly attention-span-challenged public's need for controversy. Just as quickly as they would pour into town, the tide of journalists would ebb. Sam briefly considered what he would say to them, then contrasted that with what he would like to say, then discarded his mindset as unproductive, alcoholic/addict thinking. One day at a time.

His attention returned to the task at hand, and he again scanned the documents he would have Cassie, his secretary and receptionist, file to memorialize his representation of Daniels. "Once more into the breach," he mused, and sipped cold coffee from a mug emblazoned with the 101st Airborne Division (Air Assault) "Screaming Eagles" logo. He placed the cup on the mat on his desk and briefly reflected upon a promising military career cut short by an improvised explosive device and a Taliban rifle round, then signed next to the "Sign Here" stickers Cassie had affixed to the papers.

2

Sergeant Vic Woodhouse had been a detention officer at the county jail in Custer for almost fifteen years. In that time, he'd seen a cross-section of bizarre behaviors and casual weirdness that most never do: drunks and tweakers and the mentally ill; cowboys and hippies and roughnecks and city dwellers passing through; men and women and the gender dysphoric; and young and old of all shapes, sizes, and ethnicities. Through it all, the jail had adapted—but the jailing of a former judge was presenting unique challenges.

As a threshold matter, Sheriff Neil Walsh had taken a personal interest in seeing to Daniels' jailing. "I want him bunked in booking so you can keep an eye on him," the sheriff had said. The booking area was a confined part of the jail where each cell was observed twenty-four hours a day by detention officers. That was beneficial from a detention officer's standpoint, but detainees hated it as the lights were perpetually on and the noise stemming from the booking of new arrivals was continuous.

Woodhouse had objected. "Sheriff, we're full up right now. I—"

"Then either talk with the county attorney and Judge Downs and bounce somebody, or assign someone else to a cellblock," Walsh had directed. "I want eyes on Daniels twenty-four-seven. I'm not going to have him shivved on my watch, and I don't want y'all to find him hanging in his cell."

"Well, I suppose we could move Mason," Woodhouse had said.

John Mason was a longtime resident of Custer who had spent the better part of his adult life in and out of custody doing, as one wag put it, "a life sentence sixty days at a time." Walsh had dealt with Mason on the street twenty-five years ago as a young deputy. "Has he stopped throwing his feces at the guards?"

Woodhouse had acknowledged Mason's improvement. "Yeah. Worst he's done lately is insult some of the female staff."

Walsh briefly considered the situation. Mason's chronic drug and alcohol abuse had taken its toll on the man's physical and mental health. He would be at risk in the general population, but less so than Daniels. "Well, they'll have to get over it," he decided. "But keep an eye on Mason, too—I don't wanna see him get hurt."

Woodhouse had followed instructions and Daniels had now spent just shy of two days in booking. His cell door remained open, but the painted cinder blocks, green metal bunk, and stainless steel, lidless toilet were reminders that this was no five-star accommodation. Sitting quietly in his cell, Daniels could see detention officers peer in at him from time to time. He knew he was under special watch, which would entail his remaining in the booking area for his safety.

Woodhouse had worked the weekend and was glad to be going off shift on this Monday morning. He decided to check on the old judge one last time. "You okay, sir?"

"I'm fine, Sergeant," Daniels said. He was sitting on his bunk with his feet crossed on the floor, his hands in his lap. He'd spent much of the past two days in that exact position.

"Well, okay. You haven't eaten much."

"I don't have much of an appetite."

"Understandable, but you gotta keep up your strength. Some guys waste away in here pretty quick. I recommend push-ups."

"Understood."

"Anything you want me to tell Corporal Toner?" Woodhouse asked. "She'll be on until tonight. Then I'll be back."

"I hope I'm not here tonight." Daniels looked to Woodhouse for the first time.

"Well, yeah . . . I'm just saying if you are and if there's anything you need—"

"No special treatment, Sergeant," Daniels instructed. "Do not put yourself—or me—in that position. Please don't do anything for me you wouldn't do for any other inmate."

Woodhouse watched Daniels for a moment, then nodded. "Got it."

When Woodhouse was gone, Daniels stood and stretched, then walked to his cell door and looked at the clock on the wall behind booking. Ten a.m. In another three and a half hours he'd face a judge for the first time in his life. The irony.

"Judge, er, *Mister* Daniels?" It was Corporal Toner, apparently already on the job. Short and officious, she was not an advertisement for the department's fitness program.

"Yes?"

"You've got a call," she said. "You'll have to take it over there." She indicated a phone hanging on the wall. There would be no privacy. "Sorry."

"It's fine," he said. He crossed the large room to the phone on the wall, conscious of the other inmates watching him enviously; they would not be allowed to take calls. A block-lettered sign above the phone reminded callers: "All Communications Subject to Monitoring." Daniels wondered briefly how many inmates would understand the message. "Hello?"

"Judge, it's Julie—Julie Spence."

"Julie, how are you?" Daniels asked. It was good to hear her voice.

"I'm—I'm terrible!" she said, and he could hear her sniffle. "Judge, this is all my fault! I never should have—"

"Julie, stop. It wasn't your fault," Daniels said. "I'm—I was—her husband. It was my responsibility."

"I know, but I knew you were exhausted. I should have checked—"

"Julie!" Daniels interrupted. When she had been quiet for a few seconds, he asked, "What can I do for you?"

"I'm just calling to see if there is anything I can do for *you*. I have so much respect for you and after all you have done for me—"

"I'm fine," Daniels assured her. "Don't talk with anyone about what you saw, heard, or whatever until we get you an attorney—do you understand?"

"But I already have," she replied. "The night that Marci—"

"I know that, and it's fine. Just hold your tongue now until you are told differently—understand?"

"I—I do," she said. "I want you to know that all I told them was that it was her time, that it was an accident and you did everything right—"

"Fine, fine," he said. "Now, thanks for calling—and remember to keep quiet."

"But I want to help you!" Julie insisted. "Like you said, Marci didn't want to live that way."

Daniels took a deep breath. "I know that. But for now, just do what I'm telling you. Someone will be in contact, I'm sure."

"Okay. Well, she is in a better place now—just like you said she would be," she said. "We both know she didn't want to live like that. Please let me know if there is anything I can do. You know I'll do anything to help after . . . after all you've done for me."

"Fine," Daniels said.

"Okay. Bye."

"Bye." Daniels hung up the phone, turned, and walked quickly back to his cell, then sat and took up the same position he'd maintained earlier.

In an office behind the wall where new inmates were processed, Toner watched as the young detention officer removed her headphones. "Did you get it?"

"I did," the rookie said.

"Good. Get me a copy," Toner said. "Lee said to get him every one of Daniels' phone calls."

———

An hour later, Lee removed a wireless headset and looked to Cates. "See? I'm telling you they were either in on it together, or maybe he had her do it unwittingly."

"Why do you think that?"

"Didn't you hear her?" Lee asked. "She said she was in a better place —*just like you said* she would be."

"Well, yeah. But couldn't that be taken a couple of ways?"

"In a vacuum, maybe. But given everything else we have, no," Lee decided. "Hell, she said they both knew she wouldn't want to live that way. She said it was her time and that *he did the right thing!*"

"I thought she said *he did everything right.*"

"Same thing," Lee said.

"Are you sure?"

"Absolutely. This is just one more nail in Daniels' coffin. It's intuitively obvious to anyone with half a brain that Daniels killed his wife to get her out of the way. We know she had been dying, we know her illness had drained the family finances, and we know she had a large insurance policy. Add this conversation to the mix and the jury will connect the dots."

"Johnstone will say all that proves is that Julie was a loyal employee saddened by Marci's death. That's what I'd say."

Lee measured Cates. He'd yet to be first chair in a trial and had no idea what the hell he'd say. "Somebody—Daniels or Spence at Daniels' direction, to be specific—gave her too much medication. With what we have, no jury will buy an accident."

3

Mary Perry dabbed at red-rimmed eyes with the tissue she had clutched in her hand—she'd been bawling for the better part of a week. For almost twenty years she had served as the judicial assistant (and informal confidante) to the district court judges of this part of the state. She'd seen them at their best and at their worst. Daniels had been her favorite. Mercurial on the bench and hard drinking after hours, he nonetheless had a heart of gold and behind the scenes had ensured that his employees as well as the custodial staff were well taken care of by the county commissioners and state legislators. She had done what she could to temper his drinking, especially after Marci got sick, but when he resigned she had lost the ability to monitor his activities. She recalled seeing him during a chance meeting last month: "I'll be fine, Mary," he'd told her. Now this.

She was at her desk in the outer office when Walton Bridger, Daniels' successor, came in—as always—at precisely seven a.m. He nodded curtly in her direction and brushed past her desk on his way to his chambers. "I've got a call in to the supreme court. No interruptions, please."

"Understood," was all she could respond before the door to his chambers closed behind him. She had two or three letters to prepare and his docket to distribute by eight a.m. It would have been nice if he had given her his reaction to the news, but they had never developed the close relationship she had enjoyed with Daniels. She expected he was in a panic and trying to get on the line with the chief justice to gain guidance regarding what to do when Daniels' case was inevitably bound over from Judge Downs to him.

In fact, Walton Bridger didn't know whether to be elated or disappointed. On the one hand, Saturday's arrest of his predecessor had been a tremendous shock. On the other, it went a long way toward dispelling the myth that he couldn't fill the old man's shoes, now didn't it? But with that behind him, he was again torn—this time whether to preside over the trial. He'd never really known Daniels, and didn't particularly care for him, so he felt as if he could and would be neutral and fair. However, the mere appearance of unfairness could be damaging to the criminal justice system in Custer. More importantly, no matter how the case turned out, people would be angry with him. He didn't need this, he finally decided—especially in an election year. Accordingly, he had placed a call to the Wyoming Supreme Court, seeking advice.

Bridger felt his stomach tighten when Chief Justice Richard Park picked up. "Chief, it's Walton Bridger. Thanks for taking my call."

"No problem, Wally."

Bridger hated being called "Wally"; in fact, in his entire life perhaps only Park had ever called him that. Best to let it go. "I'm calling to talk about Judge Daniels' situation—have you heard?"

"Yeah, I heard about that," Park clucked. "Poor bastard. I'd heard Marci was sick and that he was taking it poorly, but holy crap!"

"Yeah, so . . . ummmm . . . I was wondering what you thought I might do when the case gets bound over."

"What's the problem, Wally?"

Bridger took a deep breath. "Well, he was my predecessor. I think I could be fair, but the public's perception might be otherwise."

"Yeah," Park mused. "Could be."

"So, uh, should I preemptively begin to look for another judge to hear the thing?"

Park laughed. "Not yet, Wally. Not yet. A couple of things. First, if I'm Daniels' lawyer I'm going to look real hard at a change of venue. Second, remember: the canons of judicial ethics say you cannot pass on a case just because it's ugly. You gotta have a reason."

Bridger was thinking fast. "Well, er, I'm thinking I do."

"Yeah?"

"Perception. There will be a perception that I'm favoring him."

"Then do what you can to squelch it, and quick."

"But—"

"Just hang in there, Wally. We'll getcha someone to help up there when the time comes. 'Til then, suck it up, son," Park said, and rang off.

Bridger listened to the dial tone for a few seconds, then hung up and rummaged through his desk in search of an antacid.

4

4.

Just after lunch, Miller and Jensen were sitting in an unmarked car, watching a suspected drug house for activity. For the better part of two years, law enforcement had suspected a Colorado man named Trent Gustafson was transporting heroin and methamphetamine north from the Denver area to distributors in Custer. Despite their best efforts—which included twisting arms, offering deals, and threatening recalcitrant potential witnesses with harsh sentences—law enforcement had been unable to find anyone to testify against him.

Jensen was normally assigned to the patrol unit but due to an illness had been temporarily assigned to assist Miller. It was good duty. He drank coffee from a Styrofoam cup and offered some to her.

"Styrofoam? Really? Where'd you even find that stuff?" she asked.

"I didn't know you were such a greenie."

"I'm not, Mike, but holy buckets! In a thousand years, some future life form is gonna be looking at Styrofoam and asking, 'What the hell is that?'"

"I denounce myself," he replied, and they laughed while watching the front door. Over the course of an hour they'd seen nothing. Jensen side-eyed Miller uncertainly. "How was the rest of your weekend?" he asked.

"Lame," she said. "Laundry, shopping . . . stuff like that." She stole a quick look at him and knew. "Go ahead and ask." She sipped flavored water from a plastic bottle.

"It's about the judge," he said. "The arrest, I mean."

What else? "What about it?"

"I don't know. I just felt like it wasn't right—he's an old man, you know?"

"Old people kill people all the time," she replied. "You know that. What is it really?"

"Well, it was Judge Daniels," he hedged. "I mean . . . I just can't see it."

"You were there; you heard the same responses I did."

"I know," he said. "I guess I'm just saying I'm having a hard time with it. He always seemed so . . . straight, I guess."

She looked at Jensen and smiled indulgently. "The longer I'm in the business, the less often I am surprised at my being surprised," she said. "You heard him. I think he was tired and frazzled—he admitted as much—and dealing with a terminal wife for too long. Maybe he really did forget. Maybe the change in prescriptions gave him an out; maybe he just lost it for a few minutes and decided to put her out of her misery."

"But they seemed to really love each other," Jensen insisted. "How do you kill someone you love?"

Could he really be this naïve? "Maybe to end her suffering? She was weak and near the end; all he did was expedite it. He's rationalizing it right now, but I think that at some point he will admit it. And to be honest, I think it probably happens more often than we think."

Jensen was thinking about his grandfather, a Vietnam combat veteran whose losing battle with lung conditions stemming from exposure to Agent Orange had been a long and dreadful one. He had seen the toll his grandfather's illness had taken on his grandmother as well as his own father. "I know, but it just seems . . . unreal."

"Oh, it's real," she said. "Look, you said yourself that when he was in the back of your car, he apologized multiple times."

"Oh, he did. But it was more like he was talking to her rather than me—you know? He said, 'I'm sorry,' three or four times. Talked about how she wanted to die with dignity and how he had failed her."

Miller wholeheartedly agreed with Punch and Lucas that before it was all over Jensen would be a fine officer, but at present his life experience and exposure to the criminal mind left something to be desired. "I hear you, Mike. But we know he played some role in killing his wife—right? And it's only natural that rather than face it directly he would almost immediately begin to rationalize his actions. We've got his statements; we've listened to them and looked at the evidence. When we did all of that I made the decision to charge him." Jensen drank coffee and said nothing. "Say it," she encouraged him.

"I'm just thinking that Lee . . . well, Lee kind of pushed this, I think. That's all."

Miller swallowed hard. It was true enough, but it was her decision, damn it. "I made the decision to arrest," she said tightly. "I'm the one who is going to have to take the stand and testify. I'm the one that's gonna have Sam Johnstone smiling at me and eyeballing me like a rattlesnake looking at a two-legged bunny."

"I know, right? But Lee thinks—"

"Mike, I'm a big girl. I've been doing this for a while. I think I've got enough experience to know when I've got sufficient evidence to make an arrest. Besides, I ran it by the chief. He said he'd cover me if it comes to it."

"I know, but involuntary manslaughter was the right call, if you ask me."

"Not our call," she said. "Besides, you know the game; Lee probably plans to plea bargain it down."

Jensen finished his coffee. "Lee is so focused on beating Sam Johnstone in court that—"

"There he is!" Miller pointed to Gustafson, who had exited the house and was walking quickly toward a late-model sports coupe.

"Not trying to hide, is he?" Jensen said, as Gustafson backed the yellow car out and took off in a northerly direction.

"Just don't lose him. Stay back a ways and let's see if we can observe a traffic violation. I'll call the K-9 guys and maybe we can do a free air sniff when we get him pulled over. He's gotta have something on him."

"Roger," Jensen said. He goosed the four-door sedan slightly to try and keep a visual on Gustafson.

5

The attorney-client conference rooms in the county's jail were at the end of a long, spartan hallway that reminded Sam of the hundreds of similarly stark buildings he had occupied as a soldier. Tile floors, painted cinder block walls, and naked light bulbs gave the space a dour feel. The detention officer who escorted Sam wasn't one he recognized and made no effort to introduce himself, so the walk was accomplished in silence. When the door was opened, Daniels, wearing an orange jumpsuit, was seated at a gunmetal gray table with a plexiglass pane that would serve as a divider between them. Sam immediately observed that Daniels was chained to the table. "Is this really necessary?" Sam asked.

"Rules," the guard said before closing the door.

Sam turned his attention to Daniels. Seeing the older man, he swallowed hard. "Hi, Press. How ya doin'?" he croaked. He had, of course, visited dozens if not hundreds of defendants here in the past couple of years, but this was different. "Such bullshit!"

"Lee's just doing his job," Daniels cautioned. "Same as you would if you were in his position."

"I don't think so. I don't think you—"

"Oh, I killed her," Daniels assured Sam.

"Jesus, Press! Don't say that!" Sam scolded, involuntarily scanning the walls and ceiling. Attorney-client rooms were not monitored, but Sam was concerned, nonetheless.

"I'm responsible for her death, Sam." Daniels spread his hands. "It's as simple as that."

"You know better than I that there's a world of difference between being morally responsible and criminally culpable," Sam said. He watched as Daniels looked at his chained hands and rubbed each wrist. "How are they treating you?" he asked, changing the subject. He'd heard horror stories regarding the treatment of law enforcement and judicial officials in custody.

"Pretty good." Daniels shrugged. "They have me in a cell by myself right next to the control area."

"Excellent." That position would eliminate—or at least minimize—the possibility of anyone getting to Daniels without the detention officers knowing about it. "We need to talk about what happened after Corporal Jenkins arrested you."

"You saw it all," Daniels replied. "They cuffed me and put me in the back of the car."

"Did they say anything on the way to the jail?" When Daniels didn't respond, Sam changed his tact. "What did they say?" he probed.

"I don't want to get anyone in trouble."

Unbelievable. "Let me get this straight: you have been wrongfully arrested for killing your wife—"

"I'm not sure that's true—"

Sam let it pass for now. "And you're worried about getting someone in trouble? Who is it?"

"I've worked with Jensen for a long time," Daniels explained. "I think he is a good cop, and he was only doing what he was told."

True enough. "What did he say?" When Daniels didn't answer, Sam pressed him. "It's all gonna be on the dash and vest cams; do I need to watch them for myself?"

"He said he was sorry and that he personally didn't believe that I killed Marci."

Sam held his breath after he posed his next question. "And you said?"

"I told him it was okay—that it was my fault."

Christ. "Why? . . . Oh, hell. Never mind that. Then what?"

"We got to the station, and they processed me. Did a good job, too," he added. "Then they asked me if I wanted to make a statement."

"You declined, of course."

"You're gonna be pissed," Daniels said, shaking his head ruefully.

"You have got to be kidding me!" Sam exclaimed. Anyone with a basic understanding of criminal law knew better. The man was a judge! "What the hell were you thinking?"

"I was thinking I've known Mike Jensen for a while now, and he deserves to know the truth."

What was done was done. "Which is?"

"Which is that I think I killed her."

Sam sat quietly, watching his client. "Tell me that you didn't use those words."

"Sam, I can't tell you that."

Sam sighed heavily. "You didn't do anything intentionally." It wasn't a question.

"Of course not. That would be murder. I didn't murder my wife."

"Do you see why the cops are confused?"

"No. Words mean things."

"You weren't wanting to put an end to her suffering?"

"Not at my hands," Daniels said. "But obviously I wanted it to end."

"You didn't do it for the insurance money?"

"Don't be ridiculous."

Sam ignored the response. "Then it was an accident," he concluded.

"Well, yeah," Daniels allowed, and Sam filled his lungs with air again.

"So, what happened?"

"I didn't change out the prescription, so Julie administered too much morphine," Daniels said. "The day before, the doc told me if I gave her the same amount it would kill her."

"Christ! Did you tell Jensen that?"

"Miller, I think. Maybe Jensen, too. Oh, hell, Sam, it's going to come out —what Doc told me. She's got to cover her own ass."

She certainly did. "Did you tell Lee and his people this?"

"Haven't spoken with any prosecutors." Daniels shrugged. "But I told everyone the same story, because it was the truth."

Sam sat back in his chair and looked at his hands, then to Daniels. He had to know. "Press," Sam began carefully. "I need to know something."

Daniels was eyeing Sam warily. "Yeah?"

"Before we go too far down this road together, I need to know: Do you have a death wish?"

When Daniels merely shook his head and smirked, Sam got irritated. "Are you going to fight? Are you willing to help me defend you? Because if you want to punish yourself or let Lee punish you for this, maybe I'm not the right guy to help."

"Sam—" Daniels began, but was interrupted by a knock at the door.

This time, the detention officer was Tom. "Sam? About five minutes, okay?"

"Thanks, Tom. We're just about through here." Sam turned his attention back to Daniels. "Let's go," he directed. "But two things. One, let me do the talking. Two, let me do the talking—got it?"

Daniels' face had reddened. It had likely been decades since anyone had told him what to do. But his jaw soon relaxed. "Got it, Sam. And thank you."

Sam stood and knocked to get Tom's attention. If nothing else, he now understood why Daniels had been arrested, and what he was up against.

6

Just before one-thirty p.m., Downs made a last check of her appearance. As a circuit court judge, she oversaw a criminal docket that while procedurally repetitive was comprised of defendants fresh off the street, many of whom were still under the influence, and all of whom were desperate to get out of jail. Accordingly, she oversaw multiple hearings per day that brought emotions ranging from terror to disgust to hilarity to the forefront. In contrast to the district court—the court of general jurisdiction, having the ability to hear limited numbers of high-profile criminal cases and notable civil cases—circuit courts operated in relative obscurity, handling high-volume and lower-dollar value matters such as misdemeanors and small claims. But as the first stop for accused felons, from time to time high-profile matters came along, and for a brief instant the circuit court judge would be under the spotlight. Today, she would see Daniels and have her every word examined for nuance. As she looked out the window of her chambers, Downs saw out-of-state television crews setting up in areas designated by Custer police. She took a last look in the mirror in her private lavatory and was generally satisfied. She'd been working out regularly and had gotten some sun watching Emma participate in various activities, but with her fortieth birthday in the rearview mirror and her innate body image issues, she would never be completely happy with how she appeared.

The gallery would be full today. With a retired judge of local renown charged it was going to be a circus. She was running his initial appearance at the same time as those of regular defendants to give the process a semblance of normalcy; however, she'd had a clerk call Sam Johnstone's and Grant Lee's offices to ensure they were prepared to go first. Thereafter, for both safety and practical reasons, she would take a recess and allow the gallery to clear.

She was signing a stack of orders granting default judgment against debtors who had never replied to lawsuits when one of her clerks knocked on her office door.

"Everybody is here, ma'am."

"Fine," Downs replied. "I'll be just a minute." When the door closed, she took and held several deep breaths to relax. Aside from the assembled media presence, she was apprehensive in advance of what she was certain would be a contentious hearing between Lee and Johnstone.

Sam had a sour stomach, so he palmed then swallowed two antacids with tepid water from the plastic pitcher that had been placed on the defendant's table. He made a face as the concoction made its way to his gullet. Lee had studiously ignored Sam and Daniels when entering the courtroom; between that and Rebecca's absence, Sam anticipated the hearing would be ugly. He and Daniels stood with the others as Downs entered, looking fit and tanned. She had settled into the job nicely, and Sam enjoyed appearing in the courtroom of the calm and collected young judge. He noted a slight tremor in her voice as she called the court to order.

"Good morning, ladies and gentlemen. Circuit court for the 12th Judicial District is in session. We are on the record and here for in-custody arraignments and initial appearances. The State is present and represented by Mr. Lee. The first matter before the court is captioned 'State of Wyoming versus Preston Daniels.' The defendant is present, and the court notes its receipt of an entry of appearance filed earlier today by Mr. Johnstone. We are here for an initial appearance on a charge of murder. Mr. Johnstone, will the defendant waive a reading of his rights?"

Sam was already on his feet. "Yes, ma'am." He considered telling her Daniels would waive a verbatim reading of the allegations but knew she would insist on putting the reading on the record. No reason to irritate her.

Downs nodded and picked up a thick book containing annotated statutes. "Defendant is here pursuant to an arrest warrant signed by this court," she said as she thumbed the book in search of the correct law. "The allegation is that on or about the ninth day of April, the above-named defendant, in Custer County, did purposely and maliciously, but without premeditation, kill Marci Daniels, to wit: did kill Marci Daniels by intentionally administering or causing to be administered an overdose of controlled substances. This is murder in the second degree, punishable by imprisonment in the penitentiary for not less than twenty years, or life."

When she completed reading, she looked up to the gallery until the murmuring ceased. "The defendant has waived an advisal of rights and has now been advised of the charges. He has retained counsel. The court will not take a plea today as it lacks jurisdiction to do so." That part of her speech was for the benefit of the assembled media, most of whom would be unfamiliar with Wyoming legal procedures and would likely be expecting a dramatic expression of "not guilty" from Sam or his client. "Let's turn, then, to the issue of pre-trial release," she said, looking expectantly to Lee. "Mr. Lee, does the State wish to be heard?"

"Yes, Your Honor, we do," Lee said as he stood to his full height. He was slightly taller than Sam, although somewhat thinner. Sam had heard somewhere Lee had competed in track in college, and between what looked to be about a thirty-six-inch inseam and a deeply competitive spirit, Sam could see Lee as a middle-distance runner of some ability.

"I'll be brief, ma'am," Lee began. "Mr. Daniels is charged with a serious crime—among the most serious crimes on the books. This is a crime that is appalling not only as a function of its nature but also because of the sheer helplessness of the victim. While it is true the defendant held a position of trust in this community for decades—a fact Mr. Johnstone will surely emphasize—from the State's perspective, that, combined with the malicious nature of the crime, shows the defendant to be calculating to a degree rarely seen in this jurisdiction. Accordingly, while a defendant of his age and length of residence might not normally be viewed as a flight risk, we view these as exceptional circumstances, believe he poses a continuing danger to the community, and would ask the defendant be held without bond."

Sam was surprised by the brevity of Lee's request, although the bottom line—no bond—was predictable.

"Mr. Johnstone, does the defendant have a differing opinion?" Downs asked, knowing full well Sam did.

"We do, Your Honor," Sam replied before he was fully on his feet. "We believe the defendant should be released on a personal surety bond subject —" Sam was interrupted when Lee laughed aloud. He turned to face Lee, and then squared back up to the podium. "Subject to conditions the court is empowered to emplace that will ensure his appearance and the safety of the community. If—"

"Your Honor, the State opposes any bond, let alone—"

"I'm talking!" Sam snapped. "You have no right to interrupt me."

"Judge, this is absurd and a waste of everyone's time," Lee appealed to Downs.

"Gentlemen, I'll not have this back-and-forth in my courtroom," Downs said. "All comments will, per the rule, be directed to the court. Mr. Johnstone, please continue."

Sam had been knocked off stride, but Downs' tongue-lashing had given him time to review his notes. He argued earnestly for Daniels' release, citing his lack of criminal record, history of public service, declining health, and lack of finances. "Your Honor," he concluded, "my client poses no risk of flight and no danger to the community. He is presumed not to be guilty. For these reasons we ask he be released immediately, so that he might properly assist counsel in defending against this charge. Thank you." Sam watched Downs carefully; her doubt was obvious. Feeling Daniels' hand on his sleeve, he leaned over to hear from the older man.

"Nice try," Daniels praised. "But she won't—"

Unaccountably, Lee was on his feet. He'd already made his argument. "Your Honor, may the State be heard?" he inquired.

Downs looked hard at Lee. "For what reason, Counsel?" she asked.

"To rebut the comments of counsel, of course," Lee said. Ignoring the judge's glare, he continued. "Mr. Johnstone has casually mentioned his client's prior position, clearly expecting this court to grant bond as a favor to the defendant. That would be a bond no other comparably situated defendant would have the gumption to seek."

Sam was on his feet. "Your Honor!" he began. "Mr. Lee is questioning the court's—"

"I hear him," Downs said, her face flushed. "And I must say, Mr. Lee, your rather transparent attempt to paint this court into a corner is improper on face and is not appreciated." Sam could sense the excitement amongst the assembled media.

"Judge—" Lee began.

"Be quiet, Mr. Lee. I've heard quite enough," Downs said sharply before turning her attention to a form she had been completing before the attorneys began sniping at each other. "The Wyoming rules of criminal procedure prescribe the considerations a court should make before setting pretrial conditions," she began. She then outlined her rationale and the conditions, and ordered Daniels released upon the receipt of one hundred thousand dollars commercial surety, meaning Daniels or someone on his behalf would have to pony up approximately ten thousand in order for a bail bonding firm to file a commercial surety with the court. Judges sometimes ordered a defendant be released only on a commercial surety to ensure a third party—the bonding agent—would keep an eye on the defendant in order not to have the bond cashed and forfeited to the court if the defendant failed to appear or otherwise violated the terms of the bond. When she had completed outlining the terms and conditions Daniels would have to abide by should he make bond, she stood and left the bench. When the door behind her closed, the courtroom erupted. Sam put an arm on Daniels and waited for the gallery as well as Lee and his entourage to depart.

"Boy did he step in it," Daniels observed.

"I'm surprised," Sam agreed.

"Well, good for me."

"Can you make the bond?" Sam asked.

"I think so."

"Let me know. I can help if you need it."

One of the court security officers approached. "Sam, we gotta get him back."

Sam nodded. "Okay." He turned his attention to his client. It was probably unnecessary, but best to say it anyway. "Press, don't say anything to anyone." He waited until Daniels had been escorted from the courtroom before standing and gathering his materials. His phone was in the breast pocket of his suit jacket, and he felt it vibrating. Retrieving it, he saw a text from Rebecca and scanned it. He wasn't surprised but sent a response acting as if he was.

After a brief press encounter, he slowly made his way to the office, stopping briefly on the Cavalry Creek bridge to look for fish. He was at his desk an hour later when Cassie marched into Sam's office and unceremoniously dropped the print-out from the local newspaper's website on his desk. The headline of a story credited to Sarah Penrose read, "County Attorney Resigns."

Sam looked up at Cassie. "Rebecca texted me about an hour ago."

"And you didn't tell me?"

"I was sworn to secrecy."

"Sam Johnstone, I simply cannot believe you are keeping secrets from me of all people!" Cassie stormed.

Sam quickly changed his tone. "I'm sorry, Cassie, but I promised her, just as I would you."

Cassie put her hands on her wide hips and stared at him for a long few seconds. At last, she seemed to relax. "Well, I guess if you promised, it's okay."

"I did." He held up a hand as if he was taking an oath.

She nodded. "So tell me this: Sarah's story says Rebecca denied she resigned because of Grant Lee—is that true?"

Sam debated briefly before answering. "Not from what I understand."

"I knew it!" Cassie cried. "I gotta tell Raylene." She turned to leave Sam's office.

"No attribution," Sam said to her backside.

"I heard it from a little birdie," she replied without looking back.

7

Cathy Schmidt had been busy in the weeks following her resignation as a deputy county attorney. While she had taken great pride in representing the people of Wyoming as a prosecutor, the arrival of Grant Lee, along with his misogyny and questionable ethics, had spelled the beginning of the end for her. She'd discussed the situation with Rebecca Nice, of course, but the county attorney had seemed surprisingly unwilling to do anything about him. There were the usual rumors—standard fare anywhere men and women worked long hours and side by side. In the end, Cathy's decision to resign brought her relief, especially after Sam had prevailed in the trial of Mike Young. No one wanted to be on a losing team.

She had Kayla to care for, of course. She had subsequently looked at job opportunities across the state and had entertained an offer from a law school classmate to prosecute in Sioux Falls, but after some consideration over several days and glasses of Chablis she decided to stay in Custer, mostly because Kayla was doing very well in school. On Sam's recommendation she had spoken with the courthouse custodian, Jack Fricke. He was a creep, but just as Sam said he would, Fricke had an insider's knowledge of commercial real estate availability. She had registered the name of a new limited liability company and a new professional corporation, then signed a lease for a small office in a building up the hill from the courthouse. She had taken out a small business loan with a local bank and was now in the process of getting things organized. The place came partially furnished, but the walls were bare, and on this early May morning she was hanging her law school diploma and license in what would become her office when she heard sounds in the small front reception area.

Must be the manager with the additional chairs she had negotiated as part of the deal. She removed a small nail from her mouth. "I'm back here!"

When the footsteps she heard approaching on the old wooden floors ceased, Cathy turned to face a woman who was not the manager but Misty Layton, and she was—to be kind—a mess. Cathy had been prosecuting Misty off and on since her arrival in Custer some years back. Fortyish, heavyset, with loud pink hair that was generally drawn back in an unkempt, graying ponytail, Misty had been in and out of abusive relationships, drug treatment centers, and jails for decades. Cathy's relationship with Misty had been contentious, and more than once Misty had left a courtroom under guard and with a sharp word for Cathy. The fact that Misty was now standing between Cathy and the door was discomfiting.

"Relax, Counselor," Misty said, looking around the office. "This place ain't much," she added. She was wearing a black T-shirt with the sleeves removed, probably to show her many tattoos.

"Are you offering to help decorate?" Cathy asked, with more brashness than she felt.

Misty snorted. "'Course not. I'm here to hire you."

Cathy couldn't hide her surprise. "You want to hire me?"

"I do," Misty explained. She raised an arm and scratched at an armpit. "You know me as well as anyone. And I know you. You and I might disagree on stuff, but I know you are a straight shooter."

Cathy looked at her watch. She had things to do, and Misty would never be able to pay. "Well, I appreciate that but—"

"And you know I wouldn't do nothin' to hurt no kid," Misty said. "Especially my own grandkid."

Not intentionally or directly, anyway. Addicts never understood the second- and third-order effects of use and addiction. They weren't focused on the long game. Cathy looked at Misty closely; chronic methamphetamine use resulted in rapid, uncontrollable weight loss. Given her size, it was clear Misty was not using right now. Wouldn't hurt to listen.

"Have a seat," she directed, and pointed to a chair she felt could handle Misty's load. "What is the charge? I'm kind of on the outs with the county attorney's office."

"So I heard," Misty said. "They said I was endangering children. Me! Can you believe that shit?"

She could if there was meth in her house. "What happened?"

"What happened was my son OD'd while he was watchin' my daughter's kid. I was workin' as always."

These people. "Where's your daughter?"

"In prison."

Oof. "So your son—"

"Kyle."

"So Kyle was watching his nephew—your grandson—and he overdosed?" Cathy asked. When Misty nodded, Cathy voiced the obvious question. "How'd you find out?"

"My grandson—his name is Aristotle—he FaceTimed me. Put it in front of Kyle's face. Said 'Daddy's blue.'"

"Daddy?" Good Lord.

"Not what you think. Kid calls any man 'Daddy.'"

Maybe not as good an explanation as she thought it was. "I see. So you called it in?"

"I did. Tol' Ari to unlock the door. Cops showed up, and when I got home—I had to have my manager come in and I can tell you she was pissed —they already had a warrant, so I told them where I thought the drugs'd be so they wouldn't tear up my house. Then they took my grandson!"

"I understand and—"

"Do you?" Misty asked. She pushed a lock of pinkish hair off her forehead and looked at Cathy expectantly.

"Well, kind of. I mean, I'm a mom."

"Then you know I wouldn't do nothin' like they're sayin'."

"Was there meth in the house?"

"Oh yeah! But it wasn't mine!"

Wouldn't really matter if she knew it was present. "Did you know it was there?"

"I figured as much, to be honest," Misty said. "Kyle's been actin' funny since maybe two days after he got home."

"Why didn't you kick him out?"

"Cause I got no one else to watch Ari!" Misty cried. "It ain't like I can afford no daycare. No daycare, no job."

"Where was Kyle before he came back?"

"Prison. Some bullshit child porn charge."

The woman was leaving her grandson with her son, who was a tweaking pervert. Cathy wanted no part of this, and quickly considered her options. She could do a limited appearance and then line Misty up with a public defender. "So you got cited?"

"Cops don't cite people like me," Misty snorted. "They arrested me. Luckily, I got ahold of my neighbor, and she pawned some'a my furniture to get the two hundred bucks so I could make bond."

What the hell. Maybe she could meet with Kyle and see if he would own up to it to get his mom off the hook. Somewhere in his drug-addled brain there might be a shred of responsibility left. "Look," Cathy began. "I'm not going to make you any promises, but I'll work with you. When's your next appearance?"

"I think in two weeks or so. I got a letter on my fridge."

Cathy would call the court tomorrow. "Okay. Let me look into it. For now, follow the terms of your bond. Here's a card." It was the first business card Cathy had handed out. "Call me here next week."

Misty started to leave and then turned to face Cathy. "I heard you was gonna be a private attorney and I tol' my friends I was gonna come see you. A lot of 'em said you'd never take on a poor person, but I told 'em, 'I bet she will.'" And with that she was gone, leaving in her wake the acrid odor of booze and cigarettes.

With her first client on her way, Cathy put the nail back in the corner of her mouth and walked to the wall to finish hanging her diploma and license.

8

Kenneth "Punch" Polson had been the detective sergeant with the Custer Police Department until a couple of years prior, when he had been detailed to the Wyoming Division of Criminal Investigation. He had taken the job with some reservations, as he suspected—correctly, it turned out—that the job would require odd hours and take him away from family activities. The kids were getting more involved in sports and school activities, and he hated missing games and practices, so he was thrilled to be back in Custer working a case.

Miller hadn't done much with his old office. In fact, there was a cardboard box filled with expired manuals and yellowed office memoranda that he had placed there, intending to put it in the dumpster. He'd not gotten around to it before his reassignment took effect, and Miller apparently hadn't had time, either.

"Coffee?" she offered.

"Is it any better than it was when I was here?"

"If it is, it must have been putrid." She smiled briefly, then changed the subject. "So, did you have a chance to look at my report?"

"I did." Miller had filed a report regarding her observations of a suspected drug dealer named Trent Gustafson. Punch was well-acquainted with Gustafson. Long suspected of being one of the primary meth dealers in Custer, he was thought to be bringing the drug in from Denver on a regular basis. Federal authorities had him on their radar, as well, but had asked that local and state law enforcement observe and report, as they wanted to catch the bigger fish. "Good work."

"So what is it going to take for us to get the okay to move on this guy?" she asked. "He's bringing that shit in by the pound."

"I know it, and I want you to know it pisses me off, as well," Punch said. "But the pencil-pushers want us to wait. I spoke with our head and he's getting leaned on by someone in the Attorney General's office, who in turn is getting pressured by the US Attorney's office."

"So in the meantime, he can continue to deal that crap?"

Punch took a deep breath and considered how much he could tell her. He'd had the same frustrations when he was in her position. "Look, I know it is frustrating, but you've got to understand that in the big scheme of things he is a pissant."

"I get that," she said. "But he's gotten brazen and the fact that we can't ring him up is making us look like amateurs and raising some eyebrows, even among the tweakers."

"I know," he said. "And believe me, I've passed on your concerns to the task force. You're being heard." The task force was a confederation of law enforcement officers from various state and federal agencies working to get a handle on the distribution of illegal controlled substances. "I'm the chihuahua on their pantleg."

"I appreciate that, Punch," she said truthfully. "Any advice for the gal in your old job?"

"Just keep doing what you're doing. The information you are gathering, your observations of the network, will all be valuable."

"Someday."

"Right," he said, sipping coffee.

"Meanwhile, he's starting to deal fentanyl and people are dying. And I'm not going to lie; he starts dealing fentanyl, all bets are off."

"Understood," he said, looking at his watch. "I gotta get to practice."

"Enjoy yourself. And thanks for everything. Not everyone would be so . . . helpful."

"We're all on the same team. It's hard to believe that at times, but it's true. And I've been there. I get it," he said as he left. If he hurried, he could pick up Rhonda on the way.

9

Cathy's antiperspirant had failed her. It could be the unseasonably warm spring day or the quirky thermostat in her office. But more likely, it was the phone call she had made to Lee. She'd been placed on hold by a legal assistant named Sierra, whom Cathy heretofore considered a friend. But Sierra's business-only tone today had ended that. The music that played while Cathy waited was urban rap, of all things, and she was about to hang up and walk to the courthouse to see Lee when she heard him pick up.

"Lee," he said.

"Grant, this is Cathy Schmidt," she began, pausing to allow him to offer a greeting. When it was clear none was forthcoming, she continued, "I represent Misty Layton. She's charged with a felony—"

"I know who she is."

"I've been looking at the allegations. I've spoken with my client, and it seems like although she had an idea there were drugs in the home—"

"Then she's guilty," Lee interrupted.

Cathy looked dolefully at the phone. This wasn't going to end well. "You and I both know that unless she testifies—which she won't—the best the jury can do is to infer she knew."

"She led the cops right to the drugs." Lee laughed.

"It was her house; it has like five rooms. She knew which room was his; therefore, she knew where the drugs were," she explained.

"She's an addict; she's got six prior convictions for drugs. Two felonies. You've prosecuted her yourself. You know all that."

"None in the past three years," Cathy pointed out. "People can change." When he didn't respond, she continued, "Look, Grant, she has been trying to change for her grandson's sake. She has a job, she's doing NA—can you cut her some slack? I can get her to plead no contest to possession, I think, if you'll drop the endangering children."

"No dice," Lee said. "I want a full confession. I don't want her around children if she is using or tolerating drugs in the home."

He was relentless. "Grant, it's not that simple. Her daughter's in prison; the baby daddy is nowhere to be found. If my client gets locked up it's not unlikely the kid is going to end up in foster care."

"That sounds like an acceptable option," Lee said. "In any event, it's not my problem. She should have thought of that before she allowed drugs in the home."

What an ass. "If she boots her son, she's got no daycare."

"Not my problem."

"This is a woman who has been beat down and kicked around by every man she has ever known!" she exclaimed. "Now, for once in her life, she is taking responsibility on behalf of her grandchild and you—the guy responsible for justice in this county—are prepared to see an injustice be done!"

"I don't see it the same way you do—obviously," Lee said. "She is guilty in the eyes of the law, Cathy. Perhaps your inability to see that is what kept you from being a truly effective prosecutor," he added gratuitously. "I have a duty to protect this community, and I intend to exercise that responsibility to the fullest extent of the law."

Cathy thought of Rebecca. No wonder she had called it quits. She took a deep breath and was thinking about what she shouldn't say when Lee continued, "Good talking to you, Cathy. Cold plea or we try the case."

She viciously slammed the phone into its cradle. "Damn it!"

Lee was basking over Cathy's loss of self-control and reading the accounts of Daniels' initial appearance and Rebecca's sudden resignation when the receptionist called him and told him Sarah Penrose, the law enforcement reporter for the *Custer Bugle*, was here for her appointment. He'd been expecting her, of course, and was excited to get some things on the record. He'd spent an hour looking at stories under her byline and decided that her writing was acceptable: clean, crisp prose efficiently mixed multi-sourced information with insightful inference to create stories that were cutting-edge and entertaining.

She entered accompanied by Cates. "Aiden, I'll handle this," Lee said. He watched and waited until the door closed before turning his attention to Penrose. She was still standing, looking at the bare walls of his office. "Have a seat," he offered. "I don't decorate much," he added. "Decorations can be a distraction and tend to focus one's attention on the past. I like to remain focused on what's ahead. Now, what can I do for you?"

"Obviously, I wanted to talk with you about Rebecca Nice's resignation last week—I've been trying to get in to see you for some time."

"I've been busy."

"What can you tell me?" she asked.

"A real tragedy." Lee shook his head as if in sorrow. "I think she did a lot for this department—probably what she could," he added.

She removed a small digital recorder from her vest. "You don't mind if I record our conversation, do you?"

"No, no, not at all." Lee forced a brief smile and wondered why she hadn't brought along a photographer. "I've got nothing but good things to say."

"Interesting," Penrose said. She put pen to a lined notebook and scribbled something, waiting for Lee to speak. It was an old trick—one he'd obviously seen before, as he said nothing and the plastic smile never left his face. "So, how did you learn of Ms. Nice's resignation?" she asked when she determined he wasn't going to fall for it.

"She, uh, indicated to me she was giving it some thought."

"When?"

"I'm not sure—a couple of days before she announced it, maybe?"

She nodded as if accepting his explanation. "I'm told you are the odds-on favorite to be appointed to fill the chair until the next election," Penrose said. "Your thoughts?"

"Well, I am the chief deputy, so it would make sense," Lee agreed. "But that decision will be made by the county commissioners, of course."

"Of course. But assuming you were appointed, would you serve?"

Lee flashed a smile. He was prepared for this question. "Assuming I was appointed, of course. I have spent the better part of my professional life seeking justice. I will always seek fair and equal justice for the residents of Custer while maintaining high standards of transparency and account-ability."

"What do you mean by accountability?" she asked.

"Well, I mean that . . . we must be tough on dangerous criminals and prosecute them to the fullest extent of the law."

"Are you saying that hasn't been done previously?"

Actually, yes. "What I am saying is that I have concerns—concerns that the county needs a level of leadership and dedication that it has perhaps been lacking."

"Some say Rebecca Nice was a progressive—a reformer with a unique and innovative style," Penrose said. "Do you oppose that approach?"

"I can't say I oppose it, because I do not. What I can say is that results count," he said. "I think that the time-honored tradition in this country is that the imposition of immediate and certain consequences for ill-consid-ered behaviors has proven most effective."

"Is there empirical evidence to show that?"

"I think that as a matter of experience in the affairs of life most of us know that to be true."

"What kind of experience do you have?"

"I have several years' experience as a prosecutor," he said, warming to his task—which, in his view, was talking about himself. "Before that, I did civil litigation, so I think it is fair to say that I know my way around a court-room. But more than that, I think I have the knowledge necessary to lead this office and the good people who are still here. And I can promise you this: I will always be a learner. I'm not going to tell you I have all the answers." That sounded modest, didn't it?

Penrose raised an eyebrow. "I hear what you are saying, but what changes do you think you will make?"

"I'm not sure at this point, except to say that communication is extremely important, and I promise to try and improve our communications among and between all stakeholders." Gibberish, of course, but she seemed to buy it. He watched as Penrose smiled in understanding and looked at her list of questions. Perhaps he should tell her a little more about himself. He flashed his brightest smile. "You should know that I—"

"Ms. Nice says that you—as her chief deputy—filed charges against Judge Daniels without clearing it with her first," Penrose stated. "Is that true?"

Lee's smile remained on his lips but no longer extended to his eyes. "I will admit there was some inter-office disagreement regarding the timing and propriety of filing charges."

"What does that mean? Did you file without her permission?"

Lee looked upon Penrose indulgently. "I'm going to reject the premise of your question," he began. "As the chief deputy prosecutor, I believed—and I still believe—that I had the discretion to make decisions in that area," he explained. "As far as who said what and when . . . well, it would serve no purpose—"

"Except to explain what really occurred," she said. When it was clear he wasn't going to clear it up, she asked her next question. "And discretion is a power granted, is it not?" Penrose persisted. "As the boss, she had the right to make the final decision, didn't she?"

Lee looked around his office in response. "As I made clear when we started, my focus is on the future, not the past. Ms. Nice's reasons for resignation are her own, and I wouldn't begin to try and tell you what they were. I'm not sure it is important."

"But the inference is that you don't follow orders; you do what you want. Isn't that important to the taxpayers and county stakeholders to know?" she pressed. "Can the commissioners be assured that if you are appointed you will act as they wish and not in accordance with your own desires or even conscience?"

Lee made a show of looking at his watch. "I've another appointment here momentarily," he said. "But I can say this before I go. The people of

Custer can count on me to do my best every day to draw a line that if crossed by hardened criminals—no matter how rich they are or benevolent they may have been—will be enforced. Under my watch, everyone will be treated equally under the law."

"Are you saying that didn't happen before?"

Lee sighed demonstrably. "I'm looking to the future, Ms. Penrose. Now, as I have mentioned, I have another obligation."

"But clearly you are drawing a distinction between how you imagine things will be and how they have been."

"I'm not imagining anything, Ms. Penrose. I'm telling you flat-out that's how it is going to be," he said, standing. "Now, if you would be so kind—"

"I'd like to finish this interview—"

"I think we're done for now."

"Can we talk again?"

"Stop at the front desk and see my receptionist. I should be able to make some time. But you surely understand that, as the acting county attorney, and in the wake of two recent attorney resignations, I'm extremely busy right now." He pushed a button and when Cates appeared looked to Penrose, then to the young attorney. "Aiden," he asked sweetly. "Would you show Ms. Penrose to the door? We're done here."

"No need," Penrose said tightly as she turned to leave. "I've been here before."

When she had departed, Cates looked to Lee. "Anything I can do, boss?"

"No," Lee said. "I've got a handle on it."

"Do you think you'll get the appointment?"

"Of course," Lee said. He took clippers out of a desk drawer and stared fixedly at a hand. "Who else?"

"Well, I guess with Cathy gone and Mike Shepherd getting treatment—"

Lee looked up sharply. "What difference would that have made?"

"Uh. . . none, I guess," Cates said uncertainly. "I'm just saying that with them gone—"

Lee's eyes narrowed. "You've got things to do, don't you?"

"I—I do," Cates agreed. He watched Lee uncertainly and put a hand on the door. "Open or closed?"

"Closed."

When Cates was gone, Lee sat back in his chair and put his feet on his desk. "Cathy or Mike," he sneered. "Christ."

10

Sam had spent the hour following Cassie alerting him to Cathy's pending arrival trying to pick up around his office. He was dusting his shelves and failed to notice Cassie breach his doorway.

"Give it up," she advised. "This place needs professional help."

"Or maybe for you to do your job?" he teased.

Cassie sniffed. "Not in my job description."

"I think it is," he disagreed. "I wrote it."

"I don't think so. I signed it. Besides, at this point the terms of our employment agreement have been modified by mutual assent." She must have noticed Sam's raised eyebrows. "Don't be surprised," she said. "Can't help but learn a little law listening to you people flapping your lips."

Sam smiled briefly. "Is Cathy here?"

"Yes. Want me to get her?"

"Only if it's in your job description."

"I don't believe it is, but I like her, and I suppose at this point it can be presumed by—"

"Prior performance and mutual assent?" Sam finished.

Cassie smirked, then went to retrieve Cathy. Sam was on his feet when they appeared in his doorway. Cathy came in and took the chair directly across from him. She looked around briefly, then at him. "You hire a cleaning lady?"

"What makes you think it wasn't me?"

She smiled briefly, ready to deliver a smart remark, then sobered. "I need some help," she said without preamble.

Sam shrugged. "Ask."

"It's about Grant."

No surprise. "What about him?"

"He's playing hardball." She explained the situation with Misty Layton, her recovery and seeming turnaround, the presence of the drugs in her house, and Lee's refusal to recognize that and extend an offer.

His takeover hadn't taken long. "Can't say I'm surprised," Sam observed.

"Me neither. But it's not right."

"I agree," he said. "But he does have prosecutorial discretion. How can I help?"

"I don't know," she said. "Got any advice how to handle a difficult prosecutor?" She grinned before he had a chance to respond.

"Now where would I have learned anything along those lines?"

Her smile lit up her eyes. "I wouldn't know. Probably wherever you were before you came to Custer." She looked at her hands and then to him. "But seriously, I was hoping somehow, somewhere along the line you had learned something about representing innocent people."

Sam sobered. "So you believe her?"

"I really do. I think she is aging out of the game."

Sam understood. As a general rule, there were few recreational methamphetamine users. Accordingly, they either got the addiction under control, aged out of it, died, or were permanently incarcerated as the result of one or more crimes committed in furtherance of their habit. "Honestly, the best advice I have is to counsel your client carefully, paper it, and prepare for trial. If all he is offering is a cold plea, your client has nothing to lose. Bridger is a straight shooter—he won't hold a trial against her."

Cathy nodded in agreement. "That's true."

"Hell, who knows? You might get a jury to see it your way," Sam opined. "If what your client says is true, the jury would have to infer she knew—

juries don't like to do that. This is the age of CSI—they want ironclad proof. You can play that up. Who knew there were drugs in the house?"

"Well, her son Kyle, of course."

"Would he rat out his own mother?"

"I don't know."

"Talk with him and find out."

"I will. And what I'm thinking is this: if he doesn't testify, I won't put Misty on." Cathy shook her head. "No way. Everything on her record would be in play."

Sam considered the evidentiary rule while he reluctantly sipped water from a cup. Like a lot of alcoholics in recovery, he had gravitated toward sugar and was putting on weight. His sponsor had suggested he try drinking more water to keep the urge for sweets at bay. Cathy was right, of course. If Misty testified, much of her criminal past would likely be deemed relevant by the judge and Lee would eviscerate her. Fortunately, the State couldn't call her, so if Cathy didn't call Misty she wouldn't testify, meaning Lee would have to infer Misty knew where the drugs were—unless Kyle testified.

"I can't see it," Sam said, "If he's got any brains at all, he's gotta know he won't do a lot of time. With jail and prison overcrowding, everyone's all about rehab. Plus, he would have to admit his own stuff."

"What pisses me off is Lee not making an offer. He's made it clear there won't be a deal."

"Well." Sam leaned forward in his chair. "I have to believe that with you on the other side this one will be . . . personal for him."

"Why?"

Wasn't it obvious? "Well, you're a woman, for one."

She looked at herself in feigned surprise, then back at Sam. "I am!"

He laughed with her. "And you dated."

"Wrong," she said quickly.

He raised his eyebrows. "I thought—"

"You thought wrong."

"Huh," Sam said. "Well, I sense a degree of dislike. You'd best be prepared to battle that aspect, as well. I don't trust him."

She leaned forward in her chair. "You shouldn't."

"Meaning?"

"Meaning that Grant hasn't lost a lot of cases and he has taken the most recent one personally," she said, referring to the acquittal of Mike Brown.

"Then he needs to blame the jury," Sam said. "I'm just a lawyer doing my job."

"That's not how he sees things. He has it out for you. I think he has a plan."

"Wasn't it Mike Tyson who said, 'Everyone has a plan until they get punched in the mouth?'"

"No violence, Sam."

He spread his hands, showing his palms. "Who, me? I'm talking figuratively. Remember, I'm sober now. I'm a new man. I'm a smiling cloud," he joked.

Without smiling, she changed the subject. "How's your case going?"

Sam recalled Cathy's history as a point guard for the University of Wyoming. Given her competitive athletics background and prosecution experience, she was more than equal to the task of competing against Lee. "About the same as yours," he admitted. "I need to call Lee back; he left a message for me. I think he wants to continue the prelim."

"Screw him."

Sam laughed. "You think maybe I should give him the same sort of consideration he would give me were the roles reversed?"

"Like I said." She stood and prepared to leave.

"You need anything for your office?" Sam asked.

"Couple of clients. Ones with easy cases. Big money types—got any to spare?" She showed straight white teeth.

"All out of those," Sam said. "I do have a guy who came home wasted. Somehow his wife had figured out he was at the nudie bar all night, so she told him to go back there and sleep. He got pissed, went outside, jumped in his truck, and drove through the front door."

"Nudie bar?" She laughed. "I like that. Anyway, he showed her, huh?"

"I guess. To be honest, the dude has a surprisingly clean record. I've already got him in counseling and the like. So far, he is doing everything I asked. You want him?"

"Sam, you know as well as I do that guy has no respect for women—I don't care what his criminal record is."

"Don't say I didn't offer," Sam said. "Hey, I got another guy with a charge of public obscenity—his fourth. Seems his pants keep 'accidentally' falling off in front of attractive young women."

"Hard pass."

11

In Sam's estimation, Julie Spence had probably been a very attractive woman a decade ago. She was of medium height, but now much too thin. He could smell the smoke and assumed that like a lot of addicts in recovery she didn't eat well, relying instead on cigarettes and coffee to keep the urge to use at bay. She had called his office earlier today and asked to talk with him about Daniels.

"Get her in right now, before she changes her mind," Sam had instructed Cassie, who complied. It was just after lunch, and Julie was getting herself situated across from him at the table in his small conference room, where Sam habitually met with visitors as well as potential clients. It made it easier to effectuate an excuse to leave, if necessary.

"Coffee?" he asked.

"That would be wonderful," she said shyly. "Sugar."

"Make mine black," he said to Cassie.

He tried to engage Julie in small talk while Cassie made coffee, but she was guarded. She'd obviously tried to put herself together this morning, but years of bad decisions lined her face, and the eyeliner and false eyelashes couldn't disguise the sorrow in her blue eyes. She swiped at a strand of dyed-blonde hair with a trembling hand, then blew her nose with a tissue clenched in her small fist. When Cassie had delivered the coffee and closed the door behind her, Sam looked to Julie expectantly. "How can I help?"

"It's about Judge Daniels," she began. "He didn't kill Marci. At least not on purpose."

Sam wasn't surprised, nor was he particularly elated. He'd expected something along these lines. "Why do you say that?" he asked.

"Because he wouldn't do anything to hurt Marci—he loved her!"

Not helpful. "He certainly did," Sam agreed. "But Lee seems to think there is evidence that Press . . . well, that he killed her."

"That's so much bullshit!"

Sam wasn't surprised by the language, but the vehemence took him aback. "Well, again, there must be evidence—"

"But it wasn't intentional! It was an accident! I told the EMTs that. I told the cops that. I told the investigator that, but no one will listen. That's why I'm here."

"What exactly did you tell them?"

"That it was all an accident!"

Sam made a note on his yellow legal pad. "And why do you think that?"

"Because I know what happened!" She wiped her eyes with the same tissue she'd used on her nose moments prior.

Sam swiveled in his chair, retrieved a box of tissues from a small credenza, and handed the box to Julie. "I don't understand."

"According to the doctor," she began, wiping her nose again, "the prescriptions for morphine and diazepam are risky together. We—Judge Daniels and I—met with her doctor when she decreased the dosage of morphine."

"And?"

"And Press—Mr. Daniels, I mean—was supposed to replace the pre-filled syringes with the new ones having lower dosages. But he must have forgot. I—I should have checked, but I didn't. So when I gave her the morphine, it was too much."

Sam looked to his pad. "So you think he forgot?"

She looked at him plaintively. "Well, it seems pretty obvious he did—you know? I mean, she wouldn't wake up. Press said he would keep an eye on her and I said shouldn't we call the doctor but he said to leave her and that everything would be fine." She wiped her nose with a fresh tissue and threw the others in a small trash can Sam proffered. "But he didn't do it on purpose!"

Sam nodded. "And you told all this to the cops?"

"And the EMTs and the investigator—Ashley, isn't it?"

"Yes," Sam said. "What did they say?"

"Well, they really didn't say anything, but they clearly didn't believe me, or else they wouldn't have arrested him. Right?"

"Probably not," Sam mused.

"He didn't do what they are saying. I mean, she was in such terrible pain, and they'd been married so long. It was like a song or something, you know?"

"I know," he said truthfully. "Have you spoken with anyone from the prosecutor's office?"

"Yes," she said. "Some skinny, goofy-looking guy named Aiden. Christ, who names their kid—"

"What did you tell him?"

"Same things I just told you."

"Okay, let's do this. Let me think about what you've told me here today, okay?"

"Okay."

"And also, I think you might need a lawyer."

"Why?"

"Well, some of the things you've said . . . if someone took them wrong—"

She wiped again at her nose, this time with a fresh tissue. "I could get arrested?"

"Well, I don't know that it would go that far, but just to be safe."

"Will *you* do it?" she asked. "I—I don't have much money."

"I can't," he said, and explained the conflict he had because he was representing Daniels. "You could call my friend Cathy Schmidt. She just opened an office here in town."

"My testimony means that Press is innocent, right?"

Sam watched her closely. "Not exactly. But it does mean that maybe we've got some maneuver room." He looked at his watch; he had another appointment. "I've got another matter I need to attend to. Cassie will give you Cathy's number on your way out."

She wiped away fresh tears and blew her nose. "Sam, you'll get Press off, won't you?" she asked. "He didn't do what they are saying!"

"I'll do the best I can. That's all I can tell you. But I'm going to need your help."

"Anything!"

"Okay, I'll be in touch," he promised. "Thank you for coming to see me."

Right on cue, Cassie knocked and opened Sam's door. "Grant Lee on the line."

"Thank you," he said. "Would you see Ms. Spence out?"

Under the rules of criminal procedure, attorneys seeking a modification to general court guidelines or changes to schedules were required to consult with each other before asking the judge to approve a change. Lee was explaining he needed to continue Daniels' preliminary hearing because his arresting officer was out of town undergoing some training. While he droned on, Sam fiddled with a paperweight made from the lower half of a discarded 105-millimeter artillery shell.

Sam had seen countless instances whereby the prosecution called a witness to testify in a preliminary hearing who was neither on the scene nor—in extreme cases—a part of the investigation. Because the rules allowed hearsay without limitation during preliminary hearings, such witnesses were routinely allowed to testify. A preliminary hearing, after all, was on the books to force the prosecution to show the judge there was probable cause that a crime had been committed and that the defendant committed it, and experienced attorneys swore that a ham sandwich could be bound over to the district court for trial. Accordingly, Sam had his suspicions.

"What's really going on?" he asked when Lee finally took a breath.

"Just want to put the State's best foot forward," Lee replied.

Sam considered the response. He had already waived Daniels' right to a speedy preliminary hearing, hoping he might be able to do enough investigation to afford him some leverage with which to try and negotiate a plea short of a felony. Lee's request meant he was determined to try the case in the press. By firing all his guns during the preliminary hearing, he would see positive press coverage and make the unspoken case that evidence against Daniels was overwhelming, which it was not. But reporters and potential jurors wouldn't know that. Sam knew that if Lee sought a continuance, and if he opposed it, with Daniels having made bond and previously waiving a speedy preliminary hearing, the burden would shift to him to demonstrate some prejudice to his client posed by a continuance. It could prove difficult. Lee was aware of the quandary posed, of course.

"You can oppose it, but you know she'll grant it," Lee said, referring to Downs.

"Probably," Sam agreed.

"This is going to be a whole new ballgame," Lee observed. "New case, new judge, new defendant—you are going down, Counselor."

"This isn't about us!" Sam snapped. "This is about my client's life. If you want a piece of me, you know where I am. But leave my client out of this."

"Unfortunately for him, I cannot do that. Regrettably, he killed his wife in my town."

"Your town? You sound like a character in a bad western."

"Nonetheless."

"You're insufferable."

Sam could envision Lee shaking his head. "Personal attacks mean nothing to me, Counsel. I would advise you to prepare for the first of several losing arguments," he said before hanging up.

Sam had half a mind to walk to the courthouse and thump Lee's melon. But not today. He said a quick prayer and was in a solid frame of mind when Cassie knocked on his door. "Come in," he said.

"Are you okay?" she asked, seeing Sam.

"Fine," he lied. "What are we doing?"

"It's Mrs. Schumer. She wants to change her will again."

Eva Beck had been living in Bavaria when she met an American lieutenant named Jack Schumer in 1965. The two had fallen in love and married, and she had accompanied him on the many tours of duty he had undertaken during his career. She'd been naturalized along the way and was justifiably proud of her now-deceased husband's service and their ability to raise three relatively well-adjusted sons despite seventeen moves during Jack's twenty-six-year army career. Rather reluctantly, Jack had retired when he inherited the family ranch south of Custer, and he and Eva had taken up ranching until the day he died while baling hay. She had subsequently sold the ranch and moved into town, and now spent her time arguing with the neighbors over the length of their grass and squabbling with one or more of her sons.

"Which one of the boys is she pissed at this time?"

"Mike—I think."

The Schumers had named their sons Michael, Mickey and McKay— and referred to them as Mike, Mick, and Mack. It must have seemed like a good idea at the time. "Is that the one who wears boots?"

"No, that's Mick."

"Understood," he said, not understanding. "Any idea what he did to irritate her?"

"He got a DUI last week—didn't you see it in the paper? I'm sure that pissed her off."

"You know I didn't." Sam made it a practice to consume as little news as possible. He missed trying his hand at the daily crossword; on the other hand, being blissfully unaware of what was going on in the world made it much, much easier to remain sober. "All right—she ready?"

"I got her some coffee," Cassie said. "She's says it's weak."

"Wonderful," he said. "It will give her one more thing to bitch about. Give me a minute, please."

12

Cates had just finished one of the many memoranda of law Lee had assigned to him in the past few days. Lee had assigned this one yesterday afternoon, so Cates had remained in the office most of the evening, dining on a courthouse vending machine burrito and flavored water. He'd slept little, arrived early to review his work, and had enclosed it in a folder and was walking down the hallway toward Lee's office when he heard his boss on the phone.

"Oh, yeah," Lee said. "Gonna be a good day. Got things well in hand here."

Cates stopped outside Lee's partially open door, unsure how to proceed. "Rebecca resigned last month," Lee continued. "I've got a few months to get some things done. The election is in November, of course, but this is a one-party county, so August's primary will be the real election."

Cates was about to return to his office and try again later when Lee began talking again. "I have no idea," he said. "There is an older fella who clearly doesn't have the stones to run, and a couple of deputies who don't have what it takes. Had a solid female prosecutor, but she resigned a while back and I can't see her running. Got a young deputy working for me now, but he doesn't know shit from shinola. I think I'm it, so give it some thought. I'll need a number two here soon, and you've got the job if you want it."

At the mention of himself, Cates turned in anger and shame and returned to his office. He slammed the door behind him and wiped at tears of fury.

Finishing his phone call, Lee made a note to call human resources, then pulled documents from his inbox, looking for a memorandum of law he had assigned Cates the day prior. Not seeing it, he looked at his watch, then called Cates on the office intercom. "I'm looking for the memo on lesser included offenses," he said.

"I've got it right here," Cates said.

"Well, bring it down!" Lee ordered. "You were supposed to have completed it by start of business. It should have been on my desk when I came in," he added, and then hung up. While he waited, he browsed an online office catalog. He was going to need a new chair—preferably in brown leather. He was rehearsing an argument to the county commissioners when the knock came at his door. Sighing heavily, he said, "Come in!" When Cates appeared, Lee pointed at the chair on the other side of his desk. "Have a seat and let me take a look."

Lee accepted a copy of the memo and ignored Cates while he perused it. When he had seen enough, he looked to Cates and noted the red face and watery eyes. Allergies? "Well?" he asked expectantly.

"Because the charge is second-degree murder, the lesser included is intentional manslaughter." A lesser included charge was one that shared many of the same elements as the charged offense but was less serious. "Of course, there is also the possibility of involuntary manslaughter. If Sam gets that in, there's a lesser included charge of criminal negligence—"

"That isn't going to happen," Lee assured Cates. "We've got enough to show a reasonable person this wasn't an accident."

"I'm just saying *if*," Cates replied carefully.

"I don't think that way."

"Well . . . fine. What else do you need?"

"Anything on the change of venue?"

"Yes. In general," Cates began, "trials must occur where the crime occurred. But where there is—and I'm quoting here—so great a prejudice against the defendant that the defendant cannot obtain a fair and impartial trial, a change of venue may be granted."

Lee was considering Sam's options. "When is the motion proper?"

"They—Sam—could file it anytime," Cates replied. "If he files it before the trial starts, he's got a heavy burden—gotta show pre-trial publicity was extremely prejudicial and not factual. Basically, you've got to show manifest prejudice against the defendant in pre-trial news reports."

"So—"

"More likely he'll bring it after voir dire. During jury selection he'll ask a lot of questions about whether jurors have seen news reports."

Lee was scanning the memo. "And then?"

"And then he'll file his motion after voir dire but before the peremptory challenges have been made. He'll make a big deal about jurors having heard or seen media accounts of the trial. But it really doesn't matter unless the media has been reporting falsehoods or has otherwise been one-sided in its coverage."

"Okay," Lee said. "Good work. Are you okay? You look a little flushed."

"Just . . . tired, is all."

"Okay," Lee said, putting the memo into a one-inch-thick manila folder. "Well, you've got things to do. Anything else?" When Cates merely stared at him, he prompted the young attorney. "Anything else?"

"I spoke with Julie Spence like you said," Cates began. "Here are my notes and a transcript of the interview." He placed a stack of papers on Lee's desk.

"Did you ask the questions I gave you?"

"Yes."

"In the order I gave them to you?"

"Yes."

Lee was watching his understudy, who seemed irritable. "You didn't follow up or pose any others, did you?"

"No, you told me not to," Cates replied. "I mean, a couple of times she tried to explain something, so I cut her off and moved on—just like you said."

"Good. Thank you, Aiden. It's important that my people do exactly as I tell them." Lee looked back to the document he had been working on.

"Excuse me, Mr. Lee?" Cates said.

Lee looked up at the tall, young attorney. "What is it, Aiden? You can tell I'm busy, can't you?"

"Yes, sir. But I am just wondering why you had me do that interview. It seemed like there was plenty of opportunity to follow up and to obtain more information—"

Lee had been watching his young deputy closely and was beginning to question whether he possessed mental toughness to succeed, or if, like Cathy, he might be better suited elsewhere. Some people just weren't cut out to make the hard calls. "Plenty of time for that later."

"I gotta say it seemed to me like she was telling the truth," Cates ventured. "And if that's true, then I don't see—"

"Aiden, let me explain something to you. No witness holds a monopoly on the truth. The truth—if it can be determined at all—is what the jury says it is."

"But if she testifies—"

"She'll recount her version of events—nothing more or less."

"But if her version is consistent with what she experienced, then it is the truth—right?"

Lee sighed heavily. "No. It only means she testified consistent with her subjective experience and understanding of events. Nothing more."

Cates was stroking his hairless chin. "So what you are saying is that there is no absolute truth—there can't be."

"I am saying there is an indeterminacy of truth for all but select expert witnesses," Lee explained. "Lay witnesses are merely relating that which they saw, heard, felt, or otherwise experienced. Our job is to seek the truth en route to obtaining a conviction, which we do by presenting evidence to a jury. The jury, in the final analysis, will determine the truth."

"But according to the rules of professional conduct we have a duty to independently investigate anything and everything a witness says, especially where the witness' testimony could be exculpatory."

Technically, Cates was right—but it was so much more complicated than that. "Aiden, I've got to finish this brief. It's due to the Supreme Court tomorrow. We can talk another time."

"Okay, but I'm just concerned—"

"Leave your concerns with me," Lee directed. "You just do what I tell you and everything will be fine." He indicated the door. "Now please close the door behind you."

13

Cathy looked at her landline when it rang but didn't recognize the number. She was putting finishing touches on an entry of appearance in a possession case and didn't really have time, but she needed the business. "Schmidt and Associates." It was presumptuous, but what the hell.

"Is—is this Cathy Schmidt?"

"Yes," Cathy answered. "Who is speaking?"

"My name is Julie Spence. I got your number from Sam Johnstone. He says I need an attorney. Sam thinks—"

"What are you doing right now?" Cathy asked. She saved and closed the document she had been working on.

"Well, nothing really," Julie said. "My boss . . . she's cut my hours way back. I—I have some time now."

"Do you know where my office is?" Cathy asked.

"No."

Cathy explained the location and told Julie to just come right in. "I've got to make a call. Just have a seat in the waiting room when you get here, okay?"

"Okay."

Cathy hung up and called Sam.

"Hey," he said when Cassie had switched him in. "What's going on?"

"I just got a call from Julie Spence—she told me you recommended she come see me. Wanted to say thanks," Cathy said. "Thought you'd want to know."

"Good. She there now?"

"She's coming over now," Cathy said. "I'm thinking ahead. If everything we've heard is true—"

"We could have a conflict."

"Possibly," she said. "I'll let you know. I mean . . . if I can."

"Right," Sam said.

Cathy was making notes on a yellow pad. Julie Spence could well end up either indicted on her own, or—more likely—viewed as a co-conspirator. Lee would certainly try and pressure Julie, and Sam . . . well, he had a duty to Daniels. "I appreciate the referral," she said, scowling at her notes. "I'll be in touch."

"Thanks."

When Sam hung up, Cathy stood and picked up around the office. The "waiting room" she had referred to when talking to Julie was a chair in the foyer inside the door. She had to meet whatever clients she had in her office. Hearing the door open, she made her way to the front. "Julie? Good to see you. Come on back. Can I get you anything?"

"No, I don't think so," Julie said. "Did you just move in?"

"Is it that obvious?" Cathy laughed.

"Kinda."

"Okay, well, why don't you just tell me what's going on and we can decide if you need a lawyer, and if you do, whether I am the right lawyer for the job. So what happened? Since Marci died, I mean."

"So, I was home and a guy named Aiden or Kaiden or something shows up. Says he was from the prosecutor's office and had some questions to ask me. So I had him come in and he asked me questions, I answered, then he got up and left. That was it. Kind of a doofus, you know?"

Cathy smiled. It was Aiden Cates. "I do," she said. "What did he ask you?"

"Really, just a bunch of the same questions that the EMTs and that detective Ashley asked me. What happened and like that, you know."

"Okay. So you answered his questions and then what?"

"Well, he was recording what we said on his phone, so when we got done, he turned his phone off and left."

"No one else was there?"

"Nope."

"No cops?"

"Nope, just the one fella," Julie said. "I think he was reading the questions from a list or something."

"Why?"

"Because he read each and then when I tried to explain he'd cut me off and go to another one," she explained. "Kinda like one of them old phone marketers."

Why wouldn't Lee do it himself? He didn't trust anyone to do anything. Why this? "Okay, so you told him—"

"Same thing I've told everyone. Marci was so sick." Julie shook her head sadly. "When the doctor changed Marci's prescriptions, Press was supposed to exchange the syringe he had for ones filled with less morphine. He forgot, and I—I gave her too much. It was an accident!"

Cathy watched Julie closely for tics or other tells. She had seen more than one good liar in her years prosecuting, and addicts were particularly prone to the telling of untruths. "You said he forgot—how do you know?"

"Well, I mean, he said he would change the syringes . . . she died. . . then he told me later he forgot."

So Julie really didn't *know*. "You got a dollar?" Cathy asked.

"Yeah?"

"Give me a dollar and I'll have you sign a retainer agreement," Cathy explained. "I'll be your attorney provisionally, but we'll have to discuss the full terms when you decide you need me."

"What's that mean?"

"Means we're agreeing to look at me representing you, and that for now you can tell people that I'm representing you."

"People?"

"Cops. Don't talk to them without me there," Cathy said. She realized she was pointing and put her hand down.

Julie's eyes followed Cathy's hand. "Even if they say they aren't arresting me?" she asked.

"Maybe especially then," Cathy affirmed. "I happen to like cops, but nothing good comes from talking with them in other than exigent circumstances."

"What?"

"Emergencies."

Julie nodded. "Okay, got it."

"So, what are you going to do now?"

"I'm gonna go to work. I'm afraid they're gonna let me go. I have benefits and everything, but my boss says her insurer told her they might have to let me go." She shrugged. "Apparently, I might be seen as a liability now."

"Not unless it is shown you did something wrong," Cathy fumed. "You let me know of anything your boss says on that subject, okay?" Wyoming was an at-will employment state, but there were still wrongful termination laws on the books.

14

Justice Richard Park had been the chief justice of the Wyoming Supreme Court for almost four years now—a standard term. As it happened, he would turn over responsibility to a new justice in a few months and reach the mandatory retirement age shortly after that. He had fervently hoped to glide into retirement without any controversy, but with the arrest of Press Daniels up in Custer that wish was being dispelled quickly.

If a judge being accused of killing his wife wasn't bad enough, the judge up in that district—Wally Bridger—was in a near-panic at the thought of presiding over the case and had been calling virtually non-stop since Daniels' arrest. To put him off, Park had agreed to begin pulsing retired judges to gauge their interest in presiding. He looked up from a crossword puzzle he was completing when Janae, his assistant, knocked.

"Justice, I've got Alec Van Devanter on the line," she said.

"I'll take it," Park said. "Close the door, please." He waited while Janae went back to her desk to pass the call through. They'd been through this several times over the past week: Janae contacting a retired judge and asking them to speak with Park regarding a "sensitive matter." The old judge would call, and Park would explain he might need someone to preside over events involving Daniels. Inevitably—citing health concerns, long-planned vacations, or family issues—the old judge would gracefully bow out. He had a feeling about Van Devanter, though. "Al, how the hell are you?"

"I am well," Van Devanter said.

"And grammatically correct as always," Park teased. When Van Devanter didn't reply, he continued. "Al, I've got a bit of an issue. You heard about Press Daniels up in Custer, of course?"

"I have."

"Well, Wally's got his boxers in a bunch. He's certain he's gonna have himself a trial up there and he wants no part of it."

"Did he have a relationship with him?"

"I don't think so, but he's wrapped around the axle regarding perception."

"Well, he is a newer judge," Van Devanter observed. "It seems to me that one or both parties will move for a change of venue. That would resolve the issue."

"I would think so, too. But I'm told they have a new prosecutor up there who is hell-bent on making his reputation on this one. Defense counsel is relatively inexperienced but has tried some cases and gotten some verdicts. And . . . well, hell . . . Press was the senior district court judge in the state when he retired."

"I remember."

"Right, so I'm wondering what you might be doing for a couple of weeks this winter. It's beautiful in Custer that time of year," he joked.

"Chief, you and I both know that's not true," Van Devanter said. "And there would be more to it than that, of course. I'd have to hear all the pre-trial matters."

"Got a computer? Since COVID we've been doing a lot of hearings via videoconference," Park explained. "The judicial branch has come a long way technology-wise since you and I were riding the bench."

"I would prefer to hear the matters in person," Van Devanter said.

Of course he would. The ongoing fiscal crisis had Park seeking budget cuts in every area. But Alec was the first retired judge to not try to immediately wriggle off the hook, so he needed to be careful. "I could examine the budget and see if we could support a couple of quick trips up to Custer," he ventured.

"Standard rates plus per diem, I'm assuming?"

"Yes," Park replied tightly. Van Devanter had been a humorless prick since they'd been in law school together more than forty years ago. He was well-known among his peers for both his brilliance and his own opinion of his brilliance. "But budgets are tighter than a new four-strand fence."

"I'm not renowned for wasting time or dollars."

True enough. "So, it sounds like you're willing to take a look at it?" Park said hopefully. "Let me ask you, will Daniels swear you off? Any bad blood or history between you?"

"I never gave him much thought; not sure how he might feel about me."

Park rolled his eyes. "Well . . . good," he said. "I'm going to pencil you in if it comes to that. I'll keep you posted—fair enough?"

"That is acceptable," Van Devanter said. "Why are you contacting me just now? Didn't this happen in April? Daniels was arrested soon after, right?"

"You're right on both counts." Of course. "But Daniels bonded out and waived a speedy preliminary hearing. I expect his attorney wanted to see if he could negotiate his way out of it." A thought occurred to Park. "By the way, will you need a law clerk? I think Bridger is between clerks right now."

"No, I will not," Van Devanter said. "Frankly, I found law clerks an impediment to the efficient administration of justice. During my career, I spent more time explaining things than would have otherwise been necessary, and because their work was generally not up to my standards, I ended up with a duplicity of effort."

Of course he did. "Okay . . . well, we'll cut an order. I'll be in touch," Park said, and rang off.

15

On the last day of May, Misty sat across from Cathy, waggling her foot at several beats per second. Like many addicts, Misty's drug use was in part an effort to self-medicate—likely for anxiety and depression. She was chomping on gum provided by Cathy, who had summarily refused her request to smoke. "How long we gonna be?" she asked. "I need a heater."

"As long as it takes to come to an agreement regarding how we're gonna proceed."

"I ain't coppin' no damned plea."

"Well, let's talk about that," Cathy began. "You don't have the money to pay for a trial."

"Can't you front me?"

"Look around you." Cathy gestured. "Do I look like some deep-pockets law firm? I've got overhead to pay, not to mention a daughter who goes through a pair of shoes a week."

"I referred a coupla cases to you—didn't you get 'em?"

"I'm not sure—who was it?"

"Billy Eden."

"He the guy who lives out in the country? Dogs ate the neighbors' chickens?"

"Yeah, that's him," Misty said. "Me and him . . . Well, we was an item back in the day," she explained proudly. "And Levi McNeil—did he come by?"

"Not yet," Cathy said. "What's his deal?"

"Domestic. His old lady—"

"That's good enough." Cathy raised a hand to stop Misty. "I'm going to consider myself a success if I never have to defend an abuser."

"Oh, hell, Levi didn't abuse her."

"How do you know?"

"Easy. Levi's old lady says he punched her in the nose—right?"

"I have no idea."

"Well, trust me," Misty assured her. "That's what she'll say. That's what she always says."

Cathy measured Misty. She knew she would regret asking the question, but she couldn't help herself. "How do you know it didn't happen that way?"

"Cause Levi is a little person. Unless he was standing on a chair or climbed up her leg, ain't no way!"

Cathy bit her tongue and broke eye contact. Better not to encourage her. "Let's get back to talking about your case," she said. "Lee has indicated to me that any plea will be cold."

There were no degrees in Misty's past, and no letters behind her name, but she was shrewd and thoroughly versed in criminal procedure. "Then there ain't no reason *not* to go to trial, right?"

Except money. "Well, there is the little matter of my fee."

"It always comes back to that, don't it?"

Cathy couldn't help herself. "You know what? You can walk your ass right down to the public defender's office and file an application—"

"I don't want a public defender. They're—"

"Committed to helping people like you? Experienced trial attorneys? I'll tell you what, the taxpayers of this state pay millions—millions—of dollars every year to provide free attorneys for people like you and all you do is bitch about it. I'm sick of it."

"Whattaya mean, people like me?"

"People accused of crimes. People who want an attorney but don't expect to have to pay for it." Cathy picked up a bottle of water, unscrewed the lid, and drained it in one pull. She tossed the plastic bottle in the trash and turned her attention to Misty, shocked to see her tearing up. "What's your problem?"

"I'm not like some of them. I—I've had some tough times; I've made some bad decisions—"

"Welcome to the club," Cathy snapped. "We've all got junk in our trunk. Most of the time it's called 'consequences.'"

Misty wiped her nose with the palm of her hand and then swiped her hand on her pants. When Cathy offered her a tissue, she shook her head. "What do I owe you? I'm gonna pay you for what you done so far," she said. "I got one a them cards that you put money on."

Oh, crap. "Look, Misty," Cathy began. "I'm just a little stressed—okay? I've got things going on and maybe I said some stuff. I don't need your money."

Misty stood. "I'm gonna pay you. Send me a bill," she said, turning to leave. "But I want you to know that I thought when I came to see you that you might be different, but now—"

"Misty, sit down," Cathy instructed. When Misty had reseated, Cathy apologized. "I'm sorry. I didn't mean to insult you, but you struck a nerve. I'm worried about making it; you know, paying my bills and all—"

"Welcome to the club," Misty mocked.

Cathy almost laughed. "Truce?" she asked. When Misty nodded curtly, Cathy continued. "Let me talk with some people and I'll see what I can do."

"What's that mean?"

Cathy sighed. "It means that I'm going to talk with my banker and see if I can get a short-term signature loan. In the meantime, I'll start getting ready for trial."

The tears flowed again. This time, she accepted the proffered tissue. "I knew it! I knew you was a good person!"

A good, broke person. "Let's meet a week from today, okay?"

16

Daniels showed up for the meeting on time, but with his hair disheveled and his shirt sleep-wrinkled. His red-rimmed eyes indicated either a lack of sleep or a surfeit of drink. Because Sam could smell the booze, he suspected the latter. He looked at his watch—just before nine a.m. When he was a company commander, he and his first sergeant at the time shared a philosophy: if you could smell booze before nine a.m., you could attribute the odor to events of the prior evening. If the guy was still reeking after nine a.m., well, it was probably an eye opener.

"You okay?" Sam asked Daniels.

"Fine," Daniels said. He had a large paper cup filled with what might be steaming coffee. "What's going on?"

"Wanted to talk with you about where we go from here."

"What are you thinking?" Daniels asked. He took the plastic lip off the cup and indicated he wanted to trash it. When Sam proffered the bin, Daniels dropped it in. "Hate those sippy cup lids." He put his mouth tentatively to his cup, took a sip, and smacked his lips.

"What do you think about not guilty by reason of mental illness?"

"I think you're nuts," Daniels said without irony.

"You were tired, you were stressed, the love of your life was dying a slow and painful death," Sam began. "We'll bring in a couple of experts who will say that at the time you weren't in your right mind." He watched closely for a reaction. Daniels licked his lips but said nothing. "Look, you've already admitted culpability. Your statements to the EMTs, law enforcement, and anyone else are all coming in. The only question for a jury will be what they mean."

"Lemme think about it," Daniels said. "But I'll tell you up front I don't like it."

As expected. "Fair enough," Sam replied. "How do you want to handle the preliminary hearing? You want to waive it or what?"

"I don't know," Daniels said. He drank from his cup and wiped his mouth with his hand. "Think we can make any hay?"

"Maybe," Sam said. "Normally, Lee would play it close to the vest. But I think he wants to put on a show for the press. He's wanting to bring in the big guns."

"Think she'll allow you to do a little fishing?" Some defense attorneys attempted to use a preliminary hearing as an opportunity to discern the strength of the State's case. In the vernacular of the courts, it was known as "fishing."

"Doubtful," Sam said. "If you want to waive the prelim, I'd like to let her know as soon as possible. We're set for a week from today."

"Got it." Docket time was valuable. Nothing irritated a judge more than getting a waiver at the time of the hearing—as Daniels knew. He put the cup on Sam's desk and bent over so his elbows were on his knees, hands clasped in front of him.

"What's going on, Judge?"

"I'm just thinking, Sam. One, I don't really want anyone looking into my head. I don't want to pay for it, and I don't want to undergo it."

"I understand, but—"

"Two, I don't think I'm being honest if I do that. I think I was fine in my decision-making, given what was going on and all."

"I hear you," Sam said. "But why not let an expert make that call?"

"Because even though I'm no longer an officer of the court, I still feel like one, and I believe I would be perpetrating a fraud by going that route."

"Not if we have a good-faith basis for the plea."

"I don't think we do," Daniels said, shaking his head.

Sam measured his words carefully. "Judge, I don't know how to say this—"

"Then just say it, damn it!"

"You were a mess before Marci passed," Sam said. "You were disorganized, short-tempered, drinking too much—"

"Well, wouldn't you be?" Daniels snapped.

"I imagine so," Sam concurred. "But my point is you weren't yourself."

"But that doesn't mean—"

"I know it doesn't necessarily mean you weren't responsible, but why don't we look into it? What's the worst thing that happens?"

"I pay some shrink a boatload of money to examine my brain housing group, and he then tells me I am legally responsible for my actions?"

Sam laughed despite himself. "I get it; but tactically speaking, the worst that happens is they say you are okay. If they do, we'll change your plea and move on accordingly."

Daniels reached into his coat pocket and withdrew a plastic half-pint of vodka, just as Sam had suspected. He added a couple of capfuls to his cup. Seeing Sam's stare, he bristled. "What?" he challenged.

"I didn't say anything. I'm an alcoholic in recovery who had a fondness for vodka," Sam explained. "Maybe you mistake my licking my chops as some sort of judgment."

Now Daniels laughed. "Sorry. I'm a little tight . . . and a little tight."

"Keep an eye on it," Sam advised. "I need you at the top of your game."

Daniels measured Sam. "Not many folks tell me what to do."

"On the other hand, most of my clients listen to me," Sam advised. He softened when he saw what might be hurt in his friend's eyes. "Press, you've suffered a terrible loss, and you have a right to cope however you see fit. Just try not to make my job harder than it is, okay?"

When Daniels nodded his acquiescence, Sam grinned quickly and concluded, "Meantime, think it over and let me know what you think about the preliminary hearing and the plea."

Days later, Sam was waiting on Lee to pick up the phone. He'd received no response to multiple emails he'd sent to see if Lee had spoken with Julie. He looked at his watch. He'd been on hold for two minutes and was just about to hang up when the prosecutor picked up.

"Lee."

"Sam Johnstone."

"How can I help you, Counsel?"

"Have you spoken with Julie Spence?"

"I have not," Lee said. "I had one of my deputies talk with her."

"You should speak with her. She has information that I believe is exculpatory." Exculpatory information was information that tended to show a defendant was not guilty.

"Ashley Miller spoke with her," Lee said blandly. "Aiden Cates spoke with her. Miller made the decision to arrest your client after speaking with her, and based on what Cates told me it was the right call."

"You and I both know Miller's not trained in the law, and Cates . . . well, I don't know what he knows," Sam said. "Grant, I believe Julie has information that shows Press is not guilty of voluntary manslaughter, let alone second-degree murder."

"I understand what you're saying, but based on the information I've seen and heard, I concluded your witness is biased and not credible," Lee explained. "She was and is in the employ of Daniels—at a minimum."

"What the hell does that mean?"

"It means I'm looking into all possibilities, just as any prudent prosecutor—or attorney, for that matter—would."

"Jesus, Grant! The most likely possibility is that she is telling the truth!"

"It is certainly a possibility," Lee allowed. "But as you know, we've already had people explore that, and it is our collective belief that she is not telling us the full story."

"Will you talk with her?"

"Do you represent her?"

"No. Cathy Schmidt does. I'm in contact with her and I could facilitate a meeting."

Lee had quieted when Sam mentioned Cathy. "I'll think about it," he said. "Although I feel certain it will be of little use."

"Why are you hesitant to have direct contact with a witness who undoubtedly has direct evidence to give? Christ, from our standpoint, it would generally be inadvisable to invite this sort of questioning, but we feel certain—"

"I'm under no obligation to reveal any aspect of trial status strategy, Mr. Johnstone."

"Trial strategy?" Sam was incredulous. "You're telling me it's strategy to ignore a knowledgeable witness?"

"I'm telling you I believe that I already possess the information she could provide—I already know what she knows. I will talk with her when and if I deem it necessary and appropriate."

"But if you will talk with her now, it could all go away. Judge Daniels wouldn't have his life ruined, because even if he is acquitted—"

"He won't be."

Sam took a deep breath, held it, and let it go—just as Bob had coached him. "Even if he is acquitted," he said at last, "the specter of suspicion will be hanging over his head for the rest of his life." The silence on the other end of the line was telling. "What's this really all about?"

"What do you mean?"

"I mean what are you trying to get out of this?"

"Justice. That's it."

"Then it is incumbent upon you to interview Julie and to hear her story. It might well be dispositive!"

"No, it won't," Lee said. "Mr. Johnstone, I don't bring charges unless I am certain I have sufficient evidence to convict—"

"That's not the job! You are an officer of the court!"

"And in this case, as an officer of the court, I believe the evidence of your client's guilt is overwhelming, despite Ms. Spence's efforts to get her employer—and whatever else he is—off."

The inference was obvious. "Look, just interview her. You'll see my client might—might, I'm saying—be guilty of negligence. But there was no intent to harm Marci and you can't prove there was!"

"That is obviously where we disagree."

Sam was certain that if they were in person, he would observe a smirk on Lee's face. "Okay, be seeing you," he said, and hung up. He stood up and tossed a stapler off the opposite wall.

Within seconds, Cassie opened his office door. "Is everything okay in here?" she asked. Seeing the broken stapler, she fixed her hands on her hips. "Sam Johnstone, that temper of yours is going to get you in trouble one of these days. And I'm not picking that up," she added as she slammed the door behind her.

17

Days later, Sam and Daniels were in Sam's office for what had become their weekly meeting. "Did you talk with Lee?" Daniels asked. He stood and walked to Sam's credenza, opened it and squatted, expecting to find a bottle. Seeing none, he looked at Sam questioningly.

"I haven't been on a resupply mission of late," Sam explained, then watched while Daniels nodded in understanding but nonetheless retrieved a glass from the cabinet. "What are you—" Sam began, then quieted when Daniels sat and pulled a plastic bottle of vodka from a sock.

"I always keep a spare for just such an occasion," Daniels explained.

Sam watched while the judge unscrewed the cap, poured the contents into a tumbler, and drained half. He was wiping his mouth with the back of his hand when he noticed Sam's stare. "What?" he challenged.

"Damn," Sam remarked. "It's early."

"It is," Daniels acknowledged. "Is there a problem?"

Sam recalled his own issues. "Only insofar as I wanted to discuss some things with you. How many have you had?"

"I'm not counting," Daniels said calmly. "Did you talk with Lee?"

"I did."

"Did Lee talk with Julie?"

The old judge could hold his booze, of course. It was probably safe to talk. "No, and I don't think he is going to," Sam said.

"I see," Daniels replied. "He doesn't want anything to get in the way of prosecuting me."

"That's what it looks like," Sam agreed. "I'm struggling to figure this out. I think he's probably got an ethical obligation to talk with her—"

"Assuming he cares," Daniels said quickly, wiping his eyes with one hand while swirling the remaining contents of the glass with the other. "I'm not so sure that guy is playing by the same set of rules as the rest of us. Maybe he sees that if he does talk with her, he might be facing a truthful witness issue."

"I thought that was a defense attorney thing?"

"Theoretically, yeah." Daniels put the glass down and leaned forward in his chair. "Most of the literature out there discusses the ethics involved when a defense attorney knowingly tries to discredit a truthful witness. The debate stems from the ongoing discussion regarding the first duty of defense counsel—whether it is to the court or the client."

Daniels watched Sam for evidence of his understanding. Seeing Sam was following, he continued. "Obviously there is a duty to the court— defense attorneys are officers of the court and sworn to uphold the constitution. On the other hand, defense attorneys have a duty to do what they can to force the State's hand. A *vigorous defense*, as they say. What we end up with is a guy like yourself—an officer of the court sworn to help discern the truth—who simultaneously owes a duty to a client in whose interest the truth might not lie."

Perhaps recognizing the implication behind his lecture, he smiled wryly. "In theory, of course." When he observed Sam's sardonic return smile, he continued. "One school of thought is that the defense counsel can and should do whatever she can within the bounds of the law to see to it her client is not convicted."

"Sounds reasonable," Sam observed.

"It is, except that under that philosophy, the truth is secondary—a trial becomes a contest, a game." Daniels finished the contents of the glass, smacked his lips, and looked around Sam's office before apparently remembering. He bent over and pulled a small plastic bottle from the other sock.

"Jesus!" Sam said.

"Relax; I've only got two legs." Daniels uncapped the bottle as he continued. "Alternatively, the argument is made that attorneys have an unalterable obligation to the truth, because the system only works when all parties—judge, jury, and counsel—seek only the truth. Only when truth prevails, the argument goes, does society win." With that, he eschewed pouring, drank the contents from the small bottle, and tossed it in a nearby trash bin.

Sam gave a quick thumbs-up in appreciation of the accuracy shown. "Where do you come out?" he asked.

Daniels laughed. "Truthfully?" he asked. Sam nodded. "For the entirety of my career up to now I would have told you option B," Daniels said. "But now that it is my ass in a sling, I'm all for option A."

Sam smiled broadly. "But Lee is a prosecutor," he pointed out. "The responsibilities are different—true?"

"Abso-freaking-lutely!" Daniels said. "A prosecutor's duty has been, is, and always will be to see to the accomplishment of justice. If that results in a conviction, swell; if it results in an acquittal, that is the way it is. Assuming the trial was fair for both parties, the result is immaterial. From a prosecutorial perspective, a fair and impartial process is what is important."

Sam mulled Daniels' response. "So, if Lee improperly challenges a truthful witness on the stand, we could report him to the board of professional responsibility?"

"We could," Daniels agreed. "And we could likely challenge my conviction. But at that point it'll be more than likely I'll be learning a trade—like making license plates, or maybe upholstery."

Sam didn't want to think about that, so he followed up on the discussion from days prior. "What are you thinking about on the prelim?" he asked, referring to the preliminary hearing. "I need to let Downs know if we're going to waive."

"I've given that some thought," Daniels said. "Screw 'em. I want my hearing. I want to hear what they've got."

"We might not get much," Sam replied.

"Probably not," Daniels agreed. "But maybe we just show 'em I'm not going down easy."

Sam smiled. "Great," he said. "And on the subject of not going down, I've got another question."

"I'm listening."

"What do you think about moving for a change of venue?"

Daniels smiled. "I don't know where I come down on that. On the one hand, there's been a lot of publicity, and a lot of it hasn't been good. That damned Miriam—"

"Right," Sam interrupted, not wanting Daniels to get wound up.

"On the other, I served these people for forty years as an attorney and judge."

"Could be good or bad," Sam mused. "Every divorce had a loser; every criminal had a family."

"Every victim saw justice; every divorce had a winner," Daniels countered. Seeing Sam's steady gaze, he continued. "I think we wait until we see what kind of panel we draw."

"Can we do that?" Sam asked. "I've not looked at the rule in a while."

"Oh yeah," Daniels said. "We can do it anytime up to selection of the jury. There was a case over in Gillette—can't recall the caption—where that was decided."

Sam heard "deshided" and determined Daniels was feeling the booze. Better finish up quick. "So, we could see what the final jury panel looks like and file the motion—"

"After voir dire but before the peremptory challenges are of record," Daniels concluded.

Sam considered the options. "That would piss off the judge, I bet."

"Oh yeah," Daniels agreed. "But judges take an oath to uphold the constitution as well as the rules that are written to ensure its protections are afforded even when it is inconvenient and perhaps absurd. That's just one reason why as judges we're always about half pissed-off."

Sam laughed. "That explains it?"

"About half the time, yeah."

"And the other half?"

"Lawyers," Daniels said without missing a beat.

"Right." Sam laughed. "You need a ride?" he asked, concerned that his client might drive drunk.

"No," Daniels replied. "I walked. I'm trying not to violate bond."

"Good idea," Sam agreed. "Lee will have a field day if you bust bond."

"I know," Daniels said, standing.

"One last thing," Sam said, holding up a hand. "The mental health evaluation—"

The old judge shook his head a little too vigorously. "I'm not gonna do that," he said. "I'm fine."

"Look, Press . . . If what you say about Marci's death is true—"

"It is."

"Then the State has enough to convict you for involuntary manslaughter right out the gate."

"Well then that's what they ought to charge. Hell, if they do that, I'll plead. Tell your boy Lee I said that."

If only it were that easy. "Lee isn't satisfied with that—he filed second-degree murder."

"I'm aware. I was there, remember?"

Sam ignored the snark. "Then you know you're risking at least twenty years for—"

"My part in killing Marci," Daniels finished. "Look, Sam, I know damned well it might be in my best legal interest to talk with a shrink and try and convince her I was out of my mind when Marci died. But I'm not going to do that. I'm not going to say I was something that I wasn't."

"That's not how it works, and you know that," Sam insisted. "We'd have the burden—"

"No," Daniels said. "I'm not going to get on the stand and say, 'Woe is me.' You change my plea and I'll refuse to cooperate with an exam."

"Press—"

"I'm okay with you papering it up," he said, referring to Sam preparing a memorandum for record or other document to protect himself against a later claim of ineffective assistance of counsel. More than one lawyer had counseled a client who ignored the advice and subsequently sued for legal malpractice, claiming he'd never received the advice he had ignored. "Hell, I'll draft it if need be."

Predictable. Sam made a note to himself: "Prepare a memo." He looked to Daniels as the older man stood. "What about a plea?"

"To what?" Daniels asked, looking down to Sam.

"Involuntary manslaughter?" Sam asked, and waited while Daniels considered. "Do you want me to make an offer?"

Daniels had a hand on Sam's doorknob. "Maybe, but it's going to depend on the judge. I don't think I'd risk it with Bridger, he's too political. I think that at the very least we wait to see who the judge ends up being."

Made sense. "Fine," Sam concurred. "Let me see where we are, and I'll get back to you." When Daniels was gone, Sam put his foot on the desk and thought about their exchange, scratching absentmindedly at his prosthetic leg. He could change Daniels' plea to one of "not guilty by reason of mental illness or deficiency" without his client's permission, of course, but the burden would then shift to them to prove he was not competent at the time of the events leading to Marci's death. Daniels had made it clear he was not going to cooperate with any examination, however, so it appeared as if such a move would be tactically futile.

Not to mention it would eliminate any trust between Sam and Press.

18

Miller didn't like Lee, and she didn't like being in his office. It was all she could do to fake nonchalance. But Chief Lucas had made it clear that she couldn't avoid Lee, so here she was. She had waited until ten minutes after her appointment and had just gotten to her feet to leave when Lee came out and retrieved her. "Detective, I'm ready."

Miller swallowed a sharp comment and followed him into his office. Decorations-wise, nothing had changed since she'd last been here. She looked around the bare walls and then at her phone while he made a show of signing papers before at last turning his attention to her.

"Have you met Aiden Cates?" Lee asked, indicating a young man sitting nervously in a chair against the wall.

"Kinda," she said.

"He's going to sit in today, if you don't mind," Lee said to the papers on his desk.

Miller looked at Cates, who stared back at her hopefully. "No sweat," she said. Might be better to have a witness.

"Paperwork." He shrugged, finishing with a signature. Finally looking at her, he began. "The reason I asked you here was to see if you have any information about Julie Spence."

"Did you already look at your office's files?"

He sighed. "I haven't had time. I've had Aiden on it, but I thought speaking with you might result in a level of detail that I wouldn't find in the files."

"Like what?"

"Your impression of her."

Miller thought about it. What could it hurt? "Troubled. Undereducated, underemployed, bad history with men. Lots of bad choices, chief among them methamphetamine."

"I can work with that," Lee mused.

"You can," Miller agreed. She looked at Cates and considered her next statement. What the hell. "The big issue in this case is that I believe her."

Lee raised his dark eyebrows. "About what, exactly?"

"Everything," she said. "I think she is telling the truth about everything."

"You made the decision to arrest," Lee said carefully.

That much was true. "I did," she agreed. "I didn't say I believe *him*. But as you know, I recommended involuntary manslaughter—maybe voluntary at most. Depends on whether the jury believes him. It was *you* who bumped it up to second-degree murder." She looked to Cates and saw understanding.

"Because I think we can show enough to the jury to merit second degree. In any event, that's my problem now," Lee said. "Tell me a little more about Ms. Spence."

"Lifelong resident," Miller began. "Dropped out of Custer High in the eleventh grade. Followed that up with a series of dead-end jobs. Got knocked up a couple of years later, then developed a meth habit. In and out of jail for a while. Finally got busted for a felony. Took a plea and did treatment court and was doing well for a while, but then her boyfriend got wasted and punched her out. Cops got called and there was meth in the house—she claimed it was his. Whatever." Miller shrugged. "She signed over her kid to her mom so the kid didn't go into a foster home. Took a plea for probation in exchange for testifying against the boyfriend. Then got on the stand and couldn't remember her name."

"Good stuff," Lee remarked.

"Except from everything I hear, she's been good the last couple of years," Miller cautioned. "A public intox is all we show. Looks like she got her high school equivalency while she was locked up, then took advantage of some program for single mothers and got herself qualified as a health-care aide. She works for a home health care agency here in town, and has for some time. That's why she was at the Daniels place. Regular attendee at N.A. and sober for years, by all accounts. Even got her kid back."

Lee was taking notes. "Did she know Daniels before going to work for him?" he asked.

The answer seemed obvious. "Well, he was the only district court judge in the county for twenty years," Miller said. "She had a couple of felonies—seems like he must've been her sentencing judge, right?"

"Probably," Lee said, raising an eyebrow. "But that's not what I'm asking, Detective. I'm asking if he *knew* her."

She side-eyed Cates, who was checking his shine. "You are barking up the wrong tree there, Counselor."

Lee stared at her levelly. "Meaning you know that for a fact, or you are making assumptions based on his prior position in life?"

She met his stare with one of her own. "Meaning the latter, but I'd stake my reputation on it."

"How about your job?"

Asshole. "What else?" she asked.

"That's it," he said, standing and towering over her—as he knew he would. "Let me know if you think of anything else."

"Sure," she said as she left.

When all that remained was an uncomfortable silence, Lee turned to Cates. "Aiden, I have another job for you."

"What's that?"

"I need you to see what I need to do to get a license to carry a concealed weapon."

"Why?"

"I'm beginning to think I might make some enemies in this job."

19

On the first day of June, Downs took a deep breath and held it in an attempt to relax. Weeks prior, she had docketed Daniels' preliminary hearing, and with any luck in about an hour this matter would be behind her and someone else—a retired judge named Van Devanter, according to courthouse scuttlebutt—would have to deal with it.

She had been surprised Daniels hadn't waived the hearing altogether. As a former judge, he had to know they were of little evidentiary value and the one-sided presentation of evidence would likely ensure that media coverage reached a fever pitch—especially if, as she expected, Lee played things to the hilt by featuring the most damning and inflammatory evidence he had to draw maximum media interest. In turn, Sam would cross-examine witnesses, seeking to discover information he had yet to receive. She would grant Lee's objections to Sam's discovery efforts, and then—after a brief argument by the attorneys—she would bind the case over for arraignment and trial in the district court and be done with it.

And that was exactly how things went—for a time. She took evidence for an hour, after which the attorneys had each argued their position. Downs nodded and began to build her record. She outlined the contents of the criminal rule covering the subject, then stated the facts she had gathered in evidence, then applied the facts to the rule's requirements.

"Now therefore," she said, "having heard and considered the evidence and the arguments of counsel, the court will find there is probable cause to believe that on or about the 9th day of April, the defendant committed murder in the second degree. The court finds the State has met its burden and will transfer the matter to district court for all further proceedings." Good riddance. "Bond will—" she was concluding, intending to continue the bond she had set at Daniels' initial appearance and be done with it, when Lee interrupted her.

"Your Honor, might the State be heard on bond?"

She was literally one word from being done with this matter. She suspected Lee wanted to make a show for the media. "It's rather unusual, isn't it?"

"It is, but this is an unusual case, ma'am," Lee said.

"I don't think it's any different than any other murder case," Sam said.

She hadn't seen him stand and was surprised by his tenor and tone. "Just a minute, Mr. Johnstone—"

"You already set bond," Sam stressed. "Nothing has changed."

"I think she should decide—" Lee said to Sam.

"You are—"

"Gentlemen!" Downs all but shouted. When they stopped talking, she stared down all in the courtroom until the excited uttering had abated. "I'll not have this quibbling in my courtroom!"

Sam was angry. "Your Honor, this is nothing but—"

"Silence, Mr. Johnstone! I'll hear from both of you." She looked to Lee. "You wish to be heard?"

Lee was at the podium quickly. "Your Honor made the initial bond decision with little information before it. Today's hearing showed only the barest portion of the evidence the State will ultimately place on the record. In so doing, we showed defendant Daniels willfully murdered his helpless wife. We ask you hold the defendant without bond, or up the bond to an amount that—"

Sam was again on his feet; seeing him, Downs raised a hand to silence him. "Counsel, I know what you are going to say—"

"That my client's guilt or innocence isn't the question?"

"Of course it's the question," Lee sneered.

"Gentlemen—"

"My client is presumed to be not guilty until a jury says differently!" Sam shouted.

"Gentlemen—"

Veins in Lee's neck bulged as he stressed, "That's a presumption that will soon—"

"Gentlemen!" Downs yelled. She had the gavel in her hand. "I've had enough!" she said when she had gained their attention. She again stared down the crowd until all noise abated. "I'll not be disregarded or talked over. I've heard the State's motion and the basis for it—"

"My client has a right—" Sam began, but finally quieted under her withering glare.

"And I find the State has shown no good cause for this court to change the bond amount, terms, or conditions. Bond will continue as previously set," she held. "Mr. Johnstone, please prepare an appropriate order."

After she had departed, Lee turned to Sam. "That's the last favorable ruling you'll get from a hometown judge," he said as he turned to walk out of the courtroom, no doubt to conduct a quick press conference.

Sam was about to reply when he felt Daniels' hand on his sleeve. "Let it go."

"What a sorry—"

"Let it go," Daniels re-advised. "She denied the motion."

"It should never have been made," Sam argued. "Under the rules—"

"What rules?" Daniels asked. "The rules of criminal procedure?" He indicated the bench. "Or the rules of real life?" He pointed in the general direction of what they both suspected was Lee's ongoing press conference.

Despite his anger, Sam smiled. "You're right," he admitted. "Sorry about getting hyped up, but that guy pisses me off."

"Obviously."

Sam knew a visit to his sponsor was in order. "Look, Press . . . just . . . behave yourself. I'll see you next week, okay?"

"Yes, boss," Daniels said, then turned to leave before being stopped by Sam's hand on his sleeve.

"That way," Sam said, indicating with a thumb the judge's chambers. He'd arranged with Fricke to allow Daniels to leave through a fire escape in the back to avoid the media and the inevitable awkward video of a sullen, closed-mouth suspect leaving a courthouse with no comment.

Or—in Daniels' case—worse.

20

Mary Perry was as skittish as a cow with a bucktoothed calf. Having never met retired Judge Alec Van Devanter, she wasn't sure what to expect. The plan as she understood it would be to put the judge in a spare office down the hall while he was in Custer and have him use the main courtroom for the trial—if it came to that—while Bridger took care of day-to-day matters. The big issue would be coordinating both dockets, setting hearings, and the like. She had called a couple of Van Devanter's former clerks, but they were guarded in their comments about him—which probably said more than they realized. She had sought guidance from Bridger on how he wanted things organized, but he had told her to use her own judgment. The extra office was used sparingly and furnished with only a desk, a rickety wooden chair, and a credenza. The walls were adorned with faded photographs of familiar Wyoming landmarks. On the desk was a paper calendar/planner from 2014. Mary had just finished a quick dusting of the extra office when she felt a presence in the doorway. Turning, she saw a spare, bespectacled man holding a briefcase in one hand and a judicial robe in the other.

"Who are you?" he asked, and without waiting for an answer, continued, "Do you have a hanger? Where can I put this?"

"I—I'm Mary Perry," she said. "I'm Judge Bridger's judicial assistant. You can hang it in there." She indicated the door to a private restroom that featured a small closet area.

"That's an odd name—given or married?" he asked.

"Uh, it was—is—my married name," Mary said. "I'm a widow," she added.

"Too bad," he said as he hung the robe. Turning, he looked quickly around the room. "I'm Judge Alec Van Devanter. You may address me as 'Judge.' I'm going to need a computer and a printer."

"Okay . . . well, we don't have any spares."

"Call Chief Justice Park. He'll get you whatever I need. I'll need a box of pens—I like blue. And a package of yellow legal pads."

Mary was trying to decide what to do first when Van Devanter looked at his watch. "Do you have any coffee? I usually have a cup at eight, ten, and two."

"It's in the break room," she said. "Down the hall."

"Fine," he said. "I'll take it black. I don't like paper cups, by the way. I hope you've got something in resin or ceramic?"

"I—I'll check," Mary said, her face reddening. "Anything else?"

"More than likely, a key to the building and the office—I generally arrive and leave later than the staff."

"You'll have to talk with Jack Fricke—he's the head of the building."

"Can't you talk with him for me? I really don't have time for that."

"Well, I suppose I could," she mused. "There will be paperwork to sign and—"

"Go ahead and prepare it if you would. Error-free. Please understand I'm very particular about what I will sign. In my opinion, one of the few benefits of computers has been the ability to revise to perfection—don't you agree?" He sat in the chair. "Oh, this won't do. I will need a new chair."

"We don't have any others."

"Were you not listening? Call the chief—he'll get one on order," Van Devanter said. "Leather is preferable. Cloth is so hot—don't you think?" Without waiting for an answer, he continued. "Now, when you get that coffee, come back and let's talk about your responsibilities, shall we?"

He began to unpack his briefcase. Taking that as a sign to leave, Mary walked stiffly to the break room, found a cup, and was pouring the coffee when Bridger entered and put his lunch in the refrigerator. "Did you meet Judge Van Devanter?"

"Kind of," Mary said. She wiped droplets of coffee from the mug.

Bridger turned from the refrigerator to look at her. "They tell me he's brilliant but somewhat eccentric."

She stared at him, uncertain what sort of response he was looking for, until he shrugged and left the kitchen, whereupon she sighed heavily and headed for Van Devanter's office with the cup.

"Gentlemen, I called you in for what I'll term a pre-pretrial conference because I wanted to speak with you in chambers to facilitate expectations management," Van Devanter began. He was seated behind Bridger's desk, in Bridger's chambers, with Sam and Lee sitting in Bridger's uncomfortable wooden chairs. Sam had his feet on the floor, portfolio in his lap, with pen at the ready. He snuck a peek at Lee, who sat adjacent to him, back in his chair, with one long leg crossed over the other.

Sam watched as Van Devanter leaned forward, rested his elbows on the desk, and clasped his small hands in front of him. There were no rings on his fingers, and the nails appeared to have undergone a recent manicure. "As I understand it, there have been some difficulties in court with the two of you," he began. "I want to impress upon you that while I appreciate vigorous advocacy, in my courtroom attorneys are expected to comply with the rules of professional conduct and the rules of the court. In short, if anyone is going to be a jackass in my courtroom, it is going to be me."

Sam started to laugh, but quickly stifled it when Van Devanter turned his attention to him. "Mr. Johnstone, my sources tell me that you have enjoyed a great deal of success in your short time here. I am made to understand you are a fine trial lawyer, with a reputation for ethical behavior." Sam felt himself relax. "But," Van Devanter continued, "I've also been told that you are hot-tempered and impatient with process." Sam began to defend himself but clamped his jaws shut when the judge continued, "Well, so am I, and I can assure you, you are no match for me."

Sam could see a grin forming on Lee's face, but he sobered when Van

Devanter's focus shifted to him. "Mr. Lee, I've been informed that you are an arrogant, imperial attorney who displays a cavalier attitude toward authority in general and judges in particular." He raised a hand to stop Lee from interrupting. "You should know that my own arrogance knows no bounds and that—in contrast to yourself—I have reason and record upon which to base my high opinion of myself." Lee uncrossed his legs and sat straighter in his chair, mimicking Van Devanter's body language.

"Now that we all know where we stand, be advised that my courtroom will run as I see fit, which is in accordance with all applicable rules and statutes. I have no patience for fools or showmen playing to the jury. I've heard that Daniels himself had little patience for the same, so—aside from my propensity to call out such behaviors more vigorously than another jurist might—you should have little trouble anticipating my reaction to any attorney shenanigans. Questions?"

Sam and Lee silently shook their heads.

"Good," Van Devanter continued. "Now, if you don't know you should, but I wrote the trial manual used to teach trial practice at the school of law." He stood and leaned over the desk to hand Lee and Sam a copy each. "Take this, read it, and conduct your cases accordingly. I'll want your copies back whenever we conclude our proceedings."

"Judge, I—" Lee began.

"Mr. Lee, I haven't asked for questions or otherwise indicated I might entertain them, have I?"

"Well, no, but—"

"Then it should be intuitively obvious to you that I neither welcome them nor will I consider them at this time," Van Devanter said. "Gentlemen, thank you for visiting with me. I will see you in court for the arraignment next week."

When Van Devanter stood, Sam and Lee did the same. "Thank you," Van Devanter said again, and Sam took the hint and left, followed by Lee.

When Van Devanter had closed the door behind them, Lee looked to Sam. "Holy crap!"

"Now there's one thing you and I can agree on," Sam said.

21

In contrast to most judges, Van Devanter walked all the way to the bench and took his seat before looking to the assembled crowd and ordering them to be seated.

"Good Lord," Daniels muttered. Sam allowed himself a brief smirk.

"Good morning, ladies and gentlemen, my name is Alec Van Devanter. I am a retired judge whom the chief justice of the Wyoming Supreme Court has assigned to hear the matter before the court, which it appears is captioned State of Wyoming versus Preston Daniels. It is the twentieth of June, and we are here today for Mr. Daniels' arraignment. He is present and represented by Mr. Johnstone. The State is present and represented by Mr. Lee. Mr. Lee, is the State prepared to proceed?"

Lee stood at his desk and nodded. "We are, sir."

Van Devanter looked to Sam. "Same question, Counsel—is the defendant prepared to proceed?"

"We are, Your Honor."

"Good," Van Devanter said. "Then let's begin."

He then embarked on an extended and detailed recitation of Daniels' constitutional rights. When Daniels had stated he understood those, Van Devanter instructed Daniels on possible pleas, and on the procedure Van Devanter would follow. Lastly, he explained to Daniels the charges he faced, the elements of the crime, and the minimum and maximum possible penalties. It was all unnecessary, of course, but the rules made no exception where a retired judge was the defendant.

At last, he looked to Daniels. "Mr. Daniels, do you have any questions?"

"No, Your Honor," Daniels said.

"Then would you and your counsel please stand?" When Sam had assisted Daniels to his feet, Van Devanter looked over his rimless glasses at Daniels and continued, "You've indicated you understand your constitutional rights, the elements of the charge, and the maximum possible penalty. To the allegation then, that on or about the ninth day of April you committed second-degree murder, to wit: the murder of Marci Daniels, how do you plead?"

"Not guilty, Your Honor," Daniels said.

Sam was pleased with the tone and strength of his client's plea. He loosened his grip on the older man's elbow.

"Very well. You may be seated," Van Devanter said. When Sam and Daniels were re-seated, Van Devanter looked to Lee. "Are there other matters to be discussed?" he asked. In Sam's view, Van Devanter was clearly expecting Lee to simply respond in the negative. The old judge's heavy eyebrows rose briefly when Lee stood.

"Your Honor," Lee began. "I'd like to visit the issue of bond."

Sam couldn't help himself. "Judge, this is the second or third time he's raised the issue," he pleaded. "He's got some sort of fascination with having my client—"

"Mr. Johnstone, sit down. Now." Van Devanter's voice was restrained but his tone was crystal clear. When Sam had obeyed, the judge looked to Lee. "Mr. Lee, what new information do you have for the court that might induce it to modify a bond that was set by a court and reviewed once previously by the same judge?"

"The State has information that the defendant now has the means to leave the State of Wyoming and has expressed an interest in doing so."

Van Devanter scanned the file in front of him, then looked back to Lee. "The bond in place prohibits out-of-state travel in the absence of court permission," he pointed out. "What is it you seek?"

"We don't think the current bond is sufficient to ensure the defendant's—"

Sam shrugged off Daniels' arm and was out of his chair when Van Devanter saw him and barked, "Sit down, Counsel! I will not ask you again!"

When Sam was again seated, Daniels leaned over. "Don't do this. He is not screwing around."

"Mr. Lee," Van Devanter began. "I expect attorneys to provide the court with substantive evidence and citation to law in support of any motion. I am uninterested in conjecture, thoughts, or feelings."

Lee looked at Miller, who shrugged her acquiescence. "The State has information the defendant may be preparing to leave."

"Go on, Counsel."

"In a conversation with a source, defendant Daniels said, and I'm quoting here, 'I'm going to hit the bricks here one of these days.'"

Van Devanter looked up sharply as audible murmuring poured from the gallery. "Ladies and gentlemen, those of you who are particularly perceptive may have already surmised that I am not a patient or forgiving man. Accordingly, you'll understand when I tell you that another outburst like the one I just heard will likely result in my emptying the courtroom. These attorneys—and this defendant—deserve my undivided attention." He looked around the courtroom, seemingly meeting every set of eyes. "Please continue," he said to Lee.

"Well, that's it, really," Lee said.

"Do you have an affidavit?"

"Um, no, sir."

"Mr. Lee, are you asking me to modify a bond entered by a judge who is familiar with the defendant on the basis of an ambiguous statement allegedly overheard by an unknown source?"

"Yes, Your Honor."

"Well, I'm not going to do that, Counsel. That is not good cause, and it smacks of an agenda I'll not be part of," Van Devanter said. "Now, I am assuming there is nothing else to come before the court?"

Seeing no indication from Lee or Sam, he stood and left the bench. When he had departed, the excited utterances from the gallery were such that Sam and Daniels could scarcely hear one another. "This way," Sam said, tugging at Daniels' sleeve. He had again arranged with Fricke for access to the fire door. As Sam and Daniels approached the door, Fricke swung it open in preparation for their exit.

"Press! Press Daniels!"

Sam turned and saw Miriam Baker and Sarah Penrose approaching. He pulled at a resisting Daniels. "Let's go!" he hissed.

"No," Daniels argued. "I'm not going to run."

By now, Miriam was in Daniels' bubble. "You killed my sister!"

"Miriam—"

"It's true! You admitted it! Only today, with your lawyer, have you denied it!" Miriam looked meaningfully at Sarah.

Daniels shook his head. "Miriam, I loved your sister—you know it," he said. "And yes, I'm responsible. But it was an accident. Please accept my—"

"No! I will not accept your apologies!" Miriam was yelling at the top of her voice now. "You killed my sister for money and because she was an inconvenience! I'll see you rot in prison!"

"Press! Let's go!" Sam urged as Miriam's hysterics began drawing a crowd. "Now!" he again urged, pulling at Daniels' sleeve.

Flecks of spittle flew as an enraged Miriam continued her diatribe. "You told me you knew what she wanted! You said she told you she wanted to die! And then—voila!—she dies and you act as if you had no part in it! Well, I know you did, and I'll see you pay!"

She balled her fists, and Sam feared she would strike Daniels but was restrained by her husband. "I think it's best you leave, Press," David said.

"I agree," Sam added.

Daniels looked to David and then Miriam and shook his head sadly. "Miriam, I cannot believe you would think that I would harm Marci." He didn't struggle as Sam pushed him out the fire door timely opened by Fricke. "Can you believe that?" he asked Sam when they were alone.

"Yes!" Sam replied. "People do crazy things when they are grieving."

"Bullshit. She hardly even knew her," Daniels said. "They hadn't seen each other half a dozen times in forty-five years."

"She wouldn't be the first surviving family member to lionize a loved one with whom she'd not gotten along," Sam observed. When he saw

Daniels nodding in agreement, he continued, "And I'm just going to say she's got a voice like aural root canal."

At their regularly scheduled meeting two weeks later, Sam was pleased with what he saw in Daniels. "You look good," he said.

"I've still got Julie on the payroll; she's been cooking for me."

"You sure that's a good idea?" Sam asked. "That's grist for the rumor mill."

"Screw 'em."

"Well, generally, I'd agree with you, but the same folks who are hearing and passing the rumors might well be in the venire."

Daniels bristled. "Then you can sort that out, can't you?"

"I suppose, but I don't know why you want to play with fire."

"You ever eat my cooking?"

"No."

"I can make chili, grill a burger, and throw something in the microwave—that's about the extent of it," Daniels explained. "Besides, Julie needs a little extra money. Her employer cut her hours way, way back. I'm expecting them to dump her any time now. Just trying to help the kid out."

Sam knew to pick his battles. "Now that we have a judge, I wanted to talk about maybe approaching Lee with a plea agreement." Because Daniels had declined a mental health evaluation and instructed Sam to hold off on a change of venue, the remaining options were to prepare for trial or seek a plea agreement. "What do you think?"

"I'll plea to involuntary manslaughter. But I didn't kill her on purpose, and I'm not pleading to anything that says I did."

"Understood," Sam said. "Could we offer to plea to criminal negligence?" Criminal negligence was a misdemeanor, punishable by up to one year in jail.

"It's a lesser-included of involuntary manslaughter," Daniels observed. A lesser-included referred to a crime that shared many but not all of the elements of a similar, more serious crime. "Lee won't agree."

"If you plead to involuntary manslaughter, you'd have to admit you demonstrated a reckless disregard for Marci's life, whereas if you plead to criminal negligence, you could simply say you failed to recognize the dangers of your actions—or inaction, actually."

"A judge told me years ago that the difference between involuntary manslaughter and criminal negligence is the same as the difference between being an asshole and being a dumbass." Daniels smiled briefly at the quip, then sobered. "But Lee won't agree to my pleading to a misdemeanor. No way. He wants my head on a pike."

"Can't hurt to ask," Sam offered.

"Unless you're gonna get all teary-eyed when he tells you to take a long walk on a short plank."

Sam laughed. "Planks and pikes! I'll be okay—we're not exchanging Christmas ornaments, sharing the location of our favorite fishing spots, or anything like that."

22

Cathy had asked for another meeting, and Sam had again spent time cleaning his office. He now sat back in his chair, hands clasped, trying to appear casual and relaxed. When he knew she had seen him, he unclasped his hands and rocked forward in his chair, putting his elbows on the desk. "How goes it?"

She took a chair without being asked. "It's going okay. Got a few clients coming in the door. How're you doing?"

"Doing well. You up for a beer one of these days?"

"Great minds think alike," she observed. "I was going to ask you. Right now, I need to pick your brain for a minute."

"What's up?"

"I'm still undecided on my case with Misty Layton."

"The drug grandma?" Sam asked, fiddling with a grass- and dirt-stained baseball.

Cathy frowned. "The ex-drug grandma—c'mon, Sam. She's trying."

"Sorry," he said. "What are you thinking?"

"There's still no offer from Grant," she said.

What a clown. Sam tossed the ball in the air and caught it. "Well, you've looked at the thing now. Any chance of an acquittal?"

She shrugged. "There's always a chance."

"Well, yeah," Sam acknowledged. "But realistically?"

She held her hands up, indicating he should toss her the ball. "Not much. The issue—like we discussed—will be whether they can convince a jury she knew."

"Right," Sam acknowledged. He tossed the ball and watched in appreciation as she reached forward and caught it deftly. Soft hands. "Ever play?"

She shook her head. "Not much. Between high school ball and AAU, I was pretty much basketball twenty-four-seven." She tossed the ball back to him.

"You talk with the kid?"

"Kyle?"

"Yeah."

"He's not going to help." She caught the ball he tossed. "He's gonna roll over and show his belly."

"Seriously?"

"That's the vibe I'm getting."

"Then it's a swearing contest," Sam observed. "I'm sure you've taken down plenty of lying witnesses before, right?"

"Well, yeah."

"What's the issue?"

"I just think that generally, usually, normally, juries want to hear from the defendant," Cathy said.

"Agreed," he said. "But what if you wait and see how your cross of the son goes? If you think you are on solid ground, sit her. If you think she might get rung up, she'll have to testify."

"I guess."

Sam tossed the ball and caught it. "I seriously don't think you've got a lot to lose by trying the case."

"Except time and money," she groused.

"A cold plea gets you nothing; a jury verdict might have your client walking, and if not, well . . . I just don't think Bridger will hold her exercising her rights against her. He's seen Lee in action and has to know he's a pain in the ass to deal with."

"Yeah," she said, and caught the ball Sam tossed to her. "I guess I can lose the case *and* not get paid."

The implication was clear. "Don't tell me you didn't collect a fee up front?" When she didn't answer, he laughed. "Been there, done that—we all have. Every defense attorney gets bit in the butt at least once. We all want to save the world; takes some experience to figure out it takes money to do it. Any chance you can talk her into hiring the public defender?"

"Nope. She's been through 'em all."

"How about Mike Sharp?" Sharp was a private defense attorney who contracted with the local office of the public defender. Sam didn't care for him, but it was an option. "He's gotta need clients."

"I wouldn't allow him to defend my worst enemy," she said. "And he's a creep. That's the last thing she needs."

Cassie was on the intercom. "Sam?"

He looked at the clock on the wall. It ran five minutes slow. "Oof. You know what? I've got another client," he explained, getting to his feet. "Let me know when on that beer."

"When," she said quietly.

"What's that?"

Cathy was now on her feet as well. "Kayla's at a school event. I've been looking for a reason to ditch it."

"Are you sure?"

"Positive."

He looked at his watch, and then at his inbox. "Give me forty-five minutes. I'll get us a table at the Longbranch."

"You really know how to treat a girl."

The Longbranch Saloon had been on Yellowstone Avenue in downtown Custer for more than a century. Featuring a bar that ran from the front door to the back, it hosted thirsty patrons from Custer's various walks of life (who sat toward the front), as well as tourists, who generally preferred the repurposed saddles near the back door which served as seats. The ceiling was covered with bills of various denominations featuring the donors' signatures and the occasional pithy quote. The walls were adorned with tin beer signs and pictures of customers and staff celebrating everything from

Halloween to Saint Patrick's Day. Like everyone else trying to operate a business in the post-pandemic world, Gino was having trouble hiring and retaining good help. Tonight, neither of his new hires bothered to show—or call. He was pulling the tap for a couple of boisterous coal miners when he was able to make eye contact with Sam.

"What'll you have?" he asked when Sam had maneuvered his way within earshot.

"Moscato for the lady, club soda for me, two burgers medium rare," Sam said, trying not to yell but wanting to be heard.

Gino flipped a sullied dishtowel over his shoulder while he wrote the order on a slip of paper. "Be a minute on the burgers—help didn't show up."

"We've got all night," Sam said. He was about to return to the table when he felt a hand on his forearm.

"You don't recognize me, do you?"

Sam hadn't even looked at the man. Before he could respond, Gino leaned forward over the bar and tapped the man on the shoulder. "Jake, I'll not have any trouble from you. Sam is my lawyer, and he's my friend. Anything comes out of your mouth that's anything other than friendly and you're gone."

"I was jusht gonna tell him thanks for walkin' me, was all."

"No problem," Sam said. He remembered Jake now. He also remembered Jake was on probation with a "no alcohol" prohibition. Job security.

"Fine," Gino said. "Tell him and be done with it—and then let him go sit with his lady friend."

"Everything okay?" Cathy asked when Sam returned, having endured Jake's rambling thanks.

"Fine." Sam toasted Cathy. She raised her glass and touched it to his club soda with a twist of lemon. "Are you okay if I drink?" she had asked.

"Of course," Sam had replied.

She drank deeply. He took a sip of the bubbly water and was thinking how much he'd appreciate a glass of vodka straight up when he noticed her looking at him. "What?" he asked self-consciously.

"I was just wondering if it ever bothers you."

"What's that?"

"Being sober."

"Truthfully?"

"You're under oath."

"Sometimes," he said. "Sometimes I'd like to think that on a special occasion—like this—maybe I could have a glass of wine or a beer or a drink to mark it. But that's fantasy—I never, ever had just one drink."

"Never?"

"I drank with a purpose, and that purpose was to get drunk—or at least comfortably numb."

"I'm flattered you think this is a special occasion." She looked at her glass and then steadily at him. "I—I'm just going to say that I find it hard to see you so . . . undisciplined, I guess, when it comes to drinking. I mean, being a soldier and all—"

"A lot of folks mistake being an alcoholic with a lack of discipline, but the exact opposite is true," Sam countered.

"I didn't mean to offend—"

"None taken," he said, waving off her attempt at an apology. Most people didn't understand. "It takes discipline to watch your weight when you are drinking heavily. It takes discipline to set your alarm, to polish your boots, to remember your briefcase—really, to do all of the things that regular people do daily without a second thought. As an alcoholic, if you're going to be functional, you've got to make and execute plans to live what appears to be a normal life."

She laughed, and he decided he liked that sound. "I never thought of it like that."

"Oh yeah," he assured her. "If you're going to have your briefcase, you've first got to recall where you left it. Same goes for your car, your keys, your wallet—" He stopped and enjoyed her renewed laughter.

"Was it really that bad?"

"Sometimes," he admitted. "Sometimes it was much, much worse," he said, remembering the hospitalizations. Her glass was almost empty; he looked for the waitress. Sometimes it seemed he'd spent half his life waiting for the waitress to bring another round.

"What are you looking for?"

"Oh, nothing," he lied. When a waitress appeared, he ordered her another wine and himself a diet cola. "I'm switching to the hard stuff," he joked.

When their meals arrived, Sam dawdled self-consciously, hoping to see how she handled the ridiculously thick burger. Only when she began eating did he follow her lead. "So," she began between bites. "I wanted to ask you about my trial."

"Layton?" he asked. She nodded her agreement as her mouth was full. "How can I help?"

"Well," she said when she had finished chewing. "Because this is my first trial from the dark side, I wanted to run a couple of ideas by you." She then laid out a trial strategy that he found insightful and thoughtful, but potentially over the top. "What do you think?" she asked him at last.

"Truthfully?"

"You're still under oath."

"Well, I think you've got the ninety-percent solution, but I want to remind you that as defense counsel you don't have to *prove* anything. Your job is to poke holes in, and highlight the shortcomings of, the State's story."

She dipped a fried potato in ketchup. "But we agreed the best strategy was to not call Misty and to focus on the State's inability to prove her knowledge?"

"Right," Sam replied. He dipped a fry in mustard and popped it in his mouth. "From what you've told me, that's about all you've got. Just remember: a little bit of doubt goes a long way. Don't try to be too aggressive."

"Yuck!" she said, indicating the mustard on his plate. "Really?"

"What can I say?"

She signaled the waitress for a refill. "Enough about work. You'll give me a ride?" Her nose was red and her eyes were watery—just like the cops always said as part of a driving-while-intoxicated bust. She caught him watching her. "What?"

"Just thinking about another time and place," he assured her.

"Fine," she said. "Keep your secrets."

"I don't have any secrets." He drank the last of his soda and shook some ice into his mouth, thinking about the many secrets he did have.

"I know that isn't true," she said. "We all know."

"Who?" he asked, genuinely interested.

"Everybody," she replied with a sweep of her arm.

She was bombed. "Kayla home?" he asked.

"With her dad," she said, finishing off the third glass. "'Member? I told you that. But don't get any ideas. Just a ride home," she emphasized with a finger wag. "No funny business."

"I wouldn't think of it," he said, trying not to think of it.

23

On the last day of November, Cathy stood with Misty as Bridger appeared at precisely nine a.m. and made his way to the bench. He ordered all to be seated and looked over the courtroom. "Good morning, ladies and gentlemen," he began.

"Good morning," was the polite but unenthusiastic response.

"My name is Walton Bridger, and I am a District Court judge here in the 12th Judicial District of Wyoming," he said. Like many judges, he had a script that he followed during a trial, which began with thanking the jury panel. Getting out of jury duty, it seemed, was a modern-day art form. For this portion of the trial, the parties were sitting on the side of the table opposite the usual, facing a gallery filled with potential jurors. As Bridger spoke, Cathy eyed them carefully, associating faces with names. Several days prior, Violet Marshall, the clerk of court, had provided each side with questionnaires completed by each potential juror. Cathy, with some assistance from Misty, had spent time reviewing each questionnaire and gathering background on the jurors. Misty's lifestyle would be an issue for many jurors; Cathy wanted to know which of the possible jurors might struggle to give her the benefit of the doubt.

"Momentarily, the clerk is going to call the names of twelve of you to be seated in the jury box. If your name is called, please come forward." Bridger indicated the jury box with a wave of his hand. "The bailiff will direct you to your seat. Madam Clerk, would you seat a jury, please?" After twelve potential jurors were called and seated, Bridger continued, "The case that has been called for trial is the State of Wyoming versus Misty Layton. The defendant in this case is present and seated at the counsel table to the Court's left next to her attorney, Ms. Schmidt.

"Ladies and gentlemen, we will now proceed to select a jury through a process called 'voir dire'—which means 'to tell the truth.' The purpose is to select a fair jury. Mr. Lee will first ask questions of you as a group; he may follow up with questions to you individually. When he has finished with his questions, Ms. Schmidt may ask questions as well. Mr. Lee, please proceed."

Lee stepped to the podium and for the next two hours asked questions of the jurors relating to their knowledge of the case, the players, and the process, along with their predisposition toward conviction and/or acquittal. He inquired of the jurors regarding their schedules, their state of mind, and their willingness to participate. He asked several questions of the potential jurors designed to ensure their willingness to judge others. He concluded with several questions designed to elicit potential jurors' opinion on illicit substances and drug laws. When he had completed his questioning, Lee looked to the judge. "Pass the jury for cause, Your Honor."

Bridger nodded and looked to Cathy. "Does the defense care to inquire of the panel?"

"Yes, Your Honor." Cathy stood and smoothed her slacks, as much to dry her wet palms as anything else. She was, of course, a veteran trial attorney, but this was her first trial on the side of the accused. "Ladies and gentlemen, because Mr. Lee did a fine job of asking questions, I'm only going to ask you a few more. First, is there anyone here who believes my client is guilty simply because she has been accused?" Cathy watched as most of the jurors shook their heads. "Can we all agree to judge my client only by the facts presented here in the courtroom?" This time the jurors nodded in unison.

"Okay," Cathy said, warming to her task. "I'm going to tell you up front that this case will involve illegal drugs. Methamphetamine. My client does not dispute that. My client does not dispute that methamphetamine is a dangerous drug or even that it was found in her home. Now, some of you may believe those simple facts are enough to find her guilty. Does anyone here believe that it was her responsibility to know drugs were in her house?"

A woman in the front row tentatively raised her hand, and seeing her, others raised their hands as well. "Fair enough," Cathy acknowledged, and looked to her list. "Now, Ms. Shelton, let me ask you this: given your belief that a person should know, are you willing to listen to the circumstances in this case and keep an open mind to see if there might be reasons why my client didn't know?"

"Of—of course."

"Fine, thank you," Cathy said, then set about probing the jurors, looking for agendas or bias. After an hour, she finished with, "Ladies and gentlemen, thank you for your patience." Turning to Bridger, she said, "Defense passes the panel for cause, sir."

Bridger thanked Cathy and excused the potential jurors so the attorneys could select the jury. When the jury that would hear the case had been reconvened and sworn, Bridger looked pointedly at the clock. "Well, ladies and gentlemen, you are the jury which will hear this matter. It's been a long morning, so we're going to take a long lunch. We'll start again at two o'clock. But before we take our break, I'm going to read you an instruction regarding your conduct during daily and evening recesses."

Bridger proceeded to read an instruction warning the jurors against following news accounts, discussing the case, or performing their own investigation. When he concluded, he looked to the jury for acknowledgement. "The bailiff will tell you where you need to be and when you need to be there." He stood, and everyone followed suit. "Thank you for your attention. Bailiff, you may escort the jury."

Two hours later, Cathy looked around the courtroom and noted the lack of observers or media. In contrast to murder trials, drug trials were unfortunately frequent events and generally attended—if at all—only by members of the accused's family. Not surprisingly, in this case—with Misty's daughter in prison and her son a potential co-defendant or a hostile witness—no one was seated on her side of the courtroom, although there were representatives from the Department of Family Services across the aisle. When the jury had been recalled and he was seated, Bridger read the introductory instructions to the jurors and then looked to Lee. "Mr. Lee, does the State wish to make an opening statement?"

"We do, Your Honor." Lee was already on his feet and took with him to the podium a yellow legal pad and a bottle of water. "May it please the court," he said to Bridger. Nodding to Cathy, he continued the customary introduction. "Counsel."

"Counsel," Cathy replied.

Lee then made what Cathy heard as a rather perfunctory opening statement, outlining what witnesses, testimony, and evidence he would introduce and what he believed it would show. "Ladies and gentlemen, when we have concluded here in the next day or so, I will ask you to return a verdict of guilty," he concluded.

Bridger nodded at Lee, then directed his attention toward Cathy. "Ms. Schmidt, does the defense care to make an opening at this time?"

Cathy rose. "We do, sir." She made her way to the podium, took a long drink of water, and made eye contact with each of the jurors before she began to speak. She had little to work with—just the State's burden, really, so she had decided to highlight it during a brief opening.

"Good morning, ladies and gentlemen. I'll be brief. I think it is important that you understand that as a former prosecutor, I was struck by Mr. Lee's espousing his certainty of my client's guilt. There is always reason for doubt, in my experience. Moreover, you should understand that under Wyoming law, there are generally very few surprises in a trial. The defendant has the right to see the evidence of her supposed guilt. I have. And despite having seen the evidence, I find myself nowhere near as certain as Mr. Lee with respect to Ms. Layton's guilt. In fact, I think there are some glaring and gaping holes in the evidence. Most importantly, I want you to focus on the State's burden in one particular area: whether they can show that my client *knew* of the presence of illegal drugs in her home. At the end of the trial, I think you will agree that the State has failed to meet its burden and I will ask you to render a verdict of not guilty. Thank you."

When Cathy was seated, Bridger ordered Lee to proceed.

"Your Honor, the State calls Ashley Miller," he said.

After Miller was sworn, Lee conducted the direct examination of the young detective. Miller's testimony was crisp; her responses were brief and certain. Lee's questions were generally chronological and led Miller through the brief investigation in exhaustive detail, culminating in Misty's arrest and booking. After almost two hours of direct examination, Lee looked to Bridger. "No more questions, Your Honor," he said as he took his chair. "Tender the witness."

During his questioning, Lee had studiously avoided the subject of why she had arrested Misty. Although the testimony wasn't particularly damaging, Cathy felt she needed to bring the issue to the fore.

Bridger nodded to Cathy. "Ms. Schmidt, does the defense care to inquire?"

"Yes, sir," she said, standing and turning her attention to the witness. "Detective Miller, I have just a few questions."

Miller watched Cathy carefully. "Fine."

"You testified about your investigation, the call received and the basis for it—didn't you?"

"Yes."

"And you testified as to the evidence found, and the location where you found it?"

"I did."

"And you testified that the substance was confirmed by the Wyoming state laboratory to be methamphetamine?"

"Yes."

"And if I recall correctly, you testified that the methamphetamine was found in a room in the defendant's house?" Cathy asked. She realized only after the question was posed that she had referred to her client as "the defendant."

"I did, yes."

"Not in Misty's room?"

"No."

"Not in a common space?"

"No, but she owned the house," Miller said, seeing what was coming.

It was objectionable and Cathy could move to strike the explanation, but they would have to get there eventually. "Was anyone else arrested in connection with the methamphetamine located?"

Miller's eyes quickly fixed on Lee and then returned to Cathy. "No."

"Did you charge Misty with possession of methamphetamine?"

"No."

"Why not?"

Miller chewed her lip for just a second prior to responding. "Because in my opinion we wouldn't have been able to prove she knowingly and intentionally possessed the drugs."

Cathy nodded. It was the right answer. "And yet, you charged her with endangering children."

It wasn't a question, so a wary Miller sat quietly, awaiting Cathy's follow-up.

"Why?" Cathy asked.

"Because I felt like that was the proper charge."

"Why?"

"Objection," Lee began. "The question calls for a legal conclu—"

"Overruled," Bridger said. "You can answer," he continued, looking to Miller.

Miller nodded to the judge, then turned to the jury and delivered her response. "Because while we didn't believe we would be able to show your client possessed the drugs, we felt we had enough evidence to show she knew or should have known about them being in the house."

Cathy took a deep breath. This was it. "Detective Miller, do you know the difference between direct evidence and circumstantial evidence?"

"I do," Miller said. She looked to the jury, then back to Cathy.

"Direct evidence is testimony from actual knowledge, like a witness who sees or smells something. Is that right?"

"Yes."

"And circumstantial evidence is proof by way of evidence from which the finder of fact can infer facts—like maybe footprints in snow proving someone walked there—true?"

"Yes," Miller said warily. "As I understand it," she hedged. Cathy sensed Miller could see the next question coming.

"Detective Miller, what direct evidence of my client's knowledge did you have when you decided to arrest her?"

"She told us she knew about the drugs," Miller said.

Out of the corner of her eye, Cathy could see several of the jurors making a quick note. "She did?"

"Yes, she—"

Cathy walked over to the defendant's table, picked up a file, and made a show of thumbing through it. "I asked the State for any and all admissions my client made," she said. "I'm going to represent to you I didn't receive any. Do you know why?"

"I don't." Miller shrugged, then looked to Lee. "Maybe because she didn't actually admit to anything?"

"I thought you just said that my client's statements were the reason you arrested her?"

"Objection—mischaracterizes the evidence," Lee said.

"Sustained," Bridger ruled.

"I'll re-phrase," Cathy said. "You just told me that the evidence you had of my client's knowledge was, at least in part, comprised of her statements —true?"

"I did."

"What exactly did she say and when?"

Miller sat quietly, apparently calculating. "I can't recall exactly."

"Would it be in your report?"

"I think so."

Cathy wanted to stop Miller's equivocating. "If you were to look at your report, might it refresh your memory?"

"I think so."

"Your Honor," Cathy said, extracting a document from the file. "May I approach the witness?"

"No objection," Lee interposed.

"You may," Bridger allowed.

Cathy handed the document to Miller and returned to the podium. "Please review your report, and when you've refreshed your memory, let me know."

Miller turned pages until she found what she was looking for, then looked to Cathy and nodded.

"Did you find it?" Cathy asked.

"I did."

"What did Misty say?"

"She said she knew Kyle—that's her son—was using," Miller said, and sat back in the witness chair.

Cathy stood silently, knowing the jury was watching her. "That's it?" she asked when she felt she had their attention. "Anything else?"

Miller was once again upright in the witness chair. "Not that I recall." She looked to Lee for help.

"Misty didn't say where her son was using, or how, or when, did she?"

"Well, no, but—"

"She didn't say that she knew there was meth in the house, did she?"

"No."

"So you really don't *know* what she knew, or when, do you?"

"There was meth in that house; it was obvious to anyone," Miller insisted. "I've been doing this—"

"Move to strike, Your Honor. Not responsive."

"Sustained," Bridger ruled. "Jury will disregard the response. Answer the question, please."

"No," Miller admitted.

That was as good as it was going to get. Cathy moved to her chair. "No more questions, Your Honor."

Lee's redirect examination was brief and focused entirely on Miller's understanding of what she had heard. When he had completed his questioning, Bridger looked pointedly to the clock and called for the afternoon recess. "We'll reconvene at four p.m. Ladies and gentlemen, please follow the directions of the bailiff."

The State's next witness was a technician from the Wyoming state laboratory. Cathy pulled a file from her banker's box and quickly reviewed the single page torn from a yellow legal pad. There wasn't a lot to contest here. She'd rely on her experience as a prosecutor to raise a single issue—that the lab was reliant upon the investigators afield.

Lee made quick work of obtaining the laboratory technician's training and experience, then moved on to his findings. "Based upon your training and experience, did you make a determination as to the identification of the substance you were provided for examination purposes?" Lee concluded.

"I did," the man said. "It was methamphetamine."

"Your witness," Lee said to Cathy.

She was at the podium quickly. "You didn't collect the samples?"

"No."

"You don't know from where they were sourced?"

"Just what it said on the package."

"All you know is that whatever was given to you, and wherever it came from, was meth?"

"Well, I mean, I know the amount."

"But you cannot say whether my client knew anything about the existence of the meth, can you?"

"No."

"No more questions, Your Honor," Cathy said, having established the State couldn't say with exactitude what Misty knew. She would emphasize the point at closing.

"Any redirect?" Daniels asked Lee.

"No, Judge."

"All right," Bridger said to the witness. "You may step down." When the witness had departed, Bridger called for the evening recess.

24

Lee spent the next morning calling witnesses to corroborate the basic elements related by Miller: that there was both meth and a child in the house. Unstated was the idea that Misty knew or must have known about the methamphetamine. Cathy passed on cross-examination of most, as there was little to be gained. "If the witness didn't hurt you, let it go," one of her mentors had instructed her early in her career. It was sound advice, but difficult for defendants to stomach.

"Go after these people!" Misty implored Cathy at one point.

Cathy thought she smelled alcohol on her client, but let it go. "The evidence is what it is."

"Well, it will be if you don't do nothing," Misty protested.

"I need you to trust me," Cathy said. "As a prosecutor, the biggest lesson I learned was that Wyoming juries take the State's burden seriously. They are expecting to see conclusive evidence of your guilt—*CSI*-type scientific evidence. They can't prove you knew the meth was there. That's the issue."

When Lee was done, Bridger gave the parties a lengthy recess, allowing Cathy time to consult with an angry and distraught Misty. "Have some faith," Cathy counseled. "A trial is a back-and-forth thing. Sometimes things will look like they are going their way; sometimes they will look good for us. We need to stay steady."

"We're losing, aren't we?"

"I can't say," Cathy said, then—seeing Misty's look of dismay—continued, "Juries are impossible to predict. We've made the points we need to make, but you never know."

"Well, that sucks," Misty said. "Maybe if you were cross-examining the witnesses—"

"I'm doing my job," Cathy said. "I'll remind you that it was you who refused a plea. You can change your mind right now. Otherwise, you need to trust me."

"That ain't no real choice, now is it?" Misty snarled.

Sam had warned Cathy that it wasn't unusual for defendants to panic during a trial. Still, it was disconcerting to be on the receiving end. "No, it isn't. But you made your choice when you allowed your son to remain—"

"I told you, I didn't have a choice!"

Cathy, already regretting her words, let it go. "This isn't productive. Go get your smoke in before we start again."

While Misty was outside chain-smoking, Cathy quaffed a small container of lukewarm yogurt and some celery sticks. She was reviewing her outline and feeling her stomach gurgling when her phone began to vibrate. It was Sam. "What's up?" she said, trying to remove celery from her teeth with her tongue.

"Checking in," Sam said. "How's it going?"

She fiddled with the yogurt container while she spoke. "You know how it is. I've made clear to the jury that the State can't prove its case, but I'm not sure they are getting it—you know?"

"I do," Sam said.

Cathy wondered if that was true—she'd never seen him lose a jury trial. But hey, at least he cared enough to commiserate. "What's the word on the street?"

"I wouldn't know," Sam said. "I've been stuck writing a motion on a real estate case I got myself roped into—how anyone does real property law for a living is beyond me. I'd rather sit naked on a cactus."

"Yikes!" She smiled in spite of herself.

"Need anything?" he asked.

"Nope."

"Well . . . good luck—not that you need it," he added quickly. "And let's get a beer when this is over. I mean, I'll buy you a beer and—"

"I know what you mean," she said, and tossed the yogurt container six feet into the wastebasket. Still got it.

"See ya," he concluded, and was gone.

She was about to leave when there was a sound at the door. Misty stepped in and closed the door quickly behind her. "I gotta say somethin'."

"What is it?"

"I think you quit on me," Misty said. "You're afraid of that Lee guy, and you're gonna let him put me in jail and take my grandkid for something I didn't do!"

"Misty," Cathy began, "sit down. What in the world has gotten into you?"

"You and Lee," Misty said. "You used to work together. Word is you was—"

"Enough!" Cathy said. "There was and is nothing between us." She was eyeballing her client closely. Something wasn't right. "Who've you been talking to?"

"Well, Kyle for one. He says—"

"Kyle?" Cathy interrupted. "Are you kidding me? He's the one who created this entire mess. He's the one who OD'd while watching your grandson—his own nephew. He's the one who is going to testify against you to save his own skin. And despite all of that, you're going to listen to a man —a boy, really—who is willing to let his own mother take the fall? Are you kidding me?"

"He has two convictions! Third time and he'll be in big trouble."

"And whose fault is that?" Cathy asked. She should let it go. "As far as I am concerned, the best thing you can do is kick that clown out of your house, and out of your life!"

"He's my son! You can't talk about him like that!"

"I can and I will," Cathy replied. "He's almost thirty years old. It's time he started acting like a man."

Misty was tearing up. "You don't understand, Cathy. It's not his fault," she said, pulling a tissue from her sleeve. "It's mine. I made some bad decisions and set a bad example and—"

Cathy was about to interrupt Misty's exercise in self-loathing when she heard a knock at the door. It was court security. "Counsel? It's time."

"Thank you," Cathy said through the door. "Dry your eyes and let's go," she said, and waited impatiently while Misty reapplied mascara. "Let's go!" Cathy urged at last. When Misty was finally ready, Cathy placed a hand on the small of her client's back and guided her into the courtroom.

"Looks like reality is setting in, eh?" It was Lee, who had apparently been walking behind them. "I've seen it before," he added, indicating with a hand that she should precede him down the aisle.

"After you," she said, studiously ignoring his comment.

She hurried to her client's side, arriving just as Bridger was announced. After ordering all to be seated, Bridger looked at the attorneys in turn. "Shall we call for the jury?" With the assent of both, Bridger called for the jury. When they were seated, he looked to the prosecution's table. "Mr. Lee?"

"Your Honor, the State calls Kyle Layton."

Cathy felt Misty stiffen beside her. "He can't; he said he wouldn't—"

"Shh," Cathy said. "Let's just see what happens here."

Cathy held Misty's hand as Kyle swore an oath, took the stand, and got settled in without ever looking toward his mother. Lee led him through a series of questions designed to show that he was a pitiful—if not despicable—young man with an out-of-control addiction to methamphetamine.

"So, on the evening in question you'd been living with your mom for how long?" Lee asked.

"I guess a coupla months—since I got out of prison," Kyle replied, looking everywhere in the courtroom except toward Misty.

"And you were in prison for?"

"Possession."

"And to be truthful, you'd originally been given a probationary sentence, but had . . . trouble on probation. Is that right?"

"True."

Lee followed up quickly. "Why?"

"They said I came up hot on a couple of piss tests."

"So, you got out of prison, and you came back to Custer to live with your mom?"

"Yeah," Kyle said. "I was gonna get a job and then help out with my nephew while she worked."

"Where is your sister?"

"In the women's pen."

"Do you know why?"

"Same as me." Kyle shrugged. "Meth."

Lee allowed that to stand, knowing the jurors would judge Misty's parenting skills. "Have you ever been to treatment?"

"Oh, yeah."

"Fair to say it hasn't worked for you?"

"Fair."

"When's the last time you used?" Lee asked.

"The night Mom got arrested."

"You were home with your nephew?"

"Yes."

"Alone?"

"Yes."

"And you used while you were there?"

"Oh, no," Kyle said. "I used while I was out, and then I came home to watch Ari while Mom went to work."

"Did you see your mom before she went to work?" Lee asked.

"Oh, yeah. We talked."

"How did that go?"

"Not so good. She knew I'd been using, and she told me to keep that shit—sorry—outta her house," Kyle said, with a quick glance toward a frowning Bridger.

Lee was watching the jury carefully. "Did you keep meth in her house?"

"A little," Kyle said, looking toward the jurors. "I mean, I ain't got no car —where else am I gonna keep it?"

Lee ignored the question. "And she knew that?"

"Apparently."

Not good enough. "What makes you think that?"

For the first time, Kyle snuck a quick look at Misty. "She tol' me."

"That's not true!" Misty hissed, loud enough for Bridger to hear.

"Ms. Schmidt, please get your client under control," he said.

Cathy already had a hand on Misty's forearm. "Yes, Your Honor."

Lee had been observing the events with a smirk. "No more questions," he said. "Tender the witness."

Cathy was at the podium quickly. "When is the last time you were convicted of a felony?"

"Uhhh, not sure?"

"Was it three years ago in this very courtroom?" she asked, knowing it was.

"Maybe."

"For drugs?"

"Yeah. That's about all I've ever been convicted of."

"Are you pending charges right now?"

"What's that?"

"Are you facing any charges right now?"

Kyle looked to Lee. "Not right now."

Bingo. "Have you made an agreement with Mr. Lee here that he will not charge you with possession if you come in here and testify against your own mother?"

"She knew the drugs were there!" Kyle said.

"Answer my question, please. Did you do a deal with Mr. Lee?"

"There's no way she couldn'ta known!"

"Your Honor, move to strike. Nonresponsive."

"Sustained," Bridger said. "The jury will disregard the answer. Mr. Layton, please answer the question."

Kyle snuck a look at Misty, who was staring at her hands. "Yeah, I did a deal—okay?"

Cathy allowed that to sink in with the jurors. "Since you got out of prison this last time, you've been living with your mom—have you seen her use?"

"No."

"Have you seen her high?"

"No."

"Seen her in your stash?"

"No."

"Any of your stash disappear?"

"No."

"She been in your room?"

"Not that I know, but it's her house," he said. "She can go where she wants."

"But you have no reason to believe she has gone through your belongings or been in your room, do you?"

"Well, 'cept for when she's picking up my laundry."

"She does your laundry?"

"Objection, Judge. Relevance," Lee said.

"I'll withdraw," Cathy said quickly. "No more questions."

Lee followed up briefly and was done in short order. "Your Honor, the State rests," he said.

Bridger appeared to have anticipated the move but made a show of checking his watch for the benefit of the jury. "Ladies and gentlemen, this trial has moved along nicely and we're ahead of schedule. We're going to take an early, lengthy lunch. After that, the attorneys and the court have some business to attend to that will not involve the jury. Let's have everyone back by two p.m." When the jury had departed, he ordered everyone to re-seat. "Ms. Schmidt, does the defendant intend to testify?"

"I'm not sure, Judge," Cathy replied truthfully. "I was planning to have that decision made at the next recess."

"All right," Bridger said. "We are there. The court will meet with counsel at one o'clock this afternoon to get the jury instructions straight so that we'll be ready to go when the time comes. I'll expect your answer then. I don't want the jury moving back and forth like it's on a string."

During the ensuing recess, Cathy and Misty debated whether Misty should testify. Misty, of course, wanted to take the stand, and felt certain that if the jury heard her story she would be acquitted. Cathy was less sure. Most defendants overestimated their ability to withstand cross-examination, and

Cathy was certain Lee would be ready, willing, and able to eviscerate Misty on the stand. Still debating the matter during the instructions conference, Cathy was anxious, distracted, and irritable. When the conference was completed, Bridger looked to Cathy. "How has your client decided?"

Cathy looked at Misty, who nodded fiercely. "Judge, my client will testify," Cathy said, almost feeling Lee at his table rubbing his hands together in glee.

Bridger gave Misty the standard, cautionary instruction reminding her she did not have to testify. "Do you understand?" he asked her afterward.

"I do, sir."

"Fine," he said. "Call the jury." When the jury was present and seated, Bridger turned to Cathy. "Call the defendant's first witness."

Cathy stood and reluctantly called Misty. When her client was seated, Cathy began with a series of simple, straightforward questions designed to elicit minimal evidence while putting Misty at ease insofar as possible. Lee, seeing through the tact, stood. "Your Honor, the State will stipulate to the witness's biography and the reason she is here."

Bridger looked blankly at Lee. "If that was an objection, Mr. Lee, it is overruled," he said, then turned his attention to Cathy. "Counsel, please approach." When Lee and Cathy were at the bench, Bridger looked to Cathy. "Counsel, while this court is generally loath to interrupt counsel on direct, I would suggest that you move it along a bit."

Cathy nodded, and when the parties had returned to their places, she got right to the heart of the matter. "Misty, you've heard the testimony here today?"

"I have," Misty replied, then opened her mouth to follow up but stopped short of saying anything in light of Cathy's steady stare. They'd been over this: "Answer and shut up," Cathy had instructed her.

"Have you heard anything untrue?"

"Not really," Misty said.

"Have you heard anything that bothers you?"

"Yes."

"Let me ask the question straight out, then: did you know for a fact that there was methamphetamine in your home?"

"No," Misty said, stealing a quick glance toward the jury.

It was unconvincing. "That is going to seem hard to believe for some of the jurors," Cathy opined, stating the obvious. "How could that happen?"

Misty looked at her hands, then to the jurors. "Look, he got outta prison and after a few days I suspected somethin' was up," she explained. "But I was workin' two jobs and wasn't around much. I tol' him to keep it outta the house on account of Ari. I was expectin' him to follow my rule."

"Did you check on him?"

"When could I?" Misty pleaded. "I'm workin' two jobs, doin' the shoppin', no washer and dryer so I gotta go to the laundromat, NA meetings . . ." Her voice trailed off as she smeared her mascara with the palm of a hand.

Cathy watched the jury closely. There were a couple unconsciously nodding in sympathy. "Just to be clear," she asked again, "you didn't know for a fact there was meth in the house when your grandson was there?"

"I did not," Misty said, shaking her head vigorously.

That was as good as it was going to get. "No more questions," Cathy said. "Your witness."

Bridger looked at his watch. "Mr. Lee, cross-examination?" he asked, apparently satisfied with the time.

Lee was already at the podium looking at a red-faced Misty, who clearly had something to say. "Just a few, Judge," he promised. "Ms. Layton, you've got some experience with methamphetamine, haven't you?"

"When I was younger."

"By younger, you mean when your last conviction was?"

"Yeah," Misty allowed. "Before that, actually."

"And that was only a few years ago, true?"

"I guess."

"Well, you pleaded guilty to possession of meth about four years ago, didn't you?"

"Yeah."

Lee side-eyed the jurors, none of whom were looking at Misty. "You were in possession of meth prior to being convicted—true?"

"Of course. It couldn't happen the other way around," Misty griped.

Lee smiled indulgently. "And you're telling the jury you've been straight since?"

"I have."

"But you know what meth looks like—"

"Yeah."

"You know how it's kept and stored?"

"Yeah. So?"

"So if there was meth in your house, you'd know."

"Only if I was looking for it or came across it."

"Well, you just said you suspected something was up—why?"

"Cause he was tweakin'."

"Under the influence of meth?"

"Yeah."

"How do you know?"

"He's my son," she said. "I raised him. I can tell when he ain't right."

"And at some point before your arrest, you observed your son and he 'wasn't right,' to use your words—true?"

"Yes."

"At your house?"

"That's where I seen him, yeah," she said. "Otherwise, I was at work."

"Was the child ever home with your son when your son was high?"

"I don't know; don't think so—'cept for maybe when I was arrested," Misty said. "But since I wasn't there, I don't know."

"But you didn't try and find out?"

"I was workin'."

"Every day?"

"Damn near," she said. "Someone's got to."

"And you didn't look for meth?"

"Hell no!"

"Why not?"

"Because it weren't really none of my business."

Lee smiled tolerantly. "Ms. Layton, isn't it true that you didn't look for meth, and didn't ask your son about the presence of meth, because you didn't want to know?"

"Would you?" she retorted angrily, while Cathy tried to make eye contact with her.

"Move to strike," Lee said. "Nonresponsive."

"Sustained. Ms. Layton, you need to answer Mr. Lee's questions," Bridger instructed. "The jury will disregard the answer."

Misty pointed at Lee with a shaking hand. "Why?" she asked Bridger. "He's tryin' to trick me!"

Bridger's face was flushed. He took a visibly deep breath. "Ms. Layton—"

"I can't be convicted if I didn't know, right?"

That did it. "Ms. Layton! Stop interrupting me!" Bridger scolded. "I'll not have it!"

"I'm just trying to—"

"You are interrupting and delaying the proceedings!" Bridger said. "I'll not have it. Should you decide to interrupt either me or Mr. Lee again, you may well see yourself held in contempt of court. Do you understand?"

"Well, yes, but—"

"And if that were to happen, you very well might sit in jail until I decide otherwise. Do you understand?"

"Yes," Misty said.

Bridger nodded curtly, then turned his attention to Lee. "Counsel, proceed."

"Ms. Layton, it is true that you ignored the possibility that your son was using meth in the house, isn't it?"

Cathy watched as Misty sat quietly, thinking it through. Like many addicts, she was capable of quickly calculating the advantages and disadvantages of a situation—and of deflecting responsibility for her decision. If she would simply respond "Yes," Cathy could likely salvage the testimony on redirect. But she wasn't capable. "Yeah—but I had to for the sake of Ari."

Cathy watched as Lee let Misty's answer hang while the jurors shifted uncomfortably in their chairs. The implication was clear: she knew. "No more questions," he said.

Bridger looked to Cathy. "Redirect?"

Cathy could feel twelve sets of eyes on her. She could still argue her client didn't know. "No, sir," she said quietly.

"You may step down," Bridger said to Misty. When Misty was seated next to Cathy, he instructed Cathy to call her next witness.

"Defense rests," she said.

Bridger nodded approvingly. "Ladies and gentlemen of the jury, the evidence in this matter is closed. The court is going to release you a little early today so that we can prepare for instructions and closing remarks. Recall my earlier admonitions, please. We will reconvene tomorrow morning at eight-thirty a.m."

25

Just before eight-thirty the next morning, the parties reassembled in the courtroom. Cathy was tired and irritable; she'd spent most of the evening rehearsing her closing remarks. Along with Misty—who didn't look as if she had slept much better—she stood when Bridger entered, right on time.

"All right," Bridger began. "We're back on the record. Are there any preliminary matters before we call for the jury?" Seeing no indication from either counsel, Bridger asked the bailiff to conduct the jury into the court-room. When the jury was seated, Bridger spent the better part of half an hour reading them the instructions they were to follow. Concluding, he took a sip of water, then turned to Lee.

"Mr. Lee," he said. "Ladies and gentlemen, we will now hear closing arguments from the parties, beginning with the State. We will then hear from Ms. Schmidt on behalf of the defendant and then—because the State has the burden of proof—we'll hear from the State in conclusion."

As Cathy expected, Lee's remarks were pointed and accusatory. Speaking at length, he reviewed the testimony of each witness and the importance of each exhibit. He placed a chart on an easel containing the elements of the charge, and marked a large red "X" next to each as he detailed the facts he believed satisfied each element. "Ladies and gentle-men," he concluded, "I want to remind you of the judge's instruction. The

State was required to prove Ms. Layton's guilt beyond a *reasonable* doubt, not beyond *all* doubt. Now, Ms. Schmidt will no doubt argue that we failed to meet our burden. She may or may not explain why. But bear in mind, if she offers a theory, and if it is unreasonable, you must find the defendant guilty. If she doesn't offer a theory at all, but merely asserts we failed, well, use your common sense. I'm convinced that if you do so you will find Misty Layton guilty of endangering a child. Thank you."

When he had been seated, Bridger looked to Cathy. "Ms. Schmidt."

Cathy stood and began by thanking the jury for their attention. She then laid out her view of the evidence, highlighting the lack of forensic evidence against her client as well as the entirely circumstantial nature of what evidence the State did have. "Most importantly, ladies and gentlemen, do not forget that there is no evidence that my client knew of the presence of the methamphetamine in her home," she said. Retrieving a black marker from her pocket, she walked to the easel where Lee had made his marks in red and circled the word "knew." "There is no proof she *knew*," Cathy emphasized. "That is an essential element they failed to prove. You heard the judge. You must follow the law, and if you do that, my client must be found not guilty. Thank you." She sat and drank water. Her client was hanging by a thread.

"Rebuttal, Mr. Lee?"

"Briefly, Your Honor," Lee said. He then took a few minutes to neatly dissect Cathy's argument, focusing on the nature of circumstantial evidence and the jury's right to draw reasonable inferences therefrom, concluding, "It is World Series time, folks. So, like the players on television, do one thing: don't take your eyes off the ball. And if you do that, you'll know what to do."

Cathy had Misty accompany her to her office to await the verdict. As she opened the front door to her small office, her phone rang. It was Bridger's judicial assistant, Mary Perry. "We have a verdict," she said.

"What's that mean?" Misty asked, seeing Cathy's startled look.

She couldn't lie. "It's probably not good," Cathy surmised. "But you never know."

"Jesus!" Misty said. "What can we do?"

"Nothing," Cathy said. "Let's go and see what they decided."

"But if they convict me, I'm going to jail!"

"Not necessarily," Cathy replied.

Together, they made the short walk to the courthouse in silence. When all parties were present in the courtroom, Bridger entered and approached the bench. When he had been seated and the jury had returned, he turned to them and asked, "Has the jury reached a verdict?"

"We have, Your Honor." It was a short woman who Cathy had supposed would have been the last juror selected as foreperson, and it didn't bode well for Misty.

"Please give the verdict form to the bailiff," Bridger instructed, and when the bailiff had retrieved it and given it to him, he read it to ensure it was properly completed. Satisfied, he handed it to the clerk. "Ms. Layton, please stand." When Misty and Cathy had complied, Bridger looked to the clerk. "Ms. Marshall, please read the verdict."

Violet Marshall stood and with shaking hands and a quiver in her voice, read: "As to the charge of endangering children, we the jury find the defendant, Misty Layton, guilty." Cathy placed a hand on a shaking Misty's elbow. For a fleeting moment, she feared her client would attempt to flee.

Bridger thanked the jury and released them, then formally adjudicated Misty guilty and—over Lee's objection—set a small commercial bond pending sentencing. "I'm innocent!" Misty said repeatedly despite Cathy's attempts to settle her.

When Bridger and Lee and their entourages had departed, Cathy spoke quietly. "We did what we could," she assured Misty.

"I'm gonna lose Ari, ain't I?"

Cathy saw the court security officers approaching and shook her head. She needed a minute. They backed off uncertainly. "Let's take this one step at a time, okay?"

"Why? Why should I listen to you?"

"Because I'm all you've got," Cathy said. "Now, just go with these men. I'll get you a bond posted, and you'll be released later today. Come see me tomorrow first thing."

26

The Longbranch wasn't particularly loud three hours later, but Sam and Cathy took a booth in a corner, anyway. When Gino approached their table, Sam stood and shook his hand.

"It's been a while," Gino said.

"Been busy," Sam replied. "You remember Cathy?"

"How could I forget?" Gino asked. "What'll you have?"

"Crown Royal. A double. On the rocks. Beer chaser."

He raised a pair of gray eyebrows. He remembered her drinking Moscato. "What kind?"

"Surprise me."

Gino smiled and turned his attention to Sam. "The usual?"

"Yeah. Twist of lime."

"That's new."

"I'm trying to break out of my box."

Gino flashed a wry grin and left to fill their orders. Sam sat back down and slid into the corner of the booth. "So, double Crown plus? I'd ask how you're doin', but I think I know the answer."

"I'm tired," she admitted. "Tired and crabby and pissed off and frustrated—"

"That's fair."

"I'm just . . . angry I couldn't get the job done."

Understandable. "She didn't give you much to work with," Sam said. "You can't make chicken salad out of chicken crap."

She sat quietly, looking at her hands. "I shouldn't have called her. He peeled her like a banana." Suddenly, she slapped the tabletop. "I knew that would happen!"

Sam was initially startled, then self-conscious, knowing the other patrons were staring. They looked like just another squabbling couple. "She has the right to testify," he reminded her. "And it is not your decision."

"I should've talked her out of it."

"One, not sure that could have happened; two, not sure it would have made any difference," he counseled. "It's hard for regular people—which I'm defining as people who don't deal with addicts and their families—to conceive that someone could have drugs in the house and not know anything about it."

"People have serial killers in their homes—"

"I hear you."

"Well—"

Without thinking, he put a hand on hers, but awkwardly removed it when she looked at his hand. "Hey, rule number one for trial lawyers, remember? No Monday morning quarterbacking—or whatever the point-guard equivalent is," he counseled, referring to her former athletic career. "Like golfers, shooting guards, pitchers, and cornerbacks—we need a short memory."

She was looking at the table, where his hand had been on hers. She looked up. "You know what really pisses me off?"

"What's that?"

"The fact that I'm pissed off," she said. "I mean, you know she's guilty; I know she's guilty; the jury knows she's guilty. Hell, she knows she's guilty! So why do I feel like a loser?"

"Well, the verdict was against you," he reasoned. "You're a competitive person."

"Yeah, well, I don't know how you do this."

"What's that?"

"Defend guilty people."

"Remember, you are representing—"

"Their rights," she said with disgust. "Yadda, yadda, yadda."

Gino arrived with their drinks. "Enjoy," he said. Sam and Cathy touched glasses while he watched approvingly.

"Gino, while you're up, go ahead and bring me another—the same," Cathy said, after draining her shot glass and handing it to him. When he raised his eyebrows, she gestured to Sam. "He's driving." She turned her attention to Sam when Gino had gone. "Right?" she asked.

"Right," he assured her.

"Just a ride," she emphasized.

"Understood," Sam said, not understanding at all.

27

On New Year's Day, Sam was standing thigh deep in a trout stream two hours from Custer. A spring creek—a rarity in Wyoming—the flow was spring-fed and for that reason never froze. As a result, the water was accessible and fishable year-round—another rarity.

Unfortunately, the stream was in the bottom of a deep canyon it had carved since time immemorial, and the wind blew incessantly. There was little run-off, so the water flowed clear and at a leisurely pace. Above the canyon's rims, hawks and eagles competed for airspace. Their presence, combined with the slow flow and plentiful food, made the fish both wary and selective.

Sam didn't particularly care for this stream—between the wind, the high banks, and the wily fish, it was not at all unusual to cast for hours between fish. On the other hand, it was so notoriously difficult that he usually had the place to himself, which appealed to his misanthropic nature. Because it was the dead of winter, he'd slept in, timing his arrival for mid-morning, hoping to catch a hatch of insects of some sort.

He was both surprised and pleased to note the lack of wind as he unloaded his gear, but—as always—by the time he'd donned his waders and vest, strung his rod, and affixed a tiny nymph to his tippet, the wind was its usual, roaring self and he put on a knit watch cap featuring crossed rifles—the centuries-old insignia of American infantry. He walked the two hundred yards to the stream and was ruing his earlier decision to wear fingerless gloves. The tour in Afghanistan had resulted in frostbite on his right hand, and now even the slightest cold resulted in throbbing protest from that index finger. He was wondering whether he had an extra pair of gloves in his vest when he saw the tell-tale sign of a fish feeding on the surface.

A big one.

Over the years Sam had seen several extremely large trout in the stream. But given their wariness, he had largely ignored them in favor of their smaller, less wary cousins. Standing motionless, he watched as the big brown trout surfaced repeatedly, sipping tiny flies from the surface. He looked with disgust at the nymph he had tied on earlier, and briefly debated whether to change flies in what he sensed would prove a fruitless effort to fool the big fish. Deciding it wouldn't be worth his while, he flipped the nymph in the general direction of the brute and watched in anticipation as the fly sank in the gin-clear water and floated slowly toward the bottom, until it was devoured by a large rainbow trout he hadn't seen.

The cold water had slowed the trout's metabolism, and the big fish was soon in Sam's net, exhausted and eyeing him warily. Sam placed the net carefully in the water with one hand and felt for his phone with the other. He needed to have proof of this, lest fishing companions doubt him at his word later. Quickly realizing he had left the phone in his truck, he debated a dash for it, but harm to the fish was probable so he regretfully resuscitated the fish and released it unharmed.

A half-hour later, he sat back on the brown grasses, exhausted and sated. In those thirty minutes, he had caught and released four more fish, each more than twenty inches long. The trout—two rainbows and two browns—were thick, brutish fish with brilliantly hued flanks, tails the size of the brooms used to sweep home plate, and clear eyes registering the shock of the cold air. Each time Sam netted a fish he would look quickly for another fisherman—someone he could ask to record the moment for posterity. But it was not to be, and the action was over as quickly as it had begun. He fished for another two hours, catching a half-dozen smaller-sized trout. As the late afternoon sun began to go down, the temperature dropped, and he made the decision to call it a day. A great day.

He stopped at a convenience store and while filling his truck went inside and purchased a hot dog, a cup of coffee, and a bag of potato chips for the ride home. Not healthy choices, but better than the celebratory booze and pills he would have opted for just months prior. Back on the road, he took a bite of the hot dog, placed it on the console between the seats, slipped a Clint Black CD into the player, and chewed the roller dog. Warm, dry, and with a full stomach, he drove into the setting sun, and was weighing stopping for another cup of coffee as he pulled into Custer but decided instead to run by his office. He parked his truck and was standing in front of his office trying to find the right key in the streetlight when a figure moved in the recess in front of his door. Startled, Sam drew a pistol from his shoulder holster.

"Whoa!" The man raised his hands. "Dude, I was just trying to get out of the wind."

"Step out in the light where I can see you," Sam said. He noticed a faint tremor in his hands. "Now."

"I'm on it," the man said. As Sam gestured with his gun, the man stepped into the streetlight. To Sam's astonishment, he was wearing only a T-shirt emblazoned "Army." "I'm sorry; it's cold and I just got off the bus."

"Why didn't you get back on?"

"You wouldn't believe me."

"Try me."

"So, you know where the bus station is, right?"

"I do."

"There's that bar next door?"

"Right."

"Well, the bus was supposed to gas up and we had a few minutes, so I ran into the bar to get a drink and to see if I could buy a bottle—for the ride, you know?" he asked, running a hand over his grizzled chin.

He knew. "And?"

The man smiled sheepishly. "So, I saw this little gal and I bought her a drink. Next thing I know, I missed the bus. Well, she didn't have any interest in taking me home, and the shelter was already full and anyway I'd been drinkin' and so here I am."

Bad decisions rang true. "That your shirt?" Sam asked.

"It is."

"What's your name?"

"Clayton Pierce. Call me Clay."

Sam lowered the small revolver. "When did you serve?"

"'06 to '14."

Right age. "Branch?"

"Army."

"MOS?" That was the acronym for military occupational specialty—an alphanumeric indicator of one's job title.

"Thirteen Bravo. Cannons."

"Redleg," Sam said, using the time-honored nickname among soldiers for artillerymen.

Clay's eyes widened in recognition. "You?"

"Infantry."

Clay surveyed Sam briefly. "You don't look like a grunt," he said, using the age-old nickname for infantrymen.

"Been some time," Sam said. One more question should do it. "Where'd you do basic?" The correct answer was Fort Sill. More than once, Sam's questions had revealed a poser.

"Sill," Clay replied.

Satisfied, Sam put the gun away. "What are you doing?"

"I told you, trying to—"

"No," Sam interrupted. "What are you *doing*?" When Clay didn't answer, Sam asked, "Need some help?"

"Maybe," Clay said. "A little something to tide me over."

"How about I get you a room and something to eat?"

"That'll work. I—I'll pay you back when I can."

"No sweat," Sam said. "I've been there." He nodded toward his truck. "Get in."

The Horseshoe Motel was a small, locally owned place that rented rooms by the hour, day, or week. Sam had represented one of the desk clerks, and he figured he could get a discount. He side-eyed Clay as the man fidgeted and scratched at his forearms and face. Not good. "How long has it been?"

"What's that?" Clay asked.

"Since you used methamphetamine?"

"Been clean for months, man."

"I'm not a cop," Sam replied. "But I'm not oblivious, either. Don't blow smoke up my tailpipe."

Sam could feel Clay's eyes on him, so he turned his head and met the gaze. Clay's pupils were constricted to pinpoints. As Sam pulled into the parking lot, he considered simply dropping Clay off, but an offer was an offer. He turned the truck off and shifted in his seat to face his rider. "This ain't Oregon; they don't go for that stuff here." When Clay began to protest his innocence, Sam held up a hand to stop him. "I'm not gonna argue with you, and I'm not judging you. I'm just telling you how it is," he said. "You be you."

"You was an officer, wasn't ya?"

"I was."

"I can tell."

Sam ignored the insult. "Let's go," he said. He led the way into the Horseshoe's small registration area. He held the door for Clay and as he entered immediately smelled burned coffee. He looked and saw a carafe that had boiled dry on the hot plate of an inexpensive coffee maker perched on a cheap end table next to a dusty philodendron.

"It ain't the Ritz, is it?" Clay remarked.

"Well hello, Sam," the clerk said warmly. Sam had gotten her a deal on a possession charge some time back. She had put on about twenty pounds, which was a good thing. Women using meth got bone-thin fast. "You two checking in?" she asked, looking meaningfully at Sam and then Clay.

Sam laughed. "I'm gonna spot my friend here a room. Three nights. I'll pay up front, of course."

She looked closely at Clay as he shifted his weight from one foot to the other and scratched at a sore on his forearm. "Sure he's your friend?"

Sam watched as Clay struggled to maintain. "I am," he said. "We've been to some of the same places," he added while trying desperately to remember her name.

"You can swipe it or insert it," the clerk said to Sam. "We don't abide no drugs here, mister," she said to Clay. "It ain't no different for you 'cause you know Sam." She handed Clay a key card. "Down the hall; last door on the left by the pop machine."

Clay shook Sam's hand. "I owe you one."

"No sweat," Sam said. "Take care." He watched as Clay shouldered his backpack and walked quickly down the hallway to his room.

"I gotta have a phone number," she said. Sam gave her his number. "Haven't seen you down at the Longbranch lately," she added.

Started with a K. Seemed as if every woman's name started with a K or a C. Kelly! Her name was Kelly. "Well, Kelly, I've been busy," he said.

She brightened when she heard him use her name. "Well, you get un-busy and you want some company, let me know—okay?"

"You bet," he said, hurrying to leave. "Let me know if you have any issues with him."

"Will do."

28

Like many small businesswomen, Cathy didn't have the luxury of taking federal holidays off, so she was in her office on Equality Day. She was scheduled to meet with Misty to cover what would happen at tomorrow's sentencing. Together, they would review the pre-sentencing investigation and—more importantly—try and re-establish trust between them. Cathy had met with Misty occasionally since the trial and was concerned with her client's increasingly sullen, withdrawn demeanor.

Notwithstanding, she was shocked at Misty's appearance that morning and quickly reflected on a recent discussion with Sam about clients and sentencing. "The first thing they need to understand is that it is possible they will go to prison," he had explained. "Most of them convince themselves they will walk. And most of them are right—there is a lot of pressure on judges to find a way to keep people in the community, especially with a drug crime. Your client's crime is drug-related, but because she allowed her grandson to be around drugs, I'd have her prepared to do some time."

"She's gonna be pissed."

"Of course. She's convinced life dealt her a bad hand. Minimal coping skills," he said. "I'd remind her what the maximum possible sentence is—get the bad out first. Then talk about the possibility of probation only—

that's best case. Then, walk through the Department of Corrections' recommendation. Then promise only—*only*—to do your best. That's it."

"Case like this, what do you think?"

"Bridger usually follows the recommendation from the DOC," he said. "Assuming your client doesn't do something to piss him off, that's the most likely scenario."

She had thought about it and made some notes for herself to follow during her discussion with Misty. But seeing her client in this condition had Cathy off-center. "Misty, are you . . . okay?"

"Whattaya mean?"

"Well . . . you don't look . . . right."

Misty sat heavily in the client chair. "I'm fine, sister."

Good Lord, the woman had been drinking! "Christ, Misty! You've been drinking!"

"Only a little," Misty said, holding up her hand and showing Cathy an index finger and a thumb an inch apart. "What're they gonna do? Throw me in jail?"

"That's exactly what Bridger could do!" Cathy said. "He finds out you've been drinking he could send you to prison! Show up like that tomorrow and he could hold you in contempt."

"Big effing deal."

"It is a big deal! That's time that wouldn't count toward your sentence!" As a prosecutor, Cathy had seen plenty of defendants show up to court drunk. Many lacked coping skills—that was the reason they were in trouble in the first place—but this was the first time she'd had to worry about it with her own client.

"What the hell were you thinking?" Misty didn't answer; instead, she began waggling her foot. After a few seconds, Cathy saw tears. "Misty, what's—"

"I don't want to go to prison!" Misty wailed. "I've done everything right! I've tried to change. I went to treatment, I've been going to NA, I work two jobs, and I'm trying to be a good grandma for Ari. But with my record . . ." She wiped at her nose with the palm of her hand.

Cathy handed her a tissue. "I hear you. But jail's not a sure thing. Probation and Parole recommends you do a split and then get probation." A *split* was vernacular for a sentence whereby the defendant would be sentenced to a term of prison, but in lieu of serving time in the penitentiary, the defendant would be sentenced to serve a shorter period in the local jail, followed by a lengthy period of probation. "You've already done—"

"Oh, my God!" Misty was on her feet. "I've got to get outta here!"

"Sit down, Misty!" Cathy's tone got Misty's attention. "Sit," Cathy repeated. When Misty was again in the chair, Cathy continued, "We can argue for less. We can argue for straight probation, and we will. Here's how it will go." Cathy then explained their roles during the sentencing hearing. "You've got to keep your poise and you've got to be strong. This is not the time to give up," she counseled. "I need you straight tomorrow. No booze or drugs—do you hear me?"

"Yes." Misty wiped her eyes. "I'm scared."

"I get it, but don't give up on me. Worry is the price for sweating things that probably won't happen," Cathy advised. "Understand?" When Misty's blank look convinced Cathy of her client's inability to think in the abstract, Cathy gave her a piece of gum. "See you tomorrow."

Misty was on time the next morning and—except for red-rimmed eyes and the slight odor of booze—appeared prepared for court, although somewhat surly. Cathy stopped Misty outside the courtroom, had her toss the gum she had given her moments before, and patted her forearm reassuringly. At the defendant's table, Cathy nodded to the court reporter as she and Misty took their seats. The courtroom was empty except for a couple of women from the Department of Family Services, a representative from Probation and Parole, and Lee.

"Take a couple of deep breaths," Cathy whispered to Misty. "It will be fine," she added, not at all certain that would be the case. She touched Misty's elbow when Bridger entered, and they stood together.

Bridger had everyone be seated, called the case, and asked Lee, then Cathy, if they were prepared to proceed. Satisfied that everything was in order, he looked to Lee. "Mr. Lee, what is the State's recommendation?"

"Thank you, Your Honor," Lee said as he moved to the podium. "I know you have reviewed the pre-sentence investigation, and the State has done so, as well. I have to say that, given this defendant's long history with drugs, I was somewhat surprised by the leniency recommended. In my opinion, the people of the State of Wyoming have done what they could to support this defendant. It appears efforts were made at first to help, and later to coerce, her to mend her ways. Apparently, those efforts were for naught, as she continues to involve herself with drugs."

A low growl emitted from Misty and Cathy put a hand on her arm to restrain her. "Be quiet!" she hissed. "We will get a chance here in a minute."

Citing Misty's past offenses and state expenditures on her behalf, Lee continued to set the stage for his recommendation. When he stopped to drink from the plastic glass on his table, Cathy knew he was about to make his recommendation. "Your Honor, given the defendant's history, as well as her refusal to show any remorse or regret—or to simply accept responsibility for her actions—the State would recommend three to five years in the penitentiary, imposed, followed by three years of probation. Fines and fees at the court's discretion."

Cathy wasn't surprised. Given the facts it was an extreme recommendation, but well within the allowable range for the crime. She watched as Bridger made notes and thumbed through what appeared to be his copy of the pre-sentence investigation. He put down his pen and looked to Cathy. "Ms. Schmidt?"

Cathy stepped to the podium. "Your Honor, as you might expect, the defendant has an entirely different view," she began. She then recited a list of Misty's accomplishments since her prior arrest, including finishing her high school equivalency, obtaining a job where she had recently been promoted to management, and her successful completion of treatment. "Your Honor, I think it is important to note that my client is by all accounts safe and sober. She has passed several urinalysis tests, and there was no testimony that would indicate she was anything other than a mother and grandmother trying to keep what is admittedly a troubled family together."

Cathy looked to Lee, who was looking at Bridger. "Mr. Lee's recommendation appears to us to be the result of his anger at my client's daring to exercise her constitutional right to a trial. It makes sense that she would not show remorse or regret; she said at trial, and she'll say again today, that she didn't know about the drugs. She understands the jury decided otherwise, and she respects their right to do so. But that doesn't change anything. The bottom line is this: after a full trial and after having heard the entirety of the evidence, what we know is, my client—at most—turned a blind eye to her own son's relapse. That's the extent of her wrongdoing. And for that," Cathy continued, "Mr. Lee wants to see her sent to prison. Well, Your Honor, that's not what prisons are for. Prisons are for people who are dangerous. My client is not a danger to the community or anyone in it."

Cathy picked up the pre-sentence investigation and held it aloft. "Rather, the evidence and this pre-sentence investigation show that my client has done everything right for the past several years. The report itself notes she is a good candidate for probation. Now, for some reason, it asks that you impose a split sentence—I'm not sure why given the remainder of its contents. We'd ask you to give my client whatever term of incarceration you wish, but that you suspend any prison sentence in favor of probation subject to terms you deem appropriate. I would ask that any fines and fees be minimal as she is the sole working adult in the home. Thank you."

Bridger nodded and looked to Misty. "Ms. Layton, is there anything you'd like me to know?"

Misty stood and joined Cathy at the podium. "Judge, I just want you to know I'm doing everything I can to get back on my feet. I made a mess of things, and I'm trying. I've got a job and I'm going to NA and I'm working hard. Goin' to jail will set me back. And I'm worried about Ari—I'm all he's got."

Cathy touched Misty's elbow. That was what they had rehearsed, and it seemed to Cathy that Bridger was watching Misty approvingly. It was time to sit down. She touched Misty's elbow again in an attempt to have her sit, but Misty shrugged her off.

"This man," Misty said, pointing to Lee, "is wrong about me. He don't know nothing about me. And I'm not going to forget—"

"Ms. Layton," Bridger interrupted. "I'm not going to hear any personal attacks against Mr. Lee."

"But you heard him attack me for days!"

Bridger sighed visibly. "Thank you, Ms. Layton."

"And I ain't gonna forget it! You will get yours, *Mister* Lee."

Bridger had visibly reddened. "Ms. Schmidt, get control of your client, please."

Cathy stood, put a hand on Misty's shoulder, and gently seated the still-protesting Misty. She sat next to Misty and placed a hand on her client's thigh. "Stop," she ordered under her breath. "Or you're gonna talk yourself into a cell." Turning her attention to Bridger, she smiled tightly. "We're ready, Your Honor."

"Would the defendant please stand?" When Misty and Cathy were on their feet, Bridger put on his reading glasses. "It is the judgment of this court that the defendant be sentenced to a term of three to five years in the custody of the Department of Corrections," he began. Cathy felt Misty stiffen and put a hand under her client's arm in support. Seeing this, Bridger softened. "Ms. Schmidt, you and your client may be seated." When Cathy and Misty were seated, Bridger looked to his notes and continued. "I will suspend the sentence in favor of supervised probation for a period of five years."

Cathy felt Misty nearly go limp with relief. "Sit up," she whispered.

"Ms. Layton, for the next five years, you must follow these terms," Bridger said, and then explained the terms and conditions under which she would be required to live. "Finally, let me say this: I am ordering you to have no contact with any minor—including family members—under the age of eighteen except as permitted by the Department of Family Services. You will follow their orders, undertake any training, and accept any conditions placed upon you. Do you understand?"

Misty had gone rigid and now sat quietly, staring straight ahead. Bridger prompted her before Cathy could do so. "Do you understand, ma'am?"

"Does—does that mean I can't see Ari?" she asked quietly.

"Not necessarily," Bridger replied. "It does mean that you will only see him under the conditions they deem appropriate—for now. We can discuss any modifications of their terms at any time."

Misty's lip quivered and her eyes watered. "What the hell do they know?" she asked, shrugging off Cathy's hand on her forearm. "They don't know shit! They haven't walked in my shoes!"

"Ms. Layton, please control yourself," Bridger said. "This is my order, and I'll not have that kind of language in my courtroom."

"They don't know anything about Ari or what he's been through," Misty insisted. "I've been there every day for him until they—and you—took him away. He needs me, damn it!"

"I've made my decision," Bridger said, determined to end the hearing. "Is there anything else?"

Misty started to stand but Cathy had a grip on her. "No, Your Honor," Cathy said quickly.

"No, Judge," Lee said, gathering his materials and standing in anticipation of Bridger's departure.

"We'll be adjourned," Bridger said, and quickly departed the courtroom.

Misty was on her feet immediately. "I will get you, you sorry bastard!" she said to Lee.

"Ms. Schmidt, I believe your client is communicating a threat," Lee said calmly. "Please control her."

Cathy saw the court security officers approaching and held up a hand to stop them, then placed her hand on Misty's shoulder. "Misty, stop."

Ignoring Cathy, Misty was focused on Lee. "I'm not a dog, Mr. Lee. And I'm not someone who can be controlled. And you are going to regret treating me like a misfit loser."

"I have given you the degree of respect you deserve," Lee said, then turned and left.

By now, Cathy was holding Misty's arm so tightly she feared it would bruise. "Let him go, Misty. It's okay. It's fine."

"It's not fine!" Misty shouted at Cathy, then, seeing the representatives from the Department of Family Services, she yelled to them, "What I gotta do to get Ari back?"

"We'll—we'll talk about that tomorrow," a small woman in a gray pantsuit responded. "Can you be at our office by nine a.m.?"

"I'll make sure she is there," Cathy said to the woman. "Wait for me outside," she said to Misty.

When the courtroom's double doors closed behind the two scurrying women and Misty had been escorted out—ironically, by her son Kyle—

only Cathy remained. She took a deep breath, then blew her nose and tossed the tissue in a small wastebasket. She was thinking Misty had resigned herself to the sentence when she heard Misty yelling in the court-yard, "I'm going to kill that sonuvabitch—and the judge, too!" Alone in the courtroom, Cathy sat heavily in the defense counsel's chair and stared at the ceiling fan twenty feet above.

29

When a week before trial Cassie knocked, opened his door, and guided Julie and Cathy into his office, Sam could see Julie was as nervous as a rescue dog on July 4th. "Have a seat," he said. "Can I get either of you anything?"

"Xanax would be good," Julie said.

Sam and Cathy laughed politely, then exchanged a welcoming acknowledgement of the other's presence. He indicated with a wave to Cassie that she could go. When the door had closed, he looked to his star witness. "Are you okay?"

"Just nervous."

With good reason. Lee would be hard on her. "I understand; that's why we are doing this," Sam explained. "But remember one thing: all I'm going to do is have you testify to the truth. If you simply tell what you know, it will be fine," he assured her. "Cathy's going to be with you the whole time."

Julie was chomping on a wad of gum. "O-Okay," she said. "I don't really want to do this. I hate freaking lawyers—no offense," she said, looking to Cathy and then Sam.

"None taken," they answered in unison.

"Sometimes I don't care for them myself," Sam added.

"Courts suck," Julie said. She blew a bubble and popped it with her tongue.

He made a mental note to be sure she didn't have gum with her when she testified—Van Devanter would blow a gasket. He had done background on her. In addition to her many drug- and alcohol-related run-ins with law enforcement, she had been in the system for both divorce and custody matters and had been both the petitioner and respondent in cases alleging domestic violence.

"I understand," he said. "But this time it should be a little different. You're only a witness here."

"So, that attorney—the tall one—he won't attack me?" she asked, looking to Cathy.

"Well, he'll cross-examine you, but I'll make sure it is done appropriately. That's my job," Sam explained, flashing what he hoped was a winning smile but quickly sobering when she didn't respond. He watched her staring at the desktop. She wouldn't be a great witness, of course—she had far too much baggage and a tremendous distrust of the system. "Today, I just want to talk about some simple rules you'll need to follow when you're on the stand, okay?"

"Are you going to tell me what to say?" she asked. "That'd be good—I don't know what to say."

"Just listen," Cathy urged her.

"No," Sam assured her. "It doesn't work that way. For one thing, I don't think it is ethical to do too much coaching. For another, I want the jury to hear your story. Thirdly, if I tell you what to say it will not be you testifying. It will sound unnatural, and Lee will sniff it out."

"Well, what do you want me to say?"

"Let's look at it this way. The first rule is this: tell the truth. Good, bad, or indifferent—whether you think it helps Press or not. I can deal with anything they throw at me, but if you get caught in a lie, the jury can disregard all your testimony. So no matter what, tell the truth—can you do that?"

"I—I think so," she said.

"Good. Now, one thing you have to do is trust me. Lee will try and get you to agree to half-truths," Sam predicted. "He'll ask the 'Have you stopped beating your wife?' questions. That's what I'm here for—to keep it fair. Got it?"

She was still studying the desktop but looked quickly at Cathy, then at Sam long enough to nod before again focusing on his desk's embarrassingly dusty surface. "Next thing: answer the question and then shut up. Do not expand on an answer; don't try and explain anything. Just answer the question that was asked."

Again she looked to Cathy and then to him, no doubt recollecting prior court experiences. "Okay, but what if he asked something that needs explaining?"

Sam nodded in understanding. "You just answer what was asked; I'll come and get the explanation out of you later. That will show the jury he is trying to be tricky."

He watched while she blew another bubble, popped it, and resumed chewing. "Next rule," he began. "If you don't know, say so. Do not guess or speculate." While he spoke, she drew herself into a ball, with the soles of her feet on the chair and her arms wrapped around herself.

Again, Sam and Cathy made eye contact, and when he nodded imperceptibly, she spoke. "Julie, you want to help Judge Daniels, don't you?"

"I do, but I'm afraid."

"That's perfectly understandable," Cathy said. "I'd be more concerned if you weren't."

Julie put a hand to each temple and rubbed vigorously. "That attorney —Lee? He's an ass."

Cathy smiled briefly. "I can't disagree with that. But he is what he is, and you are just going to have to work around him for the sake of Judge Daniels."

"But I'm afraid he is going to tear me to pieces!" Julie said.

Sam was afraid she would break into tears. "He'll try, but again, that's what I'm here for," he said. "And you should know that as a truthful witness, there is only so much he can do."

"What do you mean?"

"I mean there are rules of ethics for attorneys," Sam explained. "The rules expressly hold that while an attorney can cross-examine a truthful witness, there are limits."

Julie shook her head vigorously. "Legal gobbledygook," she said. "I've been in court, and I've been on the stand. I know how the system treats people like me."

"This time it will be different." As soon as Sam said the words, he regretted them.

She had unwrapped her arms, but her feet remained up on the chair. "It was partially my fault, you know. He told me he would take care of replacing the syringes. But I—I should have checked. If I would have, none of this would have happened."

"Maybe," Sam allowed. "But we don't know for sure."

Julie was street smart. "It's better for Pre—Judge Daniels—if I say he was real tired and forgot to replace the syringe and I forgot to verify, isn't it?"

Indeed it would be. "Well, the best thing is that you testify to what you *know* to be true," Sam hedged.

"Exactly," Cathy added.

Julie removed her gum with two fingers, looked at it, then reinserted it into her small mouth. "What kind of trouble could I get in if I admitted screwing up?"

"I can't tell you that," Sam said. "I *can* tell you that if you testify falsely, you could get charged with perjury—lying under oath."

"Everyone lies under oath," Julie snorted. When neither Sam nor Cathy reacted, she continued, "So you're telling me—"

"The same thing I told you before: testify truthfully to what you can recall," Sam finished.

"What if I can't remember?"

That would hurt. "Then say that; it's okay," he replied.

"But that would hurt your case, wouldn't it?"

It wouldn't do Daniels any favors. "Well, yes. But not as much as he would be hurt if you get caught making up a story. Now, nothing says that between now and then you can't try to remember one way or the other. In fact," he said, looking at his watch, "it's probably best you go and think things through. But remember: the first rule is to tell the truth and only the truth—got me?"

"I do," Julie said. She looked to Cathy, expecting her to depart Sam's office with her.

"Rule two is answer the question and then shut up," Sam reiterated. "Rule three is—"

"—If you don't know, say so," Julie finished.

"Right," Cathy said approvingly. "Now go on home. I'm going to stay and finish some things up with Sam," she added. "I want to pick his brain about another matter."

Julie looked at Cathy for a moment, then at Sam before standing to leave, apparently with some reluctance.

"Problem?" Cathy asked.

"No," Julie said. "I'm just scared."

"Understood. You want me to get you home?" Cathy offered.

"No, I'll be fine," Julie said. "See ya."

When she was gone, Cathy looked to Sam. "How are you?"

"I'm good," he said. "Just hanging out."

"That doesn't sound good—for you, I mean. Been getting out at all?"

"Not really," he said. "But the playoffs are underway."

"So?"

"So if sitting around in my boxers watching football games and eating cheese puffs on my couch is wrong, I don't wanna be right."

"Pretty picture," she said.

"You're welcome to join me."

"Pass."

30

On the morning of trial, Fricke had arranged for Sam and Daniels to enter the courthouse through one of the alternate entrances. Even so, when they breached the second-floor hallway, public contact was no longer avoidable. Courthouse security had emplaced dividers on the stairways and in the main corridor to keep foot traffic flowing in one direction, but the size and enthusiasm of the crowd was making the maintenance of order difficult. "You got 'em, Judge!" and "Good luck, Yerhonor!" were among the favorable expressions offered; there were less flattering sentiments aired as well as Sam and Daniels followed two of Custer County's beefier deputies through the throng. The price of small-town fame.

Bridger's courtroom—which was where Daniels' future would be decided—was a large, square room devoid of windows. At the front of the courtroom were the judge's bench, the witness stand, and a box for the judge's law clerk. At floor level and immediately in front of the law clerk's box was an area reserved for the court reporter. The jury box, complete with fourteen chairs (counting the two reserved for alternate jurors) was to the judge's right. A lectern positioned in the center of the courtroom was flanked by two library-style tables reserved for the attorneys and the parties from the prosecution and defense. Adorning the walls were framed portraits of the grim-faced, unyielding men—to date no woman had served as a district court judge in the Twelfth Judicial District—who had presided and their dates of service. Behind the tables, and serving to separate the spectators from the participants, was a waist-high divider known as "the bar." Since the mid-twentieth century, all courtrooms in Wyoming had been required to feature the same.

In the last few moments before trial, Sam's habit was to sit quietly and take it all in. Even given his experience with pomp and ceremony stemming from military service, he always found himself awed by the spectacle of trial by jury. He looked about the large courtroom, his eyes resting briefly on the wainscotting complementing the carpeted floors. Two ornate ceiling fans circulated air far above the participants and observers, and Sam knew that outside the courtroom the public's footsteps would echo on clean marble floors as court security officers struggled to control the crowd of curious onlookers hoping to see the judge—the judge!—who had been charged with murder.

Sam stole a quick glance at Lee, who last fall had been elected county attorney, and noted Lee's navy-blue suit, white shirt, cordovan shoes and matching belt, and power red tie. The package was loud, statement-oriented, and would contrast with Sam's own subdued gray suit. Cates, Lee's young deputy, was sporting a green suit and sweating profusely. For his part, Daniels sat calmly and outwardly composed. Although Sam could smell the faint odor of booze, his thinking was that at this point Press probably operated best with a slight buzz.

When at ten minutes after the hour Van Devanter strode into the courtroom, Sam and Daniels stood with the others until Van Devanter ordered them seated. "Finally," Daniels muttered under his breath.

Van Devanter looked over the packed courtroom. "Good morning, ladies and gentlemen," he began.

"Good morning," was the usual polite but unenthusiastic response.

"It is nine-ten a.m. on Monday the seventh day of February. My name is Alec Van Devanter, and I am a retired Wyoming district court judge. I was asked to preside over this matter for obvious reasons. I am therefore happy to be here, but as a man with some experience in the affairs of life and in reading people, it is obvious to me that most of you do not share my enthusiasm." He waited for nervous laughter to abate before continuing. "That's a

shame, because what you are about to do is fulfill one of the most important civic duties a citizen may be asked to perform, and that is to serve on a
jury." Van Devanter then provided a brief history of jury duty in Wyoming
before moving on.

"You must understand and be prepared for reality in this courtroom.
And the reality is that in the real world, trials are not generally as depicted
on television or the movies. If you are selected for this jury you will have
one job only: to decide the truth—a truth with consequences, one that
directly affects the lives and liberty of those who are involved."

Van Devanter looked at the notes in front of him. "Ladies and gentlemen, the case that has been called is the State of Wyoming versus Preston
Daniels. The defendant in this case is present and seated at the counsel
table to the Court's left next to his attorney, Mr. Johnstone." Daniels sat
calmly next to Sam, looking straight ahead. Sam smiled politely at
everyone as Van Devanter continued. "Seated at the other table is county
attorney Grant Lee, who is lead counsel in this matter. Also present is
Caiden Yates, assistant county attorney. They are the lawyers for the State
of Wyoming; the burden of proof in this case rests with them." Lee stared
straight ahead as Aiden reminded him the judge had botched his name.
"Mr. Daniels has been charged with one count of second-degree murder in
the death of one Marci Daniels on or about last April 9 here in Custer
County.

Van Devanter looked up when—at the mention of her sister's name—
Miriam Baker wailed from her seat in the front row of the gallery. "Madam,
I will ask you to control your emotions in this courtroom."

"Yes, Your Honor," she said meekly.

"Christ," Daniels muttered. "She—" he began, but quieted under Sam's
glare. "Mr. Daniels pleaded 'not guilty,' and as you look at him right now
you should understand you are looking at an innocent man, and he'll
remain so until and unless you decide otherwise."

Having ensured that the gravity of the task at hand was apparent, Van
Devanter explained the process for jury selection, concluding, "At this time,
the clerk is going to call a number of you to be seated in the jury box. If
your name is called, please come forward. The bailiff will direct you to your
seat. Madam Clerk, would you seat a jury, please?"

When the first potential jurors had been called and seated, Van Devanter continued. "You will note there are fourteen of you seated. A jury is twelve members, of course, but fourteen persons will hear the case, including two alternates, in case someone gets ill. Moreover, the fourteen men and women now in the box will not necessarily be the jurors to hear this matter; the attorneys will direct their questions to those members of the venire seated in the gallery, as well," he added.

Turning his attention to the lawyers, Van Devanter continued, "Ladies and gentlemen, we will now proceed to select a jury through a process called 'voir dire,' which means 'to tell the truth.' The purpose is to select a fair jury. Mr. Lee will first ask questions of you as a group; he may follow up with questions to you individually. When he has finished with his questions, Mr. Johnstone may ask questions as well. Mr. Lee, please proceed."

Lee stepped to the podium and for the next hour asked questions of the jurors intended to reveal their knowledge of the case, the players, the process, and any predisposition toward conviction or acquittal. He inquired of the jurors regarding their schedules, their state of mind, and their willingness to participate. In addition, he asked questions about judges and the law in general, and Daniels in particular. Several jurors were struck for cause or convenience, and—except for a ninety-minute recess for lunch—Lee's questioning continued until just after three p.m.

Van Devanter looked wearily at Sam. "Does the defense care to inquire of the panel?"

"Yes, Your Honor," Sam said, standing and buttoning his jacket. "Ladies and gentlemen, because Mr. Lee did a thorough job of asking questions, I'm only going to ask you a few more. They will be simple and straightforward, for all my client seeks is a jury of fair-minded people. So, here we go. First, is there anyone here who doesn't like judges—anyone who believes they are a part of the problem?" Sam watched as most of the jurors grinned and then shook their heads. "So, can we all agree to judge my client not by his former profession but instead by applying the evidence to the law the judge will instruct you on later?" Again, each juror grinned and nodded.

"Thank you," Sam said, looking at each juror in turn. He then spent time probing the potential jurors' knowledge of Daniels, either personally or by reputation. All admitted they had heard of him; some admitted they knew him. A couple acknowledged they didn't care for him. "Let me ask you this," he asked of those. "If you were my client, would you be comfortable having yourself as a juror? Could you set aside your personal feelings and decide in accordance with the law?" Some of the jurors shifted in their chairs and snuck a peak at Daniels; some smiled slightly, but all met Sam's stare and eventually nodded their assent.

Having set the baseline, Sam inquired of the prospective jurors for more than an hour. Some were excused for cause and new ones summoned to fill their place, whereupon Lee and Sam asked questions of them, as well. Sam questioned potential jurors extensively on their use of media and knowledge of the case, trying to determine if media coverage had predisposed any to a verdict. All steadfastly denied media coverage having had any influence.

As the process wound down, Sam asked two final questions. "Is there anything that any of you would prefer to discuss in private? Raise your hand if you'd like to meet with us in private." No hands were raised, so Sam continued, "Is there anything we haven't asked you that you think we should know?" Seeing no hands, and nothing but blank stares or head shakes, he finished up. "Ladies and gentlemen, thank you for your patience." Turning to Van Devanter, he said, "Defense passes the panel for cause, sir."

"Thank you, Counsel," Van Devanter replied. "Ladies and gentlemen, I am going to release you here momentarily so that we might select that jury in your absence. We'll do this as quickly as possible, but it sometimes takes some time," he continued, smiling at his word play. "Do not leave the courthouse and follow the directions of the bailiff. Bailiff?"

When the venire had left the courtroom, Sam asked for a moment. Van Devanter had expected the request and granted the time. Sam and Daniels walked to a corner of the courtroom. "If you want to move for a change of venue, now is the time."

"I don't think it's gonna fly," Daniels replied. "I wouldn't grant it. The prospective jurors who admitted to knowing about the case all said they could set what they knew aside and decide based on the evidence produced at trial. Besides, if I'm going down, I'd rather it be right here."

"You sure?"

"I'm sure."

"Okay," Sam said. "I agree." He guided Daniels to the defendant's table. "Thank you, Your Honor," he said when Daniels was seated. "The defense is prepared to proceed."

Van Devanter nodded his approval, and the parties quickly selected the jury and the alternates. When the jury that would hear the case had been reconvened and sworn, Van Devanter looked pointedly at the clock. "Well, ladies and gentlemen, you are the jury which will hear this matter. It's been a long day, so we will go ahead and take our evening recess and we will hear opening arguments and get started in the morning. First, I'm going to read you an instruction regarding your conduct during daily and evening recesses. Please listen closely." When he concluded, he looked to the jury for acknowledgement. "The bailiff will tell you where you need to be and when you need to be there." He stood, and everyone followed suit. "Thank you for your attention. Bailiff, you may escort the jury."

When the jury had departed and the members of the panel not selected had been excused, Van Devanter looked to the attorneys. "We'll begin promptly at eighty-thirty," he said, and departed quickly.

Sam and Daniels spoke quietly until the courtroom was empty. "Cassie, can you see the judge home?" Sam asked.

"Of course," she said. "Ready?"

"Ready," Daniels said as he stood. "Sam, I just want you to know that however this turns out, I appreciate your efforts."

31

At eight-forty-five the next morning, Van Devanter finally arrived in the packed courtroom. Daniels looked at his watch and shook his head. "Christ, how imperial can you get?"

Sam suppressed a grin as Van Devanter took his chair. After calling the case, he read several introductory instructions to the jury. "Now, ladies and gentlemen," he said at last. "We'll begin with opening statements. We'll hear from the State first. Mr. Lee?"

"Thank you, Your Honor. Ladies and gentlemen, this case really began a couple of years back with Marci Daniels, then about sixty-two years old, adjusting to a new life with her husband, retired judge Preston Daniels, home. I'm sure you all know Mr. Daniels better than I do—I've only been here a little less than a year. But in that time even I have come to know the long shadow cast by this man," he said, pointing to Daniels. "I've heard the good; I've heard the bad. I'm sure you have as well. But no one knows what went on behind closed doors."

Sam watched the jurors; all eyes were on Lee as he moved from one side of the podium to the other, aware he had everyone's attention. "But you will soon find out. Because you will hear from the victim's sister, Miriam Baker, who will tell you that Marci was apprehensive about spending all day, every day with her husband. You'll hear that while he was a good provider and a good or even great judge, she found him an angry, sullen man behind closed doors, a man her sister, was—for all her love of the man—afraid of."

Sam generally shied away from objecting during an opening statement, but he had heard enough, and he wanted to bring the jury's attention to the fact that Lee wouldn't have evidence to back this claim. "Objection. Argumentative and speculative."

Van Devanter looked dolefully at Sam. "Counsel, this is opening statement. Overruled."

"He can't possibly know or have any evidence of what Marci thought of my client," Sam argued, watching the jury closely and knowing he was on thin ice.

"Mr. Johnstone, this is his opening statement," Van Devanter repeated tightly. "I previously informed the jury that statements by counsel are not evidence. Overruled."

Lee smiled at the jury and continued. "In any event, we know that Marci Daniels got sick. And you'll hear just how sick she was, and how—despite her making some progress—her husband despaired of it and began taking her back and forth to Mexico for experimental treatment. You'll hear how those treatments took time and resources and began to wear on Marci—all at the expense of FDA-approved treatment available right here in Custer. The same treatments that perhaps you and your family have undergone."

Sam watched as Lee made eye contact with two female jurors who had disclosed their own bouts with cancer. "But it didn't work, and you'll hear from several people that as Marci got worse, Mr. Daniels here got angrier and angrier. You'll hear that he told people that Marci 'wouldn't want to live like this,' that she 'deserved to die with dignity,' and that 'if the doctors wouldn't do something, he would.' You'll hear that at some point, the defendant hired a woman named Julie Spence to assist him. Now, you'll hear that Julie didn't have any real qualifications for the job. It seems she was hired because she had a previous relationship with the defendant."

"Your Honor!" Sam began. "He cannot possibly know why the couple hired Julie Spence, and it's irrelevant in any case."

"Overruled," Van Devanter said. "No more, Mr. Johnstone."

"Thank you, Judge," Lee said unnecessarily. "As I was saying, the motive for her being hired was unclear, as were her credentials. In any event, a very ill Marci was home with her husband and his . . . assistant and under their care." Lee walked to the State's table and pretended to drink water. Sam knew he was watching the jury to ensure they understood the implication. "And you'll hear from the medical experts. They will tell you that Marci died from an overdose of the drugs she was prescribed to deal with the pain of her terminal cancer. You'll hear that despite her increasing needs, the defendant refused to give her professional care, and instead insisted on taking care of her himself . . . well, I should say with the help of Ms. Spence. And you'll hear from law enforcement and the emergency medical technicians regarding what Mr. Daniels had to say on the scene and later, during recorded interviews. You'll hear that he admitted killing her. He did. You'll hear it for yourselves," Lee assured them.

Sam and everyone else watched as Lee moved to retrieve his water again. He drank quickly, put the cup down, and squared up at the podium. "And ladies and gentlemen, you'll find out about the million-dollar life insurance policy and hear of his relationship with Julie Spence." Lee smiled slyly. "And when you've heard it all, we believe that you will be convinced—as I am—that Preston Daniels is guilty of the murder of his wife Marci. Thank you."

Sam watched as Lee moved to his chair, flashing a satisfied smile toward Cates. Without looking at Daniels, he could tell the older man had moved close and was leaning toward him. "Be calm," Daniels whispered.

Van Devanter was watching Sam and Daniels. "Thank you, Mr. Lee. Mr. Johnstone, does the defense care to make an opening, or would you like to reserve?"

"Your Honor, we'll make an opening statement at this time," Sam said. He moved quickly to the podium and took a deep breath. "Thank you. Members of the jury, I want to begin by offering thanks on behalf of myself and Judge Daniels for your appearance here today, and your promise to the court to serve to the best of your abilities. Let's begin by covering a few things that I think are important—specifically, the concepts of reason and common sense, and how that will apply to the evidence you will see and hear during this trial. Reason is an idea that is central to our system of justice. As you will see, it formulates the foundation of our system of jurisprudence. As we go through the trial, I will from time to time ask questions intended to remind you what reason is, and what is reasonable."

Seeing the jury was listening, he continued. "Common sense is exactly that. Common sense tells you that there are two sides to a story. The judge will tell you to listen to your common sense. In fact, he will issue several instructions on that subject. He will tell you to listen until all the evidence is in before making your decision. As the trial progresses, you will see that we will stipulate to a lot of the evidence, and you may well wonder why I'm not objecting to a lot of the testimony like you would see a lawyer do on TV. Well, here's why: in the twenty-first century, there are few "Aha!" moments in a trial. We know who the witnesses are going to be, and for the most part we know what they are going to say. We know what exhibits the State wants to enter into evidence. We have already seen them. We have stipulated to most of it, and the reason that we have done that is that we do not disagree with a lot of it. Does that surprise you?" Sam asked.

The question was rhetorical, of course, and he continued. "You will be told that on the evening in question, my client told people he had killed his wife. We don't argue that—he did tell people that. You will see that from minute one Judge Daniels accepted responsibility for Marci's death. But what you need to do is listen to the testimony and place it in context using reason and common sense. If you do that, it will become clear to you why my client said what he said—and what he meant," Sam continued. "And what he meant, in his grief-stricken state, was that he felt he was responsible for her death. You'll find that he said he *killed* her. You'll also find that he did not say he *murdered* her. He never, ever admitted intentionally harming her, and intent—as the judge will instruct you later—is critical to the State's case. In fact, it is the difference between guilt and innocence."

Sam moved to Daniels' side. "At the conclusion of the evidence, you will be instructed by Judge Van Devanter as to the law and what the State has to have proved for you to find my client guilty. And when you have reviewed the evidence and testimony, and when you have heard the law you are to apply to the facts you have found, and when you have applied reason and common sense, I am certain you will conclude there is only one just verdict, and that will be to find Preston Daniels not guilty of second-degree murder —or anything else. Thank you."

Van Devanter looked quickly at the clock. "Thank you, Mr. Johnstone. I think now would be a good time for our morning recess. Let me remind you of a few things," he began, and again admonished the jurors regarding their responsibilities during recesses before leaving the bench.

Sam and Daniels had stood with the others while the judge departed. "It's damn sure a different look from here," Daniels said.

32

When Van Devanter had returned and the jury had been re-seated, he looked to Lee. "Please call the State's first witness."

"Call Ashley Miller," Lee said. He turned and watched as Miller entered through the double doors and held the waist-high door at the bar for her. When Miller was sworn and seated, Lee began. "Please state your name for the record."

"Ashley Miller."

"Are you employed?"

"I am."

"What do you do?"

"I am a detective with the Custer Police Department."

"How long have you been employed as such?" Lee asked.

"I guess almost two years now," Miller ventured.

"What did you do prior?"

"I was a patrol officer with the Casper police."

Sam was watching Miller closely; she appeared far more polished and confident than she had been when he had cross-examined her during the trial of Lucy Beretta.

"And how long were you with them?" Lee asked.

"About ten years."

"Any other law enforcement experience?"

"Yes, I was with the military police when I was in the air force. I finished my time at Warren Air Force Base near Cheyenne."

"Are you a certified law enforcement officer in the State of Wyoming?"

"I am, since 2010 or so."

"Were you certified in April of last year?"

"Yes."

"What position did you hold at the time?"

"Same as now: detective."

"What are your duties?"

"I respond to patrol officers' calls and conduct investigations when a serious crime is suspected to have occurred. I also train our officers in investigative techniques."

Through the questions and responses to this point, Lee had established the foundation for her responses to the questions that would follow, including questions where he would be seeking not just her recollection of facts but her opinion as well. Sam expected Miller would be a persuasive witness for the State; his intention was to limit the damage through careful questioning and with a narrow focus on steps she *hadn't* taken and by drawing the jury's attention to what the evidence *didn't* show.

Lee now moved on. "Do you know the defendant, Preston Daniels?"

"I do," Miller said, looking to the jury when she responded.

"How so?"

"He was a judge here in town when I got here."

"How else do you know him?"

"Well." Miller shifted in her seat. She stole a look at Daniels and then returned her focus to the jury. "I arrested him."

Lee waited for the murmuring to die down. "You arrested him on suspicion of murder—is that correct?"

"Yes."

"Do you recall when?"

"It was . . . after his wife's funeral."

"Do you recall the date?"

"Yes. It was April thirteenth."

"And your arrest came after you had conducted an investigation?"

"Yes."

"Let's go back in time, then," Lee suggested. "Do you recall what started your investigation?"

"Chief Lucas called me and told me—"

"You are referring to William Lucas, the chief of police?" Lee interrupted.

"I am."

"Please continue."

"Well, the chief said Marci Daniels' family had started calling almost immediately after she died—like within hours, I think. They didn't believe she had died accidentally. They told people he killed her."

"By 'he,' you mean the defendant?"

"Yes."

Lee let that stand for a second before continuing. "Now you had been on scene almost immediately after the decedent passed?"

"Yes." Miller turned her attention to the jury. "She passed at home, so I went to the home and spoke with folks there at the time."

"Did you speak with the defendant then?"

"No."

"Why not?"

"He wasn't . . . around, I guess. I talked with the doctors and the EMTs, but nothing seemed concerning at the time."

"Then what?"

"Then the next morning the chief called."

"And what did you do next?"

"I went to the defendant's home."

"Was there anyone with you?"

"Corporal Jensen."

"And what did you do when you got to the defendant's home?"

"I asked to speak to the defendant."

"Who did you ask?"

"Julie Spence."

"Who is Julie Spence?"

"She was their . . . home health assistant, I guess you'd call it."

"Right," Lee said. He looked to the jury and cocked an eyebrow. "Were you allowed to speak with him?"

"Oh, yes."

"Do you see the individual you met with here today?"

"The judge?"

Lee's ears reddened some; he had, of course, directed Miller not to refer to Daniels as "the judge." "The defendant, yes."

Miller pointed. "He's sitting at the defendant's table wearing a gray suit next to Mr. Johnstone, his lawyer."

The identification had been made, so Lee moved on. "You spoke with him at his home?"

"Yes."

"Was he free to leave?"

"Yes."

"He wasn't under arrest?"

"Not at the time, no."

"And what happened?"

"Well, I told him that I wanted to talk with him—to clear some things up."

"And what did he tell you?"

"Well, he said that on the day she died he hadn't been feeling well himself, so he set the medication out and Julie—er, Ms. Spence—was to administer the medications. He told me when he checked on Marci three hours later she was cool to the touch with her eyes open. He said he knew she was . . . had passed, so he called 9-1-1."

Lee was watching the jury. "Did you ask him what he told the 9-1-1 operator?"

"I did."

"What did he tell them?"

"He told them he killed her."

Lee had expected the murmurs and he allowed them to die down before asking his next question.

"Did you ask him why?"

"I did. He said he had forgotten to change out her medications. Apparently, she had gotten new dosages prescribed. He said that because the dosages were in conflict at that level—"

Sam had heard enough. "Objection. Hearsay."

Van Devanter agreed. "Sustained."

"Thank you," Lee said to the judge, as if he had ruled in his favor. "Let me ask you this, Detective Miller. Did the defendant tell you what he did after he called 9-1-1?"

"He did."

"What did he say he did?"

"He lay down in the bed next to her and waited for the ambulance."

This time the talking and whispering was louder, so Van Devanter stepped in. "Ladies and gentlemen, this is a trial, not a movie theater. I must therefore insist that you keep your emotions and reactions to yourself. Continue, please, Counsel," he directed Lee.

"He said that he killed her?"

"He did."

"He used those words?"

"Yes."

"Why didn't you immediately arrest him?"

"Because when I asked him why, he said that it was his fault because he had forgotten to change out the prescription and that he failed to check on her," she explained. "He also blamed himself for her not going to the doctor sooner and for taking her to Mexico for treatment. But he denied murdering her."

"He admitted to you that he had said she would be better off dead?"

"He did, but—"

"He admitted having a large life insurance policy on her, didn't he?"

"He did."

The questions were leading, but the information would come in one way or another, so Sam let them go. Lee knew Sam was watching and took the lack of objections as a cue. "Did you find that unusual? A large life insurance policy on a woman that age?"

Sam was beginning to rise in objection. It was doubtful Miller had a knowledge base such that she could have an opinion, but Miller solved the problem for him. She pursed her lips. "I don't have any idea whether that would be unusual."

Lee had seen Sam getting to his feet, and he waited for Sam to re-seat before continuing. "Did you ask him about the decision to hire Julie Spence?"

"I did."

"You questioned him about their relationship?"

Sam was about to stand when Miller replied, "I did. He denied anything untoward."

Sam watched as several jurors looked quickly to Daniels, and then back to Lee. "You continued to investigate?"

"Yes."

"You spoke with Julie Spence?"

"Yes."

"You spoke with the EMTs who responded initially?"

"Yes."

"You spoke with members of Marci Daniels' family?"

"Yes."

"And you spoke with the coroner?"

"No," Miller corrected. "I talked with the medical examiner."

Lee smiled wryly in the general direction of the jury, then looked back to Miller. "And after all that, you arrested Preston Daniels for the murder of Marci Daniels."

Miller stared at Lee for a long time before responding. "I did."

"Tender the witness," Lee said, taking his chair.

"Thank you, Mr. Lee," Van Devanter said. "Mr. Johnstone? Cross-examination?"

Sam was making a note. Miller's delayed response to the last question had raised a question. "Thank you, Your Honor," he said. He stepped to the podium, carefully arranged a file and a pen thereon, then focused on the jury and smiled. None returned his smile, and he turned his attention to Miller. "Detective, in your initial meeting with my client, he flatly denied murdering his wife, didn't he?"

"Yes."

"He took responsibility for her death because of errors he made, but denied deliberately killing her, didn't he?"

"Yes."

"And in making those admissions, he exposed himself to both criminal and civil liability, didn't he?"

"Well. . . yes."

"He told you he forgot to change the medicine out?"

"Yes."

"He felt as if he waited too long to check on her?"

"He did."

"He lamented taking her to Mexico?"

"Yes."

"And you didn't arrest him right away, did you?"

"No."

"Why not?"

"Objection!" Lee said. "Relevance."

"Your Honor," Sam began. "It is—"

"Gentlemen, please approach," Van Devanter ordered. On command, Sam, Daniels, and Lee made their way to the bench. Technically, all criminal defendants had the right to listen in on bench conferences, but since the conferences generally consisted of arguments on points of law, very few did. Daniels, of course, could be a significant asset, so Sam had ensured the parties understood he wanted Daniels included. Van Devanter would have expected no less. "Mr. Johnstone, where are we going?"

"Goes to the weight of her testimony. If she didn't believe she had enough to arrest, it shows there may have been other motives for his arrest in play."

Lee was furious. "Judge, I object! That's an unwarranted attack—"

Van Devanter looked at Lee sharply. "Mr. Lee, stop. The idea that law enforcement or prosecutors may have an ulterior motive isn't exactly plowing virgin ground—and you know that," he scolded, then turned to Sam. "Mr. Johnstone, I'm going to allow it, but you need to develop your theory quickly." He made a note and then looked up. "Overruled. Return to your places." When the men were back in place, he looked to Miller. "You may answer."

"I—I can't remember the question," Miller said.

Van Devanter stared down the laughter, then looked to his reporter. "Please read the question that was posed."

The court reporter nodded and nervously read aloud, "Question: And you didn't arrest him right away, did you?"

"Because I didn't think I had enough to charge a crime," she said. "I wanted to talk with my boss about it and maybe the county attorney."

"Did you in fact do that?" Sam asked.

"Yes," Miller said. Her eyes went from Sam's to Lee's and back again.

"Both?"

"Yes. I talked with the chief and then with Mr. Lee."

"And then you prepared your affidavit of probable cause?"

"Yes."

"And that's a document you swear to, isn't it?"

"Yes."

"And you told the truth in that document?"

"I did."

Sam was watching Miller closely. In order to convict a defendant of second-degree murder, the State would have to prove that the defendant killed the victim purposely and maliciously. Miller's affidavit of probable cause didn't contain strong evidence of either, and in fact recounted Daniels' strong denial of having killed her either purposely or maliciously. The better charging decision would have been either involuntary manslaughter (alleging Daniels had acted recklessly) or criminally negligent homicide (alleging Daniels was criminally negligent and Marci died as a result). In fact, based on Daniels' admissions, there would be virtually no defense to either. Miller was an experienced officer. She had to have known that.

"You spoke with the chief and with Mr. Lee prior to signing the affidavit?" he ventured.

"Which affidavit?" Miller asked.

The mystery was solved. Sam followed the scent. "Was this the first affidavit you had signed?" he asked, holding aloft her signed affidavit.

"Objection," Lee said.

"Overruled," Van Devanter ruled without waiting for Sam. "Answer."

"No," Miller said.

"Did you sign this one after consulting with the chief and Mr. Lee?"

"Yes."

"Fair to say the first didn't charge him with murder?"

"Yes."

Good enough. Sam could argue she'd been coerced. "Thank you, Detective."

Sam took his seat while Van Devanter made a note. When the judge looked up, he was surprised to see Lee already at the podium. "Mr. Lee?"

"Just a few questions on re-direct," Lee said. Van Devanter merely nodded, and Lee bore in. "You are not a member of the bar, are you?"

"No."

"Ever been to law school?"

"No."

"It's customary, is it not, for the county attorney's office to make the final charging decision, isn't it?"

"Yes."

Sam sat quietly, watching the jury. Lee had been successful in communicating to them that there was nothing untoward or nefarious about charging a crime the arresting officer didn't necessarily believe in.

"No more questions," Lee said, and sat down.

"Let's take our lunch recess," Van Devanter ordered. When he had given his admonitions and departed, Sam and Daniels stood with the others, then made their way through a side door to the attorney conference room, where Cassie was waiting with sandwiches and bottles of water.

"Good job," Daniels said. "That was about what we were gonna get."

———

While Miller was testifying, Punch was in Casper attempting to get his boss to allow him to move on Gustafson. Having watched Gustafson for a couple of months, Punch had developed an intense dislike. More importantly, he considered Gustafson a significant danger to the community. Like Miller, he was sick of him and the damage he was causing.

He had argued long past efficacy with Mitch Packard, his supervisor, that Gustafson needed to be taken down. "He's a one-man dispensary," he had argued.

"I know, Punch. I'm not an idiot, but the feds are telling me he is the tip of the iceberg; they are asking for a little more time to find out his sources," Packard had said. "I think once they are able to narrow that down we'll get the go-ahead."

"Christ, what is the problem?" Punch had asked. "I follow the guy once a week—he's not even trying to hide what he's doing. He's as brazen a dealer as I have ever seen. Are you telling me that at the other end he's some sort of secret squirrel or goes underground?"

Packard groaned audibly. "I'm not telling you anything, and I'm not going to second-guess the feds' methods or anything they are telling me."

"They need to get off their asses and do something!"

"Well, thanks, Punch," Packard said. "That's pure genius. Got any more bright ideas?"

"Yeah, while they're at it they need to pull their heads out—"

"This isn't constructive," Packard said. "Look, I've got to work with these guys. Besides, they've got some serious say-so in the funding that comes our way. I don't pull these grants—like the one that funds you—out of my wazoo."

"I hear you, Mitch, but people are literally dying here because of the shit Gustafson is pushing."

"Punch. I'm on your side. Just keep collecting the evidence and I promise you will get a shot at the little bastard," Packard had concluded.

Now, on the way back to Custer, Punch drove quickly, watching the clock and hoping that he could make his son's game.

———

Bridger was at his desk eating an apple and going through his mail when Van Devanter happened by. The two had spoken little since Van Devanter's arrival; Bridger had invited the older judge to lunch as a courtesy, and had even extended an invitation for dinner at his home, but each invitation had been politely declined. "Judge, how is it going?" Bridger asked.

"Satisfactorily," Van Devanter replied. "It's evident counsel do not care for each other; as a result, I've been much more involved than I would wish."

"You got that right," Bridger agreed. "Since Lee's arrival those two have been crossing swords on an almost daily basis." He smiled. "I heard you gave them both the what-for on arrival. I think we all appreciate that."

"How did you—" Van Devanter began, stopping short when Mary appeared in Bridger's doorway.

"Your Honor, I—I think you should see this," she stammered, indicating an envelope in her hand. "I opened it because I thought it was official mail."

"Bring it here," Bridger ordered.

"I'll be going," Van Devanter announced, and quickly left Bridger's chambers.

Bridger accepted the envelope from Mary and extracted the single piece of paper from within.

Dear Judge Bridger and Mr. Lee,

Please let me see my grandson, Aristotle. There was no reason for you to put that part of the sentence on me. Are you friends with the criminals out there, or are you bought? By not letting me see Ari you have ruined your credibility. So please understand, I have been punished enough. My Ari needs me more than you can know, and if I don't get to see him soon bad things are going to happen to you.

Thank you,

Misty Layton

When Bridger had finished reading the letter, he initialed it and gave it back to Mary. "File it and make sure Lee gets a copy."

"What are you going to do?" Mary asked. "Do you want me to call court security?"

"No, I don't. She's just distraught. If she does what she is supposed to, she'll get custody of her grandson soon enough."

"But she is threatening you!"

"That's one way to look at it," Bridger acknowledged. "But if confronted she could always say she was just referring to karma, or something," he explained. "Now, if you would, I need a couple of minutes to prepare for my next hearing." When Mary had closed the door behind her, Bridger sat back in his chair, closed his eyes, and tried to think of better days.

33

The first witness of the afternoon session was Dr. Ronald Laws, the county's contracted medical examiner. Sam didn't expect to have many questions. He reviewed his notes and fidgeted for an hour while Lee got the preliminaries out of the way, finally perking up when Lee began asking the pertinent questions.

"What is the medical examiner?"

"The physician assigned to the coroner's office. The coroner is an elected position and does not have to be a licensed physician," Laws said. "I head the office overseeing investigations into two major types of death: non-natural deaths—the accidents, suicides, and homicides that take place in a community—and sudden unexpected deaths—deaths where there was not a doctor in attendance who might be in a position to sign a death certificate."

"Do you also perform autopsies?"

"I do."

"How many autopsies have you performed?"

"Well over one hundred, I would think."

"Let me take you back to April 12—were you employed as medical examiner on that date?"

"I was."

"Did you perform an autopsy on an individual named Marci Daniels on or about that date?"

"I did."

"Other than yourself, who was present during that autopsy?"

"I have an assistant who was present. Detective Miller might have popped in, as well. I'd have to look at my notes."

Lee led the doctor through an extensive recitation of the steps he had taken in conducting the autopsy. "Now based on your training and experience and your findings from the autopsy, do you have an opinion as to the cause of death of Marci Daniels?" Lee asked.

"I do."

"And what is that opinion?"

"I believe the victim died from respiratory failure as the result of a fatal drug interaction—morphine and diazepam, to be exact."

"So she overdosed?" Lee asked.

"There was an interaction of the drugs in her system that resulted in her death."

"Did you visit the scene of Ms. Daniels' death?"

"I don't know," Laws replied.

The response took Lee by surprise. "Excuse me? I thought I saw in your notes that you visited the crime scene?"

"Well, I visited the residence where the decedent was found," Laws replied. "I don't know anything about a crime scene or anything like that. That's law enforcement's job."

Lee blushed and moved on. "Did you determine a cause of death?"

"Yes. I just told you. She died of a fatal interaction of drugs."

Lee was now flustered. "Let me re-phrase the question," he said through clenched teeth. "Did you make a determination as to *manner* of death?"

"I did," Laws answered. "I determined following consultation with law enforcement that the cause of death was homicide."

"Your Honor, those are the State's questions," Lee said, and sat down.

Van Devanter looked to Sam. "Mr. Johnstone?"

"Briefly, Your Honor." Sam had cross-examined Dr. Laws on many occasions and found him utterly irascible. He had one point to make—the doctor's inability to contribute to the manner of Marci's death. "Doctor

Laws, you cannot say who administered the drugs that killed Marci Daniels, can you?"

"No."

"You cannot say why the drugs were administered in the combination they were, can you?"

"No."

"And in fact, your conclusion that the manner of death was homicide was based on information provided by Detective Miller and the toxicologist —true?"

"True."

"And homicide means what?" Sam saw that Laws looked quickly at Lee to see if an objection was forthcoming. "Surely you know?" Sam prodded.

"Of course I do," Laws snapped. "It means the killing of one person by another."

"But not necessarily an unlawful killing—true?"

"True."

"So you can't say that Marci Daniels was murdered, can you?"

"I cannot," Laws replied.

Sam knew he needed to keep his eye on the ball. "No more questions, Your Honor," he said, having established Laws had nothing to contribute regarding Daniels' culpability in his wife's death.

"Any redirect?" Van Devanter asked Lee.

"No, Judge."

"All right, Dr. Laws, you may step down," Van Devanter said. When Laws had cleared the box and was leaving the courtroom, the judge looked to Lee. "Call your next witness."

Lee called the 9-1-1 operator who had taken Daniels' call on the afternoon of Marci's death. The furtive-looking woman testified briefly regarding the call's contents and what actions she took in response.

"Cross-examination, Mr. Johnstone?" Van Devanter asked when Lee had completed his direct.

Sam didn't think the witness had done any damage, but checked with Daniels, who simply shook his head. "No questions, Your Honor."

Van Devanter nodded approvingly. "Let's take our evening recess," he ordered. It had been a short day; Sam and Lee exchanged a look, but the course of a trial was solidly within the discretion of the judge. Van Devanter reiterated the instructions applicable to jurors during overnight recesses, and left the bench quickly.

Minutes later, Sam had his hand on Daniels' elbow and was guiding him to the attorney-client room when his phone rang. He didn't recognize the number, but he had a feeling. "Cassie, will you accompany Press to the conference room?" he asked, and without awaiting an answer took the call. "Sam Johnstone."

"Hi, Sam. This is Kelly. From the 'Shoe."

"What's up?"

"Your guy Clay?"

"Yeah?"

"I think he's using drugs," she said. "I mean, I seen him with Gus—or at least Gus went into his room. Him and some young chick."

"Gus?"

"Well, Gustafson. Trent Gustafson. He's a dealer."

"I know," Sam said tightly. From the Davonte Blair case. "Listen, I'm in trial right now. I'll try and figure something out later."

"Well, don't wait too long," she said. "Cops are across the street, watching. I mean, they're trying to be all sneaky and shit, but everyone in town knows Punch Polson."

Sam laughed despite himself. "Okay, Kelly. Thanks. I'll come by later, okay?"

"I'll keep watchin' if you want," she offered. "Maybe we can get a drink and I'll fill you in?"

"Thanks; we'll see. Bye."

34

The next morning, Lee called his toxicologist. "Your Honor, the State calls Dr. Cameron Black." When his witness was sworn and sitting in the witness box, Lee began his questioning.

"Please state your name for the record."

"My name is Cameron Black."

"Mr. Black, are you employed?"

"Yes, I am."

"What do you do?"

"I am a toxicologist with the State of Wyoming laboratory."

"Your Honor, may I approach the witness?"

Van Devanter nodded. "You may, Counsel."

Lee handed a paper to Sam en route to the witness box. "Mr. Black, I am handing you what I have marked as State's exhibit 14. Please take a look at it and let me know when you are ready to proceed." Lee watched the toxicologist until Black nodded. "Doctor Black, do you know what that document is?"

"I do. It is my curriculum vitae."

"Doctor, I would like to go through some of your educational and research history. Can you provide a brief history of your educational background?"

"I can. I have a bachelor's degree in chemistry and a master's degree in analytical chemistry from the University of Colorado. Then I attended the University of California where I studied biochemistry. I have a PhD in biochemistry, and I did some postdoctoral work at the University of Oregon School of Pharmacology."

"Can you provide a brief history of your employment in the field of toxicology?"

"Yes," Black said. "I was hired by the University of Oregon in the Department of Environmental Science to teach a class in toxicology. I then went to work for the United States Department of Agriculture as an environmental toxicologist. I had an interest in forensic toxicology, so when I had the opportunity to come to Wyoming and work in the laboratory I did so. I have been here for ten years."

"Are you teaching now?"

"I teach toxicology for students who are majoring or considering majoring in environmental health or pharmacology."

Lee then spent what Sam felt was an inordinate amount of time covering the expert's credentials. "Doctor, let me now turn to your opinions in this particular case," Lee finally said. "In the course of your preparation for your appearance here today, did you familiarize yourself with the available information?"

"I believe I did."

"Are you familiar with the drugs that appear to be at issue in this matter?"

"I am."

"Did you read the autopsy report prepared by Dr. Laws?"

"I did."

"Do you have any issue with the method by which Dr. Laws obtained his results?"

As Sam began to stand to object, Black saw him and quickly negated the need. "I am not a medical doctor, and I'm not qualified to comment on the method used by a physician to conduct an autopsy."

"Let me ask the question this way. You make determinations regarding matters of toxicology using samples drawn by others—is that true?"

"That is true."

"So you do not generally draw the samples you are analyzing."

"No, I do not. I review samples, or reports made from samples."

"In this case, did you review samples, or reports made from samples?"

"I reviewed blood samples."

"Are you aware who provided you with the samples?"

"I believe it was Dr. Laws."

"How so?"

"Because his typewritten name and a signature were on the plastic bags containing the blood samples that I received for analysis," Black said. "In addition, he and I had spoken telephonically while the samples were in transit."

"You received the samples and you analyzed them?"

"I did."

"What did you discover?"

"I discovered high levels of both morphine and diazepam in the samples provided."

"When you say high levels, what do you mean?"

"Well, levels indicating a prolonged use of each. Levels that in my mind were unsafe in combination."

"What do you mean?"

"Drugs interact, and certain drugs enhance the effects of certain others. A symbiotic effect, if you will."

"And?"

"Well, from my understanding, the deceased was under palliative care for terminal cancer. It was not surprising, then, that I would find any number of controlled substances. Of particular interest to me was the level of morphine in her blood. It was a level such that in combination with the prescribed dose of diazepam it would have almost certainly been fatal. For most people, anyway."

"Dr. Black, based on your examination of the samples and your review of the autopsy report, have you formed an opinion as to the cause of death for the decedent?"

"I have."

"And what is your opinion?"

"Based upon my experience, education, and examination of the materials in question, I have concluded that Mrs. Daniels died from a fatal combination of morphine and diazepam that resulted in profound sedation, respiratory depression, coma, then death."

"Does that mean she stopped breathing?"

"It does."

"Have you formed an opinion as to the manner of death?"

"I am not qualified to do so."

"Could the decedent have administered the level of drugs that you observed in her blood herself?"

"I can't say with certainty. What I can say is that given the levels that I have observed, she would have been unconscious almost immediately if she would have been able to administer them at all."

Sam saw Lee study the jury. The implication was clear: if she didn't do it herself, someone else had to administer the drugs. The who would be placed on the record in short order. The how would similarly be easy enough to prove. But Lee had to know the *why* was the key. Not surprisingly, Lee shut his examination down. "No more questions, Your Honor. Tender the witness."

"Mr. Johnstone?" Van Devanter said.

Sam rose and made his way to the podium, reminding himself not to try and make this witness any bigger deal than he was. All Lee had shown was that Marci had stopped breathing due to the combination of drugs in her system. "Dr. Black, you are not a medical doctor, are you?" He watched the man closely for his reaction. Some PhDs were very sensitive about any inference that they weren't *real* doctors.

"I am not," Black allowed.

"Your expertise is in how drugs affect bodily functions—not in the underlying science of the functions themselves, true?"

Black studied Sam carefully. "True," he said at last.

"In fact, isn't it true that because everyone is different, the effect drugs have on individuals is different, as well?"

Black smiled slightly. "Of course," he allowed. "But within reason."

"Some people react differently than others, true?"

"As far as that goes, yes."

"With some drugs, a person can actually develop a tolerance, true?"

"Yes."

"Both morphine and diazepam are such drugs?"

"Yes."

"And you don't know a lot about Marci's health, do you?"

"I know she's deceased," Black retorted.

The laughter in the courtroom was short-lived, as spectators realized it was in poor taste. Sam laughed with everyone else, then sobered. "You don't have any first-hand information about her drug use, do you?"

"No."

"Did you perform a comprehensive review of her prescription history?"

"I did not."

"So you cannot say what her tolerance for a particular drug might have been?"

"Not really," he said. "I mean, there are studies that show—"

"But those studies merely make generalizations, true?"

Black exhaled impatiently. "True, but generalizations made as the result of scientific study, of course."

"Indeed, and you don't know, with absolute certainty, *why* she died—do you?"

"That's not the standard, Counsel," Black said, feeling confident now.

"Move to strike," Sam said. "Non-responsive."

"Sustained," Van Devanter said. "Answer the question, Dr. Black."

Black shook his head as if indulging a child. "Not with *absolute* certainty, no."

"Yours is an opinion, true?"

"An educated one, yes."

"And you have *no* first-hand information regarding who administered the drugs in question, or why, do you?"

"I do not."

"So, fair to say that you don't know who administered the drugs, why or when, or what effect they had on Ms. Daniels—true?" The question was compound and objectionable. Sam hoped Lee would take the bait.

"Objection," Lee said. "Compound and confusing."

Perfect.

"Sustained," Van Devanter ruled.

"I'll re-phrase, Judge," Sam said. He could now break it down into bite-sized pieces for the jury. "You don't know who administered the morphine?"

"No."

"You don't know why the morphine was administered?"

"Presumptively, to treat her," Black said.

"But you don't know that, and you certainly cannot assign a motive of malice, can you?"

"No."

"You don't know when the morphine was administered?"

"No."

"In fact, all you know is that there was a certain level of morphine and a certain level of diazepam in Marci Daniels' system at the time of her death, and that those drugs in a person's system at the levels observed are generally toxic—true?"

"Objection," Lee said. "Compound, confusing, argumentative."

"Withdrawn," Sam said, taking his seat before Van Devanter could rule.

Van Devanter looked at his watch. "I think that's enough for today, folks." He gave his admonitions and excused the jury. "The court has another matter to attend to, ladies and gentlemen. Anything else?"

When neither Sam nor Lee replied affirmatively, Van Devanter departed.

35

Sam had slept poorly and was dehydrated and hollow-eyed at trial the next morning. In contrast, Lee appeared fresh and ready to go. "Call Miriam Baker," Lee said. Sam watched as Miriam stood and stepped through the bar. He had anticipated her being called, of course, and had visited with Daniels about her.

"What is she going to say?" he had asked.

"She's going to say I am a terrible person," Daniels had explained. "She'll tell anyone who will listen that I killed her sister—murdered her."

"Why does she think that?"

"I'm not certain she believes it," Daniels had explained. "But I think I mentioned some time back . . . I was dating her and then I met her younger sister Marci and, well . . ."

"You dumped her for her sister."

Daniels sat quietly for a second and then smiled broadly. "Best decision I ever made!"

"I'll bet," Sam said. "So . . . how have things been between you and Miriam since?"

"Tense," Daniels admitted. "It got better after she got married, of course. But let's just say the holidays were not my favorite time of the year."

"What about Marci and Miriam?"

"They were okay," Daniels had said. "I think there was some resentment, but she put the blame on me for the most part."

"Sounds fair."

"It was," Daniels had agreed. "I mean, it wasn't anything against Miriam . . . It was more that when I saw Marci it was all over for me. I loved her from the moment I saw her until . . . well, you know."

Now, as Miriam made her way down the aisle toward the witness box, Daniels sat rigidly, staring straight ahead. When she had been sworn and seated, she spent a moment arranging her dress before looking around the courtroom like a squirrel on a four-lane highway.

Lee had gone over Miriam's testimony with her, Sam suspected, but a good trial lawyer knew that family could be unpredictable, so he approached carefully, beginning with the basics. "Please state your name for the record."

"Miriam Elizabeth Baker."

"Baker is your married name?"

"It is."

"Mrs. Baker, where do you live?"

"Fort Collins."

"Do you know the defendant, Preston Daniels?"

"I do."

"How so?"

"He killed my sister."

"Your Honor—" Sam said before he was on his feet.

"Sustained," Van Devanter said. "Mrs. Baker, please answer the question. I think you know that answer wasn't proper. The jury will disregard the witness's response."

"Mrs. Baker?" Lee asked.

"He was married to my sister," Miriam said.

"Your sister was, of course, Marci Daniels?"

"Yes."

"Tell us a little about your sister," Lee asked.

As Sam expected, Miriam commenced a long narrative about the wonderful relationship she shared with her sister and the future that had been cut short "because of him," she finished, pointing at Daniels.

"Christ," Daniels muttered. "She—"

Sam leaned over and whispered into Daniels' ear, "Smile and let it go."

Lee had followed Miriam's point with his eyes, ensuring the jurors would do so as well. "Mrs. Baker, you've made some serious allegations against the defendant."

"I have."

"You really believe Mr. Daniels killed your sister?"

"I do."

"Why?" Lee asked, knowing exactly why.

"Because he told me he was going to, and he told me after he did it."

"This is so much—" Daniels began.

"Stop," Sam cautioned Daniels. "Hold your poise."

"He told you he was going to kill her?" Lee asked. "He used those words?"

"Well, he didn't put it like that exactly," Miriam admitted. "But he made it clear what he was going to do. He said 'she wouldn't want to live like this,' and he 'wished she wasn't in pain,' and stuff like that, you know?"

"And you took that to mean what?"

"That he was going to get rid of her—and he did."

"You need to object," Daniels hissed.

"Not yet," Sam replied.

Lee pressed the supposed advantage. "You testified he 'told you after he did it'—what do you mean?" Technically, the testimony was hearsay, but the law allowed such testimony where, as here, a defendant had made a statement apparently against his interests.

"He said he killed her." Miriam removed a tissue from her sleeve and wiped at a tear.

Lee watched his witness, knowing the jury was doing the same. When she had replaced the tissue, he followed up. "When did he say this?"

"When he called me to tell me she had . . . passed."

"And he just said, 'I killed her?'"

"No, he said, 'It's my fault, Miriam. I killed her.'"

"What did you understand that to mean?"

"Just what he said, of course," she snapped. "He killed my sister."

Daniels leaned over and whispered in Sam's ear, "Good call." Sam nodded. She hadn't used the word *murdered*.

Lee appeared to ponder his next question. "What did he mean—"

Sam was ready. "Objection, Your Honor. Calls for speculation."

"Sustained," Van Devanter ruled.

"What do you think he—"

Sam hadn't gotten seated. "Same objection."

"Sustained," Van Devanter repeated. "Move on, Counsel."

Lee nodded his acquiescence. "Can you tell me what the loss of your sister will mean for you and your family going forward?"

It was improper at this point in the proceedings, but Sam let it go. It had opened the door for his own questions. Miriam embarked on a long narrative centered on the loss she and everyone else would feel following Marci's death. "It's ruined our family," she concluded.

Lee made eye contact with the jury and decided that was enough. "No more questions," he said. "Your witness," he added, turning to Sam.

"Be careful," Daniels advised.

Sam nodded and stood and walked to the podium. The jury understood he had a job to do, he knew, but it was one that had to be done in a way that wouldn't appear to validate everyone's opinion of defense attorneys. "Mrs. Baker, I just want to clear up a couple of things. First, can I ask you when the last time you saw your sister was?"

"Alive, you mean?" Miriam snapped.

"Yes," Sam said. He followed up quickly with a leading question. "It had been more than five years, hadn't it?"

"I—I don't know," Miriam said. "I just know my sister is dead."

"How many times did you come and see her after you knew she was sick?" Sam asked.

"I—I don't know."

"Five? Ten?"

"I—I'm not sure?"

"Mrs. Baker, the truth is you didn't make a single trip from Fort Collins to visit your sister, did you?"

"We talked!"

"Who called who?"

"It doesn't matter."

Sam made a showing of picking up a sheath of papers and thumbing them. It was time for a bluff. "If I was to show you Marci's phone records, could you show me when you called her?"

Miriam was eyeing the papers. "Probably not," she admitted. "I'm not rich like them."

Sam put the blank stack of papers on the podium. "And my client kept you updated via email on Marci's condition, didn't he?"

Miriam looked at Daniels before responding. "Maybe. I'm not sure. I don't spend all day on a computer."

Lee was on his feet. "Your Honor, I fail to see the relevance—"

"Overruled, Mr. Lee. You broached the subject of family relationships," Van Devanter ruled. He turned his attention to Sam. "Mr. Johnstone, I will say we are about there."

"Thank you," Sam said. He turned his attention to Miriam. "And he told you that Marci was tired, and that she was in pain—true?"

"Yes, and that he wanted to put an end to her suffering!"

"When did he tell you that?" Sam asked softly. "And how?"

"On the phone. I don't know when."

"What did you understand that to mean?"

"Just what he said! What he did! That he was going to kill her!"

Sam stood quietly until he felt the jurors' eyes on him. "Did you call law enforcement?"

"No," she snapped.

"You didn't?" he asked. "Are you telling the jury that my client openly threatened to kill your invalid, helpless sister, and you didn't call law enforcement?"

"It wasn't like that!"

Sam watched her closely and saw what he felt were likely specks of wine-infused, venomous spittle forming in the corners of her mouth. "You mean he was just blowing off steam and stress?"

"Objection!" Lee said. "He is putting words in her mouth."

"I'll re-phrase," Sam said. Van Devanter nodded his approval. "Mrs. Baker, isn't it true that you didn't call the police because you knew that Mr.

Daniels was simply frustrated with the medical help he was getting for Marci?"

"I don't know! I don't know any of that. It wasn't my job to watch her—or him!"

"How long were your sister and my client married?"

"I'm not sure."

"Did you go to the wedding?" Sam asked, knowing she had not.

"No."

"Why not?"

"I was busy."

"You don't like my client, do you?"

"I don't care one way or another!"

"In fact, you hate him because he dumped you in favor of your sister—"

"Objection! Not relevant!" Lee was saying.

"—and that's the reason why you are here testifying, isn't it?"

"Mr. Johnstone!" Van Devanter barked. "There is an objection on the floor!"

"Sorry, Your Honor," Sam said.

"It's one I'm going to sustain," Van Devanter continued.

"It goes to bias, Judge," Sam argued. "She's a woman scorned—"

"Objection!" Lee said, and stomped his foot.

"Sustained!" Van Devanter said. "Mr. Johnstone, no more."

"Yes, sir," Sam said, turning his attention to Miriam. "You testified my client said, 'It's my fault, Miriam, I killed her'—did you not?"

"I did."

"He didn't say he *murdered* her?"

"No."

"He didn't say he did it purposefully or intentionally?"

"No."

"And you'll agree with me that by saying he killed her he could simply be admitting responsibility, couldn't he?"

"Objection," Lee said. "Calls for speculation."

Van Devanter shook his head. "I think the question is fair as phrased. You may answer," he said to Miriam.

"I don't know what he meant," she said, picking up on the clue Lee had given her.

"That wasn't the question, Mrs. Baker," Sam said. "The question was whether he might have merely been trying to accept responsibility."

"I don't know."

"You mentioned a life insurance policy, didn't you?"

"Yeah," she said. "He gets a million dollars now that she's dead, unless—"

"Unless what?" Sam asked quickly.

Miriam looked at Lee. "Unless he is found to have killed her, which he did."

Sam put a hand to his face and stroked his chin, trying to appear thoughtful. "And if he was found guilty, what would happen then?"

"I don't know."

"You would inherit, would you not?" When she failed to reply, he pressed her. "Wouldn't you?"

"I don't know."

"You do know, because my client sent you a copy of the policy in case something happened to him, true?"

"Yes!" she said at last.

"Fair to say, then, that aside from revenge for being dumped, you have a million reasons to see my client—"

Lee had heard enough. "Objection, Your Honor! The question is compound and argumentative."

Van Devanter looked to Sam. "Counsel, could you rephrase?"

"I'll withdraw the question, Your Honor. I think the jury understands." Sam had been watching the jurors. Most were looking at their hands in their laps. He'd shown Miriam's bias, although he had been harsher than he intended to be. "May I have a moment, Your Honor?"

"You may," Van Devanter said.

Sam walked to the table and bent at the waist. "Anything else?" he asked Daniels, who shook his head. Sam stood straight and looked to the judge. "No more questions."

"Thank you," Van Devanter said. When Lee indicated he had no re-direct, Van Devanter turned his attention to the jury. "Ladies and gentlemen, I think now would be a good time for our morning recess. It's been a while, so let me again remind you of the actions you may and may not take upon recess." He then reiterated his earlier instructions and released the jury to the custody of the bailiff. When the door closed behind the jury, he excused everyone and rushed from the bench.

"Any idea what that's all about?" Sam asked Daniels.

"None," Daniels replied.

36

Lee and Cates had hustled down to Lee's office for the recess. Cates sat nervously while Lee used the men's room. When he exited, wiping his hands on his pants, Cates quickly looked away.

"If you were me, would you call Julie?" Lee asked. Cates sat quietly, until prompted by Lee. "Well? More than once, you've told me what you'd do if you were driving. Now's your chance."

"I don't think I would," Cates said at last.

Good choice. Was it luck? "Why not?"

"Well, here's what I'm thinking. If you call her on direct, you're somewhat limited in what you're going to get out of her because a lot of what she knows could be kept out. It's hearsay. You also have the problem of her being hostile," Cates finished, and looked at Lee, expecting a reply.

"Go on," Lee encouraged.

"Well, treating a witness as hostile always looks like bullying to me. I think Sam has to call her; I think you wait and see what she says, and then pound her on cross-examination—the jury will accept that."

"What if he doesn't call her?"

Cates was expecting the question. "He will. If he doesn't, he's gonna have to call his client. If he does that, then I think you can call Julie in rebuttal."

"What if his questions for her are narrowly tailored?"

"They can only be so narrow. Sam has to call her to try and show what a high character, good guy Daniels is. The facts are damning. He's got to make this about character. He can try that with his client, Julie, or both—but not neither. He's got to call at least one of them." Cates was warming to his subject. "The facts are ugly from their perspective."

"Good answer," Lee said.

"Thank you," Cates said. "What are you going to do?"

"I'm going to let Johnstone call her." When his phone rang, he looked at his watch. "Crap! We're late."

"Mr. Lee, now that you have *finally* arrived, please call your next witness," Van Devanter said frostily. He was fully aware—as was Sam—that the State was about to rest.

"Your Honor, the State rests its case-in-chief."

"Thank you, Mr. Lee," Van Devanter said. "Mr. Johnstone, does the defense desire to present any witnesses?"

Technically, now was the time for Sam to make a motion for a judgment of acquittal, arguing that the State had failed to put on evidence to convince a reasonable person of Daniels' guilt. By asking Sam to call a witness in front of the jury, Van Devanter had sent a message regarding the likely result of that motion.

"Your Honor, a moment with my client?"

"Certainly, Mr. Johnstone."

Sam and Daniels put their heads together. "What do you think?" Sam asked.

"I don't think it's worth your time or effort—he's going to deny it."

"I know," Sam agreed. "But what do you think?"

"Honestly, I think I'd deny it. Lee got enough on the record on each of the elements so that the judge can safely deny the motion and turn it over to the jury." He was looking at Van Devanter as he finished talking with Sam. "Or he could simply reserve on it. You're going to have to call me and

Julie, anyway—when you do that, under the rule, you'll waive any sort of remedy if he denies it. I'd say save your breath."

"We'll see," Sam said noncommittally. He stood. "Your Honor, defense calls Doctor Janel Patton."

While Patton made her way to the stand, Sam quickly reviewed his notes. Patton was his sole expert. A for-hire pathologist with expertise in the administration of drugs to hospice and other terminally ill patients, she would testify to her doubt that any action taken or not taken by Daniels could have meaningfully contributed to Marci's death.

"She was terminal," she concluded, after Sam had elicited her background, education, credentials, and opinion on Marci's cause of death. "It is my opinion that even given the high concentration of drugs in her system, because she had been taking them for so long, she may well have developed a tolerance sufficient that the dosage of morphine in combination with that of diazepam cannot be assigned as the cause of death with reasonable scientific certainty."

Sam was watching the jury during Patton's testimony. "So you are saying that even if we accept all of the testimony given by the State's witnesses, there is doubt in your mind whether the combination of drugs provided *that day* resulted in Marci Daniels' death?"

"That's exactly what I'm saying," she agreed.

"So her death may not have been my client's fault—intentionally or otherwise?" The question was improper as it called for a legal conclusion, and Lee was properly on his feet immediately.

"I'll withdraw the question," Sam said before Patton could respond. "No further questions."

While Sam moved from the podium and sat next to Daniels, Lee commenced a measured cross-examination of her, careful not to impugn her education or credentials—the seven women on the jury might frown on that. What he did do was bring to light her experience as an expert-for-hire, the number of times she had testified, and the disparity (and presumptively qualitative difference) between her scientific method and that of the Custer County medical examiner and coroner.

"You didn't draw the samples?" Lee asked.

"I did not," she admitted.

"You didn't perform an independent analysis?"

"I did not."

"You didn't harvest the organs or perform the toxicological exams?"

"No."

"Did you note any major departures from best practices during the collection of relevant samples or during the conduct of the autopsy itself?"

"No—but I only had access to the written reports, of course."

And on it went, Lee picking at nits until he asked his final question. "So, to be sure, you cannot say with a reasonable degree of scientific certainty that the misadministration of medication to Ms. Daniels . . . you cannot say that *didn't* cause her death, can you?"

"But that's not the question, is it?" she argued.

"It's *my* question, Doctor."

"No, I cannot say it didn't—but I cannot say it *did*, either," Patton insisted. "That's the whole point."

Sam was watching the jurors carefully and felt that while a couple were gamely hanging in there, most were on autopilot, and if they were listening at all, they had their minds made up. Accordingly, and to Van Devanter's obvious relief, Sam passed on the opportunity for re-direct.

"I think that's enough for today," Van Devanter said when Dr. Patton had left the stand. "Ladies and gentlemen, we're going to recess for the day. And the good news is the attorneys and I will need some time to attend to matters not concerning you first thing in the morning, so you'll have the opportunity to sleep in a little bit. Bailiff, we'll start again at ten a.m. Jurors, be here when she tells you. In the meantime, please listen to my end-of-day instruction once more."

When he had completed, Van Devanter released the jury, and then quickly departed the courtroom. "What's going on?" Sam asked Daniels.

"I imagine that Bridger needs the courtroom," Daniels said. "Dockets are full, and this isn't the only case going on. Juveniles have to be seen right away, and you've always got emergency custody matters, guardianships and stuff like that."

"Huh. Well, hang tight," Sam advised Daniels as the crowd behind them thinned. "We need to talk."

37

The next morning Sam moved to the podium when called and took a deep breath. "Defense calls Julie Spence," he said. He watched her closely as she made her way up the aisle, was sworn in, and took the witness's chair. He gave her a few seconds to settle in her chair, and when she finally looked to him, he flashed his biggest smile, hoping she would return the gesture.

"Good morning," Sam said to his grim-faced witness. When she merely nodded but didn't return the greeting, he quickly moved on. "Would you please state your full name for the record?"

"Julie Marie Spence."

"And do you live in Custer County, Wyoming?"

"I do."

"Are you more than eighteen years old?" Sam listened as the audience giggled, but noted he'd still not gotten a reaction from her.

"I am."

"Are you employed?"

"I am. I am a home healthcare assistant."

"What training and experience do you have?"

"I got my certificate when I was . . . in a program, and then I have some on-the-job experience."

"Any other training?"

"Classes on certain subjects as needed."

"Any training on administering medications by injection?"

"Yes."

"Do you know my client?"

"I do."

"How so?"

"I was assigned to work in his home—to help him with his wife."

"When?"

"Oh, I don't know . . . a year, maybe eighteen months ago—something like that? I was with them for three months before she . . . died."

"Okay, and how did you get that position?"

"I was working and one day Debra—my boss—said they had a position at the judge's house and would I be interested."

"Were you?"

"Not at first."

"Why not?"

"Because I'd been in front of him in court. This court. He was . . . mean, I thought."

Sam let the laughter subside. "What changed?"

"I saw him caring for his wife. That's when I knew there was another side to him."

Sam then spent several questions having Julie review what she'd observed between Daniels and Marci, their general routine, the nature of her illness, and the treatment that was administered. "Marci passed away on April 9?"

"Yes."

"Did you see her that day?"

"I did."

"Did you administer her medication?"

"I did, late morning or early afternoon, I think."

"Where was the medication?"

"Where it always was: on the counter."

"Did you check to make sure it was the proper medication?"

Julie's lip quivered, and she wiped her eyes and then blew her nose with a tissue. "No," she said. "I wish I had. I'm sorry I didn't."

"Was that part of your job?"

"No, but I coulda," she said. "I mean, I was with Judge Daniels when the doctor came and gave us instructions. He should have changed it out."

"Do you know why he didn't?"

"Objection," Lee said. "Calls for speculation."

"Not if she has first-hand knowledge," Sam said.

Van Devanter frowned in doubt. "I'll allow it," he said at last. "But only as to what she knows."

"I think he was exhausted," Julie said.

"Move to strike," Lee said quickly.

"Sustained," Van Devanter ruled. "The jury will disregard that answer. Move on, Mr. Johnstone."

Sam nodded and turned his attention to Julie. It was time. "You gave her the medication, and what happened next?"

"I went about my duties. I was doing the laundry and keeping an eye on her while the judge took a—"

Lee was on his feet again. "Your Honor, I'm going to object to the witness referring to Mr. Daniels as a judge."

Van Devanter watched Lee carefully, clearly annoyed by the objection. "He is a retired judge, Counsel."

"May we approach?"

"No," Van Devanter ruled. "I'll sustain. Ms. Spence, you may refer to the defendant as 'the defendant,' 'Mr. Daniels,' or by his first name—do you understand?"

"Oh, I could never call him by his first name to his face!"

Even Van Devanter cracked a smile. "Okay, well, you heard me—right?"

"Yes, sir."

"Proceed," Van Devanter said to Sam.

"He took a nap?"

"Yes."

"Then what?"

"Then he woke up and went to check on her."

"How do you know?"

"Because I watched him go into their room, and that's what he always did."

"Then what?"

"He came out and said—"

"Tell me what he did," Sam directed, to avoid a hearsay objection.

"He ate lunch. And then he went back in her room about an hour later. And then I heard him yell her name. And then I ran in the room, and I heard him call 9-1-1."

"And then?"

"And then he lay down next to her and cried."

"No more questions," Sam said. "Your witness."

Sam expected Lee to go right after Julie, and he wasn't disappointed.

"I have quite a few questions for you, Ms. Spence," Lee began. "Now, your testimony was that when you came to work that day you put your coat away and went to the kitchen, wasn't it?"

"Yes. That's what I said because that's what I did," Julie replied. Sam tried to make eye contact with her—she was already talking too much.

"It was already light outside, wasn't it?" Lee asked.

Julie chewed her lip, obviously trying to remember. "I think it was."

"And the defendant was already awake, right?"

"Oh yes, he's always awake by then," she said. "He doesn't sleep well." She smiled at Lee and then made eye contact with Sam, who wasn't smiling. Realizing she had gone beyond simply answering the question, she dropped the smile.

Lee saw the exchange of glances between Sam and Julie and then looked at each overtly, as if he was shocked to see her look toward Sam. He watched the jury out of the side of his eye, and when he had their attention, he asked his next question. "Ms. Spence, did you prepare for this hearing with Mr. Johnstone? He told you what to say?"

"Oh yes," she said, and then made eye contact with Sam, who was halfway to his feet. "No!" she corrected. "He didn't tell me what to say, he—"

"Well, let's not get into communications between you and Mr. Johnstone. Thank you," Lee said. She shut down, as he knew she would. "Let me ask you this," Lee transitioned. "You testified there was daylight, and that the defendant was awake when you got there—true?"

Julie had spent her life getting fooled by men. She could smell a trap. "Yeah," she said, and waited.

"Did you turn the lights on in the house?"

"Of course not. I already said it was light outside."

"And you saw the defendant?"

Julie stared at Lee before responding. "I already told you I did."

"He looked okay to you?"

Sam could see where this was going. He stood. "Objection. Relevance."

Van Devanter looked to Lee.

"Background and preliminary, Judge," Lee said.

"I'll allow it. Overruled." Van Devanter looked to Julie. "You can answer."

"He seemed fine to me," she said carefully.

."Was he drunk?" Lee asked.

The jury shifted uncomfortably, and muted laughter emanated from the gallery behind Sam.

"No!" Julie said too quickly. She had taken the bait, Sam knew. Lee would now reel her in.

"How do you know?" Lee said simply.

"Because I've seen him drunk!" she snapped, before realizing her mistake. "I mean, not a lot, but . . . you know."

Lee knew. "So, it's your testimony that he was sober, awake, and feeling well," he said. "Was he drunk the night before?"

"I—I don't know."

"Well, let me ask you this: do you know any reason why—"

Sam was again on his feet. "Objection. The question asks her to speculate."

"Your Honor," Lee said before being asked, "I am just asking if she knows of a reason why the defendant would have forgotten to change the medication."

"It is speculative," Sam argued.

"Overruled," Van Devanter held. "You can answer—if you know," he said with a nod toward Julie.

"No," Julie said, shifting uncomfortably in her seat while Lee stared hard at her. As he knew she would, she filled the void. "I can't imagine," she said, making Sam cringe.

"You can't imagine?" Lee smiled.

It had been asked and answered, of course, but Sam was in a bind. If he objected, it would bring her response to the jury's attention. He recalled the musings of Daniels one night at his kitchen table when the old judge was halfway through a bottle. "The issue isn't whether something is objectionable—any idiot can figure that out. It is whether it hurt you. If it didn't hurt you, let it go." Sam knew he would hear it again but decided to let it go.

"Of course not," she said.

Sam was thinking along with Lee, who had Julie boxed in. Now, as the questions got harder, if she tried to offer an excuse, it would appear to be a lie. Lee knew it as well. "So you don't know of any reason, and you cannot imagine any reason, why the judge would forget to change out the syringes?" Lee pressed.

"No . . . I—I don't. I mean—"

"Now, let's talk about how you got the job, shall we?" Lee began. "What training do you have in the medical field?"

"Well, my certificate."

"How did you afford that?"

"Objection," Sam said. "Relevance." It was relevant, of course, but unduly prejudicial, as Julie had attended the course while doing time.

Van Devanter evidently agreed. "Sustained," he ruled.

"You were hired by the defendant?"

"No," she answered. "I was hired by a home health care firm. They assigned me to assist Press—er, Mr. Daniels and his wife."

"Your job was what?"

"Help him with Marci."

"And how long did you do that?"

"A couple of months is all," she said. "He was tired and needed help."

"How did you know he was tired?"

"Anyone could tell."

"Did you know the defendant before you went to work for him?"

"I didn't work for him."

"Thank you," Lee said. "I stand corrected. Did you know the defendant before you were assigned to help him?"

Julie looked quickly to Daniels, then back to Lee. "Not personally."

"But you'd met?" Lee pressed.

."You know we had."

"I do in fact," Lee agreed. "How?"

"Well, he was a judge . . . Lot of people knew him."

"Fair to say you knew him better than most?" Lee asked, then quickly followed up. "In a professional capacity, I mean?"

It was objectionable, but again Sam decided to let it go. "I dunno," she said. "I was struggling. He was tough but fair. He saved my life."

"Oh, were you in trouble?"

She nodded vigorously. "Oh, yes, for a while—just drugs and stuff. But Judge Daniels—er, Mr. Daniels—he helped me. A lot."

"Really?"

"Yeah. The drug court program he started . . . well, it saved my life. I mean, everyone thinks he's such a hard ass, but he is really a nice man."

Lee nodded as if in understanding. "So, you testified you gave Marci Daniels her last dose of medicine?"

"I—I did," Julie acknowledged. She wiped her eyes with a tissue.

"What was the process by which you—by your own account a convicted drug abuser—were allowed to handle dangerous drugs?"

It was gratuitous but fair, Sam knew.

"He had syringes with certain amounts of the drugs in his safe. He placed them on the counter and would tell me what to give her and when. He had it all written down."

"So you didn't measure anything?"

"No, he did."

"How did you administer the medications?" he asked her. She stared at him questioningly. "Did you give her a shot?"

"For some medications, yeah. For others it was a pill."

"Fair to say she took a lot of medication?"

Again, she had no way to know. "It looked like a lot to me," she said before Sam could object. The answer was good enough, so he remained seated.

"Do you know what all she was taking?"

"Not really. I mean, I knew she was taking morphine and diazepam, because the doctor came and told us that combination was . . . sketchy, I guess."

"Sketchy, huh? We'll talk more about that later," Lee assured her. "So, you just gave her a shot or a pill that was prepared for you by the defendant?"

"Yeah. The morphine came in prefilled, disposable syringes," she began, having forgotten Sam's admonitions. "I usually fed her breakfast and gave her a sponge bath and helped her toilet and brush her teeth, then I gave her whatever he put out for her if he wasn't going to be around. Later, the nurse would come by and check on Marci."

"Every day?"

"Yeah."

"Did the nurse come by on the day that Marci died?"

Julie's eyes narrowed briefly. "No."

"I want to make sure that I understand everything you have said," Lee began. "You are testifying that the defendant handled all of the medications?"

"Yes."

Lee moved back to the prosecutor's table and made an elaborate show of drinking water. Sam knew the show was about to start. He watched as Lee moved quickly to the podium, about to attack. "Ms. Spence, the truth is that the defendant felt sorry for you—isn't it?"

"Objection," Sam said as he stood.

"Overruled," Van Devanter said. "Answer if you can."

"I—I don't know."

"And it's true, isn't it, that you felt sorry for him?"

"Of course! His wife was dying!"

"You wanted to help him?"

"Of course!" she said. "After all he's done for me—"

Lee nodded as if in understanding. "And you still want to help him, don't you?"

"What do you mean?"

"I think you know exactly what I mean."

It was argumentative and not a question. "Objection," Sam said.

"Sustained," Van Devanter quickly ruled.

"You said the defendant was exhausted?"

"Yes."

"And you heard him say on multiple occasions that Marci wanted to die with dignity, didn't you?"

"Well, yes. But—"

"And he told you she wouldn't want to live like that, didn't he?"

She looked to Sam and then back to Lee. "Well, yes—but he didn't mean it like that!"

"Like what?"

"Like what you are thinking. Like he wanted to hurt her."

"How do you know?"

"Because we . . . talked."

Lee feigned surprise. "He took you into his confidence?"

"I—I guess you could say that."

Lee changed tactics again. Having established at least some degree of bias, he would now attack her character. The rules allowed an attorney to question a witness's past in some circumstances. "Now, you have been convicted of a number of crimes, haven't you?"

"I have," Julie admitted, shrugging. "I was wild back in the day."

"In fact, you have been convicted of a number of felonies—isn't that true?"

"Yes."

"Do you know whether the defendant took any other felons into his home or under his wing?"

"I don't."

"He was fond of you?"

"I think so. One time he told me I was like a daughter to him."

"A daughter? Or a younger version of Marci?"

"Don't be sick," she snapped. "A daughter!"

"Miss Spence, isn't it true that you and the defendant were having an affair?"

"No!"

"Miss Spence, isn't it true that you could have double-checked the dosage you gave the decedent?"

"Well . . . yes."

"But you chose not to, didn't you?"

"I didn't think about it. I had no reason to believe—"

"That he would kill her?"

Sam had heard enough. "Objection!" He was on his feet. "Argumentative. He needs to let her finish."

"Sustained," Van Devanter intoned. "You know better, Mr. Lee. Finish your thought, Ms. Spence."

Julie sat for a second. "I had no reason to believe he would do anything to hurt her—he loved her!"

Sam groaned inwardly. He knew she had misspoken. "But you think he hurt her?" Lee asked.

"Objection. That's not what she said," Sam argued.

"Sustained," Van Devanter ruled.

Lee looked at Julie skeptically. "Isn't it true that you and the defendant were fully aware the nurse would be delayed on April ninth?"

"Well, yeah . . . she told us."

"And isn't it true that you and the defendant plotted to finish Marci off?"

"No!"

"Did you know about the life insurance?"

"No!"

"I think you did, and I think you knew the nurse wouldn't be there, and you did nothing to stop the defendant from killing his wife by the administration of an overdose—did you?"

"Objection, Your Honor!" Sam said. "The question is argumentative, compound, and it's been asked and answered."

Julie's entire body was shaking now. The question was whether the jury would notice and pity her, or view it as evidence of complicity.

"Sustained," Van Devanter said. "Move along, Mr. Lee."

"Ms. Spence," Lee began. "You knew the defendant wanted his wife dead—isn't that true?"

"No! He didn't want her dead. He just didn't want her to suffer!"

"In her condition, wasn't that the same thing?"

Sam was again on his feet, but Van Devanter was already on it. "Sustained," he said before Sam could speak. "Counsel, I am growing weary of this line of questioning," he advised Lee. "I'm looking at the clock and I think it is time for our noon recess."

Van Devanter gave his usual warnings before letting the jury go.

Lee and Cates made their way downstairs to Lee's office. Cates was staring at Lee.

"What?" Lee asked finally.

"Can you ask those questions?"

"What do you mean?"

"In law school they taught us that a prosecutor cannot discredit or undermine a witness if he knows the witness is telling the truth."

"Right."

"But she's clearly telling the truth!"

"Your opinion," Lee said. "I don't know that now, and I'm not going to know until I get some answers from her."

"But to date every single thing she has said has been corroborated by other evidence or witnesses."

"To date."

"Right."

"I don't have certainty."

Cates considered Lee's response. "Isn't that an overly narrow definition of knowing?"

It was. Lee was surprised Cates saw it. "Perhaps, but the important thing is that Daniels is going down."

"But justice demands—"

"Justice? Is it just that some people have better opportunities than others? Is it just that two people charged with the same crime can see two different results?"

"That's a systemic—"

"I'm implementing justice in this jurisdiction one case at a time. We will see justice in this case when Daniels is convicted."

"But Ms. Spence—"

"Might end up as collateral damage—I'll admit that."

38

Sam had spent the recess trying to talk Julie down, but she was understandably angry and hurt. "He can't do that, can he? You said you wouldn't let him attack me!"

"Julie, you're doing great," Sam lied. "Just remember the rules and everything will be fine. You want to help Press, don't you?"

"Of course, but even saying that is getting me in trouble!"

Now, when the parties were again present, Van Devanter reconvened the trial. "Ms. Spence, you are still under oath. Mr. Lee?"

Lee was already at the podium. "Ms. Spence, before lunch you admitted you've been convicted of several felonies, didn't you?"

"Yes."

"And it would be fair to say, wouldn't it, that you have a lengthy criminal history?"

"I suppose so," she admitted. "Not as much as some people."

"You've done time in prison."

"Yes. For drugs."

"You've done time in county."

"Yes."

"Do you understand what the words 'dishonesty' and 'false statement' mean?"

"Yes."

"In fact, you've been convicted of both—right?"

"I—I think so."

"You think so?" Lee asked snidely. "Most people don't have a criminal record, and of those who do, most can remember their convictions."

"Objection, Your Honor," Sam said. "Counsel is testifying. I won't object if he wants to take the stand, but I would like the opportunity to cross-examine him."

Van Devanter took off his glasses, sat back, and looked at the ceiling, taking visibly exaggerated breaths. "Counsel, please approach," he said, beckoning to both Lee and Sam. When they were in front of him, he stood and bent at the waist to deliver his message over the bench. "I think it best that you each understand I am reaching the limits of my patience," he began. "I've warned the two of you repeatedly about improper lines of inquiry and I've cautioned each of you regarding objections. I believe, therefore, that I am well within the limits of discretion to hold either or both of you in contempt should I again have to correct either of you. Am I clear?"

"Perfectly," Sam said.

Lee leaned forward. "Your Honor, I object to counsel's—"

"To your places, gentlemen." Van Devanter sat back down.

"Your Honor, I wish to make a record—"

"The record is clear, Counsel," Van Devanter said. Lee stared at the judge for a long moment before turning and making his way back to the podium, whereupon he resumed the attack on Julie. Reading from her criminal record, he proceeded, "In the past ten years alone, you've been convicted of burglary?"

"Yes."

"Shoplifting?"

"Yes."

"Forgery?"

"Yes, but my roommate—"

"The manufacture and distribution of a controlled substance?"

"Yes, but only weed."

Sam tried to make eye contact with Julie. She needed to resist explaining.

"And perjury?"

"Yes, but—"

"You were convicted of lying to a tribunal?"

Sam and Lee had argued the issue of Julie's perjury conviction at a pretrial conference. Van Devanter had reserved his decision until the issue arose—now was that time. Sam stood. "Objection, Your Honor. Relevance." Julie's conviction for perjury was relevant, of course, but even relevant evidence could be kept out of the jury's hearing if it was deemed cumulative or unduly prejudicial. Because the parties had agreed in advance that Sam's formulation of the objection would be on the grounds of relevance, he phrased it as such.

"Van Devanter looked pointedly at his watch. "Ladies and gentlemen, we again have a matter to discuss that does not require your presence. Bailiff, please conduct the jury to the jury room. We will be fifteen minutes or so, I expect. Please stand for the jury." When the jury had been dismissed, Van Devanter ordered everyone re-seated. "Mr. Johnstone?"

Sam had his argument ready. "Your Honor, I believe the question is both objectionable and the response inadmissible because her response— if mandated—will unduly bias the jury against her. The fact is, she took a plea, but she was in a drug-addled state and—"

"Are you saying the sentencing court didn't properly advise?" Van Devanter asked.

"No. I'm simply saying she was a different person living a different life. Her actions and decisions then are not relevant to her testimony here today. Her testimony should be received and evaluated by the jury solely based on what is related within the confines of this courtroom. Anything beyond that risks the jury's evaluation of her testimony being unduly poisoned by her past, faulty decision-making."

Van Devanter nodded his understanding of Sam's position. He turned to Lee. "Mr. Lee, I suppose your view is different?"

"Absolutely, Your Honor," Lee said as he stood. He looked about him, took a visibly deep breath, and began. "Your Honor, all of this"—he swept a long arm in front of himself—"this courthouse, this courtroom, your rope, that flag . . . all of it was envisioned, arrayed, collected, and positioned to remind us all of our solemn mission—the search for justice. And that justice, ladies and gentlemen—er, Your Honor—is just as applicable to the people as to the defendant. Certainly, the burden of proof is properly and lawfully fixed upon the State. But the burden should be one that can be borne fairly. The State has by statute and case law every right to question a witness's competence, bias, and veracity. Absent that, trials would quickly devolve into a swearing contest. We seek to introduce evidence of Ms. Spence's perjury only to show a propensity for self-interest and a willingness to lie when it will serve that interest. We ask that we be allowed to inquire into the circumstances of her prior conviction for perjury. Thank you," he concluded with a slight bow.

Sam watched Van Devanter carefully, expecting an opportunity to respond. But when Van Devanter did not inquire of Sam, but again removed and cleaned his glasses in deliberate fashion, Sam stood.

"Your Honor, may the defendant be heard in rebuttal?"

"No, Mr. Johnstone. I don't think so. You'll recall you were heard at the pretrial conference, as well." He replaced his readers and looked at two pages of paper. Placing one in a file and closing the cover, he quickly scanned the other and began reading from what was a prepared memorandum. "The court has heard the arguments of counsel and has considered the same. And while the court appreciates the defendant's argument, it seems to me that the evidence already on the record is such that any prejudice against defense will not be unduly prejudicial; rather it will be the result of the State's right to fully explore the potential bias and self-interest of a witness. I'm going to deny the defendant's motion in limine and allow the State to inquire into the circumstances of the witness's prior conviction for perjury."

By the time Van Devanter finished his explanation, Sam was out of his chair. "But Judge, the inquiry is not designed to uncover either bias or self-interest. Mr. Lee is clearly intent upon destroying the witness's credibility." Sam felt Daniels' hand on his sleeve but brushed it off.

Van Devanter stared levelly at Sam. "I've made my decision, Counsel." He stopped there, but the implicit challenge was, "Appeal me."

Sam sat angrily.

"It's the right call," Daniels whispered into his ear.

"The jury won't believe a word she says," Sam countered.

"She'll be all right," Daniels assured Sam. "She's strong."

"I think we have a few minutes before the jury will be back," Van Devanter said. "Let's take a recess of our own."

***

After Van Devanter departed, Sam and Daniels followed a smirking Lee through the double doors at the rear of the courtroom and made their way to an attorney-client conference room for which Cassie had secured a key. They each accepted a bottle of water proffered by her before taking a seat. Sam uncapped his bottle and drank deeply, draining the entire thing, then paled when Daniels leaned over and retrieved a small bottle of vodka from his sock.

"Jesus!" Sam exclaimed. "Are you kidding me? What the hell are you doing? I need your help!"

"And I need a drink," Daniels explained. He uncapped the small bottle, drank the contents, and tossed it in a nearby wastebasket.

Sam stood and threw his own bottle against the wall. Daniels watched with aplomb. "Feel better?"

"No! No, I don't!" Sam growled. "What if someone finds that and thinks it's me?"

"You been drinkin'?"

"Of course not!"

"Then you don't have shit to worry about," Daniels said. "Me . . . well, I get convicted, it may be a while. No law against booze on your breath in court."

"You should know," Sam snarled, then—seeing the startled look on his mentor's face—quickly apologized. "Judge, you know I don't mean that."

"Bullshit," Daniels said. "And don't apologize." He wiped his mouth with the back of his hand and turned to Cassie. "You got any gum?" he asked Sam's now-pale assistant. When she handed him a piece, he reached into his other sock and repeated his earlier performance with another bottle, then stuck the gum in his mouth and began chewing loudly. "In for a dime; in for a dollar."

Sam shook his head. "Christ," he muttered. "Cassie, could you go check on Julie? She's probably nervous as a long-tailed cat in a rocking chair showroom." Cassie nodded and was gone in an instant. The two men looked at each other until Sam spoke. "It's only going to get worse. Damn."

"Agreed," Daniels agreed. "Perjury convictions are rare—I only saw a couple in my time on the bench."

"So what are you thinking?" Sam asked, not needing to be more specific.

"I think I'm going to have to testify. I think the jury expects me to deny killing Marci—and rightfully so."

"You sure?" Sam asked. There were dozens of reasons a defendant shouldn't testify that Sam could recall off the top of his head. But few applied to this case; his client was well-educated, experienced in the law, articulate, generally composed, had unmatched courtroom experience, and would not be intimidated or bullied. The fact was, he probably should testify. None of that made Sam feel any better.

"I'm sure."

Cassie knocked on the door and opened it a crack. "Sam? Ms. Perry just gave us the two-minute warning."

Sam and Daniels stood and shook hands. "Sorry," Sam said again.

"Forget about it," Daniels replied. "I wish I'da quit drinking when I was your age. If I did, I might not have all the regrets I do now."

39

When the parties had reassembled and the jury had been recalled, Van Devanter looked to Julie, who had taken her seat on the witness stand. "You are still under oath," he reminded her before turning his attention to Lee. "Counsel, please proceed."

As always, Lee was already at the podium, straining at the leash. "Ms. Spence, when we took our recess, you had just admitted having been convicted of perjury—do you remember that?"

"Y-Yes," she said.

Sam was watching her closely; they had discussed the possibility of her having to discuss her criminal history in detail, but he had eschewed speaking to her during the break.

"Did Mr. Johnstone talk with you during the recess?"

"No."

Lee reacted as if surprised. "He didn't?"

"Your Honor," Sam began.

"Move along, Mr. Lee," Van Devanter ruled.

"But you remember being convicted of perjury—lying in court?"

Julie looked to Sam. "Yes."

"You lied to the court?"

"Objection," Sam said wearily. "Asked and answered."

"Mr. Lee, I agree," Van Devanter said. "The objection is sustained."

"Was this during a trial?"

"Yes."

"And were you a witness or the defendant?"

"A witness."

"In fact, you were called by the prosecution to testify against a co-defendant—isn't that true?"

"Yes, it was my boyfriend."

"And you were found to have lied, weren't you?"

Again, it was objectionable, but the value of objecting had been lost. "They said I said my boyfriend didn't have anything to do with the drugs."

"And that wasn't true."

"He threatened me."

"You testified under oath to something that wasn't true, didn't you?"

"Wouldn't you? He threatened me and my kid."

Sam held his breath. If that was all she said she had gotten the better of Lee during this exchange. Most rational people could see a person lying to save themselves or their child. Lee seemed about to cease his questioning when Julie blurted, "And I ain't a snitch."

Sam could hear the intake of breath from the jury, as well as Daniels' muttered curse. By trying to appear what passed for honorable in the drug world, she had inadvertently set herself up to be skewered.

"So, you lied to cover a co-defendant, but you wouldn't have told the truth, anyway—would you?"

"What I said was I couldn't remember," Julie said.

"But you did remember; you had in fact signed an agreement to cooperate by testifying against him—isn't that true?"

"He threatened me!"

"Move to strike," Lee said.

"The jury will disregard the response," Van Devanter said to the jury. Looking to Julie, he continued, "You need to answer the question."

"What was it?"

"You had signed an agreement to cooperate with the State in prosecuting your boyfriend," Lee said, leaning forward at the podium, "in return for which your charges were to be dismissed—true?"

"Yes."

"But during the trial you said you couldn't remember, right?"

"Yes," Julie said. "I didn't really lie, per se—I just couldn't remember anything that could help the cops. I mean, it's not like I wasn't screwed up at the time."

"But you were later overheard later on the jail phone telling your boyfriend that you lied to help him, weren't you?" When she didn't respond, Lee pressed on relentlessly. "Ms. Spence, it's your view that you merely withheld information?"

"Yeah."

"Just like you are today, right?"

"No! I've answered every question you've asked!"

"But that's not everything, is it? You haven't told us, for example, that you appeared in front of then-Judge Daniels more than twenty times, have you?"

"Well, no, but you didn't ask how many!"

Lee looked to Daniels before the next question. He appraised Julie. "In fact, you got to know each other quite well over the years, didn't you?"

"He saved my life!"

"And you'd pay him back here and now if it was possible, wouldn't you?"

"Of course!"

"You'd do anything to help him?"

"Wouldn't you?" she asked. "I already told you he saved my life!"

"You'd lie for him, wouldn't you?"

"No!"

"In fact, you've lied here today, haven't you?"

"No!"

"Ms. Spence, you are asking this jury to believe you here today—"

"I'm not asking anything. I'm telling the truth."

"—when you admit having lied before in court."

"I've told you the truth!"

"You—a proven liar—are telling us you'd do anything for the defendant except lie? Is that it?"

Sam was on his feet. "Your Honor, I object. He's merely badgering her at this point."

"Sustained," Van Devanter ruled.

Lee nodded to the judge, then returned his stare to Julie, where it remained for some time. At last, he shifted his eyes to the jurors, attempting to meet the eyes of each. Van Devanter saw through it at the same time Sam did. "Mr. Lee, ask a question or sit down," he ordered.

"Tender the witness," Lee said, and sat down as instructed.

Sam stepped to the podium and asked questions of Julie designed to show that she had changed the direction of her life since her earlier transgressions. But Julie, feeling she had been mistreated, answered Sam's questions with indignation. "I'm a different person now"; "That was then, this is now"; "I've turned my life around."

But as Sam gauged the jury's reaction, it was clear they were having none of it. He quickly discerned he was making little to no progress in rehabilitating her and brought his re-direct to a halt. "No more questions," he said, and noted obvious relief on the part of at least three jurors in response.

"You may step down," Van Devanter said to a flushed, tearful Julie, who immediately disappeared out the back door of the courtroom. When she had cleared the doors, Van Devanter looked to the jury. "I think that's enough for the week. Please listen closely while I again remind you of the dos and don'ts for jurors during breaks." When he had completed his warnings, he stood and was gone.

40

An hour later, Sam was struggling to make his final changes to a letter to a client when Cassie buzzed him on the intercom. "Sam?"

"I'm here."

"Some gal named Kelly is on the line. Says she works at the Horseshoe. Says she knows you, and that you will want to hear this."

"Send her through."

"Sam, this is Kelly. Your boy Clay overdosed. Cops were here and they hit him with naloxone. They cited him for use. He refused to go to the hospital, and I don't think they want him in jail, so he's still in the room."

Damn it. "Okay, thanks."

"You gonna get him out? 'Cause the boss don't want anyone using on the premises."

There wasn't anyone *not* using on the premises. "Uh, yeah. Pretty soon. Listen, I'm kind of overwhelmed here today, but I'll try and get down there after work."

"Cool. Maybe we can get a drink after doin' business?"

"Kelly, I gotta tell you, I don't drink anymore."

"I heard. But I'm sayin' get a drink, I mean, you know, like go somewhere and hang out. Could be my place or yours . . . you know."

"Okay, well, we'll see."

Just before six o'clock, Sam was knocking on the door to Clay's room. He pounded for a couple of minutes and was beginning to panic when he heard Clay ask, "Who is it?"

"It's Sam. Open the door. I'm freezing my ass off out here!"

Clay obliged, and as soon as Sam had stepped through the door, he slammed it shut behind him. "How are you doin', man?"

"I'm fine," Sam replied. "The question is, how are you?"

"I'm alive."

Give me a break, Sam thought. "Pity much?"

"Huh?"

"What's your major malfunction? I give you some help, get you a place and something to eat for a couple of days, and now I find out you're ODing on fentanyl."

"None-a your business, is it?"

"It is when I'm paying."

"What do you want from me?"

"A little gratitude would be good, for a start," Sam said. "Then I'd like to see you pull your head out of your ass, quit feeling sorry for yourself, get a grip, and start making some changes."

"That all?"

"For a start."

"You don't know—"

"Save that shit for someone else. I know you're a drunk and an addict. That's all I need to know, 'cause everything else stems from that," Sam said, watching Clay carefully. "When's the last time you had something to eat?"

"Yesterday at the soup kitchen."

"That's a day and a half!"

"Well, I been . . . busy."

Right. Methamphetamine use dampened hunger. "Look, there's a taco shop right down the street; I'm gonna give you some money. Will you use it for food?"

"Of course."

"One condition," Sam said, raising an index finger for emphasis.

"What's that?"

"Who sold you the shit?"

Clay looked up at Sam. "I ain't a narc, man."

"And I'm not a cop," Sam reminded him. "I told you that before." Seeing Clay's doubts, he added, "Think of it as business development."

"Dunno the dude, man. All I know is his name was Gus."

"Trent Gustafson?"

"I dunno, man. I just heard him referred to as Gus."

"Let me ask you something. You understand you got cited rather than arrested because you almost died, right?"

"That's what they told me."

"So right now, you're looking at up to six months in the clink—"

"For usin'? Man, that's bullshit."

"Yeah, well, I seriously doubt Judge Downs gives a rat's ass what you think—know what I'm saying?" When Clay didn't respond, Sam continued. "So here is what I'm thinking. If you don't want to spend six months in the local can, I'll see if I can get you probation only if you tell the county attorney you bought from Gustafson."

"I'm not a squealer, man!"

"Yeah, well, you change your mind, you let me know."

"You'll represent me if I don't squeal, right?"

"Wrong. Nothing I can do. The facts are what they are, and the county attorney is on a mission. He's not gonna deal. Doesn't like me, anyway—you're probably better off on your own."

"C'mon, Sam," Clay said. "Don't be a dick."

"Not being a dick—just business," Sam said, peeling off a couple of twenties. "Here. Go get yourself something to eat. I'll cover you for two more nights, but then you gotta go or get yourself off my tab, okay?"

"Thanks, Sam."

"See ya," Sam said as he left the room. In his truck and with one hand on the wheel, he dialed his phone with his thumb. After two rings, Punch picked up. "Punch, how the hell are you?"

"I'm well, Counselor. You?"

"I'm good. Hey, I think I have a client who might have some information for you."

41

On Saturday afternoon, Cathy was wrapping up a telephone consultation with a potential client—a local businessman who had been caught and given a citation for possession of a small amount of weed he had obtained at a dispensary in Colorado. The plan was for him to come to her office on Monday and put down a deposit, after which Cathy would file an entry of appearance, a plea of not guilty, and a demand for discovery in his case. She was opening a file and making notes when she heard the door open. She hurried out of her office and almost ran into Misty, who was walking quickly down Cathy's hallway. The smell of marijuana was immediately apparent.

"Misty, what are you doing here?" Cathy asked. "And I can smell the weed! You know you are on probation! If the judge finds out, he could revoke your probation and send you to prison!"

"Could care less," Misty said, and smiled.

Good Lord, she was high as a kite. "Sit down," Cathy ordered. "I'll get you some coffee."

"Lots of sugar," Misty replied. "I like a little coffee with my sugar."

When she had made Misty's coffee, Cathy placed it on her desk between them and took her chair. "Now, why are you here?"

Misty tentatively placed her lips on the cup. She took a miniscule sip and replaced the cup on the basketball-shaped coaster on Cathy's desk. "Hot," she said, then—noticing Cathy staring at her—smiled and said, "What?"

"Why are you here?" Cathy asked levelly.

"I can't see Ari," Misty said. "My own grandson. I can't see him."

"Why not?" Cathy asked. "Have you been following the terms and conditions of your probation?"

"For the most part, yeah. I mean, I missed an MDT meeting, and I was hot on a urinalysis last week."

An "MDT" referred to a multi-disciplinary team that had been established at Bridger's direction to ensure that Misty was sober and Ari would be safe in her custody. In addition to verifying Misty's sobriety through frequent urinalysis testing, the team would provide counseling, guidance, and support for her to get on her feet with the ultimate goal of re-establishing contact between Misty and Ari with no oversight.

"Christ, Misty! You've been through all this before; you know how important it is!" Cathy said.

"It's all a scam; they set me up to fail," Misty said. "They know no one can follow their rules."

"People can and do!" Cathy asserted. "And you can, too! But you've got to try!"

Misty shrugged and reached unsteadily for the coffee; it took a couple of tries for her to successfully get both hands around the cup. She smiled as she again put her lips to the cup.

"What?" Cathy asked.

"I dunno," Misty said. "It's just funny."

"You aren't going to be laughing if you fail another UA. Bridger's likely to cut you out."

Misty shrugged. Tears were welling in her eyes. "Don't matter. Ari's been staying with some white-bread folks what live up by the golf course. Got all new toys, big house with a slide in the yard. Ain't no way he will wanna come back."

"Of course he will," Cathy argued. "You're his grandmother and you love him—he knows that."

"I had visitation last week at the advocacy center and he said,

"Grandma, I want to go home.' And I said, 'I want you home,' and he said, 'Not with you, Grandma—with them,' and pointed to the one-way glass where the fosters were."

Ouch. "That's just kids being kids," Cathy counseled. "When—"

"No, it isn't," Misty said. "He's had a taste of the good life."

"Misty, look. Let's just take this—"

"I'm gonna shoot that sonuvabitching judge, and that lawyer, too."

Cathy knew not to overreact. "Misty, I'm sure this is all going to blow over. You've been doing all the right things." Except getting high, of course. And missing MDTs. "You can't just throw your hands up and admit defeat. You've got to fight for—"

"With what?" Misty asked. "How? I got nothin'. I got a daughter in the pen, a son on his way, and a history won't no one let me move past. I got leaks in my roof, the air coming through the windows, and a car that might not get me where I need to go any day. I can only drive at night 'cause my plates is expired." She broke into tears and Cathy watched years of bad decisions roll down Misty's cheeks. She retrieved a box of tissues.

"Look, let me give you a ride home," Cathy suggested. "Come on back tomorrow; that'll give me some time to see if I can arrange some resources to help you."

"Yeah, right," Misty said. "Ain't no one ever helped me yet."

It wasn't true, of course. The fact was the state had spent hundreds of thousands of dollars in direct and in-kind assistance, including counseling, health care, substance abuse treatment, parenting classes, subsidized meals and school supplies, job training, education—the list went on and on. But now wasn't the time to argue. Cathy succeeded in talking Misty into the passenger seat, and watched out of the corner of her eye as Misty's head bobbed to the '90s country music Cathy favored.

"You know what my favorite song is?"

Probably something cheesy. "I do not," Cathy said.

"The one about the lights goin' out in Georgia—'member that one? Gal shoots someone who crossed her," Misty said. "Somethin' about a make-believe trial. Well, that's my song."

Cathy pulled up in front of Misty's trailer and stopped. Best to ignore it for now. She turned off the lights and cut the engine. "Come by tomorrow and we'll talk."

For a few seconds, Misty didn't move. "Double shift tomorrow," she said, then opened the door and got out.

Cathy watched as Misty opened the unlocked trailer and entered, never looking back.

42

While Cathy was dealing with Misty, Julie was blocks away wiping viciously at her red nose with a used tissue she had clutched in her small, bony hand. "I don't understand!" she wailed. "I've done everything you asked. You told me yourself just a month ago I was your best employee. You gave me a raise and promised that when a position opened, you'd let me lead a team!"

Debra McIntosh nodded. It was all true. But Julie's testimony yesterday had gotten back to corporate, and the subsequent media reports had changed everything. "I know, Julie. And I'm sorry. But when word of your testimony got back to those guys in ties and the shoulder-pad-wearing shrews at corporate . . . well, they told me I needed to let you go."

"But why?" Julie repeated.

Deb looked around her small office and sighed heavily. She'd known it would be ugly, for a number of reasons. As a threshold matter, it was probably unfair to Julie. But it wouldn't do her any favors, either. Since the pandemic, it had been increasingly difficult to find good employees—everyone knew that. Losing Julie, one of the few workers who needed no oversight, would increase her own workload. She had explained all that via email to her supervisor, and had argued against this, finally agreeing to let Julie go only when the chief operations officer, Dan Moon, made clear that if Deb wouldn't let Julie go, he would find someone to put in Deb's position who would. Principles only went so far—she had a family to feed. "We can't keep her," he had said. "She is uninsurable. A lot of the stuff that came out in the trial . . . well, if we'da known that, we never woulda hired her. Now we know, so if something were to happen to another patient . . . hell, there's probably exposure right now from Marci Daniels' family. We've got to let her go. Give her some severance pay—I'll authorize up to a thousand dollars right now."

"Julie, I already explained that to you," Deb said at last. "Don't make this harder than it has to be."

"For who?" Julie snapped. "I didn't hide my history, and I passed any background checks you had, right?"

"Right," Deb admitted. "But this . . . well, this is different to the folks back east."

"But I didn't do anything wrong! Press was supposed to change her prescription. I had no way of knowing! I—I'm not a doctor or a nurse," she stressed. "I administered what he left me, just like I did every other day. I listened to the home health care nurses and did exactly what they said and what he said and now I'm the one getting screwed!"

"I'm sorry, Julie. There's nothing I can do."

"Or will do."

Deb felt her ears burning. "Julie, I feel bad about this—really. And look, I've been authorized to provide you some severance pay to help you out until you can get back on your feet. I can give you six hundred dollars— that's a week's pay." Moon would be impressed if she came in under budget.

"Whatever," Julie said.

"And I will, of course, provide you with glowing letters of recommendation," Deb said. She looked at Julie, who was now dry-eyed. She knew Julie to be street-smart and wary, and figured she was already calculating what to do with the money. "Julie, what else can I do?"

"Oh, hell," Julie said, standing. "I don't know. It's just so unfair. I bust my ass to turn things around and get myself straight, get my life back together, and just when I think I'm heading in the right direction this comes along. It's like one step forward and two steps back," she concluded, turning for the door.

"What are you going to do?"

"I dunno," Julie said. "Either get high or go to a meeting, I suppose. It's always one or the other."

"Well . . . take care of yourself, Julie," Deb said as the door closed. "You are a good person."

43

That evening, Sam was in his office and on the phone with one of the few clients who had his personal number. The man had made millions in the oil and gas industry and—like many self-made millionaires—had concluded that he was very likely the smartest person in any room in which he happened to be. Some months ago, he had gotten into a dispute with another self-made millionaire over back-ordered goods, contracts alleged to be breached, and the like. Rather than work it out, the two hard-heads had actually gone to blows. The man had shown up in Sam's office charged with battery and wanting to sue his counterpart.

"Lawsuits are expensive and time-consuming," Sam had counseled.

"I don't give a damn," his client had said. "It's a matter of principle." Like every other lawyer, Sam had heard this before and had quoted the man a five-figure retainer and an hourly rate of a few hundred dollars.

"Principles are expensive," Sam had explained.

"I don't care," his client had said at the time. Now, months later, after the retainer had long ago been used and replenished, and as Sam's bills had begun to pile up and the anger had worn off, Sam had gotten the expected phone call. "Sam, is there a way we can just dismiss all this and be done with it?"

"Maybe," Sam said. "But you'll recall that when you sued him, he filed counter-claims against you. So in order to 'dismiss all this' we're going to have to get him to agree."

"So how much is that gonna cost?"

"I'll make the calls to his attorney at my hourly rate."

There was a lengthy silence at the other end. "What if I just call Bill and see if he is willing to forget it? I mean, I've known the guy forty years. He ain't really a bad guy and—"

"I think that's a great idea. Lemme know what happens," Sam said. He hung up and was making notes in his file when his landline rang. It was a Montana area code and there was no reason to answer, but he had a feeling.

"This is Sam Johnstone."

"Mr. Johnstone, this is Dr. Ann Robinson from the Treasure State Regional Medical Center. I am an oncologist and I'm currently treating your father, Les Johnstone. Your father asked that I inform you—"

Sam's stomach was in an immediate uproar. "Yeah well, thanks, Doc. See, we are not exactly close and—"

"So he tells me. I'm sorry, but I wanted you to know that he has signed a release of information and asked that I contact you to let you know we are transferring him to a hospice unit affiliated with the hospital."

"Fine."

"He is conscious, aware of his surroundings, and not in any pain."

Sam was short of breath. "That's good. Ummm, I'd prefer that you not contact me again. As I mentioned, we are not close. That's the decision he made a long time ago."

"I'm sorry to hear that."

"Yeah, well . . . it is what it is," Sam said. "Look, can you make some kind of note or something in his file telling folks I'd rather not be contacted? And I'm sorry for your time and trouble." There. He'd said what he had to say.

"I understand."

She probably didn't, but that was okay. "Great. I appreciate your time," he said.

"I'll see to it that a note is put in the file, and I'll let your father know your wishes."

Sam had a vision of the old man in bed raging in anger. He was about to hang up when the doctor spoke up. "Mr. Johnstone, I don't mean to pry or interfere or anything . . ."

It sounded like she was going to do exactly that. "But?"

"Well, I am board certified in palliative care—that means I see a lot of situations where people who haven't gotten along well in life . . . well, toward the end. . . sometimes people reach out in an effort to make amends."

She clearly expected him to say something. "And?" he said.

"And if I may be so bold, might I offer a bit of unsolicited advice?" Without waiting for his permission, she continued. "I'll just say I have never seen anyone regret reestablishing contact. The worst it will do is reaffirm your hard feelings. On the other hand, it might help resolve some things. And if you don't at least listen, well . . . you could come to regret that later. Just a thought. Good luck to you, Mr. Johnstone," she said, and hung up.

Sam drank decaffeinated coffee and thought about some of the things he and Bob Martinez had discussed over the years. Les had wronged him— there could be no doubt. But Bob had counseled Sam should "seek to understand, not to be understood," and to "forgive, rather than be forgiven." Certainly, he had every right to be angry and hurt. But because those emotions were unproductive, Bob would advise Sam to examine his own responsibility for the situation and to understand that his fear of rejection was likely playing an enormous role in his inability to forgive. He sipped the decaf, mulling and understanding that at some point he was going to have to come to grips with his anger at his father.

44

At the last minute, Cathy had eschewed the Sunday morning church service and was grocery shopping with Kayla in tow when Julie stormed up to her. "What is it?" Cathy asked, putting an arm protectively around Kayla.

"They fired me!" Julie wailed.

Damn it! "Okay, okay, calm down," Cathy counseled, gesturing to a corner of the store near the bakery. "Wait here," Cathy said to Kayla, who obligingly stuck her nose in her phone. When they had some privacy, Cathy turned to her. "Did they say why?"

"Because of my testimony, of course!"

"I understand," Cathy said. "But did they give you a reason?"

"Something about my testimony causing them problems with insurance or something? I dunno, Cathy. I just know that I'm out of a job. I got Kira back finally, and after all the trouble I had with Department of Family Services—"

"Okay, I hear you. Try not to panic," Cathy said. "I'm not an expert in employment law, but I'll talk to someone who is and see if there is anything we can do."

"Working for Press—Judge Daniels—was perfect because he let me work around Kira's schedule. I don't know if anyone else will let me do that."

"I understand. Did you get any severance pay?"

"Six hundred."

Cheap bastards. "I think you need to start looking for another job while you've got that money. I'm sure Press will be a solid reference for you, and I will, too."

"Debra—she was my boss—said she would, too."

"Well, there you go, then," Cathy said. "Look, there are bumps in the road, Julie. But you did the right thing and you're gonna land on your feet."

Julie wiped her eyes with a tissue. "Yeah, well. That's what my sponsor keeps telling me, but I cannot help but feel like I'm getting kicked in the ass."

"I understand, but try and focus on the future. Let's get this thing turned around, okay?"

"Okay."

"I'll get ahold of Sam and see who he recommends, and I'll get back with you tomorrow."

Julie looked at her watch. "Okay, I gotta go. I need to pick up Kira and I'm late," she said as she hurried off.

Cathy watched Julie until she sensed Kayla's presence.

"Wow, Mom. That was scary," Kayla said.

45

On Monday morning—ironically, perhaps, Valentine's Day—Sam called his client. "Your Honor, the defense calls Preston Daniels." Daniels stood and made his way to the witness box. Sam was thinking how surreal it must be for the man who had manned the bench for decades to find himself in the witness box. When Daniels was settled, Sam smiled wryly. "Would you state your name for the record?"

Daniels ignored the nervous laughter in the courtroom. "Preston Daniels."

"Are you employed?"

"Retired."

"Where do you live?"

"Right here in Custer."

"Are you married?"

Daniels took a deep breath and then exhaled. "Widowed."

"You are the defendant in this matter?"

"I am."

"You are charged in connection with the death of your wife?"

"I am."

"How long were you married?"

"Forty-five years. Woulda been forty-six in June."

"Were you happily married?"

"We were."

Time to get to the heart of it. "Your wife Marci had been ill for some time before she passed away?"

"She had cancer."

"Was she under a doctor's care?"

"Yes," Daniels said. "She had several doctors."

"Were you satisfied with the care she received?"

"Not really."

"Why not?"

"Because she suffered terribly. The treatments themselves, the pain, the vomiting, the constant intestinal issues—she was miserable. It—it hurt me."

"And you felt?"

"Anger," Daniels said quickly. He wiped his face with a hand. "I find lately that anger seems to be my go-to emotion."

"So you weren't satisfied with the treatment she was getting. What did you do in response?"

"Well, at first I tried talking to the doctors—tried getting them to do more," Daniels explained. "But it was apparent that the doctors here didn't think . . . they didn't think she was going to make it."

"By here, you mean?"

"Wyoming . . . Colorado . . . Minnesota."

"What did you do when you heard the doctors in the US didn't have any answers?"

Daniels again rubbed his face with a hand. "Well, I'd been reading about some treatments in Mexico that seemed like they might help, so we went down there."

"And?"

"Well, she got the treatments but . . . didn't . . . respond."

"How did that make you feel?"

"How do you think?" Daniels snapped. "Pissed off! To begin with, we paid a fortune for nothing. Then we got back here, and we had doctors— the same ones whose own treatments hadn't done squat—telling us we were wasting time and money on treatments down there."

Sam nodded. "Let's talk about the circumstances of Marci's passing."

"I forgot to change her prescriptions—"

"Just a minute—" Sam tried to interrupt.

"—and she overdosed," Daniels finished.

"Let's walk that back—"

"That's what happened." Daniels shrugged. "It's my fault."

"—a bit," Sam managed to get in. "Tell the jury about Marci's last few weeks."

"Well, we got back from Mexico, and she was still sick. The doctors here said there was nothing they could do. I had promised her I wouldn't put her in a home, so I was caring for her."

"What did that involve?" Sam asked.

"Feeding, bathing, administering medication . . . you know, all that stuff."

"Did you have any help?"

"Not until I got Julie."

"Julie Spence?"

"Yes."

"How did you come to get her?"

"I called her employer and told them what I needed," Daniels explained. "They sent Julie."

"Did you take her on immediately?"

"Oh, no," Daniels said.

"Why not?"

"We'd, uh, met, I guess you could say."

"In court?"

"Yes."

"Did you recognize her when she showed up?"

"Not right away," Daniels said. "She'd put on some weight—that's a good sign for an addict in recovery, by the way. She told me she'd gotten straight—had been to treatment, then went to school. She looked good. Healthy."

"Different than you'd seen her before?"

Daniels nodded vigorously. "Oh, hell yes. Much better. She's a fine-looking young lady when she is straight."

"So, what happened?"

"Well, to be honest, I still didn't really want her in our house. I'm kind of ashamed to say this, but I've seen so many addicts relapse over the years that, well . . . But when I told Marci that I didn't want Julie in our house, Marci insisted we give her a chance."

"And you agreed?"

"I did."

"Any regrets?"

"Absolutely not." Daniels shook his head vigorously. "She did a great job. She showed up every day, on time and ready to go to work. That's more than I can say for a lot of folks."

Sam smiled as most in the gallery nodded in agreement. "So, what exactly were her duties?"

"Well, what I said earlier: helping me with feeding, bathing, toileting, and things like that. After a few weeks she helped with meal preparation." Daniels stopped, seeming to think of something.

"Cooking?" Sam prompted.

"Well, kind of," Daniels said, shaking his head. "Toward the end Marci didn't eat much—stomach trouble, you know? Just a lot of soft things: bananas for potassium, gave her some ice cream for the calcium—it was more just preparation, I guess you'd call it."

Time to get to it. "Earlier you mentioned administering medication—how did that work?"

"Well, it was just me for a while, you know. But apparently Julie had some training in that, so after some time I began to allow her to administer medication. First, I would set out pills for her to give Marci. Eventually, I watched her as she administered medicine with . . . shots."

"Eventually?"

"Yes," Daniels acknowledged. "I had to learn to trust her."

Sam was watching the jury. They were with him. "And how did that work?"

"I kept the controlled medicines in a safe. I'd been doing that even before Julie came into the picture."

"How did you know she was doing things right?"

"Well, we'd gone to a class for how to give the shots. And it was obvious if Marci hadn't had her medication; I'd forgotten a couple of times when I was alone—overslept, or just forgot," Daniels explained. "And I'll admit that I had installed a couple of home security cameras that weren't easy to see. I watched her."

"You didn't trust her at first?"

"Addiction's a bitch." Daniels shrugged. "I saw it my entire professional life."

True enough. Sam smiled and watched as the jury members' gazes shifted uncomfortably from Daniels to Van Devanter, whose expression never varied. "But there came a time when Julie gained your trust?"

"Yes," Daniels said. "Didn't take long."

"So, if I understand, you would prepare the meds and Julie would administer them?"

"Only when I wasn't going to be around—maybe running to the store or whatever. It's not like her giving the medication to Marci was the usual thing."

"Not her job to measure or apportion or whatever?"

"No. Most of 'em were pre-measured."

"Let's talk about what happened when Marci passed."

Daniels leaned forward in the witness chair. "I forgot to switch out the medications and Julie gave her too much."

"Let's make sure the jury understands the whole story," Sam cautioned. "Had there been a change in her medications?"

"Yes, they upped her diazepam. When they did that, they lowered her morphine. I was to get pre-filled syringes with the lower dosage of morphine in them, exchange the new syringes, and take the others back to the pharmacy."

"Did that happen?"

Daniels sat perfectly still. "No."

This was it. "Why not?"

Again, Daniels sat perfectly still without answering. Sam watched the jury members—each of whom had eyes locked on Daniels. When Daniels' silence had gotten uncomfortably long, Sam inquired. "Did you hear the question?"

"I did. I can't answer that."

"Objection!" Lee said. "The witness must—"

Daniels looked sharply toward Lee. "I don't mean *I won't*, you twit—of course I will answer," he snapped.

"Your Honor!" Lee protested while Sam and some of the jurors suppressed smiles.

"Mr. Daniels, you know better," Van Devanter said, then turned his attention to Lee. "Objection overruled. The court takes the witness's response to mean he cannot explain his actions—or inactions."

This wasn't good: Sam's expectation was that Daniels would simply reply, "I don't know," or "I forgot."

"Let me ask you to clarify your answer," Sam began. "You didn't not exchange the medicine intentionally." It was a double negative and a terrible question, but hopefully Daniels would see where he was going.

Lee saw through it. "Objection; form of the question."

"I'll re-phrase," Sam offered.

"Please do," Van Devanter said.

"Can you explain why the medicine wasn't changed out?"

"Not really," Daniels admitted. "I mean, I was tired and all, but it was my job, my responsibility to take care of her. Mine. I'd done it before—she'd been through medication changes on innumerable occasions. I just . . . I don't know. I'm sorry."

Probably as good as it would get. Sam and Daniels had discussed Sam asking questions about Daniels' statements to law enforcement and others that he had "killed" Marci to try and blunt Lee's efforts, but after a lot of thought, and now, seeing that Daniels was holding up fairly well, Sam made the decision to let it go.

"No more questions, Your Honor," Sam said. "Tender the witness."

46

Sam watched as Lee stepped to the podium, drank from a glass of water, and then stared at Daniels, who sat impassively. It was ridiculous. "Perhaps Mr. Lee doesn't have any questions?" Sam said as he stood.

"Mr. Johnstone," Van Devanter snapped. "I'll not have that." He turned to Lee. "Mr. Lee, if you do have questions, let's get to it. The noon recess approaches."

"Mr. Daniels," Lee began. "Immediately following your wife's passing—or, I should say, your having notified law enforcement of your wife's passing—you told anyone who would listen that you had killed your wife. True?"

"No."

"You didn't tell the cops, the EMTs, and the 9-1-1 operator that you had killed your wife?"

"Oh, that's certainly true," Daniels allowed.

"Then why did you just respond 'no?'"

"Because your premise was false. It is false to say that I told anyone who would listen. Given that faulty premise, the correct response to the entire question is 'no.'"

Lee's face reddened as those in the gallery tittered. "You told the 9-1-1 operator that you killed Marci?"

"I did."

"You told law enforcement you killed her?"

"I did."

"You told the EMTs that you killed her?"

"That I do not recall, but I'll accept your representation if you say I did," Daniels explained. "I have no reason to believe I said otherwise."

"You don't deny it?"

"I cannot. I don't recall."

"You oversaw your wife's treatment, didn't you?"

"No, her doctors did."

"Mr. Daniels, you took your wife to her appointments, met with her doctors, and were responsible for her care—true?"

"Responsible in what way?" Daniels asked.

"Move to strike, Judge. Not responsive."

"Your questions are imprecise, Mr. Lee," Daniels said. "Words mean things."

"Your Honor!" Lee protested.

Van Devanter looked to Daniels. "Mr. Daniels, if you do not understand the question or if you seek clarification, ask for the same, please." He turned to Lee. "Please proceed."

"Mr. Daniels," Lee began anew. "Did you see to your wife's needs during her illness?"

"I did."

"Were you guided in doing so?"

"I was."

"By whom?"

"Her physicians," Daniels said. "And a nurse came by two or three times per week to check on us."

"And they provided direction?"

"They did."

"And you followed their directions?"

"Yes."

"Except for replacing her prescription?"

Sam could hear the gallery draw a collective breath and awaited Daniels' blow-up. "I'm sure other mistakes were made," he said carefully.

"Mistakes?" Lee pounced. "Is it your position that Marci's death was the result of a mere mistake?"

"Yes," Daniels replied. "A terrible mistake made by me."

"You gave her the wrong medication?"

"No," Daniels said. "Were you not listening? I didn't give her the medication in question."

"You prepared the wrong medication for Julie?"

"No. I provided it; I didn't prepare it."

Again, the audience tittered. Lee's ears were red. "You provided a medication that Julie was to administer?"

"Yes, I believe that is accurate."

"And that medication you provided was in an amount in excess of her prescription at the time?"

"Yes."

"And you don't know why?"

"Why what?" Daniels asked.

"You don't know why you gave her—provided her—er, provided Julie the medication in an amount in excess of what had been prescribed?"

"Actually, it had been prescribed in that amount, but previously."

Lee was now visibly shaking in anger. "Your Honor, would you instruct the defendant to answer the questions posed?"

"If that was an objection or a move to strike, it is overruled or denied," Van Devanter said sharply. "I think he is answering, albeit precisely."

Lee sighed. "Why wasn't the medicine changed out?"

"Because I didn't do so," Daniels answered.

"Why not?" Lee asked immediately.

"I don't know."

"Who would?"

"I can't answer that."

"You agree it was your responsibility?"

"Yes."

"You knew you needed to do that?"

"Yes."

"You understood what could happen if you didn't?"

"Oh, yes," Daniels said. "Her doctor made that very clear."

"And yet you failed to do so. Can you explain that?"

Sam almost objected; the question had been asked and answered. But here Daniels could make some hay. "I cannot," Daniels said. "I guess I got busy or confused and I forgot." Sam made a note and underlined it. Not good; because Daniels had responded in that way, there would be no evidence on the record to support the heretofore possible lesser-included offense of criminal negligence.

"You forgot to change out your wife's medication even though you knew not changing the medication out could kill her?" Without giving Daniels an opportunity to respond, Lee continued. "Isn't it true that you didn't give her the medication because you wanted her to die? To see to it she got her medication, I mean," Lee corrected before Daniels could respond.

"No."

"You knew she was sick, and you knew she had a large life insurance policy, didn't you?"

"Compound question," Daniels said. "But yes to both."

"You needed the money?"

Daniels shook his head. "Not really."

"You spent a fortune on her treatment?"

"I would have spent everything I had and borrowed more," Daniels said. "She's gone. What am I going to do, Counsel? Take a beach vacation?"

Lee ignored the response. "Do you remember talking to Miriam Baker while Marci was sick?"

"Oh, yes," Daniels said.

"She called you and you told her—"

"She never called us," Daniels corrected. "Never." Seeing Lee was taken aback, he continued. "I asked her about it one time, and she said it was too expensive to call. She didn't visit her sister, either," he added with a glare toward Miriam.

"In any event," Lee continued, "you told her you wished Marci was dead, true?"

"No," Daniels said, shaking his head. "I told her *Marci* said she wished she was dead. Big difference. *I* told her Marci was in tremendous pain—"

"And you wished it was over?"

"Oh, yes—absolutely. Wouldn't you wish the same in my position?"

"Mr. Daniels," Van Devanter warned.

Lee moved in. "It was a difficult time for you?"

"It was," Daniels agreed. "It still is."

"And you were determined to end her pain?"

"I was," Daniels said. "I did everything I could—Mexico, alternative treatments, physical therapists—"

"And when none of that worked you took it upon yourself to put her out of her misery, didn't you?"

Daniels sat quietly, then reached up and adjusted the microphone. He took a deep breath and started to speak, then closed his mouth and glanced at the jury. Sam saw what was coming and stood to ask for a recess, but it was too late. "You are one miserable sonuvabitch, you know that?"

"Mr. Daniels!" Van Devanter said quickly. "You are out of order, and you know it!"

"I wonder how you look at yourself in the mirror?" Daniels continued. "Do you like what you see? Have you ever loved anyone in your sad, sorry life?"

"Your Honor, might I have a moment with my client?" Sam requested.

"Mr. Daniels, I'll not have that kind of behavior in my courtroom!" Van Devanter scolded Daniels, ignoring Sam. "You, more than anyone, know it is improper. You will answer the county attorney's questions and leave it at that."

"Mr. Lee wouldn't make a boil on a good county attorney's butt," Daniels said to a smirking Lee, who was standing at the podium with his arms folded. "I've seen some self-righteous dingleberries in my day, but this guy tops the list."

Sam expected that would do it, and he was correct. "Mr. Daniels, I have heard enough," Van Devanter began. "Because I know you know better, I will dispense with additional warnings and find you in contempt of court. You will apologize immediately or be remanded to the custody of the sheriff's department until you do. As you know, the rules mandate your presence, but that presence is not unfettered, and I am perfectly willing to continue this trial in your absence if you cannot control yourself."

"Your Honor, a moment with my client?" Sam asked again.

"No, Counsel. Your client is perfectly able to make this decision on his own." Van Devanter was staring fiercely at Daniels, who returned the stare.

"Your Honor, may the jury be excused?" Sam persisted.

"No, Counsel. It's too late for that."

Sam watched helplessly as the pair measured each other for what seemed like several minutes, alternating his own gaze between the two judges and the jury members, who were understandably and visibly shocked by what they were observing. At last, Daniels spoke. "Your Honor, I mean no disrespect to the court," he began. "I believe in the court as an institution with all my heart. My disrespect is reserved solely for Mr. Lee here, who I know to be an officer of the court. I was wrong to express my deep feelings of disgust and disdain for him in this forum. I apologize to you, the members of the jury, and all who are in the courtroom. I make no excuse for my actions and promise you I will not act in this manner again."

Van Devanter was visibly relieved. "Your apology is accepted. The finding of contempt stands. I will reserve my ruling on an appropriate sanction until later, but I warn you it will be largely dependent upon your conduct in this trial henceforth. Should there be another outburst on your part, it is unlikely you will be anything other than an observer for the remainder of the trial—from afar, if you understand the court's inference."

"Yes, Your Honor," Daniels said.

Van Devanter nodded, satisfied. Turning his attention to the jury, he said, "Ladies and gentlemen, it's a little earlier than the court would generally grant a recess, but given the events of this morning let's take a few minutes. Bailiff, have the jury prepared to be re-seated at eleven a.m.," he said, and was gone.

In the attorney-client conference room minutes later, Sam burst out laughing. "Holy shit! That was like something from a bad made-for-television movie!"

Daniels smirked. "Bastard deserved it."

Sam sobered. "Of course he did, but you and I both know that hurt you. I mean, the jury cannot un-see what they just saw."

"I understand," Daniels said. "I put you in a bad spot and—"

"It's not about me," Sam countered. "It's about you. Your future."

"I have no future."

That wasn't good. "Remember six months back or so, when I asked you if you had a death wish?" Sam asked. "I wasn't asking out of morbid curiosity. I was asking because I needed to know if you were in this for the long haul. I needed to know if you were going to fight."

"I need a drink," Daniels said.

"No, you don't."

"Sam, I was married to the woman for forty-five years. Do you know, I don't even know how to pay bills? I'm looking at the bills from the hospital and the providers and the insurance companies and something called a supplemental insurance company and I have no idea. I didn't pay my home insurance until my agent called me and told me my policy had been cancelled. I'm going through the motions, not understanding what the hell is going on—like a lion eating tofu."

Sam frowned. "It's to be expected. It's going to take you a while to get on your feet." He was watching Daniels carefully. "Maybe you should see a counselor. Help you deal with your grief."

"I don't need to see a damned shrink! Too much sniveling going on in the world as it is." Daniels sat quietly, and then—perhaps realizing his mistake—continued. "Aw shit, Sam. I'm sorry. I—I mean for someone like me. A guy like you—a hero—well, that's different."

This was a man who for decades had made his living, at least in part, by thinking before he spoke. "Press, look. You're off your feed today. Why don't I tell Van Devanter that you're sick and ask that we continue this tomorrow?" Sam offered. "Go home—hell, get drunk if you want—and we'll start again tomorrow."

"No," Daniels said. "Let's just get it over with."

Probably the right decision. "Lee might not have a lot left—you might have flattened your own tire there."

"I know," Daniels said. "Juries like judges."

"And that ass-chewing from Van Devanter was a direct hit—maybe below the water line."

"You're mixing metaphors."

"It's the best I can do," Sam replied. "I'm still replaying you telling Lee he's a self-righteous dingleberry. Not sure I've got that kind of creativity in me." He looked at his watch. "You ready?"

Daniels nodded and took Sam's hand. "I am. Let's do this."

"One more thing," Sam said with a hand on Daniels' forearm.

"Yeah?"

"You know we just lost criminal negligence, right?"

"I do," Daniels said. "But the jury wasn't going to buy that I'm too stupid to recognize the risk of mixing up her meds, would they?" He smiled at his own joke. "But I understand, and frankly, I think it's the right choice. If they think I killed her intentionally, then it's second degree. If they think I consciously disregarded a risk, then it's voluntary manslaughter."

"They could find not guilty on both," Sam offered.

Daniels shook his head. "That won't happen. Guys go broke betting on juries, but no way. They'll get my scalp one way or the other."

"We can always tell Van Devanter we want to do a cold plea."

"I'm not pleading to anything that says I had a bad intent," Daniels said. "And if I were Lee, I wouldn't agree to involuntary manslaughter at this point. He's got us on the ropes. If there's no deal, there's no reason not to roll the dice with the jury."

"Except for Van Devanter."

"I think he will be fair."

"For your sake, I hope you're right."

"I am," Daniels said. "He's too arrogant to care about me, the public, or anything else."

Moments later, Sam's suspicions proved to be correct. Lee waived any further cross-examination; Sam didn't dare re-direct; and Lee passed on the introduction of rebuttal evidence. He had enough for a conviction and he knew it. The evidence the jury would see and hear was on the record.

Van Devanter called the noon break. Reminding the jurors of their duty to withhold judgment, he released them with a final reminder to avoid media accounts of the trial and to not discuss the matter with anyone.

When the jury had departed, he turned to Lee and Sam. "Counsel, I'll see you in chambers in fifteen minutes. Let's get the jury instructions nailed down."

When the judge was gone, Sam turned to face Daniels. "Get something to eat, but stay close in case I need your help—do you hear me?"

"Yes, boss," Daniels said sarcastically.

"Should I ask for an instruction on involuntary manslaughter?"

"No. I'll take my chances."

"Sure?" Sam urged. "This is our last shot."

Daniels shook his head. "I'm sure. You've done a good job. I appreciate everything you've done." The men stopped talking when Lee and Cates walked by within earshot. "What a sorry piece—" Daniels began.

"Stop it," Sam said. "I'm so old I think I remember when you told me not to take any of this personally. 'He's just doing his job,' I think is how you put it."

Daniels' eyes twinkled. "Doesn't sound like me at all."

Sam looked to Cassie, who had been lurking nearby. "Cassie, will you get the judge something to eat?" He watched approvingly as she took Daniels' arm and walked him out a door normally reserved for the court staff. Cassie would, Sam knew, have pre-positioned her car outside the courthouse's back door for a quick escape.

47

After lunch, Van Devanter read the instructions to the jury. "Ladies and gentlemen, I will now read the instructions of law which will guide— indeed, direct—your deliberations. Please listen closely." For half an hour, he read instructions covering everything from what to do when delibera- tions commenced to the provision of meals, if necessary. When he had finished, he looked to the jury. "Ladies and gentlemen, we will now hear the closing arguments of counsel. Mr. Lee, because he represents the State, will go first. When he concludes, Mr. Johnstone will argue on behalf of the defendant. Then, because the State has the burden of proof, Mr. Lee will have the opportunity to have the last word. Please give your attention to counsel. Mr. Lee?"

Lee had been sitting at the prosecution table with one leg crossed over the other. He acknowledged the judge's introduction, stood, and walked to the podium. "Your Honor, may I re-position the podium so that I am facing the jury?"

"You may."

When Lee had turned the podium so that it faced the jury, he smiled briefly. "May it please the court? Ladies and gentlemen, as you know, defen- dant Preston Daniels is charged with second-degree murder in the death of his wife, Marci Daniels, last April 9 I want to begin by thanking you all for your attention here in court for the past week. I am sure each of you wishes this matter was behind you. It has been a long and emotional trial, and we appreciate your attention in this difficult matter. Before I get into the details of the evidence and testimony, I want to touch briefly on the law in this matter. Judge Van Devanter has read to you the instructions you must follow, and you'll get a copy of each of the instructions he read. But I want to highlight what I think is an important point: the idea of reasonable doubt. I can almost assure you that Mr. Johnstone will ask you to find reasonable doubt—I would. But recall what the judge just told you: reasonable doubt is doubt that is reasonable, not just any doubt. Reasonable doubt. There is none in this case, and let me tell you why," he said.

"Let's begin by discussing the testimony and evidence we heard and saw during the trial. I'm not going to go witness by witness and re-play the trial —you were here," he said. "I think it is important to recall that this investigation was not commenced by law enforcement initially. No, the fact is that the deceased's death looked perfectly natural. Expected, in fact, given her long illness. No, the investigation began at the request of her family—they alerted my office. You heard from Miriam Baker. You heard from the lead investigator, Ashley Miller. Both testified the defendant himself admitted to killing his wife. To this day he will tell you he is responsible for her death. That's what he said then; that's what he says now.

"You heard from several subject matter experts in medicine, toxicology, and forensics. Now, I don't want to review their testimony except to say that through them we learned that Marci Daniels died from a fatal mixture of morphine and diazepam administered by Julie Spence, an untrained companion of the defendant's, at his direction." Lee moved from one side of the podium to the other. "You heard from Julie Spence, the aide or assistant or whatever you want to call her. Now, about Ms. Spence, I think it would be fair for you to discount her entire testimony. Why? Well, the judge just read you an instruction that said words to the effect that if you find a witness has lied in any aspect of their testimony, you are free to disregard the entirety of their testimony—remember?"

Lee pointed at Julie, who was sitting in the audience. "And we know that Ms. Spence is a congenital liar. You heard her admit she has been convicted of lying to courts before. She is undoubtedly biased—there was

no reason to hire her; she had no real experience. She owes a debt of gratitude to the defendant, one we are unsure how she planned or plans to pay.
She knew the defendant wanted Marci to die. She knew about the insurance and knew the nurse wouldn't be in. It strains credulity to believe it just
so happened that on that particular day she wouldn't check to see if he had
decreased the dosage."

Lee pointed to Daniels. "Finally, you heard from the defendant himself,
who takes responsibility for his wife's death—there is no issue with that. He
admits responsibility. The sole question confronting you is the degree of
culpability. How responsible is he? To decide that, you need to determine
who you believe, because if you think he simply 'forgot' to change out the
medicine, you must decide one way. On the other hand, if you find that the
reason the medicine wasn't changed out was the result of malice afore-
thought, you must decide differently."

Lee began gathering his materials as he spoke. "What is clear, what is
inarguable, is that Mr. Daniels is guilty of a crime. It's up to you as jurors to
decide exactly what he is guilty of. To that end, let me help. You heard Mr.
Daniels' testimony. You must decide for yourself if he was credible as a
witness. What was his motivation? Was it to tell the truth, or was it to tell a
story to save his own skin? Ask yourself what he was trying to get across.
Thank you again for your attention."

Van Devanter looked to Sam. "Mr. Johnstone, what says the defendant?"

Sam moved quickly to the podium. "May it please the court? Ladies and
gentlemen, I too wish to add my thanks for your courtesy and attention
during this trial. My client wanted one thing: a fair trial. And thanks to you
and Judge Van Devanter, he got it. My client had the opportunity to hear
the testimony and to view the evidence the State could muster. He was able
to cross-examine the State's witnesses to show that in some cases the testimony and evidence did not add up to what Mr. Lee was certain it would.
My client was provided the opportunity to have witnesses testify and
evidence introduced on his behalf. Finally, my client was allowed the
opportunity to give his side of the story."

The jurors were paying attention. This might be one of the few trials
where a closing argument made a difference. "The system—so often
derided in the press—works well in Custer. It's those of us who operate

within it who fall short, who fail to make the system operate as designed, perhaps." He smiled and was pleased to see three jurors return the smile.

"My client, as you saw, had the opportunity to defend himself, and as you saw he took advantage of that right. He called Dr. Patton, who told you that Marci was going to die, and that she may well have died from causes other than the medicine mix-up. Her opinion was in contrast to the State's expert's, but the State's expert, of course, had all the advantages, and even he couldn't dismiss altogether the possibility that Marci didn't die from the mix-up of drugs. You heard that. Dr. Patton testified that even if everything the State says is in fact true, it cannot be said with reasonable certainty that any action or inaction by my client or others directly resulted in Marci's death. That in and of itself is reasonable doubt.

"He then presented a witness—Julie Spence—who testified to her observations and experiences as to what went on in the Daniels home, and with Marci's treatment. She made no outlandish claims, she made no bald statements, she urged no position upon you; she simply testified to what she had seen and heard while doing her job. And yet, she has been repeatedly attacked and had her testimony dismissed by Mr. Lee here," Sam said, indicating Lee. "And why? For the simple reason that if you believe her testimony, then you must believe my client's. She testified she thinks my client was tired and worn out. She testified of his love for Marci and how he expressed that love. No one else can or could testify to what went on in that house. Mr. Lee had to destroy her, because he couldn't count on cross-examining my client, because as you'll recall my client didn't have to do what he did, which was to take the stand and fight for his freedom. Mr. Lee had to try and destroy her. He had to."

Sam held up a hand. "But you saw the evidence; you heard the testimony. And nowhere did you see, and nowhere did you hear, convincing evidence that what occurred was anything other than an oversight. An accident. And ladies and gentlemen, you should know: that's not a crime the State charged. They could have, and perhaps—given what you heard—they should have. But they didn't. Very simply, if you believe my client, there was no crime. And there is no reason not to do so. He has money. He has a house and a pension. He's financially stable. He loved his wife—everyone agreed on that. He took care of her for years—everyone agreed on that. He did everything humanly possible to save Marci, and his efforts weren't enough."

Sam took a sip of water. This was it. "Finally, my client took the unusual step of taking the stand—why? Because he knew that he had to. He knew that if he did not, and if he did not directly answer Mr. Lee's accusations, you might very well accept Mr. Lee's assertions. Was it a gamble? Of course. Was my client irritable and short-tempered? Absolutely. How many of you have ever been accused wrongfully? Were you happy about it? Of course not. Well, Press Daniels took the stand, and he took the best shots a doubtful Mr. Lee could deliver. He looked him in the eye and answered his questions, and right now he's looking you in the eye and asking you to do your duty. And what is your duty? Well, remember the instructions the judge gave you: if the State hasn't proven every element of a count beyond reasonable doubt, you must acquit. Not you *can* acquit, or *should* acquit, or *may* acquit. You *must* acquit. You *must*."

Making eye contact with each juror, Sam continued in a hushed voice. "Ladies and gentlemen, you took an oath. You took an oath to find the truth and to hold the State to its burden. My client asks only that you meet your burden—that you find the truth, and that you hold the State to its burden, because he believes that if you do that, you will find that you must—you must—acquit." With that, Sam nodded his thanks to the jury and sat.

"Thank you, Mr. Johnstone," Van Devanter said. "Mr. Lee, any rebuttal?"

"Briefly, Your Honor," Lee said.

While Lee concluded, Sam sat back in his chair, exhausted. His role in the trial was for the most part complete. He took a deep breath and drank water from the plastic bottle Daniels offered him. "Nice job," Daniels said, patting Sam's forearm. "One of the best closings I've heard. I appreciate it."

Sam half-listened, perspiring heavily while Lee made his rebuttal, reviewing briefly what he might have said or done better—such was the trial attorney's lot. Unproductive, but common. When Lee had finally finished, Van Devanter gave them one final instruction and sent them to the jury room for deliberations. Sam and Daniels took their chairs, awaiting the gallery's departure. Sam looked at his watch. It was three p.m.

48

By Wednesday morning the jury had been deliberating for almost a day and a half, and while that normally was a promising sign for a defendant, Sam couldn't shake his sense of dread. Waiting for a jury was one of the toughest jobs for a defense attorney, and Sam was in his office drafting a complaint for a client on a construction litigation matter and trying to keep his mind off the pending verdict. He had bills to pay and didn't have the luxury of working one case at a time, even when—as here—he had a trial ongoing. He was edgy and irritable and the thought of another sleepless night was weighing on him.

Cassie's voice on the intercom startled him. "Sam? Mary called—"

"I'm here," he said, both relieved and dreading the prospect of a verdict. "I'll be on my way in a second."

"Take your laptop."

"Why?"

"It's not a verdict," Cassie explained. "The judge says the jury has a question."

"Oh, good Lord," Sam groused. A question at this point was unusual but not unprecedented. And in Sam's experience, the response to a question was generally quickly followed by a verdict. He'd take everything he needed.

Five minutes later, Sam joined Lee and his staff and a smattering of courthouse staff in the courtroom. Daniels—looking every bit as bad as Sam had anticipated—joined them moments later. When the door to the judge's chambers opened, the small gathering stood. It was Mary. "Judge would like to see the attorneys and the accused in chambers."

Mary held the door while Lee, Cates, Sam, and Daniels filed into Van Devanter's chambers. "Jury says they are deadlocked," he said without preamble. "Thoughts?"

"Read them the instruction," Lee suggested. Wyoming had a set of pattern jury instructions courts could use to instruct juries, one of which dealt with juries considering themselves deadlocked.

Van Devanter looked to Sam. "Mr. Johnstone?"

Sam held up a finger to ask for time. He and Daniels consulted briefly. Sam nodded and addressed the judge. "They've been at it for the better part of two days," Sam said. "If we tell them to get back at it, we may well get a verdict that's the result of their not wanting to be locked down anymore, as much as the result of an impartial examination of the evidence."

"Your Honor, that's abject speculation," Lee said. "The jury has a job to do, and you need to hold their feet to the fire until they do it one way or the other."

Van Devanter sat back in his chair, fingers steepled against his mouth. "I think the jury has already done its job, Mr. Lee," he said. "For more than a week they've sat, paid attention, listened, and now have deliberated. That said, a lot of taxpayer dollars have been spent on this trial so I am going to instruct them to keep trying. I think that's best." Lee began to stand, and the judge looked at him sharply. "But I'm telling you both right now, if they come back again telling me they are deadlocked I will declare a mistrial. Let me get the instruction ready and I'll run it by you before we call for the jury. Stand by."

"What do you think?" Sam asked Daniels as they waited outside the courtroom.

"He made the right call," Daniels said. "I'da done the same thing. And you know as well as I do most questions or holdouts come from one or two jurors, and that as soon as the question is answered, or as soon as it becomes clear the judge is not going to allow them to leave without a decision, a verdict is rendered—usually within an hour."

"What do you want to do?"

"I think we'd best stay close. Maybe just hang down at your office for an hour or so."

Sam looked at his watch. "I'll have Cassie order us a couple of sandwiches."

As they walked to Sam's office, they stopped to greet several well-wishers. Most knew both Press and Marci; none could envision his having done anything to hurt her. "Got any booze?" Press asked as he opened the door for Sam.

Sam thought about it. He had a bottle in his office. "I do," he said over his shoulder. "But—"

"Sam, this is a different situation. If that jury convicts, I'm going to jail."

"Press, don't say—"

"Van Devanter will take me into custody immediately, just as he would any other defendant. He'll make a point of it."

"We'll appeal!"

"On what grounds? Virtually every important decision has gone my way. Alec knows what he is doing."

"Inefficient assistance of counsel?"

"You aren't serious." Inefficient assistance of counsel was an appeal to the court alleging that but for ineffective representation by a defendant's attorney, he or she would have been acquitted. It was the longest of long shots. "If I'm found guilty it is in part because Lee discredited Julie, but more so because I lost my cool. You know it; I know it."

Sam poured two fingers in a glass, then added a third when Daniels raised an eyebrow at him. "I know it. That sonuvabitch!"

"Doing his job."

"No!" Sam pushed the glass over to Daniels. "His job is to see to it justice is done!"

"Sam, I made some mistakes. Perhaps this *is* justice." Daniels took a long pull from the glass and smacked his lips appreciatively. "That's good stuff."

"We all have. None of us are perfect," Sam said. "I thought Julie did about as well as could be expected."

Daniels shrugged. "Agreed. He was hard on her—just like you would have been. I haven't seen her since she testified, but I heard she got fired."

"Are you serious? They had to know who and what she was before she testified. That's ridiculous. I'll talk with her; maybe there's something I can do—a threat letter, perhaps."

"Doubt that'll work. According to her employer, she got canned because her background—and her testimony—makes her uninsurable," Daniels said, draining the glass. "Sounds righteous to me. You know how insurance companies are."

"Such bullshit."

"Agreed. Hit me." Daniels indicated his glass. "Personal injury attorneys want to be able to waste a company that hires someone with a record who then does something illegal or outside the scope of employment. They're looking for deep pockets," Daniels explained. "Of course, the same attorneys cry foul because a rule like that is naturally going to impact some groups harder than others when it comes to hiring practices. And don't even get me started on profiling." Daniels drained the two fingers and looked meaningfully at Sam as he gestured with his glass. "Again."

"Press—"

"Sam, seriously, what are they going to do?" Daniels asked. "Put me in jail for having booze on my breath?"

What the hell. If the old judge wanted to get stiff, who was he to say otherwise? "Okay, but I'm here to tell you, that stuff's expensive. Got it from Max," Sam explained. "Before he died, he shipped me half a dozen bottles. Go easy on it!"

Their laughter was cut short by Cassie's knock. They exchanged a look. "Yeah?" Sam asked. It hadn't been thirty minutes since the judge had instructed the jurors to keep trying.

Cassie opened the door. "The jury's back," she said simply.

"Told ya." Daniels chugged the entire glass before standing. "I'm ready if you are," he said to Sam. "Got any gum?"

49

Sam understood the novelty of a judge being charged with his wife's murder; still, the sheer size of the crowd that had magically assembled outside the courthouse was a shock. As he and Daniels approached, the crowd parted to allow them to pass. Inside the double doors, Sam and Daniels were confronted by microphones. "Mr. Johnstone, what do you anticipate the jury doing?" "Will you appeal if the judge is convicted?" "Judge Daniels, will you remain in Custer if you are acquitted?"

Sam refused to comment, and when Daniels began to slow in preparation to say something, Sam tugged at his sleeve. "We'll talk—if necessary—after the verdict," Sam said. He was grateful for the relative quiet of the courtroom, which became even quieter when he and Daniels entered and took their seats. As was his habit, Sam took out a yellow legal pad and scribbled with a pen to make sure it worked. Why, he wasn't sure—there would be nothing to write. Daniels poured himself a glass of water from the pitcher provided. His hands were shaking so badly that Sam considered taking over, but Daniels got it done. Lee and Cates arrived in a rush. Shortly after they were seated, Violet Marshall appeared and announced the judge would arrive momentarily.

Sam took a deep breath and held it, then looked to the ceiling and counted to ten. Releasing the breath, he closed his eyes and said a brief prayer his sponsor had suggested: "God, I ask that you remove my fears and direct me to be that which you would have me be."

Mary entered, followed by Violet, followed by Van Devanter. "All rise," Marshall ordered.

Van Devanter got to the bench in three strides and looked up before being seated himself. "Please be seated," he instructed. When all had complied and the shuffling of feet, purses, coats, and other materials had quieted, he called for the jury. When the jury had been seated, he continued. "Mr. Lee, does the State agree the jury is present?"

"We do, Judge," Lee said. Sam thought he heard a slight tremor in the normally steady attorney's voice.

"Mr. Johnstone, what says the defendant?"

Sam had observed the jury closely as they entered. Not one had cast a glance Daniels' way—never a good sign. "We agree, Your Honor," he said.

Van Devanter nodded and looked to the jury. "I have been informed the jury has reached a verdict. Would the foreperson please stand and hand the verdict to Ms. Marshall?"

A slight woman in the front row stood and proffered the form, which Marshall retrieved and handed to Van Devanter, who quickly scanned it to ensure it was completed correctly and signed, then nodded in approval and handed it to Marshall.

"Ladies and gentlemen, we are about to publish the verdict. Before the clerk does so, I want to remind everyone that this is a courtroom. There are no winners and losers, only justice being done. I will not have any demonstrations, remonstrations, comments, hoots, hollers, or the like. Any reaction whatsoever will likely result in non-parties being removed from the courtroom. I hope I am clear," he added unnecessarily, then waited a few seconds before looking to Daniels. "Mr. Daniels, please stand."

When Sam and Daniels were on their feet as instructed, Van Devanter looked to Marshall. "Madam Clerk, please publish the verdict."

Marshall held the paper tightly and brought it up to her face. "As to count one, murder in the second degree, we the jury in the entitled matter find the defendant not guilty."

Sam could sense the audience's difficulty in restraining itself. Behind him, he could hear people in the gallery excitedly whispering. "Ladies and gentlemen, please restrain yourselves," Van Devanter warned.

"As to the alternative count, voluntary manslaughter, we find the defendant guilty."

Sam felt Daniels' knees buckle slightly and he reached over and held onto the older man's elbow. Van Devanter had been eyeballing Daniels throughout the reading and observed his struggle. "Thank you, Madam Clerk. Mr. Daniels, you may be seated," he said. "Counsel, do either of you wish to have the jury polled?" Polling was a way to ensure that the verdict had in fact been the verdict of each juror.

Sam looked at Daniels, who shook his head. When Sam's turn came, he stood and indicated the same to Van Devanter, who then thanked the jury, dismissed them, and asked them to wait for him in the jury room.

"Mr. Daniels, please stand," he ordered. When Sam had helped Daniels to his feet, the judge continued. "The matter having been tried to completion and the jury having returned a verdict of guilty, the court now adjudicates you guilty of one count of voluntary manslaughter. Bond is revoked, and you are remanded to the custody of the sheriff's office pending sentencing."

Over the voices of the crowd, Sam tried to make himself heard. "Your Honor! I'd ask that you reconsider. My client is aged, presents no danger to the community. Moreover, incarceration of my client will pose a hardship on the jail staff and place my client at great risk."

"Judge, the defendant—" Lee began, but was stopped short by Van Devanter's raised hand.

"As a matter of habit, Mr. Johnstone, this court takes convicted defendants into custody pending sentencing. In that way, the court can be assured that the pre-trial investigation can be undertaken and completed."

"But you don't have to have one, Judge. You know my client and his record of service. He's done nothing but good in his lifetime—"

"Except kill his wife," Lee said.

Sam turned to face Lee as the crowd murmured loudly. Van Devanter, fearing a full-blown confrontation, sought to avoid the same. "Mr. Johnstone, I have made the decision I will make today. If you wish me to reconsider, please file the appropriate motion and I will reconsider when emotions—on all sides—are not so high."

Sam sat resignedly and put a hand on Daniels' shoulder. "I'm sorry, Press."

"You did all you could, Sam," Daniels said. The men stood as the judge departed, then made a brief plan to remain in contact while the courthouse security officers stood by uncertainly.

"Judge, uh, I guess we gotta take you over to the jail," a tall, young deputy said.

"We'll look out for him, I promise," an older deputy assured Sam.

With a last look to Sam, Daniels accompanied the men from the courtroom. Sam waited until Daniels was gone, and then turned to gather his materials. A hand flashed in front of his face.

"Good job," Lee said.

Sam looked at the hand, trying to decide whether to shake it or break it. "That wasn't right," Sam said, taking Lee's soft hand.

"You're just upset you got your ass kicked," Lee replied. "Get used to it," he added, then released his grip and dashed from the courtroom to talk with the media.

Sam sat and waited, alone with his thoughts. When he checked his watch, ten minutes had passed. That should have given Lee enough time to run his mouth. He made his way to the courtroom's double doors and was immediately blinded by lights and deafened by questions. He answered questions until he had nothing more to say, then trudged to his office.

50

Several hours later, while Cathy looked at the menu, Sam walked to the bar and ordered her a glass of wine and himself a club soda.

"You want a twist of something?" Gino asked.

"Surprise me."

Gino grinned. "Don't tempt me," he said. "Go get a seat, I'll bring your drinks."

"You don't have to do that."

"I want to flirt with your girlfriend." He smiled, indicating Cathy.

"Not my girlfriend," Sam said.

Gino said, "Stop it; last time I seen you with that kind of a look on your face you was here with Victoria or Veronica or whatever her name was."

Veronica Simmons had been a judicial assistant. She and Sam had been in a relationship for a while, but his drinking and other issues had driven her off. She had left town and he hadn't heard a lot, except that she had gotten married. The mention of her name soured him some. He looked to Cathy, who was studying the menu. "Okay, but keep it cool, will you?"

"That's my job. Christ, if I couldn't keep it cool I'd be out of business in a month."

Sam smiled and walked back to the table, nodding in recognition of a few patrons along the way. Some he had defended; some he had done estate plans for; still others he had helped in one way or another. There were even some he had sued. Small-town law. He sat across from Cathy.

"I can't decide between the chicken fried steak or the chili dog," she said.

"I think it depends," Sam replied. "You looking to die of hardened arteries or gastro-intestinal disorder?"

"What are you having, Mr. Healthy?"

"Don't know. What goes good with club soda?"

"Probably a nice beet and arugula salad."

"Kill me."

When Gino showed, they decided to share an order of fried pickles. She had the chicken fried steak. "I'm running five miles tomorrow," she said by way of explanation.

"You look good to me," he said, and was immediately uncomfortable when she smiled. He ordered a burger and fries. "I'm not running anywhere," he added.

"This is the best thing that's happened to me lately," she said. "No pressure."

"I agree," he said, not agreeing at all.

They talked about work for a few moments until Cathy suddenly turned serious. She drank deeply from the wine and then licked her lips. "Can I tell you something?"

"Well, yeah," he said. He felt his stomach tighten.

"I don't think I can do this."

"Do what?"

"Defense work."

He nodded his understanding. "Then don't," he said. "Gal could make a good living doing domestic stuff and civil litigation. A lot of local attorneys who did that stuff have aged out of the game. Not many new lawyers want to practice in rural areas. There's a real need in this town."

"I'd hang myself," she said. She took another sip, then swirled the remaining wine in her glass. "I think I was born to prosecute."

He watched her closely. "I can't say I disagree. It's a mindset."

"You know, it would be one thing if defense work was like on television —nothing but innocent clients getting screwed by the system. But—"

"In real life ninety-nine percent of them are guilty as hell."

She finished the wine. "Right? I just don't know how you do it."

"Everyone deserves a defense; maybe the guilty most of all."

"Maybe, but it doesn't have to be me." She looked around the bar until she met Gino's eyes and signaled him for another round. When she had another glass on the way, she looked at Sam. "I've been doing some looking on the state bar's website. Looks like there's some jobs in Cheyenne."

He didn't want to see her leave. "Good place to practice," he offered. "State capital's there; lots of lawyers; ninety minutes to Denver."

"Yeah," she agreed. "Kayla's settled in here and all, but I just can't see myself here in five or ten years defending tweakers, drunk drivers, and wife beaters—you know?"

He was about to respond when Lee and Cates entered through a side door. Sam closed his mouth tightly while watching Lee turn in the direction of his table, with Cates trailing behind. "Well, look who's here!" Lee said a little too loudly. "The vanquished. How about I buy you two a round?"

Sam could feel his stomach muscles tighten. "Pass," he said.

"No thanks," Cathy said. "I'm driving."

"Too bad," Lee said to her. "I would give you a ride, but guess I missed my chance, huh?"

"Call it an airball," she said tightly.

"Well, I'm sorry you two feel that way. These kinds of defeats can be hard on lawyers in private practice. No one wants to hire a loser." His gestures were a little too loose, and his voice a little too loud for Sam's taste.

"Grant," Sam said, emphasizing the use of Lee's first name. "Why don't you go celebrate with your mini-me there while Cathy and I have dinner?"

Lee's smile evaporated. "Sure, Sam. I'll leave you two to lick your wounds . . . and whatever else—"

Sam was on his feet but not before Gino stepped between the two men. "Order up," he said, and placed Cathy's food first, followed by Sam's. He took a moment to place dinnerware elaborately and deliberately on the table before standing and facing Lee. "Could I offer you and your friend a table over there?" he asked, not offering at all. "Or would you prefer to sit at the bar?"

Lee stared at Sam for a moment before turning his attention to Gino. "A table would be fine," he said at last.

Sam stood and stared at Lee's back until he had been seated at a table on the other side of the room.

"Down, boy," Cathy said. She cut a piece of steak, dragged it through the gravy, and popped it into her mouth. Sam started to say something, but she picked up one of the french fries from his plate and offered it to him. "Eat. You have nothing to prove. That's what makes you comfortable to be around."

Sam took a deep breath, accepted the offered potato, and popped it in his mouth. An accounting was in order.

"I have another question," she said after cutting and eating another piece of steak.

"Sure," Sam replied.

"I've got a client threatening to shoot him," she said, indicating Lee. "And Judge Bridger."

"Get in line," Sam said too quickly. When Cathy didn't so much as smile, he sobered. "Is he serious?"

She considered the question. "I don't know. I mean, people say things all the time, but this time—"

"You have concerns."

"I do."

"The state bar has an ethics counsel," Sam advised. "Call her and ask her what to do, then do it. That's the best I can tell you."

"Good enough," she said, looking around the bar. "See the waitress anywhere?"

Across the room, Cates was eyeing his boss. "You didn't need to do that, you know," he offered. "You won."

Lee wiped the menu with a paper napkin. "I don't need to do anything. I do what I want, and what I wanted to do was send a message."

"What was the message, exactly?"

"I've been reading the great military philosophers," Lee said. "Clausewitz said, 'No military leader has ever become great without audacity.' I want Johnstone to know his days of dominating are over."

"'Great is the guilt of an unnecessary war.' That was John Adams," Cates countered. "I would say the Wyoming analogy would be, 'If you mess with a bull, you risk a horn in the ass.'"

When Gino approached, Lee looked up at him and ordered whisky. "The best you got. A little water. And make it a double. I'm feeling good."

Gino watched him closely before asking, "Anything to eat?"

"I'll pass."

"You?" Gino asked Cates.

"Just a diet cola."

"Not hungry?" Lee asked Cates when Gino had departed.

"Not really. Listen, I just . . . I just think you need to be careful with Sam. I mean, he's troubled."

"Sam's days as the big dog in town are numbered," Lee assured his young associate. When Gino brought their drinks, he raised his glass. "To victory!"

"To victory," Cates echoed, raising his glass without enthusiasm.

"Once more," Lee said to Gino. "We're celebrating. Not sure if it's the end of the beginning," he said, gesturing with a finger to himself and Cates, "or the beginning of the end." He indicated with a thumb the general direction of Sam and Cathy. "But damn, I feel good."

Gino's expression darkened. "You drivin'?" he asked Cates.

"I am now."

51

Sarah Penrose was reviewing her notes while awaiting her interview with Lee. He had readily accepted her request after yesterday's brief press conference but was running twenty minutes late. She was about to leave when he rushed by her. She could smell stale booze in his wake. Seconds later, a clerk opened the door. "Mr. Lee will see you in just a few minutes," she said.

Good Lord. "Fine," Penrose said tightly. She had made it clear that she would be on deadline, so what was up with the power play? She was texting her editor (who was also the publisher) to see if he could hold the front page for her when the door finally opened.

"Ms. Penrose? Would you come with me?" When Sarah stood and extended her hand, Lee shook his head. "I'm sorry," he said. "Ever since the pandemic I don't shake hands."

She followed him down the hall, wondering if he urinated with gloves on, and sat when asked to do so. She looked around his office once more at the spartan decor. Aside from a couple of stock photos depicting Wyoming landscapes there was nothing to indicate where they were, and if one were to remove the framed diploma and law license it could have been anyone's office. In her experience, most experienced attorneys' offices were testaments to career accomplishments.

"You have some questions for me?" he asked without preamble. He poured bottled water into a tall glass.

"I do," she said, opening her purse and extracting a mobile voice recorder. "You don't mind?"

He apparently gave it some thought, weighing the options. "I do not," he said at last.

"My first question has to do with the recent trial of Judge Daniels. What—"

"He's retired."

"Indeed. What are your thoughts regarding the trial of *Preston* Daniels?"

"What do you mean?"

"Was justice done?"

He shrugged. "Of course. He was convicted by a jury of his peers."

"Was it the proper verdict?"

Lee dropped two tablets into the glass of water. "You were there. You saw the evidence and heard the witnesses testify. What do you think?"

"Not for me to say," she said.

"Me neither. But for the record I absolutely believe justice was done. The evidence demonstrated clearly that *Mister* Daniels killed his wife— probably for her insurance policy proceeds." He stuck a long index finger into the glass and stirred the contents, then stuck the finger in his mouth.

Sarah resisted the urge to say something along the lines of "Ew!" "And yet the jury convicted only on the lesser count of voluntary manslaughter," she countered.

"The jury likely sympathized to some extent with the defendant. Human nature." He shrugged again.

"The defendant's witness, Julie Spence—"

"Testified untruthfully. She was clearly covering for her employer," he added, then drank the concoction. "He probably had offered her something in return for her testimony." He pushed his glasses up to the bridge of his nose with a knuckle.

"But she swore to tell the truth," Sarah countered. "She seemed credible to many of us."

"People lie all the time," Lee said, then belched. "Sorry, must be some-thing I ate. Clearly, the jury didn't buy her story."

"Judge Daniels used to say that in a trial either everyone was a winner, or everyone was a loser," Penrose said. When Lee simply stared at her, she continued. "If justice was done, he would say everyone won. On the other hand, if there was injustice, everyone lost. Do you agree?"

"I think that's a very naïve way to look at things," Lee opined. "Guilty people should be convicted. Innocent people should walk. I don't charge innocent people."

"What will you recommend at sentencing?"

"I'm not going to go into all that except to say that the fact that he was a judge will not impact my recommendation. In fact, I think it is an aggravating circumstance. He needs to be made an example of."

"Do you expect Sam Johnstone to appeal?"

Lee snorted. "On what grounds? The trial was fair. The judge was impartial. I charged his client because I knew he was guilty, and the jury agreed. I'm not saying he won't appeal, you understand—I'm just saying there are no good grounds for an appeal."

"I'll be looking to hear more from you following sentencing."

"I understand."

"Thank you for seeing me."

"Thank you," Lee said. When she was gone, he sat for a long time, feeling much better and wondering why she hadn't brought a photographer.

52

On the first Monday in April, Van Devanter looked critically at himself in the mirror. He was expecting a sizeable crowd—it wasn't often a former judge was sentenced. This was going to be an emotional hearing; Lee had lined up half a dozen members of Marci Daniels' family, each of whom was expected to call for a severe sentence. Lee himself would ask that Daniels serve as an example, citing a breach of public trust and the like. Sam Johnstone, of course, would argue that Daniels had already suffered enough, that nothing would bring Marci back, that Wyoming law did not countenance making an example of someone, and the like. In sum, Van Devanter would confront irreconcilable positions and would have to make the decision regarding a man's life and liberty functionally unassisted.

"This is why they pay us the big bucks," he said as he exited the restroom adjacent to his temporary chambers.

"Pardon?" Mary asked.

He hadn't seen her. She was straightening a file rack on a credenza, getting things ready for Judge Bridger, who had taken the day off. This must be difficult for Mary. "Mary, I just want you to know—"

"You're just doing your job," she interrupted. "I've been around this business for a long time. It's not easy on you, I know."

"You were with him for years," he observed.

"Eighteen," she said, placing folders in the rack. She turned to him. "He was very good to work for, you know. A very kind and considerate man."

"I didn't know him well. We only saw each other a couple of times per year. That's part of the reason I was asked to preside," he explained. "For your sake, I wish it had turned out differently."

"Me, too." She wiped away a tear. "It's just such a . . . tragedy . . . for everyone."

"A death like this one always is," he observed. He looked at his watch. "Well, I guess we can't put this off much longer, can we? Will you let me know when everyone is in place?"

"Certainly," she said. "Closed?" she asked, referring to the door.

"Please," he said. He needed to take one more look in the mirror.

Sam had braced himself for the worst, but when court security entered the holding cell next to the courtroom and led Daniels in to meet with him, he was shocked. Incarceration took a toll on the elderly, and Daniels looked as if he had aged ten years in the weeks since the trial. Van Devanter had denied Sam's motion for his client's pre-trial release, and Daniels' pallor was now gray from a lack of Vitamin D—and wasn't helped by the stubble on his face. If he had shaved at all it had been a poor attempt. The orange jumpsuit had been a good fit at the time it had been issued, but Daniels' subsequent weight loss was evident, and the clothing sagged on his shoulders. Although Sam had visited Daniels several times since the trial, he was concerned.

"I must look pretty bad, huh?" Daniels asked as he took a seat.

"You look . . . fine," Sam lied.

"Never try to bullshit a bullshitter." Daniels laughed. "Security bubbas tell me there's a big crowd; the sharks smell blood in the water," he observed. "Ain't often you get to see a judge get his."

Sam smiled ruefully but said nothing.

Daniels examined his chained hands. "Sam, relax. The jury's decision is final. Van Devanter ran a good, clean trial. Lee did his job; you did yours. The jury found me guilty. It's that simple."

"No, it isn't," Sam seethed. "Lee is an unethical bastard who should probably be disbarred!"

"I don't know about disbarred, but I'll agree his behavior in court was probably unethical and—"

"Probably?"

"Sam, the cross-examination of a witness on behalf of a client is complicated stuff. You and I were able to observe what happened first-hand. But a bar review committee or an appellate court looking at a transcript won't see or hear the condescension, the distaste, and the disrespect he showed Julie. It's unlikely that anyone could get the full effect of just how Julie was discredited, and how it was done."

"But he is a prosecutor!" Sam cried. "He's supposed to stand for justice!" Realizing he was speaking louder than he intended, Sam involuntarily cringed.

"Sometimes your all-American attitude is endearing," Daniels said. "At others, it is almost childishly naïve." It stung, but Sam let it go. "Sam, it's going to be fine."

"It's not fine. It's a travesty."

"He'll give me a split and place me on probation—that's what the presentence investigation's recommendation is," Daniels predicted. Seeing Sam's reaction, he continued, "I know what you're thinking. You're thinking he might want to make an example of me, or he might overcompensate to show that he treats everyone the same. But Van Devanter isn't like that. First off, he is a good judge. Second, he is retired and so incredibly arrogant he could care less what anyone thinks."

They could only hope. "Okay, well, I'll see you in there," Sam said.

Daniels stood. "Thanks, Sam. For everything."

Moments later, just minutes away from learning his client's fate, Sam looked to the courtroom's ceiling fans, took and held several deep breaths, and said a brief prayer. He started when he felt Daniels' hand on his. "It'll be fine, son," Daniels assured him. "It will be what it will be."

They stood together as Van Devanter entered the courtroom and sat with the others when commanded to do so. "Good morning, ladies and gentlemen, we are on the record and are here for sentencing in State versus Daniels. The State is present and represented by Mr. Lee. The defendant appears and is represented by Mr. Johnstone. It's nine o'clock according to my watch." Van Devanter looked to Lee. "Is the State prepared to proceed?"

"We are, Judge," Lee said.

"Mr. Johnstone?"

Sam stood on shaky legs. "We are, Your Honor."

Van Devanter donned his reading glasses. "The parties were provided with the results of a pre-sentence investigation. Per the rule, it looks like the court received it in a timely fashion. Mr. Johnstone, have you and Mr. Daniels had the opportunity to review the report?"

"We have, Judge." Under Wyoming law, a pre-sentence investigation was generally required prior to sentencing for felonies. The investigation was conducted by probation and parole officers employed by the Department of Corrections and included information on the defendant's childhood and family, education, employment, and criminal history. The intent was to give the sentencing judge a look at the defendant's past and to include therein mitigating and extenuating circumstances regarding the crime, to alert the court to any aggravating factors, and to provide a forum for victim impact statements. Sam and Daniels had gone over Daniels' report, which—as one might expect—revealed a life well-led.

"Are there any corrections or changes the defendant wishes to make on the record?"

"None," Sam said. As Daniels had noted, the pre-sentence report recommended he receive a "split" sentence, meaning he be sentenced to a prison term, but that the prison time be suspended and that he serve up to a year in the county's detention center before being released on probation. Because Daniels would be credited with about fifty days served by Sam's count, if the judge adopted the recommendation, Daniels would still face another ten months in jail. When the time came, Sam would argue for time served and Daniels' immediate release on probation.

Van Devanter was making notes as he went. When he finished, he looked to Lee. "Does the State have a recommendation?"

"We do, Judge." Lee stood and walked to the podium. Nominally, he was addressing the court, but those involved knew his remarks were for publication. "We are here today as the result of a tragedy. The death of a woman who had much left to give is tragic, of course, but that tragedy is compounded when, as the evidence in this matter showed, her death was the direct result of actions taken by this man," Lee said, pointing to Daniels for emphasis, "the man whom she entrusted with her care. The very man who took an oath to care for her and to love her in sickness and in health. The other, unspoken tragedy is the loss suffered by others."

Lee then called Miriam and other family members who testified tearfully to Marci's central role in their lives. When they had completed their remarks, Lee resumed his place at the podium and delivered a soliloquy espousing his theory that Daniels had long planned to kill Marci for the insurance proceeds and that when her illness presented itself, he had taken advantage of the circumstances and had seen to it that she underwent questionable—even hare-brained—treatments rather than await more traditional ones. While Lee spoke, Sam felt himself getting angry. He took deep breaths and tried to meditate but could feel his blood pressure rising.

At one point, Daniels leaned over to him. "Easy, Sam. It's all part of the show. Be calm, son."

Sam nodded. Lee then embarked on a long diatribe regarding what he viewed as a gradual degradation in the value society placed on marriage and the lessening of respect given social institutions, including the courts. Sam doodled and tried to remain calm, but when Lee reiterated that Daniels' facilitating the treatments in Mexico was part of a scheme to see Marci die, he stood.

"Your Honor, I've never objected to a sentencing recommendation before, but counsel is espousing some sort of conspiracy that was not brought forth at trial, and for which there is no evidence."

"I'm only making observations regarding what the evidence revealed about the character of the defendant," Lee replied.

"Your Honor, he's got no right—"

"I've not only got a right, but I've got a duty—"

"To see justice done!" Sam interrupted. "A duty you apparently have no interest in!"

"Gentlemen, please approach," Van Devanter said. He took his readers off and sighed heavily as the two attorneys approached. When they were in front of him, he stared hard at each. "Counsel, your personal animosity is well known and—now that I've spent time with you both—perhaps understandable. But it is beginning to influence events here, and I won't have it. I expect each of you to be on your most professional behavior."

"Your Honor, he is putting matters on the record that are pure speculation," Sam said. "He's assigning motives and making pejorative judgments about things that—again—are not of record."

Van Devanter replaced his readers. "I'm aware of that, Counsel. I was at the trial, remember? I expect you to keep your poise, and I demand any objections to be offered professionally," he scolded. He then turned his attention to Lee, who had been enjoying Sam's tongue-lashing. "Mr. Lee, I've been sitting here wondering if your sentencing recommendation here today has any relationship to the trial of Mr. Daniels over which I presided, or if it is entirely founded upon some theory of social and connubial relationships you harbor."

"Your Honor, I—"

"I'm still talking, Counsel—do not interrupt me again! Now, what I want to hear when you get back to your place is your recommendation and the rule-based foundation therefore—you know what this court's sentencing criteria are. Please confine your argument to relevant considerations and save your opinions for yourself. I'm not interested in your theories regarding social norms, the criminal justice system, or anything else. Now, back to your places!" Van Devanter watched as Lee and Sam returned to their places. When Lee was at the podium, Van Devanter ordered him to continue.

"Judge, I think the pre-sentence investigation does a fine job of laying out mitigating circumstances. Clearly, the defendant has done some positive things in his life. But nothing can diminish the level of evil revealed in his actions. And we cannot and should not forget the victim in all of this, Marci Daniels. Marci Daniels, who took a vow to love and support her husband, and to remain faithful in sickness and in health, thinking her husband would reciprocate, never imagining he would take her life when the going got tough." Lee took a drink of water and looked at Daniels. "Your Honor, the court has the victim impact statements in front of it. Therein, you can read in those statements, written with heart-wrenching emotion, about a woman who spent her life in support of her husband; a woman who was smart and articulate and who sacrificed any thoughts of a career of her own to ensure her husband's star continued to rise; a woman who was caring and loving and singularly devoted to the man who killed her."

Sam took a drink of water and noted that his hands were shaking. He snuck a peek at the judge. Van Devanter had been on the bench for years before he retired and was difficult to read. Sam could only hope he was seeing Lee's rant as the hyperbolic appeal to emotion that it was. He looked to a stoic Daniels and wondered how the man could remain so calm while his character and reputation were being torn apart. He looked to the ceiling and practiced his deep-breathing exercises.

At last, Lee wound down. "Your Honor, we believe that the facts of the trial revealed a man not appropriate for rehabilitation and not fit to walk among those of us in society. He showed himself willing to violate the most sacrosanct of vows—that of marriage—and to commit the most heinous of crimes—the taking of another's life. For these reasons, the State recommends you impose a sentence of seven to ten years in the Wyoming State Penitentiary."

The murmuring in the audience began when Lee articulated the years and reached a dull roar when he requested it be imposed. "Thank you, Your Honor," Lee said as he took his chair, but not before looking out over the audience.

When Lee was seated, Van Devanter looked to Sam. "Mr. Johnstone, do you or Mr. Daniels desire to be heard?"

"Both, Judge," Sam said. When he was on his feet at the podium, he took a deep breath and began. "Your Honor, the jury has spoken. After a trial on the merits, they found my client, Preston Daniels, guilty of voluntary manslaughter. We don't necessarily agree with the verdict, but we respect the process. The question is, what now? What proper sentence for a man who has led a life of service. What sentence can the court impose that will be just and proper for all?"

Sam was struggling to get his breathing under control, so he stopped for a drink of water. "Your Honor, state law requires a pre-sentence investigation be accomplished prior to sentencing. You ordered it and one was prepared, and I think anyone who has seen more than a handful of these was struck by the life of the individual it portrays. My client, by all accounts, has led an exemplary life, one characterized by accomplishment and service to others. Except for the matter bringing us here today, he has never received so much as a parking ticket. By all accounts, he was a loving and caring husband for decades. How then to sentence? The books written by law professors tell us there are generally recognized purposes for sentencing in our system of criminal justice: general deterrence, specific deterrence, incapacitation, rehabilitation, and retribution. Examining each, it is easy to dismiss several. General deterrence, given today's media over-load, is a concept fading fast. Specific deterrence? Well, suffice to say my client will learn no lesson to be applied in the future. Incapacitation? My client poses no risk to the community at large—the pre-sentence investiga-tion makes that clear. Rehabilitation? My client has no bad habits or traits of character that require remediation. That leaves retribution, Your Honor. The idea that society has the right to get even."

Sam pointed to Daniels, who was sitting rigidly upright on the wooden chair. "With this man?" Sam asked rhetorically. "How does society get even with this man? This is a man who, on balance, has given far more to society than he has or could receive in return. This is a man who for decades presided over cases just like his own, and who recommended sentences with compassion and an understanding of the issues on both sides—a perspective that seems to have been lost on our current prosecutor." Sam looked pointedly at Lee and then to Van Devanter. "I'm not arguing there is no right to retribution—there is. And I'm not arguing it isn't proper in this case—it is. What I'm arguing is that this man, who gave so much, has already lost everything. Everything. First and foremost, he lost the woman he loves. He lost the respect of his family. He lost a fortune paying medical bills. He will lose his good standing in the judicial community and license to practice law. He has spent approximately fifty days in jail—at the risk of his life each day. The other inmates know who he is. His former occupation put him in contact with many of them. It doesn't take a conspiracy theorist to conjure up thoughts of one or more offenders seeking to get even. For these reasons, Your Honor, I'm going to ask that you impose a time-served sentence and place my client on probation for a duration of time and under terms as you see fit. My client will agree to and comply with whatever terms of probation you set. He poses no risk whatsoever to the community but rather is at risk while incarcerated. I ask that you sentence not to send a message or to placate the bloodthirsty among us, but that you sentence fairly and with an eye toward both my client and the crime itself. Thank you."

Van Devanter nodded. "Thank you, Mr. Johnstone," he said before turning his attention to Daniels. "Mr. Daniels, you of course have the right to address the court before I impose a sentence."

Daniels stood and took a deep breath. "I know well how difficult this is for you, Your Honor—and I don't envy you the task. I know that whatever your decision, you will be criticized for it. That's part of the job, of course. I don't have a lot to say. The jury rendered its verdict. I respect their verdict and thank them for their service. I was well-served by my friend and counsel, Sam Johnstone. I received a fair trial, one overseen by you, and I thank you for coming out of retirement to preside." He turned to face Marci's family. "To Marci's family, I can only say that I am so very sorry for the way this turned out. For more than forty-five years, I loved that woman with every fiber of my being. I wasn't the best at showing it; I regret that sometimes I took her for granted, and if I could go back in time and do it all again, I'd choose her again to be my wife."

He looked to the table and then to her family. "I alone am responsible for her death," he said, and waited for the murmuring to die down before continuing. "It was my responsibility to see to her care. I failed her. I failed you. I failed myself. For that, I will never forgive myself." He then looked to Van Devanter. "Your Honor, sentence me as you will. I deserve no less."

"You deserve to rot in prison! You killed my sister!" It was Miriam Baker, Marci's sister.

"Miriam," Daniels began.

"Madam, please be quiet!" Van Devanter barked. "If you cannot control yourself, I will have you removed!" He looked around the courtroom, his eyes searching the faces of each spectator. "Ladies and gentlemen, I ask once more that you quiet yourselves. This defendant—and this process—deserve this court's undivided attention. There will be no additional warnings. Are we clear?" he asked unnecessarily.

Seeing no response, Van Devanter began with general observations. "This has been one of the more difficult cases I have encountered in my nearly fifty years' involvement in the legal profession. Not from the standpoint of the legal issues involved—I've seen many more complicated cases. Not from the horror aroused—while it was in fact horrific for those involved, we are all aware of cases beset with facts that make our skin crawl. No, this case was one fraught with difficulty due to the personalities involved."

Warming to the task, Van Devanter continued. "The defendant appears before this court, just as he did the jury, with a commendable—remarkable, even—record of service to his fellow man. The pre-sentence report shows a man of compassion and steadiness, a man who dedicated every day of his professional life to the service of others. The report reveals an equally compassionate and service-oriented victim. By all accounts, before her illness, they were 'on their way to forever, together,' as a long-forgotten radio host used to say." Van Devanter looked up from his outline and saw a number of heads nodding in agreement—even some of those who sat behind Lee in support of the State.

"But something went terribly wrong. This court cannot know with certainty exactly what went wrong or when, but it is unquestioned that somewhere along the line something happened. This court won't comment on the propriety of the treatments sought, or the wisdom of a man attempting to see to his wife's treatment by himself—that's for others to decide. What this court can say, and what the defendant has openly acknowledged here today, is what the jury said: Mr. Daniels was criminally responsible for his wife's untimely death. This court, then, faces the task of imposing a sentence that reflects Mr. Daniels' responsibility for his wife's death as well as his history of service to his fellow man, while assessing the risk posed to the rest of us. The court agrees with Mr. Johnstone's assertion that society has a right to retribution, and the court agrees with Mr. Johnstone that this is not the kind of case that lends itself to "sending a message," as Mr. Lee would have it do. Therefore, the sentence in this matter is intended to send a message only to Mr. Daniels. Mr. Daniels, please stand."

Sam helped Daniels to his feet, placing a hand under his elbow to lift and then steady the older man. Daniels might well need some physical therapy when he was released.

"It is the sentence of this court that you will serve three to five years in the Wyoming State Penitentiary. I will suspend all but six months and will place you on five years of supervised probation. I will credit you with fifty-one days served to this point." He then explained the terms of Daniels' probation. "You will serve the balance of your imposed sentence—one hundred twenty-nine days, if my math is right—at the detention center here in Custer. You may be seated."

While Van Devanter explained his client's right to appeal, Sam sat alone with his thoughts. There was little to say to Daniels, who had been resigned to whatever punishment was coming his way. For his part, Sam was disappointed but not surprised. He had hoped for a time-served sentence, but it certainly wasn't as bad as it could have been.

When Van Devanter finished, he looked to Daniels. "You are remanded to the custody of the sheriff's office," he said, then adjourned the proceedings and departed. Most of the audience, as well as Lee and his entourage, left quickly. When Sam and Daniels were alone, they stood. Sam gave the court security officers a look, and they stepped back, giving the pair some space.

"I'm sorry," Sam said, blinking back tears of frustration.

"Sam, it's fine. You did a good job—as fine a job as could have been done." Daniels took one of Sam's hands into both of his own. "I didn't give you a helluva lot to work with," he advised. "It was inevitable."

"The sentence—"

"Was right on the money," Daniels finished.

"We'll appeal."

"No," Daniels said. "I haven't retained you to appeal, and I won't sign off on any appeal." Seeing Sam's downcast look, he continued, "Sam, look at it this way. I'll be out of jail before Labor Day. I'm ready," he said to the officers.

"Sorry," one of the officers said to Sam.

"No problem. Take care of yourself," he croaked as Daniels was led away.

"Don't worry about me," Daniels replied.

"I won't," Sam lied.

He waited for a few minutes, pondering what he would say to the assembled press. When he was sure he could discuss the subject of Daniels' sentencing without losing his temper, he stood, gathered his materials, and made his way toward the double doors.

"Tough luck," Jack Fricke observed as he vacuumed the floor between the rows of pews that observers had occupied just moments before.

Sam mumbled an acknowledgement and opened the doors to a raucous crowd.

"Bad day for Judge D," Fricke commented. He pocketed two quarters he found on a seat. "On the other hand, this might be my lucky day."

53

Punch took a bite from a sandwich that Rhonda had made him and looked at his watch. He had only been watching the room for an hour, but it seemed like he'd been in place for days. He reflected briefly on how many times he had staked out a room in this very motel over the years—ten? Fifteen? You'd think people would learn. According to Sam, his client had bought fentanyl from Gustafson and subsequently overdosed. Punch was well aware the feds were after bigger fish, but the people of Custer needed a little help. And maybe, just maybe, if he got Gustafson by the balls he would roll on whoever his supplier was. He wouldn't bet on it, of course, but Gustafson was a squirrelly little dude and Punch couldn't see him doing some serious time without real trouble.

He had drafted an affidavit of probable cause that referred to Sam's client as Confidential Informant 1 and omitted Sam's name. Lee was all over it, of course —nothing would make him happier than to prosecute someone for dealing fentanyl. Downs was a little more problematic; the idea of signing a warrant on the basis of uncorroborated, unsworn testimony from a user was unsettling, but in the end she had signed it. Punch had briefed the local law enforcement folks, and had a team that was comprised of Miller, Ron Baker from the Custer police, and himself. The plan was to pop Gustafson when he emerged from the motel room. Because they didn't believe he knew Miller, they'd parked and disabled an old Buick in front of the motel, down a couple of rooms. Miller would turn the car over occasionally, and act like she was on the phone to someone. Gustafson's car was in the other direction from the room, so if all went according to plan he would either offer some gentlemanly assistance, or —more likely—head the other way, in which case she would put the grab on him. Baker was wearing cotton utility clothes, posing as a maintenance worker.

Punch manned the radio and ate his sandwich. He was drinking the last of the lukewarm coffee from his thermos when Gustafson stepped from the motel room, looked quickly in the direction of Miller, and then—as predicted—headed in a near-run in the other direction toward his car. Miller leapt from her vehicle and quickly closed on Gustafson. Punch was exiting his own vehicle and saw Gustafson run smack dab into Baker, who used an arm bar to push the much smaller Gustafson up against the door of a room until Miller arrived and the pair quickly cuffed him. By the time Punch arrived, Baker was already advising Gustafson of his rights. "Do you understand?"

"Kiss my ass," Gustafson replied.

"Nice," Punch said. "Get him out of here," he said to Baker. "Miller, you wanna come with me? Let's go see what Sam's client has to say."

Miller nodded and together they walked to the room Gustafson had just exited, which Sam had indicated was Clay's. Punch knocked loudly. "Clay? This is the police. Just want to talk with you."

Hearing no response, he put his ear to the door. "Don't hear anything," he said, then indicated the window. "Can you see anything?"

Miller cupped her hands over her eyes and peered into the room. "I can see a foot. Looks like he's on his back on the bed. Hit it again." Punch pounded on the door anew, ordering Clay to answer. "He isn't moving," she said.

Punch tried the door and found it unlocked. "Let's go," he said, drawing his pistol. She drew her own and followed him into the room. "He's blue," Punch said. "Damn it! Gimme your naloxone."

Miller handed her device to Punch and was clearing the bathroom when she stopped. "Shit! Punch! We got another one down!"

Punch stepped over Clay to the bathroom door, peered in, and saw a young woman on her back on the floor. "Damn it! Call dispatch!" He returned to Clay's lifeless form and administered the drug. When nothing happened, he yelled to Miller, "You got another one?"

"No. Baker will have one."

"Get him in here. And then get anyone else who's got one here."

Sam had fallen asleep on his couch. The knock on the door startled him. He found the small revolver on the kitchen counter, pocketed it, and made his way to the front door, reminding himself for the hundredth time that he needed to get "eyes on"—some sort of device to see who was at his door without his opening it. He took a breath and opened the door, standing to the side for protection.

It was Punch. "Sam, I've got some bad news."

"Come on in," Sam exhaled, gesturing with his free hand.

Punch followed Sam into the kitchen and declined a cup of coffee or glass of water. "I gotta get going. I just wanted you to know, your buddy Clay? He overdosed again. I'm not sure he's gonna make it."

"Shit."

"I did what I could, Sam. Hit him with a dose of naloxone, and I even put the defibrillator on him. Doc says he's fighting."

"I'm sure," Sam said. "You know, I checked him out. Got ahold of his military file. He's the real deal. A hero."

"I'm sorry, Sam. Anything I can do?"

"Yeah. You can arrest Gustafson."

"Done. There was a kid with them, too—she didn't make it."

"A kid?"

"Yeah. I'd say sixteen, maybe seventeen."

"That's a big-time felony," Sam commented. "He'll do serious time for that. How'd you get him?"

"I got sick of seeing his smart-ass running around town, ruining lives, so me and Miller jumped him." Punch accepted Sam's offer of a fist-bump. "The chief and sheriff were against it, but with this kid dead—"

"He's hosed," Sam said, referring to Gustafson. "Grab him by the short and curlies and I'm sure he'll start talking."

"I'm not so sure."

"Why not?"

"Cause he's thinking he's got an ace up his sleeve."

"What's that?"

"He says he's gonna hire you."

Sam shook his head vigorously. "Not enough money in the world."

54

Julie closed her eyes and recited the Serenity Prayer. Her seven-year-old daughter, Kira, had been dawdling over her dinner for thirty minutes, and Julie was trying to keep her temper under control. "Finish your dinner, Kira. Now. I gotta be at work in twenty minutes!"

"Mommy, why do you have to go to work at night?" Kira asked. "Can't you stay here with me?"

"You know I can't, honey. I told you, Mommy lost her other job. I gotta work at the store until I can find something else. Now, go get your shoes and coat on. I packed you a snack you can eat at Grandma's house."

Kira folded her arms. "I don't want to go to Grandma's house. I want to stay here with you!"

"Kira, honey. Please don't make this harder than it is," Julie said. "Now let's get going. I don't want to be late."

At last, Kira complied, and minutes later they pulled up in front of Julie's ex-mother-in-law's house. Julie rang the doorbell and Jackie answered, lit cigarette dangling from her mouth. Julie frowned; she had asked Jackie not to smoke in front of Kira.

"Grandma!" Kira raised her hands, hoping to be scooped up by Jackie, but Jackie turned and walked back to a tattered recliner and sat without saying a word. She ashed her cigarette and Julie noted a tall glass filled with ice and amber liquid. "Would you have her in bed by nine, please?" she asked. "I'll be back around six-fifteen, so if you'll have her up and ready I'll get her home for breakfast and ready for the bus."

Jackie didn't answer, so Julie turned her attention to Kira. "Gimme a kiss." They embraced and Kira held her more tightly than usual. "It's gonna be fine, pumpkin. Stay with Grandma tonight. When you're in school tomorrow, Mommy is going to be out looking for a new job like the last one."

"And then you can be home at night with me?"

"In or out?" Jackie snarled. "Runnin' up my heating bill. Bad enough you can't keep a job or get one that pays and I gotta watch your kid—don't be runnin' up my bills, too."

Julie took a deep breath. "Sleep tight, sweet pea. I'll bring you something from the store—okay?"

"A donut?"

"Maybe," Julie said, knowing she would. She kissed Kira again and left quickly before the tears formed. That was the last thing Kira needed.

The twelve-hour shift had begun at six p.m., and when she glanced at her watch, she died a little inside when she saw it was only nine. Had it only been three hours? My God, it was going to be a long night. She hadn't always loved her job as a home health care worker—who would? Between holding old people's hands, telling them they would get better, cleaning up messes, feeding and bathing . . . It was a tough and largely thankless job. But it was better than this.

Following her termination, she had applied at a number of similar agencies, but word had gotten around and no one else would hire her, citing insurance issues. The natural resource industry was struggling, so after some soul-searching she had applied at a number of retail outlets, finally landing this job as the "assistant manager" of a 24-hour convenience store. And—wouldn't you know?—it was right on Teton Avenue, and every jerk she had ever met stopped by. "How you doin', Julie?" "Good to see you, Julie." "Julie, you maybe want to hang out sometime?" Made her want to barf, although not like cleaning out the restrooms did. Good Lord. Between people shooting up, passing out, and leaving messes in the toilet that would gag a maggot, she was glad she had a strong stomach.

Her boss was a wicked recovering meth addict. According to her name tag, she'd been at the store for a couple of years, and—probably because anyone in their right mind would have quit by now—had risen to manager. As Julie understood it, the woman had gotten wrapped around the axle with a charge of endangering children, and now with her daughter in treatment, her son in jail, and her daughter's baby daddy in prison, she was scrambling to get custody of a grandkid back from the Department of Family Services, which was talking about adopting the kid out. Accordingly, between her frequent smoke breaks and talking on her phone about screwed-up judges and dim-witted lawyers to what was apparently an endless supply of sympathetic ears, the manager didn't do much except nag at Julie—and tonight was no exception.

"What are you doing?" she asked Julie.

"I'm wiping down the counter," Julie said. "I can't believe the mess people make just putting sugar and creamer in coffee, can you?"

"Get used to it. Good thing for you to do," the manager said, pulling a lighter from the pocket of her filthy embroidered company shirt. "When's the last time you cleaned that shitter?"

"Two hours ago, just like it says on the checklist."

"Well, I'm gonna go have me a smoke—maybe two. When you get done with that counter, you get in there and clean off them floors in the bathrooms—they're nasty."

She put a lighter to a generic cigarette and turned to leave the store, then turned back. She reached into a display case and withdrew a large folding knife that was for sale. "Just in case some pervert decides to give me trouble."

Like that would happen. *Bite your tongue, girl*, Julie reminded herself. *You need this job.* "Right," she said, wiping feverishly and almost gagging in mere anticipation of the sights and smells she would soon encounter.

In his basement office, Lee checked his watch and saw it was a little after nine. Probably safe to leave now. As county attorney, it was his job to set the example. For too long, these people had been working eight to five. It was time to put some effort into this job, and to get the kind of results that hard work alone could bring.

Well, that and natural talent.

He shut down his computer and put the papers on his desk in neat stacks according to case or subject. He'd start with those in the morning. Satisfied all was in order, he turned out the light, locked his door, and walked out of the courthouse to his car. He was halfway to the townhouse he was renting when the fuel light came on.

"Aw, crap," he said aloud. In his hurry to be the first to the office that morning, he'd forgotten to stop and fill up. He hated putting gas in a car wearing a suit, and he hated even more going out in public wearing a suit in a town where the usual dress was steel-toed or cowboy boots to go with denim and flame-retardant shirts. On the other hand, he could use something cold. He made a left turn and pulled into an all-night convenience store located on Teton Avenue. While the tank was filling, he decided to kill two birds with one stone, and walked toward the store, intending to get that drink. To the side of the front door was a plump, pink-haired, vaguely familiar fiftyish woman with a name tag he couldn't read affixed sloppily on her shirt. She was sitting on a plastic chair next to a coffee can. She pulled on a cigarette and eyed him suspiciously with one eye, the other closed to avoid the smoke.

"Evening," he said simply as he passed her by.

"Evening," she said.

He saw in the reflection of the window that as he passed, she took a long, final drag and then tossed the butt in the coffee can. He retrieved a soda and on impulse purchased an ice cream sandwich, then made his way to the unstaffed counter. He stood for a few seconds and then looked around the store. He saw the back side of a woman with a mop and bucket, but when he said, "Hello?" she didn't turn around. He looked to the entry and saw the employee still at the front of the store, staring at him, hands on hips. Next to her, the smoke from the discarded butt rose in the cool night air. "A little help here?" he indicated with his hands as he spoke the words aloud.

The woman sighed heavily and entered the store, then walked slowly behind the counter and rang up his items. "That it?"

This woman was a peach. "That's it," Lee said.

"Run yer card, then."

Lee noted that she was watching him closely as he did so. He'd been recognized. Probably from the newspaper. There was a stack of the local birdcage liners near the door. He nodded and turned to leave.

"You don't recognize me, do you?" the woman asked.

The hair on the back of his neck rose with her words. Probably best to leave. He looked at her name tag and remembered. "Uhhh, Misty, is it?"

"It is. You should remember me, since you've spent a fair amount of time ruinin' my life." As she spoke, she moved from behind the counter to a position between Lee and the door.

"Misty, look. I don't want any trouble. I'm sure there's been some sort of mistake," he said as he backed up a step.

"No mistake. You been trying to take my grandkid. I tol' you them drugs belonged to my son Kyle, but you insisted on charging me with endangerin' children. Endangerin' children! Me! The only person who has been raising Aristotle since he was born. So now I got a felony and I'm gonna lose my job when H.R. finds out. And I'm gonna lose my grandkid because you insisted on charging me even though it wasn't my drugs!" She moved forward menacingly.

"The jury decided you knew the drugs were there," he said. "That's a crime!" He felt his pulse quicken as she took another step forward. Very quietly he told her he had a concealed firearm, but when she pulled a knife from a sleeve, he yelled in panic, "Stop! I was only doing my job!"

When she swiped at him with the knife, he drew the weapon as he had been taught and fired. He watched in horror as she fell, striking her head on the corner of a stained linoleum counter, sending discount candy bars and bags of chips flying. She struggled briefly as if she would stand, and he shot her again. Finally, she fell to the dirty floor, gurgled slightly, and went silent. Lee holstered the pistol and stood over her, unsure of what to do.

A woman's voice from the area of the restroom. "What happened?"

"She came at me with a knife!" he replied. "Do you know CPR?"

"A little."

"Come out here and take over while I call 9-1-1!" he ordered, and stepped aside, careful not to move the knife, which—along with the store's video—would be key in corroborating his story. Thinking he might retch at the sight of the blood pouring from Misty onto the cheap tile floor, he yelled for the woman, who was still unseen. "Now! I'm going to step outside for a minute."

He exited the store and quickly made the call to 9-1-1, grateful for the fresh air and for not having to look at the dying woman. When he had finished, he rang off. Was there anyone else to call? Anything else he should do? Maybe he should call the sheriff or the chief of police? No, let the authorities do their business. It would be easily dealt with. He turned back to the store and saw the backside of the woman just bending over to assist his assailant. My God, had she done nothing to help the entire time?

55

Baker heard the call and was the first officer on the scene. As he pulled up, he saw Lee standing in front of the store talking on his phone.

"What happened?"

"Gal attacked me over a case. I—I shot her."

"Is she dead?"

"I don't know." Lee shrugged.

Baker was appalled. "Counsel, you don't know and you're standing out here? Who is helping her?"

He'd been recognized. "Some woman," Lee said. "I felt like it was better to stay out here."

Baker had heard enough and went through the doors. On her back on the floor a heavy woman was lying spread eagle. Baker was about to check for signs of life when he heard a voice from behind the counter. "She's dead. I checked."

Jensen knelt and verified the victim was dead, then looked at his watch. The deceased had what looked like a small bullet hole in the front of her shirt. "Misty" was the name embroidered on the front. He called the scene in. "Is that Misty Layton?" he asked.

"Yeah."

"Do you work here?"

"Yeah. For a coupla weeks now."

"Can you lock the back door for me?" Baker asked. "I'm going to need to secure the scene."

"I need to lock her office, too—is that okay?"

"Do it," he ordered. He made calls as she first locked the register, then went to lock the manager's office. He waited impatiently until she returned. He took a quick report from her. "I really didn't see anything," she concluded.

"Right. Go on outside and wait for me. Use the back door and lock it on your way out—can you do that? I'll talk with you in a few," he said. "And take your coat."

"I'll wait in my car."

"Where is it?"

"Out the back, by the dumpster. That's employee parking," she explained.

"Let me have your key. I'll secure the front door," Baker said. "But don't go anywhere. We're going to have to take you downtown for a statement."

"Okay," she said, and filched a pack of cigarettes as she departed for the back of the store.

When he heard the back door close, he walked to the front door, opened it a crack, and told Jensen the store was secure.

———

The cop cars and ambulances had drawn a crowd. After seeing that Misty's body was covered with a sheet, Jensen pulled Lee aside to talk with him privately. "Counselor, what the hell?"

"I told you," Lee said. "She pulled a knife on me. She swung it at me, or whatever. I was backed into the store with no way out, so I—I shot her."

"How many times?"

"I don't know. I was . . . scared, I guess."

"Where's the gun?"

"Here." Lee extracted it from a shoulder holster and handed it to Jensen. "I have a concealed carry permit."

"What did you do with the knife?" Jensen asked, carefully placing the pistol in an evidence bag.

"I didn't touch it. I left it right where it was. I'm smart enough to know it is corroborative evidence," Lee explained.

Jensen was thinking about what he had seen—and what he hadn't. "Where was it when you last saw it?"

"Right next to her!"

"Right side? Left side?"

"I can't remember—maybe left side?"

Jensen nodded, then turned and walked back to the front door and knocked. Lee watched as the uniformed officer let him in. Through the window, Lee could see Jensen looking around, then saw him get down on a knee and then maneuver to his hands and knees. He spent several minutes looking around Misty's body—at one point, he rolled her over slightly, furrowed his brow, and then rose.

Lee watched as Jensen approached the front entrance through the glass. When the uniformed cop again opened the door, Jensen exited. "No knife," he said as he approached Lee.

"There has to be!" Lee replied in disgust. "It was right there when—wait a minute! Ask that woman. She had to have seen it all!"

Jensen nodded and was about to close the door and go back into the store when Lee had an idea. "Hey!" he yelled. "Uhhh—"

"It's Jensen. Corporal Mike Jensen."

"Jensen, there must be a video system on this place. Get the tape. That will show everything," he said, thankful for twenty-first-century technology.

"On it," Jensen said. Lee again watched as he spoke with the uniformed officer and nodded. The pair then walked around the corner in the store— presumptively, to the office. When they were out of sight, Lee took a phone call and explained what was going on to Cates. He finished the call and paced, awaiting Jensen. When he couldn't stand it anymore, he walked around to the side of the store and saw Jensen talking to a blonde woman sitting in an aging sedan. He decided to go and listen. As Lee approached, he saw the woman searching for something in her car.

"It's right here, somewhere," she was saying to Jensen as Lee walked up.

"Well, what did she say?" Lee asked.

"She doesn't seem to have seen anything," Jensen replied. "Said she was cleaning the bathroom when she heard an argument and then a gunshot. She says she was afraid, so she waited a few minutes before she came out. Says you told her you needed to make a call and to take over first aid. Says the lady was already dead."

"She—Misty—threatened me. You saw the knife," he said to the woman in the car, who was reaching under the passenger seat for something. "You had to!"

Jensen was watching Lee closely, but merely shrugged. "She says she never saw one."

"What?" Lee asked in a combination of fury and surprise. "She had to have moved it!" he yelled, pointing at the woman. "I sure as hell didn't!"

"I'm sorry, but I didn't see anything," the woman said, apparently to Jensen. She straightened and turned at last, and Lee recognized Julie Spence.

"You!"

"Me."

Now . . . look . . . Ms. Spence . . . uh, I don't know what's going on here, but you know exactly what happened."

"I don't believe I do," Julie replied. Turning to Jensen, she held up her lighter. "Here it is!" she said. "Meet you downtown for that statement?"

"Just a minute," Jensen promised. "Just as soon as we get a detective on scene." Looking across the parking lot, he brightened. "There's Ashley now."

Lee watched as Jensen updated Detective Miller, who made notes and occasionally looked toward Lee while Jensen filled her in. Julie exited the car to smoke. When Miller came over to speak with him, Lee was ready. "I've already given my statement to him," he said, pointing to Jensen. "And this woman"—he pointed to Julie—"saw the whole thing."

"I didn't see jack-shit," Julie said to Miller before Jensen could get a hand up to silence her.

"Now see here," Lee began, lecturing Miller earnestly. "I am an officer of the court and I'm telling you this woman saw everything! And if she says anything otherwise, you'll have her for perjury when you view the store's video!"

Miller looked expectantly to Jensen, who kicked the ground with a boot. "Well, Counselor, bit of a problem there. According to Ms. Spence, the woman you shot was the manager. Apparently, she was a big smoker. Didn't want the owners to know, so she removed the thumb drive during her shifts and replaced it when she left."

Lee was incredulous. "What? Then find that drive!"

Jensen shrugged. "We're on it," he said. "If it's here, we'll find it."

"Where the hell else would it be? That woman had a knife!" Lee cried, pointing to the store where Misty's body lay covered with a sheet. "She threatened me! There was nothing I could do! It was self-defense!" Then he jabbed a finger toward Julie. "And she knows exactly what happened! She had to have seen and heard it all!"

Miller nodded. "Mr. Lee, my people have been searching, and no one can find the knife you are talking about. We're looking for it, and we're looking for the drive. There are no exigent circumstances, so I am working on getting a warrant to search the premises. Give us some time and let us do our jobs and hopefully we can clear this up."

"Hopefully? *Hopefully*? Are you kidding me?" Lee closed the distance between himself and Julie. "Interview her!" he demanded. "Search her. I'm telling you, that woman—"

"My name's Julie."

"She—Julie—saw everything, and she got rid of the evidence!" When neither Miller nor Jensen replied, he continued, "You can't let her get away with this!" Then he turned his full wrath on Julie. "You! You'll never get away with this!"

Julie had turned sideways to Lee and was trying to light one cigarette with another in the omnipresent Wyoming wind. Having finally gotten it lit, she inhaled deeply from one and discarded the other. "Get away with what?" she asked.

"You'll testify or—"

"Or what?" Julie exhaled a combination of smoke and breath into the frosty air and watched as it dissipated in the wind. "Someone's gonna put me in jail? Been there. Someone's gonna ruin my life? Look around, Mr. Lee —this look like I'm Princess freakin' Diana?"

"My God! You know—"

"I don't *know* squat. Besides, you may have forgotten, but you made me out to be—how did you say it? Oh, yeah, a 'congenital liar'—remember? So even if I was to testify, no one would believe anything I said." She dropped the cigarette to the ground and crushed it with the toe of a well-worn flat. "You made sure of that."

CONFLICT OF DUTY

The pursuit of the truth might cost one Wyoming lawyer everything...

In the wake of a trial loss and personal upheaval, defense attorney Sam Johnstone is drawn back into the legal fray by an accused drug dealer involved in a fatal fentanyl case. The dealer's tantalizing offer? Pivotal information that could exonerate the son of Sam's former partner in exchange for representation.

As Sam ventures deeper into this moral minefield, he uncovers suppressed testimony that could incriminate a former client... and threaten his own career.

From Wall Street Journal bestselling author James Chandler comes the sixth book in the Sam Johnstone legal thriller series; perfect for fans of John Grisham, James Patterson, and C.J. Box.

Get your copy today at
severnriverbooks.com/series/sam-johnstone-legal-thriller

ABOUT THE AUTHOR

Wall Street Journal bestselling author James Chandler spent his formative years in the western United States. When he wasn't catching fish or footballs, he was roaming centerfield and trying to hit the breaking pitch. After a mediocre college baseball career, he exchanged jersey No. 7 for camouflage issued by the United States Army, which he wore around the globe and with great pride for twenty years. Since law school, he has favored dark suits and a steerhide briefcase. When he isn't working or writing, he'll likely have a fly rod, shotgun or rifle in hand. He and his wife are blessed with two wonderful adult daughters. Misjudged is his first novel.

Sign up for James Chandler's newsletter at
severnriverbooks.com/authors/james-chandler